A TIMELESS Romance ANTHOLOGY

Summer Wedding
Collection

A TIMELESS Romance ANTHOLOGY

Summer Wedding Collection

SIX ROMANCE NOVELLAS

Melanie Jacobson
Julie Wright
Rachael Anderson
Annette Lyon
Heather B. Moore
Sarah M. Eden

Mirror Press

Original Cover Design by Christina Marcano
Paperback Cover Design by Rachael Anderson
Interior Design by Rachael Anderson
Edited by Annette Lyon

Published by Mirror Press, LLC

E-book edition released May 2013
Paperback edition released March 2014

ISBN-10: 1941145086
ISBN-13: 978-1-941145-08-1

TABLE OF CONTENTS

OTHER TIMELESS ROMANCE ANTHOLOGIES

Winter Collection

Spring Vacation Collection

Autumn Collection

European Collection

Love Letter Collection

Old West Collection

Summer in New York Collection

Love Bytes

Melanie Jacobson

Other Works by Melanie Jacobson

The List

Not My Type

Smart Move

Second Chances

One

To: bree.riley@email.com
From: dal.warner@email.com
RE: Wedding drama

Can't you put your friend in check?
—Dallen

To: dal.warner@email.com
From: bree.riley@email.com
RE: Wedding drama

Can you put a force of nature in check? Is that a
thing? Because if it is, tell me how to do it and
consider it DONE—kind of like I almost am. (She's
making me crazy. Puce flowers? PUCE?! I've been a
good best friend. What did I do to deserve this?)
—Bree

To: bree.riley@email.com
From: dal.warner@email.com

No being done. You don't get to be done. DON'T
YOU LEAVE ME WITH THESE CRAZY PEOPLE
BY MYSELF. I'm counting on you to help me talk
them down from ledges. I went to dinner with her
and Slade last night. All she talked about was
changing her flowers. Because they're not just
flowers . . . (You want to finish the sentence here?)
—Dallen

To: dal.warner@email.com
From: bree.riley@email.com
RE: Wedding drama

. . . they're a symbol. Everything is a symbol.

Just remember back to the Addison you knew before
they decided to get married. She's still in there
somewhere. That's how I don't kill her. Also, not
living in Chicago with you guys helps.
—Bree

To: bree.riley@email.com
From: dal.warner@email.com
RE: Wedding drama

Stop trying to make me jealous of not living in LA.

Don't know how you're surviving the maid-of-honor
gig. I'm only the best man, and I still feel like the first
target in the line of fire. I almost punched Slade in

the face four different times this week. Only the knowledge that Addison would kill me if I broke his nose held me back.

Remember last week when the biggest problem we had was thinking of a plan to keep Slade's Drunk Uncle away from all the single ladies? HA! Now that Puce-pocalypse is upon us, gropey wedding guests seem like a cake walk.
—Dallen

P.S. Don't mention cake walks to Addison. It will become a thing.

Dallen hit send and smiled. It was true: he *was* counting on Bree, almost a total stranger, to help him manage the most stressful non-work project of his life. And it felt good. Her jokes and sense of calm had made everything more manageable from the moment they'd traded their first emails a few weeks before.

When Slade first asked Dallen to be his best man, he'd been flattered. Now he wondered if he'd just been Tom Sawyered because Slade's other friends were too smart to say yes. If Dallen had realized exactly how smitten Slade was with tiny, bewitching Addison, he might have found something else—anything else—more pressing to do that weekend. They'd seemed so normal for the year they'd dated, but the engagement had turned Addison into a crazy woman, and Slade refused to say no to anything.

Dallen sighed. They were exhausting, but the truth was there wasn't anywhere he'd rather be than standing by his best friend's side when he said his vows to the love of his life. It helped that standing there meant digging his own toes into the white sandy beaches of Maui.

He glared at the rain pelting his office window. His view of Lake Michigan was pointless half the year. Chicago's late spring rains sucked, simple as that.

He growled and leaned over the architectural blueprints. He picked up his pencil and erased a cornice, the high-maintenance bride and groom fading to white noise as he worked on perfecting the exterior of a new high rise. Changing the Chicago skyline was infinitely less stressful than being best man.

Two

*P*oor Dallen. Bree had to smile at his frustration. Addison was normally the most level-headed girl, but she was a demanding bride. It was bad enough for Bree sitting in her LA office two thousand miles away; Dallen had to listen to Addison's obsessive attention to wedding detail in person. She'd always loved the symbolism of weddings, and as crazy in love as she was with Slade, she wanted every last detail to perfectly reflect their feelings.

There had been discussions of live animals, exotic flowers, outdoor canopies, and horse drawn carriages. When they finally settled on a Hawaiian wedding, Bree breathed a sigh of relief. The location would limit Addison's insane plans; horse-drawn carriages didn't work on sand. It had still taken some fast talking to convince Addison to not enter on a white stallion. When Bree had exhausted every argument she could think of, she won on manure.

"What if the horse poops? Is *that* the symbolism you're going for?"

After she emailed Dallen with her victory, he'd sent her a GIF of an old man laughing until he cried.

If it weren't for his emails cracking her up several times a week, she'd be pulling her hair out trying to keep up with Addison's quicksilver moods and plan changes. Dallen, in exaggerating the crazy, made reality a little easier to deal with.

Her phone buzzed with a text.

Dallen: Wait. I don't even know what puce is. Help me.
Bree: Did Google fail you?
Dallen: I could ask it but it lacks your sense of humor.
Bree: The second you say I'm funny, my sense of humor locks up. Quit it. It screws with my mojo.
Dallen: Did I imply you're funny? Massive typo. Don't want to hurt your feelings, but you need help. Study these . . .

He included a link. She clicked and grinned. It was a Joke of the Day site.

Bree: Nice.
Dallen: I really am.

She snorted.

Bree: Oops. I just tried to make an emoticon for an eye roll, but it looked like . . . boobs. *Red face.*

He pinged back with the old man GIF. She smothered a laugh.

Bree: Fine. Think puke, as in imagine if someone ate an eggplant, chased it with a glass of cream, and

6

puked it back up. That's the color we're talking.

A long pause followed.

Dallen: Unfortunately, I can picture that perfectly. So . . . thanks?

She laughed, and Sarah popped her head over their shared cubicle wall. "The laughter—it must stop. Interior design is serious business. You can't treat it like a joke."

Bree raised an eyebrow. "Okay, girl who did a whole kid's room around Peewee's Playhouse."

Sarah happy sighed. "I love celebrities and their money and their willingness to do ridiculous things with it." Last fall, her work had attracted the notice of a major LA magazine with her whimsical design for the toddler of a TV star who wanted something besides a typical sports or space theme. "How's your project going?"

Bree glanced at the mockup for the upscale Melrose clothing boutique she'd been commissioned for. "Fine. Can't find the right chairs for the lounging area by the fitting rooms, but I'll figure it out."

"Not *that* project. How's the wedding coming? And by wedding, I mean the online affair with your new true love."

"Stop it," Bree said without any heat. She'd argued with Sarah's interpretation too many times to think she'd shut her up, much less win.

Sarah pointed at Bree's green smoothie. "Losing weight for someone else?"

"My bridesmaid dress."

"And the hot guy who makes you laugh ten times a day."

"I should have never showed you his picture," Bree grumbled. "I bet you wouldn't think I was losing weight for him if he were chubby and short."

"Moot point. He's gorge-until-you're-sick delicious."

"Ew. What a gross way to put it. I swear this diet is about the dress." It was most definitely *not* about the dress. Her ex-boyfriend's face flashed through her memory before she shoved it out and ordered her stomach to stop the automatic churning it did whenever she thought of him. This was about redemption.

"Your friend was nice enough to pick silk. The cut's all floaty; so you don't have to worry. If it were satin, even boneys couldn't pull it off without Spanx and airbrushing." *Boney* was what Sarah called the exercise-obsessed trophy wives that often hired them. "If you have even a tiny figure flaw, satin is the worst. Silk is easy."

"Thirty pounds isn't a tiny flaw. That's a third of a boney."

Sarah shook her head. "You look so good. I don't know why you're starving yourself. You've lost, what, fifteen pounds? Stop. You don't need to lose any more."

"I'm not starving myself." It was true. She'd started a crash diet the day after Addison called, begging Bree to be maid of honor, but that lasted all of a week after food deprivation made her so cranky she threw a pillow at her Jillian Michaels workout on TV. She'd switched from a cabbage cleanse to common-sense healthy eating and made up with Jillian. After six weeks, good eating and daily exercise had begun to feel like a treat, not a chore. Now the combination was just a good habit.

She wouldn't admit that at the seductive call of premium chocolate, the pictures of Dallen she had found on Slade's Facebook page kept her out of her emergency Dove stash. Slade had messed with Dallen by creating an album titled "Dallen the Modelizer," filled with snapshots of his friend with a dozen different thin, amazingly beautiful women. Dallen had threatened bodily harm in the comments, but Slade had fired back with, "You did it, you own it."

Bree liked looking at Dallen—his dark hair with a hint of a wave, his sexy mouth curved in a half smile, his strong jaw and broad shoulders. It was like studying candid shots of a J. Crew model. She didn't like looking at all the models he was with, although Addison promised that none of them were current models, and all of them held jobs that required brain power.

Brains *and* beauty. It hadn't made Bree feel any better about the crush she was nurturing on her wedding partner in crime. She fell into the "pretty smart and kind of pretty" category. She used to be fine with that until Grayson ground her confidence to dust with a relentless campaign to get her to lose weight. She'd been thin when they met, but the stress of joining the firm three years ago, coupled with her parents' surprise divorce, led to comfort food, and her clothes became very *un*comfortable. At first, Grayson hinted that they should get out to bike and rollerblade, but graduated to frowning at the food she ate. It got worse from there.

She'd sensed his disapproval, but it only stressed her out more, which led to more bad eating. Now all she had left of that relationship were his toxic parting words.

You can't expect me to be attracted to you when you look like this. I hug you, and I can't get past the fat roll. This is LA. You can't walk a block without tripping over a gym or a health bar. Get yourself together. There's no excuse for not looking hot.

Sarah interrupted her thoughts. "Fine. You're not starving yourself. But seriously, you look amazing. If you drop this last ten pounds you think you need to lose, you're going to be a boney. Minus the rich husband, huge house, and tiny dog in an overpriced purse."

"Leave me to my smoothie and my newest wedding emergency."

"Another one?"

"It's been twenty-four hours, hasn't it? Any idea where

to find puce flowers in Hawaii?"

Sarah's eyes widened. "She changed them again? To *puce?* She's messing with you."

Bree shook her head. "She wore a puce dress the night they met, so she wants the color reflected in the decor. It's symbolic."

"If this dude asked her out on a second date after she wore a puce dress, he's a keeper. But I'm telling you, make her get a wedding planner."

Bree turned to her computer again, ready to fire up a Google search for flowers. "She doesn't trust a wedding planner. I'm the only one who can get it right."

"No, you're not."

"No," Bree agreed. "But as long as that's what Addison thinks, I'm the one who needs to do it." She smiled up at Sarah. "I know this looks crazy—"

"It *is* crazy."

"Trust me, if the roles were reversed, Addison would have my back no matter how crazy I acted. She has since we were little kids. This is the first time I've ever seen her so high-strung, but she's love-drunk and happy."

Sarah smiled. "You're a good friend."

"That depends on if I can find puce flowers." With that, she began another Internet search.

Three

Light splash of cologne, check. Styling gel, check. Good jeans from the dryer, check.

Everything was ready to go, except his motivation. Dallen groaned and ran a hand through his just-styled hair, sending a piece poking up. It mocked him in the mirror; he didn't care. In less than an hour, he was supposed to pick up his date, but he didn't want to. He'd been out with Amanda twice already, and she was nice. Maybe better than nice—gorgeous, cultured, and fit. They'd never run into any awkward silences, but somehow conversation with her fell flat.

Instead of putting on the shirt he'd picked, he wandered to his laptop to see if Bree had emailed. Clicking his email tab was a move he made embarrassingly often. Last Friday, he'd gone out with Amanda for lobster and a gallery opening. It had been fine. But Saturday he'd stayed in and IM-ed with Bree about the footwear protocol for a wedding on the sand.

SAND-als, she'd pinged him back then said she had to go because there was a Homeland marathon on. He'd fed her fake spoilers all night and laughed much harder at her responses than he had on both dates with Amanda combined.

No email from Bree. Pathetic how much that disappointed him. He tugged his shirt from its hanger and put it on. He'd go through the motions of dinner with Amanda because it would be rude to stand her up at the last minute. But it looked like this would be strike three. Too bad. Usually it took closer to a month for him to lose interest or realize he had found, yet again, someone who deserved a bigger commitment than he was able to give.

Fine. Than he *wanted* to give.

If only he met women who made him laugh like Bree did. Funny, but she was the only woman in years to stick around for any length of time. After two months in the wedding planning trenches, he looked forward to each new crisis, because he knew Bree would make it hilarious. It was the second best thing to sunshine in the Chicago gloom.

He snatched his keys from the counter. He'd get Amanda and make the best of it, but he'd have to fight hard to not keep checking his phone for emails. He wouldn't be *that* guy. It wouldn't be easy.

Four

CALL ME.

Bree glanced at Addison's text and sighed. Luckily she had some post-workout endorphins to get her through this new crisis, whatever it was. It would definitely be a crisis. She hoped it wasn't another change in bachelorette party plans. She'd had to book three different packages so far. Shuffling the deposits around was becoming a pain.

When Bree called, instead of saying hello, Addison asked, "What's going on with you and Dallen?"

Bree had to process the words, and when their meaning sank in, her stomach sank too. "Nothing. Why?" Had he said something to Addison? Dallen seemed to find their conversations as hilarious as she did, but what if the next words out of Addison's mouth were some gentle warning about how Bree shouldn't get too invested? She'd need her entire Dove stash.

"He asked about you at brunch."

The free fall in her stomach stopped. Asking about her could be okay. "Asked about me how?"

"He tried to be all smooth, but he totally wasn't. Said he had a lame date last night with a girl who had no sense of humor, unlike you. He wanted to know what you're like so he's better prepared to work with you in Hawaii next month, but he was fishing for details way beyond wedding planning."

"What did you tell him?"

Addison would tell him only good things about Bree, but the Facebook pictures of him with a parade of stunning women flashed through her mind. She frowned at her grubby sweats. They fit better than they had a couple of months ago, but in her current state, she was no prize.

"I told him the truth. That you're the funniest, sweetest, bestest friend ever."

"Aw, thanks," Bree said, regretting all of the impatient thoughts she'd had when Addison texted, demanding a call.

"Then he tried to be all sly asking what you look like."

Bree's stomach dropped again, but Addison chattered on. "He goes, 'I like watching movies more if they're filmed somewhere I've been.' And then he said something about how it seemed weird to have talked to you so much without knowing what you look like. He was trying to be all, 'Just looking for a little context.' *Obviously* fishing."

"What did you say?" Bree tried to keep the stress out of her voice, but when Addison didn't say anything, Bree's worry spiked. "Addison?"

Addison cleared her throat. "I may have shown him a picture."

Bree groaned, knowing which one. "You suck so much."

"You're ridiculous," Addison said, her voice light. "I love that shot."

Bree imagined it, the photo Addison had taken when she visited last summer. "I miss California," she'd said. "You're the poster girl for beach living." She'd snapped a picture of Bree smiling into the distance with a palm tree and bright blue sky behind her.

Bree hated it—and every picture taken of her since gaining weight. Addison promised not to post it anywhere, but she refused to delete it. "I can't," she'd said. "I'm going to pull this up every time we get a blizzard this winter. Plus, that's your super happy smile, and I don't get to see it anymore."

"Promise not to be mad," Addison said, interrupting Bree's memories. "Slade told him how cute you are."

"'Cute,'" Bree repeated. Like a roly-poly puppy. To be fair, Slade met her once when he and Addison flew to LA to announce their engagement to her parents. Bree tugged on the loose waistband of her sweats. Not so roly anymore. And maybe less so by the time she hit the Maui beach in a month.

She couldn't explain the twin flames of hope and fear that the reality of meeting Dallen lit in her stomach. Or how the more she hoped, the brighter the fear burned. Addison's way of being supportive during Bree's weight loss had been to tell her she was crazy to think she needed it, but Bree knew better. Her efforts had become about so much more than dropping pounds. There was something deeply satisfying about getting up and doing good things for herself all day long—eating well and exercising. Her grandmother had died of a heart attack at sixty. Doing more to improve her fitness felt like the right way to pay tribute to her—by not going down that road.

Moving from clothes that were too snug, to fitting right, to becoming loose—that was good too. Great, even. But she was no Addison, the classic California blonde guys pinned up in locker rooms. Bree wasn't the tiniest bit jealous; Addison was also kind and smart and loyal. But Bree also knew from experience that guys expected Addison to run with equally hot friends. And Bree was nobody's locker room fantasy.

But not every guy was a Grayson. She'd believed otherwise for two years and hadn't gone on a single date, not because of her size but everything to do with her head.

She drew a deep breath and waded into deeper water. "I've decided to quit being stupid about my weight; it is what it is. I'm more worried about being healthy now." And if that was true, she needed to let go of some other unhealthy habits—like body shame. "Show the picture to whoever. Plaster it all over Facebook if you want."

"Uh-huh," Addison said. "I'll believe you're okay with yourself when *you* plaster it all over Facebook."

"Everyone is way more interested in pictures of my nieces and LA's sunsets than they are in pictures of me."

"Uh-huh," Addison repeated. "I know you think you're fat—"

"I don't," Bree interrupted. "Promise." It was true. Or starting to be.

"Good. Because you're so pretty. And I think Dallen is looking forward to meeting you."

"Thanks."

When they hung up, Bree pulled her bridesmaid dress from the closet and slipped it on. She stood in front of her mirror and frowned, but only for a moment. It looked good on her. *She* looked good, better than she had since college. As she thought about the picture of Dallen on Addison's Facebook, which she'd stalked way too regularly, a smile blossomed on her face. She liked him. She liked his jokes, she liked how quick his mind was, and she liked his patience with Addison.

She liked so many things about him, like the dedication he showed to his architecture career. Several nights, they'd ended up IM-ing as they each worked, drawing up plans for different buildings, him for the outsides, and her for the insides. As long as that wasn't a metaphor for the way they evaluated people, maybe Hawaii *could* be something more than an exercise in managing Addison's craziness. Maybe there was room for a romance of her own.

LOVE BYTES

To: bree.riley@email.com
From: Dal.Warner@email.com
RE: The end is near

T minus 10 days and counting.

What does T minus mean?

And how do we add days to that? Or maybe I want to subtract them all and already be in Hawaii at the moment the ceremony is over and NO MATTER WHAT, there is nothing Slade can make me do because it's ALL DONE.

I love Addison, but Slade dragged me to go watch her in court the other day instead of having lunch like he promised, and now I understand the full scope of the focus she has turned on wedding planning. She is crazy fierce. I bet she'll be the DA for Chicago in five years.

Watching her today made me sure that I never, ever want to get on her bad side. So what's left to make sure that everything goes off without a hitch? Because I'm scared.

To: Dal.Warner@email.com
From: bree.riley@email.com
RE: The end is near

You almost tricked me. I almost said we had it all covered, until I remembered that it's practically an invitation to the universe to upset Addison's

17

MELANIE JACOBSON

wedding plans. I won't be fooled. The last time I said we were all set, the ukulele player for the ceremony had open-heart surgery. I refuse to tempt fate by saying it again.

So I won't.

I couldn't even if I wanted to. Addison has decided that she disagrees with the fundamental message of bachelor and bachelorette parties. The idea that they would want to spend time apart is *no bueno* for her. Bad symbolism, I think. So now I have to figure out a way to get my party's path to cross with your party's path before the night is through.

Hitch: I accidentally believed her last time she swore she wouldn't change her mind about her bachelorette party, so I booked something with a nonrefundable deposit. You're going to have to work around that.

To: bree.riley@email.com
From: Dal.Warner@email.com
RE: You're trying to kill me, aren't you?

I will be taking an insane red-eye the day before the wedding; I land around nine. How about all the bridesmaids and groomsmen come pick me up at the airport, and we'll count it as them seeing each other during the parties. I can't think of anything else that will work, so say yes.

18

To: Dal.Warner@email.com
From: bree.riley@email.com
RE: You're trying to kill me, aren't you?

No.

To: bree.riley@email.com
From: Dal.Warner@email.com
RE: You're trying to kill me, aren't you?

You're a hard woman. We're going to do a luau for our bachelor thing. With hula dancers. If you ladies will be the hula dancers, that counts as a party intersection, right?

To: Dal.Warner@email.com
From: bree.riley@email.com
RE: You're trying to kill me, aren't you?

Okay, NOW I'm going to kill you.

To: bree.riley@email.com
From: Dal.Warner@email.com
RE: You're trying to kill me, aren't you?

Fine, I admit it. I made up the hula dancers part. We're really going to hike for a few hours (did I mention I'll be coming in off a red-eye and will probably die?), and then we're going to dinner. What are you guys doing?

To: Dal.Warner@email.com
From: bree.riley@email.com
RE: You're trying to kill me, aren't you?

Um.

I don't really want to say. Because it might involve hula lessons. Something about Addison learning a dance that tells the story of her love for Slade?

To: bree.riley@email.com
From: Dal.Warner@email.com
RE: You're trying to kill me, aren't you?

It is FATE that all of you bridesmaids hula dance for our bachelor party!!!!! AND as a bonus, it was all Addison's idea, so I can't even get in trouble for it.

But I'm not going to say that out loud, because it makes me sound like a creeper. So I propose we find a way to meet up at dinner somehow. Or at least cross paths. Will crossing paths be enough for Addison?

Check one:
_____Yes _____No

To: Dal.Warner@email.com
From: bree.riley@email.com
RE: You're trying to kill me, aren't you?

X Yes (I hope) _____No

Dallen sat back in his desk chair and laughed. Her emails never disappointed him. He'd never had such an easy rapport with someone so fast. Maybe with Slade. But this was different. Slade had definitely never made his pulse jump because his name showed up on a computer screen.

His fingers hovered over the keyboard, ready to tap out an idea for how to coordinate their party schedules, but he hesitated. The wedding was in less than two weeks, and suddenly it was the last thing he wanted to talk about. Was he bold enough to ask what he really wanted to know? It was risky since he couldn't read her face to do damage control if he was off base. Then again, when would he see her again after the wedding? It might mean a couple of awkward days in Hawaii . . . Or it could mean making Hawaii even better.

What did he have to lose? Nothing, really. But he pictured the sweet face from the snapshot on Addison's phone and decided that maybe he had a lot to gain.

❦

Bree stifled a squeal, but Sarah's head popped over the cubicle wall anyway. "What?"

"Nothing." Bree tried for a neutral expression.

Sarah's eyes narrowed. "Not nothing. But I can't tell if it's a good or bad something."

"That makes two of us."

"What's up?"

"An email from Dallen," she finally said.

"Yum," Sarah answered.

That stressed Bree out even more. Many times in college, she and Addison had sat out in the commons, watching mismatched couples walking past and joking, "Someone's being nice." She and Dallen were a classic mismatch.

"Yeah. He . . ." *Argh.* How to explain the next part? "He's wondering if I want to kick off Hawaii with an actual date. Like meeting for breakfast before he has to do his best-man stuff."

"Get it, girl!" Sarah said.

"Shhh." Bree looked around, but the chatter in the rest of the office hadn't stopped at Sarah's crowing. "I'm not sure it's a great idea."

"Why not? You guys totally click on email. He's hot. You're hot. What's the problem?"

Bree frowned, and Sarah matched it. "Don't say you're not hot, Bree, or I swear, I will climb over this wall and smack some sense into you."

"It'd probably be faster if you walked around."

"You are *hot*, is my point, and it's a correct point."

A smile escaped Bree. "I'm getting there."

"You were hot before you started your crazy diet."

Bree rolled her eyes. "Name one crazy thing I eat."

"Kale."

"It's good."

"I've given up trying to explain the wrongness of that green blight, but I'm dead right about you."

Bree peered up at her. Sarah hadn't worked here when she and Grayson split, hadn't seen the way it broke her down inside. "I love that you always say good things to me, but . . ." She couldn't bring herself to spew all of Grayson's ugliness. It was too humiliating, so she chose a different story instead. "In college, Addison begged me to let her set me up with her boyfriend's buddy. Like an idiot, I said yes. We all went out, and my date was as gorgeous as Addison had said, but we didn't click. The conversation was okay, but nothing special. We went to a movie, and when I came out of the bathroom, I overheard my date complaining to his friend that I was nice, but he'd expected someone hot like Addison, not average like me."

Sarah scowled. "He was an idiot. There's no way a quality guy like Dallen is going to be that shallow."

"It's not his fault if he's expecting someone like Addison and he gets—"

"What? Someone as awesome as you? He should be so lucky. How do you know what he's expecting? Has he seriously not seen a picture of you?"

"He has." Not a good one, but he still wanted to make Hawaii about something more than surviving the wedding. That had to count for something. Bree allowed hope to outshine fear for a moment.

"Go for it. Even if you don't like him, or he doesn't like you—which will *never* happen if he has half a brain and two good eyes—then who cares? You'll love Hawaii, and if he's lame, you never have to see him again."

Bree thought about the few days she'd be spending in Hawaii post-wedding, a treat she was gifting herself after throwing herself into one high-profile work project after another. She'd imagined long, lazy days on the beach with fruity cocktails, but lately, Dallen had been appearing in the lounge chair beside hers, shirtless and tan and charming. Mainly shirtless.

If those daydreams didn't become reality, she'd be disappointed, whether it was because he rejected her, or because she never made a move to make it happen. Which meant . . .

"Well?" Sarah demanded. "Are you going to email him back?"

"Of course."

"What are you going to say?"

"Yes." Bree stuck her fingers in her ears. Sarah's squealing still hurt.

To: bree.riley@email.com
From: dal.warner@email.com
RE: Yes.

I'm glad you're down with breakfast. Sorry I didn't call you in person, but I was kind of worried about freaking you out.

Dallen

To: dal.warner@email.com
From: bree.riley@email.com
RE: Yes.

I don't scare that easily. But thanks for thinking it through. That says good things about you. :-)

Bree

To: bree.riley@email.com
From: dal.warner@email.com
RE: Yes.

Good. Now I have to convince Addison to say nothing but good things about me, and I'm all set.

Dallen

To: dal.warner@email.com
From: bree.riley@email.com
Re: Yes.

Then you're all set. She kind of doesn't shut up about how great you are. She talks about you at least one-tenth as much as she talks about Slade, so . . .

To: bree.riley@email.com
From: dal.warner@email.com
RE: Yes.

So I'm borderline nauseating through no fault of my own?

Dallen

To: dal.warner@email.com
From: bree.riley@email.com
Re: Yes.

Refer to subject line.

Bree

Five

*Y*our fiancée is infecting your brain," Dallen said into the phone. He leaned back against his sofa and stared at the ceiling. *Choreography? Is Slade kidding?*

"She is not," Slade said, voice calm. "Say something like that again, and I'll punch you. In the throat, because it hurts worse."

"When did you become the guy who started planning ridiculous romantic gestures?"

"When I met Addison. She deserves a big moment she didn't plan. Are you in or not?"

"Big moments are for chick flicks. Has she been making you watch those?"

"Bro, shut up and wrap your head around how we're going to do this. I have to come up with a plan in three days."

"Fine. But I'm adding this to the long list of things you owe me for." After they hung up, Dallen stared at the phone. Slade's scrambled brains or not, Dallen had never seen his friend happier, but he'd be glad when there was no way for either of them to have one more "great idea" for the wedding. Slade's latest one was complicated, and Dallen had no problem admitting that he wasn't man enough for the job on his own.

He checked the time. It wasn't that late, and more importantly, this was something that couldn't wait if they had a prayer of making it happen—a prayer offered to a hundred tiki gods for a whisper of a chance. He should call her. That would be more efficient.

He reached for his cell and stopped short with a laugh.

Dude, you could text. You want an excuse to talk to her and this is it. Be real. He thought back to the email flirting they'd done that afternoon. He wasn't nervous; talking to women had never been a big deal. But what if talking to her wasn't as cool as texting? Or emailing? Or instant messaging? What if they didn't gel? Part of him wanted to wait until Hawaii to discover that and enjoy the entertainment for a few more days. But part of him kind of just really wanted to talk to her.

Yeah, okay. He was being stupid.

Dallen: *Hope you're not busy. You must stop everything and help me with the crazy people.*

Bree: *Am wandering through my kitchen while wearing a towel on my head, waiting for something to magically appear in my fridge. Towel is not, in fact, a magic turban. Guess I can put fridge stalking on hold.*

She could tease smiles from him without effort, and he dug it. Screw it. He highlighted her number and pressed send.

It rang three times before she answered. Good. Not too eager to pick up. No making him wait too long. Not that games mattered. Still, it was good form.

"Hi." Her voice was mellow and slightly husky.

"Hi, yourself. Sorry I have to call under such disastrous circumstances. Also, I air quoted disastrous."

"I won't hold it against you," she said. He could hear the

27

smile in her voice. "Are we talking an actual *Titanic* disaster, or a there-are-no-puce-flowers disaster?"

"Let me backtrack. First, it's good to talk to you."

"You too," she said, and he liked that she was direct about it instead of deflecting the compliment.

"Second, this *is* a potential disaster, but it's all on Slade's side because if this doesn't come together, Addison will never know it didn't happen. Remember how obsessed she was with finding the bridesmaids a nail polish?"

"I have nightmares about it."

Addison had flipped out trying to find something that not only matched their dresses but that had a name symbolizing love and happiness. Enter Love Blush. At least it was a pretty coral.

"Slade is at that level."

"Interesting," she said. "I've only hung out with him that one weekend when they came out for the engagement announcement. Seems kind of unlike him."

"It's *completely* unlike him. I've been underqualified for this best man gig from the start, but now I'm about to flunk out of Advanced Best Manhood."

"Lay it on me," she said. "Let's see what we can do."

Easy. It was just as easy talking to her as the texts and phone calls had been. He cleared his throat. "Slade wants to do some huge gesture for Addison to match all the effort she's put into planning the wedding."

"Not possible."

"Right. Mission: Impossible."

"We should call it Mission: Unnecessary. She doesn't need him to do anything like that."

"That's why he wants to."

"It does make it more perfect," she admitted. "Did you threaten to boycott the ceremony on the grounds that he didn't think of this sooner?"

"I should call him back and do that."

"Nah. Let's just dive in. What kind of big gesture are we

talking here?"

Dallen sighed. "I heard the words 'flash mob.'"

"Were they followed by the word 'overdone?'"

He laughed. "Worse—the words 'viral,' 'YouTube,' and 'line dancing.'"

"Yeah, you're going to need to kill that right now. Because those words are things Addison hates."

"I might have made some of that up. What he really wants to do is somehow recreate the night they met. Can you convince her to bring her puce dress to Hawaii without letting on why?"

"I can handle that. What else?"

Dallen leaned back and relaxed into the cushion. Having a teammate, especially one who could make him laugh, made everything much more doable. As he explained Slade's vague outline for a surprise, Bree made a few suggestions, and then the conversation drifted. They covered the weather, books they were reading, and what they liked to do for fun.

Dallen didn't realize how much time had passed until Bree startled him with a surprised squeak. "It's almost midnight there! You're so nice to stay on the phone and act wide awake, but I should let you go."

Was that a hint to let this conversation drop? "I'm fine." He paused for a tiny second. "You're better than coffee for keeping me awake, and that's a good thing." He winced at how stupid that sounded. He'd never been a guy to use lines with girls, but he was usually smoother than this.

"It's not that I want to get off the phone," Bree said. "It's more that I think my hair may dry into a turban shape, and it's kind of curly, so I gotta go tame it before it rebels."

He pictured the soft, medium-brown hair he'd seen falling around the pretty face laughing from Addison's phone. She had a girl-next-door quality about her that appealed to him, something much more uncomplicated than the beautiful but high-maintenance women he'd dated lately. There was a kind of . . . honesty in her look, maybe. Like what you see is what you get.

"I hate when I get turban hair," he said. "So I'll let you go. Thanks for talking me through this. If you're cool with helping, I think we can make it work."

"I hope we can make this work," she echoed.

And he wondered as they hung up if she meant making more than Slade's surprise work. Because he was beginning to hope so too. He had to wait four more days to find out.

Six

ree threw open the hotel room balcony doors and stepped into the warm wash of Hawaiian sunshine. She'd left a gray June inversion for this perfect, smog-free paradise. Even the Pacific sparkling in the near distance looked bluer and cleaner and warmer here.

The scent of hibiscus flowers tickled her nose; she plucked a purple one from the branch near her and tucked it behind her ear, laughing at herself. It had taken her all of one night's sleep in Hawaii to go native.

"I love it!" Addison said behind her.

Bree turned to smile at her best friend. "Thanks. Seemed like the right thing to do."

Addison swept her into a hug. "Thank you for being here. And for putting up with my crazy. And for being you and helping put together this wild dream."

Bree returned her squeeze. "I'm glad to do it, and I'm so happy for you." She leaned back and framed Addison's face with her hands. "You deserve it all, and it's worth being nuts to see you happy."

Addison grinned and whirled toward the balcony doors. "The nuttiness is just starting. I'm getting married in two days—two days!" she hollered at the ceiling as she collapsed backward onto her bed in giggles. "I love Slade Banks, and two days is too long!"

Bree took a flying leap, landed on the bed next to her, and swatted her with a pillow. "He's the most brilliant, handsome, talented man in the universe. He still doesn't deserve you, but mazel tov and all that. Now focus: what's on tap today?"

Addison shot up. "You mean you don't have it all committed to memory? I expected to see it tattooed somewhere on your skinny self."

Bree brushed a dark strand of hair out of her face and smiled. "Thanks for noticing." She'd landed late last night and let herself into their shared suite as quietly as possible so as not to wake Addison.

"How could I not notice?" Addison said, scanning her from head to toe again. "Stand and do a twirl for me."

Bree obeyed, sending the skirt of her white sundress floating out and ending it with a curtsy and a laugh. "You don't think I went too dark with my hair?"

"Definitely not," Addison said, eyeing the rich brown. "I think those highlights are genius, and the contrast with your eyes makes them pop. I'd kill for your green."

Bree laughed again. "Your hazel is pretty. And you got the best of everything else, so maybe it's fair I got interesting eyes."

"And curves! And fab hair! Never get skinnier than you are right now. You look awesome."

"I'm still ten pounds over what I was in college."

"You were too skinny in college. All pointy cheekbones and sharp elbows. You look great." Concern dimmed her smile. "Do you really not see that?"

Bree smoothed her soft pink sarong over her round hips and lost the fight against a huge grin. "Actually, I do."

"Work it, girl," Addison said. "Speaking of work, first up after breakfast is working on our tan. Pull out your cutest bikini, and let's take it on a tour of the pool. I'll get the other girls."

"I thought you'd be dying for the beach after Chicago rain."

Addison pointed at her toenails painted in Love Blush coral. "No way. I'm not jacking these tootsies up by dinging their paint job until I walk out on that sand for the ceremony." She narrowed her eyes at Bree. "You'd better not either."

Bree held up her hands. "No, no. The pool sounds great. I'll change."

Addison nodded her satisfaction and disappeared to rouse the girls in the suite's other bedroom. Shayla and Jen were already here, and Michelle and Whitney would be arriving later today. Addison's wedding madness hadn't extended so far as having an enormous bridal party.

Bree opened her suitcase and pulled out her new swimsuit, the fabled itty bitty, teenie weenie, yellow polka-dot bikini. Well, not itty bitty. She wasn't that bold. But it definitely highlighted more of her assets than she'd put on display in a very long time. When she'd spotted it on the rack and the lyrics ran through her mind, she hadn't been able to resist. Looking at it now, she sort of wished she had. It was tame as bikinis went—it covered all of her bits admirably—but it seemed small now that it was time to greet any poolside gawkers. She'd barely gotten comfortable running near her apartment in a tank top and shorts.

She held the swimsuit at arm's length and studied it with a critical eye. Unfortunately, she'd been so stunned by how not awful she looked in it that she'd bought three more in other prints to celebrate.

MELANIE JACOBSON

No, not unfortunately. Time to get that out of her head. She'd looked good in this polka-dot confection. She'd look even better in it today if she wore it with a little confidence, or so said the article she'd read in a fitness magazine about how confidence was the best accessory. She slipped the suit on and turned to face the mirror.

"Sexy!" Addison said, walking back in.

Bree grinned. "Not bad, right?"

"Freaking awesome is more like it." Addison's eyes glinted with mischief. "Dallen is a goner the second he sees you. Just wear that everywhere. He'll fall at your feet."

With a snort, Bree scooped up her sarong and slipped it on. "I'm eating yogurt then hitting the pool," she called into the suite's small lounge area to the other girls. "Last one down is a dirty, stinky bridesmaid."

Giggling and the soft shuffle of bare feet on carpet met her announcement as Shayla and Jen scrambled back into their room to change. Bree was scraping up the last bit of yogurt with her spoon when they reemerged in cover ups, beach bags on their shoulders.

"Ready, Addison?" Bree asked, sticking her head around their door.

"Ready." Addison looked like the poster child for glowing brides to be, her blonde hair hanging around tanned shoulders, a smile in her eyes. "Let's go. We've got three hours to relax, and then it's time to get cracking."

Bree rolled her eyes. "When you put it that way, how could we possibly *not* relax?" She grabbed Addison's wrist and hauled her out. "Better get a move on, bridesmaids. We have to *relax*, and stay on schedule!"

They joked at Addison's expense all the way to the pool. Within minutes of the girls claiming a row of lounge chairs, Bree felt Hawaii creeping into her bones, working its magic. The scent of flowers and suntan lotion drifted on the light breeze and lulled her into a delicious daydream where a

34

cabana boy who looked an awful lot like Dallen brought her a cool drink and offered to rub her back. At least part of the daydream proved irresistible—chilled fruit juice and sliced pineapple sounded like the only way to improve on heaven. She stood and made her way to the pool's bar, not realizing until she was halfway there that she'd forgotten her sarong. Huh. More progress.

A guy wearing board shorts and an appreciative grin checked her out. He elbowed his friend, who glanced at her and nodded agreement. Heat flooded her cheeks, and she was glad she'd worked on her tan enough in LA that the blush wouldn't show, especially when there would have been so much of it to see. She'd worked hard to get healthy, and now she looked good. She knew it whether guys checked her out or not.

Not that it hurt to have it confirmed.

Her smile only grew bigger when she dropped back into her chair to see a text from Dallen.

So. Breakfast in the a.m. I'm going to sit across from you and text so it feels normal.

Addison caught Bree's smile. "Let me guess. Dallen?"

"No, baseball scores. My Angels are looking good."

"Liar," Addison said, smiling back. "Let's make it a double wedding."

Bree balled up her sarong and threw it at her. Addison batted it away with a laugh. "Fine. No double wedding. But you guys are totally going to hit it off."

Bree typed a response. *If it'll make you feel better. But conversation seems to come easy, yeah? Looking forward to it.*

So much. The thought of meeting Dallen sent a warm wave rolling through her, a heat that made her scalp tingle, mixed with the giddy anticipation she used to have as a kid on the night before her birthday. She had the sense of being on the verge of something special. She'd kept far back from the edge, but their phone call and their ease with each other, added to the hundreds of times he'd made her laugh in the last two months, had yanked her to the brink. She was ready to take the next step and discover would happen.

Seven

*. . . the conversation seems to come easy, yeah?
Looking forward to it.*

Dallen smiled at the message. That's what he liked about Bree—her straightforwardness. *Looking forward to it.* He liked how uncomplicated it was to talk to her, yet how she constantly forced him to bring his A game to keep up with her lightning-quick wit. Her jokes ranged from baseball digs against his beloved Cubs to comparing wedding duties to Middle Eastern politics. The places her mind went fascinated him. *Everything* about her fascinated him. If he could have figured out a non-creepy way to ask Addison to send him the picture of Bree, he would have spent ridiculous amounts of time studying it, trying to figure out what could make someone smile with such pure happiness.

He set his phone on the hotel nightstand. He hadn't been able to wait for Hawaii, as he spent a useless day of work distracted by packing and the wedding. And by Bree, really. So he'd cleared it with his boss and come in a day early, texting Bree before takeoff and landing in time to steal a nap and re-humanize before he'd drop in on dinner to surprise Slade. And Bree. The biggest surprise of all was how much he was looking forward to that.

He lay back and stared at the lazy circles the ceiling fan made, drifting to sleep on images of warm sand, sunshine, and Bree, wondering what her eyes looked like behind the sunglasses in her picture. Big and brown, he bet. Damn, she was cute . . .

The sound of a happy shout through the open window woke him. He struggled upright, squinting at the hotel clock radio, wondering how much time had passed. Just after five. Good. Plenty of time to get ready for dinner. He sent a quick text to Slade.

Arrived early. How's dinner looking?

His phone lit up immediately with a reply. *Stoked. Dinner is looking like a pig in palm leaves. Worth the flight just for that. Reservation at 7. Find me in #429 when you're ready to grub.*

Two hours later, Dallen tapped on Slade's door, now showered, refreshed, and curious about how the night would go. Slade pulled the door open and gave him a back-thumping hug. "Glad you're here."

"Thought I'd better make sure I didn't need to hold you together so Addison had something to marry on Saturday."

Slade grinned. "Maybe I'm crazy, but I have no fear, man. I can't wait for Saturday."

"Lucky guy," Dallen said. "You didn't tell her I'm here yet, did you?"

"No. She'd spill it to Bree. They're expecting me and Deacon down there about now. The other guys get in tomorrow. Ready to do this?"

Dallen savored the rush of adrenaline in his veins. Nothing like the thrill of the hunt. "Let's get some dinner."

"And hot Hawaiian action, friendly bridesmaid style."

Dallen punched his arm. "Shut up."

Slade grinned and led the way to the dining room. The entire west side of the tiki-themed room tapered into the sand, where guys in the hotel's standard red aloha shirts tended a pit in the ground. Fragrant steam rose and drifted toward Dallen on the breeze. "You weren't kidding about the pig."

"I never joke about food," he said as his stomach growled, making Dallen laugh.

Their friend Deacon stood and waved them over, and Dallen gave Slade a sliver of attention as he recounted his wipeouts while learning to surf that afternoon. He focused the rest of his attention in a sweep of the dining room, looking for a head of wavy, light-brown hair. A few women caught his eye and smiled. On any other day, he might have returned them. A brunette seated by herself caught his eye and gave him a small smile, but she was more like the high-maintenance beauties in Chicago. He kept looking.

When the hostess seated them, he gave up and asked Slade, despite the teasing he knew it would earn him. "Where's Addison?"

"By Addison, do you mean Bree?"

Dallen shrugged, refusing to give Slade more to work with.

He grinned. "Addison's got a tickle in her throat, so she's resting and calling in every favor the universe has ever owed her to make sure she isn't getting sick. The other girls are supposed to be around here. I'll look for them."

Dallen grabbed his wrist to stop him from standing and let go when Slade plopped back in his seat. "Let's order first. You scope out the room while we wait for our food. Tell me when you see them, and I'll do something asinine like send drinks over to the table."

Slade nodded. "Make her come to you to thank you. Smart."

That's not why he'd suggested it, but Dallen didn't correct him. Bree had mentioned once that when Addison got extra crazy, Bree imagined herself sipping on a mai tai, and that got her through the crisis. He wanted to send one over to show that he remembered, not to gain some strategic advantage.

The waiter showed up to rattle off the specials, but Dallen barely heard the list of delicacies as he peered around the room again in search of Bree. It wouldn't feel like a vacation until he finally had her in his sights.

Eight

He stood there, in the flesh. Granted, half the time in her head it had been bare-chested flesh, but Bree didn't know if Dallen could look better than he did at that moment fully dressed, pausing on the restaurant threshold while he waited for the hostess to seat him and Slade. She wanted to get up and go say hi, and she pushed her chair back to do it, when his gaze fell on her. She smiled. This was it. He was here—early—and she couldn't be happier about it.

His gaze flickered a moment but moved right past her, sliding to a table full of good-looking women and checking them out.

And just like that, it was over. It had taken exactly two seconds of cold reality to deep freeze her warm, fuzzy daydreams about this week and Dallen.

Even looking her very best, she hadn't been enough to hold his attention, not with a table full of prettier women in the vicinity.

41

Awesome. He'd overlooked her as easily as if she were still hiding under a couple of layers of fat and mousy-brown hair.

Disappointment churned in her stomach, as vaguely nauseating as if she'd eaten a bucket of fried food. What now? Any moment, Slade would notice her and come over. She couldn't stand the inevitable awkwardness of trying to talk to Dallen as if everything was cool when it would be so clear that there was no chemistry between them. It would take two to create a reaction, but he wasn't feeling it.

She made a quick decision and rose from her table to slip through the French doors leading outside to the sand. Jen and Shayla wouldn't miss her; they'd decided to eat in the bar when they spotted some cute guys inside. Bree had stuck with the restaurant and its healthier options, but she wasn't hungry now.

Outside she veered toward the beach, slipping off her sandals. Love Blush would just have to get a touch up. Touching the sand was a relief, an immediate connection to the countless walks she'd taken up and down her stretch of beach back home as she thought or plotted, or simply was.

Being on the beach felt better. But it still didn't feel good. For a second, she thought she'd seen a flicker of recognition in his eyes, but she was wrong. Why hadn't he told her he was coming in early? Maybe he wasn't in the same rush to see her.

She sighed and trudged through the sand toward the water. It was low tide, the waves rolling in but petering out in white foam bubbles before they wet her toes. She sat and pulled her knees to her chest, staring into the distance to the bright orange rays the setting sun left hanging in the sky.

It was lame of her to have gotten so caught up in the possibilities. She'd spent so much time managing Addison's expectations that she hadn't put the brakes on her own.

We'll meet, it will be love at first sight, and we'll have the best how-we-met story.

She knew how it went now. They met when she'd stared at him in frozen surprise, and he hadn't seen her at all.

She stretched her feet out in front of her and studied her toes. Love Blush was intact, unlike her pride.

It was stupid to feel so let down by a twenty-second restaurant non-event. He'd seen her, he hadn't recognized her, so what? What had she expected? That they would spot each other on the beach and run through the sand, splashing in the waves as Dallen swept her into an embrace?

She turned to examine the long stretch of beach. Well, yeah. That's what she'd pictured a hundred times.

Okay, more.

Now she'd seen the reality, and it was a bummer, but she didn't have any business being offended just because Dallen didn't decide on the spot that she was his soul mate. Nope. Not even when she'd begun to sense from their emails and conversations that it was a possibility.

She wrapped her arms around her legs and sighed again. It had been so fun to live with the what-ifs for a couple of months. They'd entertained her through countless miles on the treadmill.

What if we click? What if he's as cool in person as he is online? What if we have chemistry? What if this stupid crush I have turns into something—a two-way something?

Ocean foam tickled her toes, and she drew them back, a smile escaping despite her disappointment. So they weren't going to be a thing. She was in Hawaii to witness her best friend's marriage. She drew in a deep breath of crisp ocean air and leaned back on her hands to revel in the last bit of sunset. She might as well cancel on Dallen for breakfast and dive into the nonstop schedule of pre-wedding festivities, which Addison had made her download to her iPad. Twice.

Tomorrow, when her path crossed Dallen's at Slade's big surprise, Bree would smile and crack jokes and try not to regret what could have been. Maybe she wasn't the premium-grade cover girl Dallen usually dated, but she'd worked too hard to be healthy and disciplined to waste time on regretting his narrow tastes. Let him find himself a long-legged model poolside for his plaything this weekend. Addison needed her, and she'd rather be a good friend than arm candy anyway.

Nine

Dallen: Hey. I landed a little while ago. Thought I'd surprise you at dinner, but I didn't see you anywhere. Are you up for a drink and a hello?

Bree: So glad you made it. Everything (Addison) is much crazier than I expected, so I don't think I've even got a free second until Slade's thing tomorrow night. So sorry!

Dallen sank onto his bed and stared at his phone. Something had gone very wrong between this text and the one that morning. What was it?

Someone pounded on his door.

"Open up!"

Addison? He hurried to open the door for her.

She greeted him by shoving his chest hard, forcing him to take a step back. "What is *wrong* with you?"

"Whoa," he said, taking another step back in case she decided to shove him again. "What's wrong?"

"I asked you first," she said. "You've never been an idiot before. Why would you start now?"

He frantically scanned his memory files for a wedding task he'd overlooked. "Did I forget to do something? Should I have not texted Bree?"

"No, you should not have texted her. You should have said hi when you had the chance." She stuck her hands on her hips and glared at him. "How could you walk right past her without saying a word?"

"I haven't seen her yet."

"Exactly!" she said on a near shout. "She was right in front of you, and you didn't even acknowledge her! Way to be, you idiot."

"When did I see her?" he asked in confusion. "I've only been down to the restaurant and back, and believe me, I looked."

This time only a strangled groan of frustration came out as Addison shoved her hands in her hair and tugged. "I want to punch you so bad right now."

"I can tell," he said, moving further back. "Should I call Slade or something?"

"No, you should call Bree and beg her forgiveness. I learn a lot of nasty words working in the court system. I'm trying to figure out the best one to use for you."

Dallen pushed through the mental fog that had descended with Bree's rejection text. "She was in the dining room, and I didn't see her?"

"Yes, genius."

"Why didn't she say anything?" He took another hasty step back when her face darkened further.

"Because she smiled at you, and you looked right past her. She said you even frowned. She decided maybe it wasn't the right time to say hello."

"Wait," he said, the first throbs of a headache kicking up. "What was she wearing?"

"A white sundress. She said she smiled at you, then you checked out a bunch of other women and went on to your table, where you started shoving your face with pig." Her eyes narrowed. "You are what you eat."

"Be nice. I was only looking for Bree, that's it. I know exactly who you're talking about in the white dress, and I *would* have smiled back if I hadn't thought that would mean sending signals to some random chick when I flew in a day early to see someone else. You're telling me that *was* Bree?"

Addison gave him a single, sharp nod.

"But she didn't look anything like the picture."

Addison whipped her phone out of her purse and thrust it at him. "*That* is Bree."

"Holy crap." The picture staring back wasn't a sweet-faced girl next door with light-brown hair and eyes hidden behind sunglasses. Addison's phone showed a stone-cold fox with almost auburn hair and stunning green eyes. "Holy crap. This doesn't look at all like the other one."

Her eyebrows drew together. "That's the *only* picture you've seen of her?"

"Yeah."

"Oh." She studied him for a long moment. "Why haven't you asked to see more pictures? I thought you'd probably exchanged some over email or something." She flinched. "That sounded skeevier than I meant it to."

"That's exactly why I haven't asked her, or you, or anyone else for pictures. Most people you can find plastered all over Facebook, but not Bree."

Addison's grin appeared. "You looked?"

His cheeks heated. "Sure. I was curious about who I was jumping through all your demented wedding hoops with."

That finally earned him a punch. He rubbed his ribs where she'd nailed him, but he didn't apologize. He was too confused to react.

"So, dummy," she said, waving the phone at him again. "This is what you walked away from tonight."

He groaned. "I totally saw her. I expected someone a little more . . ."

Addison's eyes narrowed again. "Average?"

"Girl next door," he said. "It doesn't matter. I feel bad that she thinks I dissed her."

Addison shook her head. "She didn't take it as a diss, exactly. She came back from dinner laughing like it was no big deal. But she's seen Slade's supermodel album of you, and she's had it in her head ever since that you're looking for something more exotic than she is, or something equally ridiculous."

He rubbed his hands over his face. "I'm going to tell you something, and I know you hate keeping secrets, but you have to keep this one. I don't want her to take this the wrong way, and I don't trust you to say it to her the right way."

Twin expressions of curiosity and annoyance crossed her face. Curiosity won. "Fine. What?"

"I did expect someone way more average. Not that it mattered. I think she's cool, and I was looking forward to hanging out with her. So it's surprising that she's hot, but it really doesn't matter."

Addison tilted her head. "I believe you because I know you. But now you have to convince Bree, because I know her even better, and I'm telling you right now that she's going to have walls up. Mile-high walls. So fix it."

He scrubbed his hand through his hair. "I'll text her again."

"And say what? 'Sorry, but I didn't realize you're hot—now that I know, I want to talk to you'? Don't text her. Tone will get lost."

"Then I'll drop by her room and say hi."

"You need a less loaded situation." She closed her eyes as if considering the options. "I'll get her out to the rose garden in half an hour. Find a way to be there, but don't tell her I sent you, and think of something good to say."

He nodded. "Thanks." He slid his hands in his pockets and rocked back on his heels, debating his next words. "I like her. I'll fix this."

She gave him a quick hug and headed for the door. "If you're smart, you will. She's one in a million," she said before closing it behind her.

He reached for his phone a dozen times, anxious to fix his screw-up, but he stopped each time, mindful of Addison's warning. *Tone will get lost.*

He tried to figure out why he would be in a rose garden at nine o'clock at night. He decided to put on his workout clothes. Maybe running on the beach would give him a good excuse? Twenty minutes later, Addison texted.

She's on her way.

He took the stairs down and followed the hotel's private path to the rose garden. The moon was so bright he didn't need the lights set artfully around the flower beds to see Bree sitting with her back to the entrance, her fall of dark hair contrasting sharply with her white dress. He cleared his throat, and she twisted around, her eyes widening when she registered that it was him. For a second, she said nothing, and he wondered if she would pretend not to recognize him, but then she turned to face him fully, her shoulders back and a friendly smile on her face.

"You're Dallen," she said. "Nice to finally meet you."

"You're Bree." *And you're smoking hot,* he wanted to add, but not at the risk of making it sound as if it mattered. Or insulting her by sounding surprised.

She nodded and offered a tiny wave. "Hi."

"Hey," he said, unable to contain a wide grin as he crossed to hug her. Her hug was cursory, the kind you give when you don't want to be rude. Yeah. Walls way up.

He stepped back and smiled. "Funny running into you here. It's weird to bump into people out of context, isn't it? I feel like it's going to take me a minute to believe that the Bree I've been emailing is right here in front of me."

Was that too subtle?

Her eyes narrowed for the tiniest fraction of a second.

He would have missed it if he hadn't been studying her so closely, but it was enough to tell him he hadn't been subtle.

She shrugged. "Yeah, it's strange." Her forehead wrinkled. "Addison made me come down to check whether this place would be better for the ceremony. What brings you here?"

Careful not to incriminate Addison, he pointed to his sneakers. "Going on a night run. Thought I'd see what was behind the fancy flower arch." He hated how stilted they both sounded—nothing like what he was used to between them, and even further from how he'd hoped it would be.

"That's good. Enjoy yourself." She settled onto the bench again, her smile and tone polite, but it was a clear dismissal. He missed the underlying current of mischief he'd heard in their phone calls.

"Sorry breakfast won't work out," he said, fishing for anything salvageable.

She showed her first signs of uneasiness. "Yeah, well. You know how Addison is."

It had nothing to do with Addison, but he let none of his frustration show in his face. "If we don't bump into each other before then, I'll see you tomorrow night."

"See you then."

With nothing left for him to say, he sketched a brief wave and left, hitting the beach path at a jog. He'd pound the sand until he figured out how to get the two of them back on the right footing. Even the way Bree handled herself when she was disappointed appealed to him. She was classy, undramatic, and even more intriguing since he knew what a funny girl hid beneath the hot-girl, detached-from-it-all demeanor. He'd figure out how to lure *that* Bree out, because he was more convinced than ever she was worth the effort.

Ten

Bree sucked in her first deep breath only after she heard the thud of Dallen's retreating footsteps. Once again he'd caught her by surprise. At least this time she'd had the good sense not to grin like an idiot. She ran their short conversation through her head several times. He'd looked so good in his workout clothes, as good as he had in his dinner clothes. Maybe better, because his hair had lost its perfect styling, so it looked mussed, and way too touchable. Thank goodness she'd kept herself together. She'd tried to act exactly like she would have with Slade, to think of Dallen as a nice guy that she only kind of knew. It had helped.

But she was going to have to come up with a much better strategy for dealing with him by tomorrow, because despite keeping him at a distance, heat had raced through her when he'd pulled her into a hug, shocking her so much it was all she could do to remember to let her arms float up and return the favor before he let her go. He'd felt so good. She'd have to try to forget about that before she saw him again, or she'd end up looking pathetic.

Deep in thought, she made her way back to her room. Addison definitely had something to do with Dallen's sudden appearance in the garden. How did she have the energy to worry about Bree's love life and still panic hourly about her wedding? The first order of business would be to make sure Addison didn't butt in anymore.

When Bree slipped back into the suite, Jen and Shayla were settled on the sofa watching a Lifetime movie with the volume low.

"Where's Addison?" she asked.

"She went to bed," Shayla said. "By the way, you're my hero now. I had no idea you were running so much interference between us and her fifty thousand last-minute changes."

Bree smiled. "She's the kind of friend that it's worth doing for."

"She's pretty great," Jen agreed. "But I'm glad she's sleeping. She's stressing herself out too much."

"Truth," Bree said, squishing onto the couch with them. "You guys ready to help with the big event tomorrow?"

Shayla nodded. "I've been practicing the moves. You sure the guys are going to do this?"

Bree shrugged. "Dallen says yes."

"And we trust this guy? He wasn't smart enough to recognize you from ten yards away."

"Maybe his vision isn't great, but he seems pretty on top of everything else. For once, if something goes wrong, it'll be more his headache than mine. He doesn't believe me that Addison is going to love it whether or not it goes perfectly."

"True," Shayla said. "She'll just think it's romantic. And then she and Slade will be nauseatingly cute about it."

Jen grinned. "They're pretty vomitous, aren't they?"

"And perfect," Shayla admitted. "I love those two together."

Bree snuggled into the sofa. "Yeah. They fit." So what if she'd spent a few weeks imagining that she and Dallen would connect the same way? No one ever needed to know that she'd had them married off and picking out baby names before they ever met. It's not like she thought it would happen for real. It was a good reminder not to let her daydreams overrule reality.

When the movie ended, she slipped into bed and prayed for Dallen-free sleep. What she got was a dream right before waking full of hungry kisses and rolling around in the sand with Dallen like they were in a Hollywood movie. She got up and dragged herself down to the beach to tackle a long run and clear her head, but every time the waves nearly got her, she remembered the dream kisses, and heat suffused her, spreading out from her middle to flush her cheeks and advertise her continuing inability to separate swoony fantasy from reality.

She ran harder, until all she could focus on was keeping her breathing even and powering through the punishing sand. By the time she returned to the hotel, her calves were screaming, but her mind had calmed. She was ready to tackle the day.

She kept it together through breakfast after Whitney and Michelle arrived, through the girls' spa day, when her mind wandered to Dallen in the garden, or Dallen and her in the sand, or even the reality of Dallen's hug. Each time, she yanked her attention back to how she'd maneuver Addison into position for Slade's big surprise. It worked, all the way through getting ready for dinner, when she slipped on the green strapless cocktail dress she'd imagined wearing for Dallen.

She wore it for herself now. She loved the way it brightened her eyes, and focused on that, pushing all thoughts of the impression she'd hoped it would make on

Dallen out of her mind. She had a delicate mission to execute anyway.

"Is that what you're wearing?" she asked when Addison pulled a brightly printed maxi dress from the closet. Her phone chimed with a text, and she stole a peek at it. Dallen.

"Hike" nearly killed us. Just got back, but we're on schedule. You ready?

Addison held her dress up. "You like it? It's nice enough for dinner downstairs, right?"

"Um, maybe," Bree said, squinting at it and pretending to think. "I mean, it's cute. But did you bring the puce one? Seems like a good night for nostalgia."

"Yeah." Addison fished it out of the closet. "You really think I should wear it?" She held up the dress she'd been wearing the night she met Slade. "I love it, but it seems too reserved for here. I can't see myself doing the hula in this."

As far as Addison knew, they were heading down for drinks at the bar before the hotel's weekly luau on the beach, complete with the hula dancing they'd learned that afternoon. In reality, there would be a big dance performance, but *for* Addison, not *with* her, courtesy of Slade's intricately planned flash mob. The hike he'd told Addison about had really been a recruiting trip up and down the beach, rounding up hotel guests willing to learn a dance and spring it on his fiancée a few hours later.

"This whole weekend is about celebrating you and Slade," Bree told Addison. "Wearing the first dress he ever saw you in on the last night before you marry him is pretty cool. Who cares if it's a little dressier than you need?" Bree wasn't sure her argument made sense, but Addison took the bait.

"You're right." She plopped down on the bed and hugged the dress to herself. "I can't believe I almost didn't go to that cocktail party. The young professionals networking thing sounded stupid, but it was fate."

Bree smiled at her friend's starry-eyed expression. "Definitely. And definitely wear that dress."

Addison bounced back up and shimmied into it, her voice muffled as she pulled it over her head. "Let's go. Where are the other girls?"

"They said they were going down to hold a table." In reality, they'd slipped out before Addison could see them in cocktail dresses more suited for the city than the beach.

Addison tugged the dress down. "I'll hurry."

When she closed the bathroom door behind her, Bree fired off a quick reply.

Bree: *Ready. Slade hanging in there?*
Slade: *So stoked he can't stand it. Don't laugh at my dancing.*
Bree: *Don't know if you're crazy or a prince among men, but you're def a good friend. See you on the dance floor.*

Addison popped back out of the bathroom, her lip gloss in place on her happy smile. "Time to see my girls."

They found the rest of the bridesmaids with fruity drinks already in hand. Bree eyed their margaritas. She wasn't much of a drinker, but maybe she should start with a couple of shots of tequila-flavored courage to settle her nerves. Dancing in public wasn't her thing. Add in her nerves over seeing Dallen again, and she was a jumble of knots. She'd spent the whole day lecturing herself every time one of his texts came in updating her on their progress, setting off flutters in her stomach.

She tried remembering the way his eyes had slid over her without seeing her the night before, but images of him in the rose garden looking sexy in his running shorts crowded that out. She tried imagining him with a parade of gorgeous women to remind herself that she wasn't his type, but instead she remembered him putting his arms around her. Somehow that image included the smell of soap and a whiff of rum.

She tapped her fingers on the table in a staccato rhythm, trying to channel her nerves, but Addison's forehead wrinkled, and a hint of suspicion crept into her expression as she took a closer look at her bachelorette party. "What's with the dresses?"

Uh oh. Bree bent her head over her phone and tapped out a warning to Dallen. *Show time.*

"What do you mean?" Michelle said, her tone bland. "You don't like them? I think everyone looks really cute."

"You do," Addison said, undeterred from her cross-examination. "But you don't look tropical. You look you're about to meet with your senior partners at a cocktail party."

A couple of the girls shot Bree veiled looks of panic. She tried to muster her nonexistent acting chops.

"Your margarita must have been strong because that's crazy talk. We'd better get some food in you." She took Addison's wrist and pulled her toward the restaurant.

"But we're eating at the luau."

Bree shook her head. "I think you need something now. Bread, maybe. Come on, girls."

A few muffled giggles escaped behind her as they rounded up their drinks and handbags. She couldn't stop her own smile from breaking out when they reached the dining room. The second they appeared in the doorway, diners at the four tables nearest them rose and moved all but one of the tables to the side, creating a large space.

"What's going on?" Addison demanded. No one answered.

How many people had Dallen and Slade convinced to do this? Bree drew Addison to the remaining empty table. A waiter stopped to offer champagne in fluted glasses, and Bree nodded at Addison to take one.

"But I didn't order this," she said.

"I did," Slade said from behind them, dressed in a business suit. Bree squelched the urge to search for Dallen. Addison turned to smile up at him, and he nodded at the hostess, who reached down and pushed a button. The soft Hawaiian background music stopped, and the opening strains of "I Believe I Can Fly" poured from the speakers, much louder than the dinner music had.

It took Addison a couple of moments, but then a huge smile lit her face.

Slade leaned down to smile back. "Is it possible that this is the worst song ever?"

Bree had heard the story a thousand times after they met; this was the opening line he'd used on her at that cocktail party.

He straightened and held up his fingers in the "okay" sign, and suddenly five other guys rose from different tables, all overdressed in business suits. Bree immediately found Dallen and couldn't look away. He wore charcoal pinstripes and a sky-blue shirt that matched his eyes perfectly. Bree swallowed. Wow.

As R. Kelly started singing about life being an awful song, the groomsmen formed a semicircle behind Slade and did some awkward soft-shoe moves while Slade lip synced. Her smile threatened to split her cheeks.

Bree tried not to stare, but she couldn't help watching Dallen. He was a pretty bad dancer, but he was committed, and she had to respect the effort as he clomped through the side steps. When the guys all executed a synchronized spin, the girls' table broke into cheers, Bree included.

Oh, screw it. She was going to have as much fun with this as anyone, and if Dallen took that to mean she was letting her guard down, that was his problem, not hers. She swayed to the beat with the rest of the girls doing some interpretive chair dancing. A handful of other diners rose and joined the suits, their tropical shirts and colorful dresses adding splash to the proceedings.

When Addison realized they knew the moves too, and that she was dealing with a true flash mob, she whooped. Slade grinned but kept up his lip sync. Cell phones appeared all over the place as people filmed the action, and Bree finally spotted the bride and groom's parents at a table off to the side, looking delighted by the whole production.

More and more diners filtered in to join the group until nearly two dozen people hopped and spun and did jazz hands to the schmaltzy words coming through the speakers. Dallen looked like he was trying not to crack up. His sister had choreographed the routine, and Dallen had IM-ed Bree for an hour one night about his epic battle waged against jazz hands. Clearly, he'd lost. She laughed. He caught her eye and winked. The chorus swelled, which was the bridesmaids' cue to break into their chair dance part of the routine, arms waving like fans, swaying heads, and all.

When the song ended, the entire restaurant broke into applause. Addison launched herself out of her chair and straight into Slade's arms, and the clapping grew louder. Slade let go of Addison long enough to gesture for the applause to die down, and he drew her to his side, his arm tight around her waist.

"Ladies and gentlemen, I thought I was the luckiest man alive when I saw the most amazing woman in the world across a crowded room last year. She talked to me even though I came up to her with the lamest icebreaker in history. But I was wrong. I'm the luckiest man in the world because Addison Morgan has promised to be mine forever when she marries me tomorrow." And with the sound of the whole restaurant's congratulations ringing in their ears, he dipped Addison back for a long, romantic kiss.

Once again, Dallen caught her eye. *Oof.* She had to fight the tractor beam pulling her gaze his way. Looking away would only make it obvious she wanted to avoid him, so she gave him a thumbs up. He did a subtle fist pump and mouthed, *Nailed it.*

"I have got to find a man like that," Whitney grumbled, watching Slade smile at Addison. "Are any of the groomsmen single?" She stood to find out.

Bree didn't care to see what happened when the curvy redhead verified Dallen's single status, so she leaned over to Michelle. "I'm going to go see if our seats for the luau are ready."

Michelle nodded. "We'll be down in a bit."

With that, Bree slipped out through the open patio and stepped onto the sand with her high-heeled sandals threaded through her fingers. A few minutes later a hotel worker verified that luau seating would begin in half an hour. Plenty of time to walk the beach and get her game face on.

She made her way to the water and smiled out at it. Maybe the Dallen thing hadn't worked, and that was disappointing. But chemistry was a funny thing. She could have been a knockout like Addison, and the spark might have still flowed only one way. That's what made couples like Slade and Addison so magical. In the huge sea of choices, they found their perfect fit. It would happen for her. She had just hoped it would happen here. With Dallen.

She sat and wrapped her arms around her knees, staring out at the last rosy glow of the sunset clinging to the horizon. This was where she'd pictured herself sitting with Dallen, the wedding madness behind them and four more sun-soaked days in heaven ahead. It was hard to imagine it with anyone else—not the guy from the pool who tried to chat her up the first day or the waiter at lunch who had asked if she was free tonight. Only Dallen made sense here. Dallen, who had made her laugh and think and laugh some more.

Maybe Addison was right about symbols. Bree should try one of her own to purge her expectations and put herself in a head space to fully enjoy reality. She picked up a handful of sand and let it run back out, forming a small pyramid beside her. How many grains were slipping through her fingers? It almost didn't matter. No doubt she had thought of Dallen at least that many times. She dusted her palm to brush off any stray grains.

Vamanos, Dallen. You were standing between me and Hawaii, but we're done now. I belong to Hawaii for the next four days, and there's no room for you.

She rested her head on her knees and studied the pile, wondering if she felt better.

A bare foot poking out from a gray, pinstriped pant leg stepped on her pile, and suddenly there stood Dallen.

"Don't run," he said when she looked up. "I'm fast on the sand, and I'll eventually catch you, but it won't be fun in this suit."

Eleven

ree stared up at him, then back down at the symbol he'd flattened. "Have a seat," she said, patting the ground next to her. "I won't run."

He sat, stretching his legs out in front of him. "It's over," he said, on a sigh of relief. "If we survive the ceremony tomorrow, we are rock stars."

She leaned back on her arms. "I pick Kelly Clarkson. You can be Justin Bieber."

"I've always seen myself as an Adam Levine."

"Fine. You can be him." That fit him way too well. For a split second, she mentally photoshopped Adam Levine's face onto Dallen's body, only to realize Dallen looked hotter. She dropped the picture and glanced away from the distracting reality to look out at the waves.

"No disrespect to Kelly Clarkson, by the way, but that's not the right fit for you either. I see Katy Perry. Except classy. And smarter."

Her cheeks warmed at the comparison. "Thanks. You're sweet to say so."

"If so, it's accidental sweetness. I'm just being honest."

Somehow it sounded true instead of like a line. "So the flash mob is done. You ready for your best-man duties?"

"Check this out." He stood and braced his feet, his hands clasped in front of him. In his suit, he almost looked like a Secret Service guy guarding his subject. He painted a serious, thoughtful expression on his face, nodded his head a few times, did a couple of courtesy chuckles that won answering laughs from her, and then mimed patting his coat pockets and looking panicked, which made her laugh harder. A moment later relief crossed his face and he dug into his pants pocket to pull out an imaginary ring box and fumble the hand off to an invisible Slade.

He sat down and smiled. "Maybe I should practice."

"Good idea."

He leaned back again and followed her gaze out to the ocean. "Is it as cool to you as it is to me, since you get to see it all the time?"

"The ocean? It never gets old," she said.

They listened to the waves in silence. She was too aware of him to relax completely, but she didn't feel the need to break the quiet. She stifled a small sigh. This is what it could have been. Plus kissing. And moonlight.

He cleared his throat. "I need to say something that's probably going to make me sound like an ass."

She turned to look at him. A soft wash of color reddened his cheeks that couldn't be blamed on the setting sun. He looked the way she had felt after giving him the big grin he'd looked right past. What did *he* have to be embarrassed about?

"Go ahead," she said.

He moved about three feet away and turned to face her directly. "I'd move even farther in case you throw sand or something, but I feel stupid enough without having to shout."

She turned and scooped up a handful of sand. "You definitely have my attention now."

"I don't blame you for being mad that I didn't recognize you last night."

It was her turn to blush. He knew she'd seen him? Worse, he knew she was mad about him not seeing her? The heat deepened and crept down her neck. It sounded like a juvenile complaint, not how a mature twenty-six-year-old would react. But it was how she felt. Disappointed hopes sucked. She didn't necessarily want to be dwelling on it anymore, but she wasn't going to pretend it hadn't been a high-grade bummer to watch parts of her fantasy crumble.

"Here's the thing," he said, and he scrambled backward a few more feet. "I definitely noticed you. I thought, 'That chick is hot, but that's not who I flew in early for.'"

He thought she was hot? She threw the sand at him anyway, not trying very hard to hit him. "I object to the term *chick*."

"I meant to say amazing woman."

"Nice save."

"Thank you. Happens to be very true. I'd only seen one picture of you, of this cute girl hiding behind sunglasses. I didn't know what your eyes looked like. You had different hair. I was looking for that girl. I was so excited to surprise her. To be honest, I should have realized it was the same smile, but . . ." He trailed off and grimaced before taking a deep breath. "When you smiled at me, I was like, 'I don't have time for hot chicks—women—because I'm looking for Bree.'"

She strangled a laugh. That had definitely not come out right, but she could see that he was trying hard to be honest.

He misunderstood the sound she made, and his head dropped. "I know. That sounds bad, like I didn't think you were hot from that picture. I'm only going to get myself in more trouble for saying this, but I've had the chance to date some really good-looking women, and a lot of them are high maintenance and personality deficient. In all of our talks or emails or whatever, you seemed way too funny to be . . . Uh, I'm going to stop now. I don't think I can go anywhere good with this."

She picked up and dropped several handfuls of sand. Her cheeks were still warm, but it had everything to do with his words. Staying distant would be safer, but everything he said was obnoxiously endearing. "I'm beginning to feel totally ridiculous about this whole situation."

"Don't," he said. "I think I'd be kind of ticked if I thought you'd blown me off. But I swear I didn't. And I'm really praying that you're getting my huge point in all of this, which is that it's nice that you're pretty, but I already thought you were pretty before, and that's not why I'm into you. You're funny, and quick, and laid back. Are you going to forgive me?"

He was into her? The rest of her was warming up nicely too.

These two days had only been awkward because she'd been so stupid about her insecurities. If getting healthy had quit being about looking good weeks ago, what was her problem? Grayson was long gone, and she needed to take back the last piece of control over her life from him, to end the grip his words had held on her sense of self, and to dictate her own happiness and well-being. Why stop at the scale?

She stood and strolled toward him. A half smile appeared on his face. She reached down, slipped her hands around his lapels, and tugged. It was enough to send him scrambling to his feet. She gazed up at him and the grin lighting his face.

"I forgive you," she said, smoothing his jacket. "Forgive me too?"

"For what?"

64

"Being lame and high maintenance."

His smile softened as his gaze grew intense. He slipped a hand into her hair, cradling the back of her head and pulling her slowly toward him to give her time to break away if she wanted to. She didn't want to.

His lips brushed hers with a touch as light as the tropical breeze, but when she didn't pull away, he pressed harder. She slipped her arms around his neck and returned the kiss. He groaned low in his throat, and his free arms slipped around her waist to pull her against him. She wondered if he could feel her heart pounding against the hard wall of his chest, but decided she didn't care.

He broke the kiss to drop his forehead against hers. "I've been wanting to do that since the first time you made me laugh out loud. I'm so glad that's not the effect funny people normally have on me because I don't think my guy friends would be into me kissing them every time they made a joke."

"I'm into it," she said, clasping her hands tighter.

"I'm into *you*," he repeated, his voice quieter now and his smile gone. He leaned down and kissed her again, harder and hungrier. Heat exploded inside her, sweeping through her in seconds as he parted her lips with his and explored the kiss even more. Her knees buckled, and he held her tight. "I'm not letting go," he said against her mouth. "We're going to look really stupid trying to dig out wedding rings and do our wedding duties tomorrow like this." He tightened his arms around her waist.

She sprinkled kisses along his jawline, loving the scrape of his five o'clock shadow against her lips. "We'd better practice then, because I don't think I could let go if I wanted to."

He kissed her until she had to pull away to breathe, and when she leaned her head against his chest to smile up at him, he brushed another kiss against her forehead. "I need to do something. Can you give me a minute?"

Now? She straightened. "Sure."

He pulled his phone from his pocket and sat back down on the sand, his fingers tapping like mad on the screen. He stopped and smiled at her, and a second later her phone beeped. He tugged her down beside him but said nothing. She fished her phone from her clutch and read the text.

This is how I hoped it would be.

She smiled and sent her answer. *How sad.*

He looked at her, startled.

She leaned over and stole another kiss. "It's even better."

ABOUT MELANIE JACOBSON

Melanie Bennett Jacobson is an avid reader, amateur cook, and champion shopper. She consumes astonishing amounts of chocolate, chick flicks, and romance novels. After meeting her husband online, she is now living happily married in Southern California with her growing family and a series of doomed houseplants. Melanie is a former English teacher and a sometimes blogger who loves to laugh and make others laugh. In her down time (ha!), she writes romantic comedies and pines after beautiful shoes. Visit her website here: http://www.melaniejacobson.net

Romeo and Julie-Ex

Julie Wright

Other Works by Julie Wright

Cross My Heart

Loved Like That

My Not-So-Fairy-Tale Life

The Newport Ladies Book Club Series

The Hazzardous Universe Series

One

People who say that everything looks better in the light of a new day are total liars. Sometimes a new day means misery.

Adam called the wedding off exactly fifty-two minutes before my wedding dress showed up on my doorstep. The doorbell for the delivery rang in the middle of me running his pictures through my paper shredder. I didn't even check the peephole before opening it. Would it matter if it had been a serial killer? I still held a couple of pictures in my fist when I answered and saw the UPS man standing there.

He had his little handheld delivery scanner held out to me and a smile on his face. "Hi there. I have a delivery for Juliet Moore. Are you Juliet?" His cheery voice made my hand tighten. The pictures crumpled into little balls. He must not have really needed me to confirm my identity, because before I could answer, he said, "If you could sign for this, ma'am . . ." He nudged the scanner thing in my direction.

I blinked, making no move to sign anything. "Do you know what's in that box?" I asked.

His brow furrowed, not that it had far to furrow—the man in brown was dangerously close to a uni-brow. "I don't really—"

"It's a dress." I cut him off and felt guilty for not feeling guilty about it. "A *wedding* dress."

His face contorted somewhere between the furrowed brow and a smile he wasn't sure he should offer. His mouth seemed to be forming the word, "Congratulations." But he never actually said it. Apparently he had enough intelligence to notice I wasn't smiling. Or maybe he noticed the black mascara trails streaking down my cheeks. His gaze slipped to the wrinkled pictures in my hands.

"A wedding dress," I repeated. "For my wedding. I spent two months' worth of wages on a gorgeous, perfect Reem Acra gown—one that would have made Cinderella's fairy godmother look like a fashion-challenged tightwad. But do you know what happens now?"

He shook his head—a slight shake. He seemed terrified to move.

"Nothing. Nothing happens now, because Adam, the groom, has a girlfriend, a girlfriend who isn't me. He has *another* girlfriend, or I guess just one girlfriend now, since I am no longer part of this equation. I am also no longer his fiancé. I will never, *ever* be his wife. So the dress you're so keen on me signing for? It's for nothing. Nothing at all."

We stared at each other. With my lips pressed tightly together, I tasted salt from dried tears. Finally, when it seemed I'd ranted the UPS man into a mute statue, I threw my arms in the air and said, "Give me that." I pulled the scanner from his hands, scrawled a vicious mark into the screen, and shoved it back at him.

He scampered off my steps without a goodbye or backwards glance. The box sat on my porch, a pathetic little tower of shame.

The dress would hang in my closet. Which would be a good thing, I supposed. No sense wasting the perfect dress on *him*—cheating, lying, son of a—

The phone rang.

I didn't answer it—*couldn't* answer it. What would I say? I'd just sobbed the most personal details of my life to a complete stranger. What would I say to someone who knew me well enough to call?

With my fingers still tightly fisted around his pictures, I managed to wrap my arms around the box and heft it into my entryway. It slipped and fell against the little table by the door and knocked over the bone china vase I'd been given at a bridal shower.

I kicked the box at the same time little white shards of pottery showered my feet. Stupid Adam! Stupid wedding! Stupid, stupid me for spending that much money on a dress I'd never wear.

The phone rang several times more.

I didn't answer it. Not once.

In my more honest moments of the entire after-break-up agony, I recognized signs of relief. His lunatic, racist mother would never be *my* mother-in-law. Score one for me. His creepy brother would never leer at me again. Score two. I'd never have to sit through another dinner at his favorite French restaurant, even though he knew I hated French cuisine. Score three.

I recounted all the reasons for relief instead of anguish, surprised that there were so *many* reasons to be relieved as I fed photos, playbills, tickets, and notes into the shredder. While the shredder did its job, I systematically deleted everything off my hard drive as well. If I could have taken an eraser to the man himself, I'd have done it.

And somewhere between the delivery of the box holding my wedding dress and the next morning, I had a mental breakdown with the realization that all of Adam's pictures had made it through the shredder, including a few where I'd actually looked good.

Why hadn't I just cut him out? Why had I shredded the whole photo? Why had I been so careful in deleting everything?

Idiot!

I fell asleep amidst piles of shredded photo paper, tape, and failed attempts at piecing one of those pictures back together.

I awoke to the chimes of my doorbell, and swiped at the shredded bits of photo paper stuck to my face. It took a moment to realize what the noise was until the chimes went off again.

"I'm coming!" I shouted in the quietest way possible; the light streaming in from the windows slashed my eyes like cat claws. *A crying headache.* I wiped at my eyes to remove the leftover saline granules and opened the door.

I stared at my best friend and roommate, trying to focus on her between the blur and the headache. "Alison? Don't you have your key?" She was a buyer for several major chain stores and travelled all over to view new clothing lines.

"Key's on the counter in my bathroom." Her eyes narrowed as she really looked at me. "What happened?" She said the words in that sympathetic voice people used when dealing with small children or the mentally impaired.

"Why would you assume something's going on?"

She tugged her suitcase into the apartment. "Juliet, honey, it's obvious. You look hung over."

I shut the door. "I do not."

She reached at something attached to my head. Feeling like she'd yanked out half my hair, I threw my hands to the offended spot as she held up a long strand of hairy tape. She shook it in front of my face. "Your eyes are puffy and bloodshot, your cheek looks like the victim of a bad tattoo artist, you've got tape stuck in your hair, and what is this? Am I walking on glass?"

She looked down at the white shards crunching underfoot as she shifted her position.

I shrugged before she could complain that we'd lose the deposit if we scratched the floors and led the way to the living room so I didn't have to explain out loud. She could see the remnants of my ruination and figure it out for herself.

A gasp sounded from behind me as she stepped into the living room. I turned to watch her as she surveyed my own personal ground zero.

Her mouth hung open, and her eyebrows bunched up into a knot above her nose. Her pity face. I both hated her pity face, and needed it at the same time.

"You didn't even open the dress to look at it?" She acted intensely more scandalized about the unopened box than the fact that Adam had dumped me.

"What's the point of looking at a dress I don't get to wear?" I slumped onto the couch, shredded photo paper falling off the cushions in a fluttery snowfall of pathetic.

She sat next to me, but I could tell from the way her feet were placed on the carpet and the way her muscles tensed that she was ready to pounce on the box and open it herself if I'd let her.

But I didn't want to see anything.

She finally realized that the permission she wanted wasn't coming and settled back against the cushions. "So what now?"

I leaned back too, rolling my head so I could stare at the ceiling. "An excellent question." It seemed I should probably cry some more, but no more tears came. I felt hollowed out and useless, like a pumpkin the day after Halloween.

"What do I do with all the shower gifts?" I asked after several minutes of us staring at the ceiling.

She turned her head towards me. "Keep 'em. If anyone asks, have them call Adam so he can explain everything. Besides, the new blender is fabulous, and now I get to share it with you."

I ignored her joy over the blender. "This was so not part of my plan . . ."

"You can't plan life. Life is that thing happening while you're busy making plans. It just is what it is."

"It just sucks."

She smiled. "That, too."

"I have to tell my parents. What do I tell them? And I have to cancel everything. The flowers, the invitations, the caterers, the reception center. All those deposits—down the toilet." I moved to my feet and began to pace, energized by the fury of this realization. I was going to end up losing a small fortune on this not-happening wedding.

"That slithering snake!" I shouted, glad to be able to channel the anger. "He insisted on the very best of everything. Only the caterers his mom approved of. A reception hall that wouldn't shame his father when his business buddies showed up. The very *best*, which translates into the very most expensive! On *everything*! And *I* was the one who paid the deposits on all of it!"

I kicked the shredded remnants of our relationship. "I'm going to kill him. Kill him, resuscitate him, and kill him again!"

"Killing people is against the law." Alison reminded me, her eyes carefully tracking my movements as I paced and kicked and threw punches into the air, imagining Adam's face.

"Not if they don't find the body!"

Alison frowned. "I still think it's against the law. It's just harder to try the case in court. You're the lawyer; you should know that."

I let fly another kick, this one landing solidly against the box with the dress.

I sank beside the box, my hand resting reverentially against the side. "Next week was going to be the big photo shoot for my bridal portraits. I was going to get my hair done, my nails done, and wear this dress." I let out a bitter laugh. "It was the only thing Adam actually paid for. He insisted we had to use this guy because he was a friend of the family, and it would upset his parents to snub their friends. I told him if he wanted that guy, he'd have to pay for it. So he did. He paid for several locations and sittings. But because they were family friends, the photographer was the only thing fully refundable." I blinked and looked up at her, shaking my head.

Alison had on her pity face again. "Oh, hon. I am so sorry." She moved down from the couch to sit next to me and my box of failed possibility, and put her arms around me.

I shook my head. "He not only ruined what should have been a great day of pampering, he doesn't even have to pay the deposit."

She stiffened and pulled back, her eyes no longer filled with pity, but something else entirely.

I knew that look. It was the one that got me constant after-school detentions back in high school. It was the one that ended up with both of us taken into police custody after she talked me into helping her spray paint her ex-boyfriend's car with the word "liar." The reason we weren't actually arrested was the same reason she'd been able to talk me into carrying out her devilish plans in the first place.

And that look was back, the one that promised vengeance of the four-horsemen variety.

"What?" I should have known better than to ask.

"He *already* paid for it?" she asked.

I nodded slowly.

"What happens if you show up at the photo shoot?"

I pulled farther away from her as if she had a disease I didn't want to catch. "What kind of loser gets bridal portraits done when they aren't going to be a bride?"

"Don't be so dramatic. Of course you're going to be a bride. You'll just have a groom upgrade when it happens. And it isn't loser-ish to think ahead. He's just giving you a wedding present for when you marry a real man."

"No!" I put all my remaining energy into that one word so she'd know I meant it.

But she acted like she hadn't even heard as she soldiered on. "Yes. You need to do this. He owes you, and you need to stand up for yourself. Do you think he's going to offer to pay his half for all the deposits you lost?"

"No . . ." This time the word was one of defeat, not conviction.

"Exactly. No. Which means it's only fair. He can't get a refund on a photo shoot that took place already."

She stood and slid her finger under the packaging tape, tugging it free from the cardboard. Big fluffy plastic bags of packaged air floated out as she opened the side wings of the box. And there, in a dress bag so elegant, it could only have come from Reem Acra, waited the most incredible gown ever designed.

Alison pulled the bag from the packaging and unzipped it. Her smile went from something feral to something soft. "It's perfect, Juliet."

"It's perfect for an actual bride." I countered.

"It's perfect for a strong, talented woman who carries herself like royalty. It's perfect for a princess."

That was the point I stopped arguing with her. I wanted to have my spa day, with my hair and nails done. I wanted to wear the dress that had made me smile for several weeks after placing the order. I wanted to feel pretty and elegant and special.

This dress gave me all of that.

And the photos would give me proof that the day had happened.

Alison made me try it on right there in the living room, and then, when I complained one last time over wearing a bridal gown, she went to my room, pulled out all my scarves and shawls and came back with her arms loaded.

She tried a bunch of different options before she finally wrapped a sheer, green scarf around my shoulders. "Now it's just a white formal. Promise me you'll do this."

"I will as long as you come with me."

She shook her head. "Not hearing the conviction. Promise you'll do this *no matter what.*"

"I promise. But you are coming, right?"

Her mouth twisted. "I can't. I'm heading out of town. But you can't back out now. You already promised. What kind of lawyer breaks their word?"

My fingers smoothed over the layers of silk as if I could find comfort in each individual thread. "Adam broke *his* word," I muttered.

"And that's why he's going to pay for your pretty pictures." She smiled, triumphant in her evil master plan.

"It's really unfair for you to have such skills of persuasion."

Alison laughed.

Two

I hadn't stepped foot inside a hair salon since I'd gone to prom my senior year in high school. Eight years had passed since that unfortunate night. The misfortune hadn't been the fault of the hair style, which had been perfect, but more the fault of the date, Nathan, who showed up to my house already trashed because he'd indulged in the limo mini bar.

At the first scent of alcohol, my dad had a talk with the limo driver, put in a call to my date's dad, and sent Nathan home.

After that night, the rumor went around that my dad was an ex-marine who'd threatened the life of my sorta-date. No guy wanted anything to do with me. Luckily there had only been a few months left of school, but that had been long enough for me to get the nick name "Julie-Ex" instead of Juliet.

Nathan came up with the name and acted pretty smug until he ended up in juvenile court with a DUI. Well, he was still probably smug about the nickname even then, but at least I felt some kind of legal vindication about the whole thing.

I tried hard not to think about the results of my last salon experience. *After all,* I reasoned, *it isn't like I'm trying to impress a guy this time.*

But the old nickname kept floating to the surface of my memories. Maybe that was my destiny. Maybe I would always be Julie-ex.

My phone rang twice during the salon visit. I jumped both times, making the stylist curse under her breath. But I didn't answer my phone. What if Adam was trying to call? What if he'd heard about my plan to keep the photo shoot appointment? The photographer was a friend of his mom's. It stood to reason Adam would've informed his family of the breakup by now. Maybe they cancelled the appointment for me.

How stupid would I feel if I showed up at the photo studio and was turned away?

Totally stupid.

These were the thoughts that kept my hands twisting in my lap as the stylist reinvented my dull brown hair into something wonderful with twists, braids, and ringlets. When she turned me around and let me look in the mirror, I gave the first real smile since Adam walked.

It had been a week since then. My parents and friends all knew of my disgrace. They all clucked tongues and cooed sympathy and offered to bump Adam off and throw him in the Hudson, which offers I appreciated, but declined. I felt guilty enough going through with the photo shoot. Hiring a hit man was really out of the question.

I paid the cab driver, hefted the dress bag out of the car, and finally stood outside the Brooklyn photo studio. The insanity of the plan made me wish I'd stayed home with a book instead. I stood there staring at my reflection in the glass door for several seconds, before deciding that honesty

JULIE WRIGHT

was the best policy. I couldn't go through with a lie. It wasn't my style.

The front door to the studio opened as I turned to leave. "Can I help you with something?"

Caught.

I turned slowly to face my guilt to meet the smiling warmth of a nice-looking guy. "I . . . um . . ."

The guy blinked a set of warm, hazel eyes at me. *Did my stomach flutter at that?* No. Of course not. I was just nervous and stupid and—

"You must be Adam's fiancé, Juliet?"

"I'm Juliet." I didn't say anything about Adam, since really, what could be said that wasn't horrifying?

"Great. You're right on time. Do you want to use some of my studio for the shots, or do you want to just go on location like we'd talked about earlier?" He smiled, waiting for an answer.

There was no way out without explaining myself. This was a just-go-with-it moment. I narrowed my eyes, trying to understand what I was seeing. He'd just said "my studio" as if it belonged to him. Adam had said the photographer was a friend of the family, which I took to mean that the photographer was some stodgy old guy in his late fifties with a bad comb-over. Sure, he'd sounded younger on the phone, but that wasn't exactly a clue. Voices didn't get gray hair and wrinkles. "You're Jack Montague?"

"Unless I'm in trouble, in which case, it's my prerogative to change my name to whatever gets me out of trouble again."

I think he expected me to laugh. Instead I said, "You're absolutely not what I expected."

He grinned at that and gave me a once over that let me know he'd checked me out before saying, "You aren't what I expected either. You're not exactly Adam's type."

I bristled. "What's that supposed to mean?"

82

He looked flustered to have made his last statement out loud. "That wasn't an insult, no matter how it sounded. Adam usually goes for vapid girls, the ones with long legs and empty heads." He paused. "I'm making this worse, aren't I? I just meant Adam has never before aligned himself with a girl wearing jeans and a button up flannel shirt."

I looked at my outfit, chosen because a button up would keep my hair intact *and* because it was comfortable. I liked comfortable. Were my clothes the reason Adam was with someone else?

No.

He chose someone else because he was a crappy human being who didn't understand the meaning of *faithful*. I wasn't going to take his blame. The week spent sorting out my feelings had been good for me.

I shrugged, realizing Jack waited for a response. "Do you have a problem with flannel?" I asked.

"If you've gotta ask, then you've never seen my closet."

"I *haven't* seen your closet," I said, hating that the idea of seeing his closet appealed to me. Wasn't I in mourning over lost love? One cute guy checks me out, and I'm suddenly over heart break? *Get. A. Grip. Juliet.*

"So how about it?"

Heat flooded my face. "Seeing your closet?"

He laughed. "No. Should we stay in the studio or go to other locations?"

I bit the inside of my lip. "Oh. Right. Of course. I don't know; can I see the studio first?"

He opened the door for me then waited for me to enter. "This way," he said, and moved past me to lead the way down a hall filled with large portraits and fine art photography.

The portraits were amazing, catching glimpses into real human life in a way I'd never seen a photographer do. I expected him to be a basic wedding photographer—the kind that took shots of the stereotypical girl in white staring down into a bridal bouquet.

His portraits depicted something else. They seemed to tell a story of the person being photographed. One family portrait had been taken from behind the father and mother holding hands while their little toddler daughter slept on her dad's shoulder.

The picture gave off the feeling of being safe.

Each picture I passed pressed an emotion through me.

"Did you do all of these?" I asked, following slowly enough to make him stop to wait for me.

"Yep. Doesn't help my business any if I put up some other guy's pictures on my wall, does it?"

I laughed, feeling good to know that I had a laugh left in me. "You have a good eye,"

"Thanks."

I finally turned my attention back to him, following him back into the studio.

Strange props filled the spacious area that made up the studio. Old chairs, ladders, paint buckets, hanging backgrounds of all kinds, fence panels, a street light, and lighting equipment littered the bulk of that space.

The props weren't anything spectacular, nothing that called out "bridal shoot" to me, so I was about to tell him that we should just go on location since I'd already planned it out with him when the appointment had first been made. I wanted my pictures done in the city I loved, featuring Central Park. But then Jack opened some wide French doors that led out to a backyard of sorts. The dense foliage of trees and meadow grasses startled me. In the city of cement, one expected to see such intense green only in parks.

Six trees planted in two rows close enough that their overhanging branches touched at the top gave the illusion that the small yard was actually much larger. Dozens of books hung from their spines in the trees, their pages rustling softly in the breeze. The books twirling slowly hanging in the air, their pages splayed out as if waiting to be plucked from the air and read, created an enchanting effect. This was a place for little girls to become princess and have tea parties. A place for little boys to become adventurers and play hide and seek.

It was a place of magic.

"It's beautiful," I said, and meant it. "Who would have guessed this was back here?"

He didn't answer, but looked on the yard-scape with a certain degree of pride. "Sorry about the books. I forgot they were out here. I friend of mine is a literary agent and a client of hers was visiting the city and wanted to get some pictures for her website. It seemed like a good enough prop. I can take them down while you change if you want to use the garden. Or we could just go on location."

"We can do both. But leave the books. I like them." The entire scene reminded me of the music video Shadow Puppets by the group Book on Tapeworm.

"Books for the bride. Great. You can do your costume change in the dressing room." He ushered me back into the studio, pointing out the door to the changing room. "I'll get the lighting set up for a few shots then we can go to the places we discussed earlier."

I nodded again, though he wasn't looking at me, and so didn't see, and entered the room he'd indicated.

He called my putting on a wedding dress a "costume change." And so it was. I was a grown woman playing dress-up for the day. Pathetic.

A large mirror hung over a dressing table with several glass apothecary jars filled with things like bobby pins, safety pins, and single use packets of lip gloss. Jack obviously understood his job.

With my dress on and buttoned up in the back as far as I could reach on my own, I realized a second person was necessary to get it buttoned all the way to the top. Originally, I'd planned on bringing my mom with me to the photo shoot, but since she knew about the break up, she'd never approve of me going through with the shoot. I'd forgotten all about the buttons.

"Idiot!" I muttered to myself. Then louder, I said, "Um . . . hello? Jack?"

It took a moment before he answered. "You called for me?"

I rolled my eyes, feeling my face heat up with my own stupidity. "This is going to sound so incredibly lame, but I can't reach all the buttons in the back, and I kind of need . . ." Words failed me.

"Help?" He finished when it became obvious I couldn't.

"Yes. Help."

"Are you comfortable with me coming in then?"

To answer, I opened the door.

He stood standing just outside the door when I opened it, which put us face to face in a way that was too close to be comfortable, especially considering what I asked him to do.

We stared at each other a moment before he blinked, shook his head slightly, lifted his arm, and made a twirling motion with his finger.

Right. He needed me to turn around. I complied, glad that the new flash of heat on my cheeks wouldn't be visible with me facing the other way.

His fingertips brushed the skin just below my bra, making me shiver, and then feel stupid for shivering, because there was no way he hadn't noticed the goose-bumps.

Good thing I bought a brand new, cute, lacy bra to wear with my dress since the thing was now doing a public debut.

Alison would laugh herself sick when I spilled the misery of this moment.

Jack didn't rush through the process. There was a hesitation between finishing one button and beginning the next. Had he ever done anything like this before? I glanced to the table with its bottles of pins and lip gloss.

Probably.

Which meant there was no reason for my stomach to feel like an entire butterfly migration had just taken to the air.

But I couldn't help it.

As the heat of his fingers brushed my skin with each button, my face radiated that heat. I stared at the floor, wishing to be less ridiculous, less vulnerable, less needy.

Once he'd reached the top button, he hesitated a moment longer, letting his fingers hover over my neck a moment. Then I felt them trace the outline of my necklace.

The movement felt insanely intimate and more affectionate than anything I'd ever felt from Adam. My breath caught.

He picked up my necklace and moved the clasp to the back of my neck.

Oh.

Right.

The clasp.

A new heat wave hit my face, which I was glad he couldn't see until I realized he was looking at my reflection in the mirror.

He had the decency to look away when he realized he'd been caught watching me. "All ready then?" he said, walking away from the dressing room door, where he pretended to be picking out props for me.

I knew he was pretending, because the prop box was labeled TODDLER and had balls, stuffed bears, and stupid hats in it. I didn't think he expected me to utilize anything from that box.

Had he felt that spark of connection too?

He thinks you're engaged, idiot.

That settled that.

He likely hadn't thought anything about buttoning up my dress, except that maybe I was a total lunatic for acting like a schoolgirl with a crush.

"Shoes," I said. "I need my shoes."

He nodded and kept his head down while he still rummaged through the toys like a man on a mission.

I turned away, lifting my dress to step into the bejeweled heels, so I wouldn't trip on my own hem.

I looked up to find Mr. Photographer watching me again. Instead of looking away when he'd been caught this time, he smiled and lifted the camera hanging around his neck. "Ready now?"

I pulled the green scarf off the hanger. "Ready."

It was a lie though. This man unnerved me in a way that made me feel like I'd never be ready.

Three

e let me lead the way to the garden.

Stepping out into the sunlight diffused by the trees, with my skirts brushing aside the long grasses, made me take a sigh of contentment I hadn't felt since Adam had basically called me worthless baggage holding him down. And really, had I *ever* felt this kind of contentment?

No.

Not really.

I always felt like I'd been weighed and measured and had fallen short of expectation—a stock purchase that didn't pay off.

Here in this moment, wearing this dress, in this place, I felt *possible*, like the future in front of me was waiting for me to reach out and accomplish great things.

How had I not realized how liberating a break up with the wrong guy could be? Adam *had* been the wrong guy. Right guys didn't cheat. I raised my face to the sun, feeling warm, comfortable, and grateful in being possible.

When I turned to see where Jack wanted me to stand, I found he was already taking pictures.

I laughed. "You ought to warn a girl when you're doing that kind of thing."

His face was mostly covered by the camera, but not enough I couldn't see him grinning. "But then I'd miss out on you acting naturally."

"Ah. I see. You're one of those sneaky photographers."

He finally lowered the camera, his grin even wider. "If by sneaky, you mean the best kind of photographer, then yes. Yes, I am." He gestured to an antique divan-styled sofa that was in the center of the trees. He must have set it up while I'd been changing. "Have a seat." He strode up to the divan and patted the red upholstery.

I sat and looked up, waiting for further instruction.

He didn't say anything else, but instead placed his hands on my shoulders and gently eased me back against the side of the divan that arced up into an elegant single wing. When I met his eyes and felt a smolder of something I shouldn't have been feeling for my photographer—especially when he was a friend of Adam's family—I hurried to look away.

Curse my red cheeks!

He lifted my arm and rested it over the top of the curved wing, brought my other arm up so my hands were close but not touching. Then he plucked a book from the tree closest to us as if picking an apple and settled it into my hands.

He stood back and studied the scene before saying, "Tuck up your legs so you look comfortable."

I did as told.

He fussed a little more, pulling up the hem of my dress so my shoes peeked out, and fixing the way the skirt fell to the ground. He then shook his head and removed the green scarf from around my shoulders.

90

"But—" I began to protest, but stopped when his smile settled over me.

"Trust me, Juliet. I know what I'm doing."

He arranged the scarf over the bottom of the divan, then drew it up over my feet where it dipped down again until it came back up at my knees then dipped down before settling over my hips.

He stepped back again and lifted his camera to his face. "Perfect. Now read the book."

So I did. Then I laughed. "Really?" I asked. "Did you do this on purpose?"

"What?" He didn't take the camera away and moved around in front of me as his camera clicked and clicked and clicked.

"Shakespeare?" I waved the book at him. He kept shooting pictures. "Romeo and Juliet?"

He laughed. "Right. Your name. That was just a coincidence. A very probable coincidence though, since all of the books in the trees are Shakespeare. I got them from an English teacher who was getting new copies for her classroom. They were old and hardback and looked cool swinging from the branches."

"Have you always wanted to be a photographer?" I asked.

"Nope. When I was five I wanted to be a pirate, but my mom told me I'd be disinherited if she ever caught me pillaging. I didn't discover photography until *way* later."

"Really? When?"

"Six."

I laughed again. Jack was funny. Funny was new. Adam was never funny.

Jack had me in all kinds of crazy poses while we talked and his camera clicked.

By the time we left to go out to the locations, I discovered that he'd been given a Sony World Photography award, that his parents weren't actually any more impressed with him taking pictures than they had been of his pirate pillaging ambitions, and that he was a dog person.

In that same time, he discovered I was willing to climb a tree in a dress that cost more than some people's cars, I confessed to not knowing what the Sony World Photography award was, explained my job of being an intellectual property rights lawyer in exhausting detail, and told him my favorite song was from an obscure band out of Utah called Shadow Puppets. He made fun of me when I told him the name of the band.

"So why a lawyer? Or was it just because you wanted to be a pirate too?" he asked with a grin.

I laughed at his lawyer joke, and considered his question as he packed up his camera and folding tripod in a carry case. What did I have to lose in admitting to my uneducated pedigree? "Neither of my parents received a higher education. None of my grandparents or great grandparents even finished high school. When I started college, my dad would brag that someday his daughter would be a lawyer or a doctor and bring glory to our family name. I knew I had to be one or the other, so I could make him proud."

"And the doctor thing didn't work out because . . ."

"I throw up at the sight of blood."

Jack laughed. "I'm with you on that. Well, sort of. I don't stay conscious long enough to know if I throw up or not." He looked at his phone, which rumbled with the incoming text. "Cab's here."

On the ride over to the park, we pointed out our favorite parts of the city.

We discussed our favorite restaurants, our favorite plays, our favorite movies.

And most of them were the same.

Alison texted me while we were walking through Central Park to see how I was doing.

I sneaked a glance at Jack and texted back. *Great. The photographer's amazing. It's sad that this is the best date I've had in years and the guy I'm with is my photographer, and he thinks I'm engaged.*

She texted, **Snort**

Which was her version of LOL.

"Are you hungry?" Jack eyed a hot dog stand as we passed.

"You want me to eat a hot dog in this dress?" I gave him a look that I hoped conveyed the absurdity of such an idea.

"You climbed a tree in that dress."

What was there to say to that? I *had* climbed a tree in it, and had fun doing it.

"Yeah, I'm hungry," I admitted. "But I left my purse back at the studio."

"It's on me." He pulled a wallet from his inside jacket pocket. Smart. He wasn't one of those idiot New Yorkers who kept their wallet in their back pockets. He grinned at me. He had a great smile. "Or, rather, it's on your fiancé. I'll add it to the bill."

I coughed and felt blood drain from my face—which was probably better than blushing. "Right. Good idea."

That settled it. I was evil. I was totally going to burn in the fiery pits of Satan's playground for this little escapade of deception. But I didn't stop Jack as he ordered his hot dog smothered with everything. I ordered mine with relish, mustard and ketchup.

"What? No onions?" Jack raised an eyebrow at my condiments.

I gave an indifferent kind of smile.

"Ah, I see. Probably planning on a steamy make-out later. Onions are the destroyer of good kissing."

I blinked for a moment trying to figure out if he meant that *he* planned on kissing me later when I came to my senses. *No, he means Adam.* Which was too bad, because onions or no onions, Jack would have been fun to kiss.

He consumed his hot dog as though he hadn't eaten in a month, then excused himself to use the restroom. I sat on a bench to wait, feeling starved, and wondering how to consume my own hot dog without getting ketchup stains on the dress. It was bad enough to have my hands so full of food I couldn't lift my skirts. I hated walking when the hem dragged the ground.

"You going to eat that?" someone asked.

As I turned to the voice, I had to keep my face in a neutral position. I hadn't noticed the street-smudged man when I sat next to him, because he'd been on the ground, wedged between a tree and a garbage can. He wore a tattered coat in spite of the growing summer heat.

I wanted to eat the hot dog, but I could eat later. This guy likely didn't have a *later* option.

I stooped down so we were at the same eye level and handed him the hot dog. When he took it, his fingers wrapped around mine, and his warm, wet eyes filled with gratitude. "Bless you, princess," he said.

I smiled at the name and stood up again. "You're welcome, dear sir."

Jack approached just then. "Back to work?"

I nodded and followed him down the path, lifting my skirts so they stayed off the ground.

"Thank you!" the homeless man called after me.

Jack raised an eyebrow. "What was that all about?"

I shrugged without comment.

We pretty well toured the entire park, taking pictures everywhere: the Swedish cottage, the band shell, on and around several bridges, benches and gardens, the carousel and at the Belvedere Castle.

Jack knew the park better than I did. He knew where to get shots without crowds of people in the background.

Together, we laced our way through the little empty corners of every garden.

It took the whole day.

In the course of a whole day, I learned that Jack cried at the ending of *Star Wars*, which was entirely corny for any guy to admit to out loud, and that his parents would likely trade him in for me, because I went to law school, while he'd been a university drop out.

From Harvard University.

"You dropped out of Harvard?" I couldn't keep the incredulity out of my voice. "Who does that?"

"A guy who doesn't want to grow up to be a clone to the men who came before him, that's who." Jack backed up a little to get the picture.

I adjusted my position on the stone stairs and tried not to laugh when a bicyclist nearly ran Jack off the walk. "Oops," Jack said. "Didn't see him."

I did laugh then. "I didn't even bother sending Harvard an application since I knew they have a magical force-field surrounding their admissions offices that automatically sets overreaching applications on fire."

"Trust me. You proved your intelligence by not applying. It's good to know who you are and what you want without strings attached. Intelligence has very little to do with where a degree came from."

I liked that he said that—liked that he wasn't one of those non-thinking, under-achieving drop outs. He really did know who he was and what he wanted. Nice.

Adam hadn't been like that. Everything with him had been about what other people wanted him to do or be.

I was not one of those things that Adam's family wanted for him. Adam had pretended he didn't care. But ultimately he did care, and ultimately, I didn't want to belong to a family full of implications and expectations.

95

"I didn't go to law school just because my parents wanted me to," I said, wanting to make sure he understood. "I went because when I was in high school, my uncle developed a tool that helped with welding. He went through the process to get a patent on it and everything but ended up becoming prey to someone who took his idea and sold it as his own. He didn't understand his rights, so the other guy won. After that, I knew I wanted to help protect people in situations like that. I wanted to help people keep their own creative ideas."

Jack made a noise that sounded like something between amused and impressed. "As a man with creative ideas, I thank you." He gave me a slight bow before moving us on to the next photo opportunity.

I watched Jack closely after that and found all of his manners to be refined and careful. He spoke well, using language that proved he was well read and well educated in spite of dropping out of college. Was his family like Adam's? Would they have certain requirements for the sort of people their children married?

Jack had become a photographer in spite of the opposition from his family. I felt certain that it wouldn't matter if a girl was what his family wanted or not. For Jack, it would only matter if she was what *he* wanted.

After only one day, I couldn't keep myself from admiring him, and feeling a little stupid for imagining such a connection after so little time.

We ended at the turtle pond with the castle in the background. My stomach growled in protest of the many hours that had passed since the hot dog that didn't happen.

"I heard that, hungry lady." Jack pointed at my stomach. "We'll be done soon. This is the last shot. I wanted to end here because of the clouds." He glanced up.

I followed his gaze to the sky where I realized the clouds were afire with the sunset.

"You knew we were going to have a pretty sunset today?"

"It's my job to know. That's why I rushed you to the cottage." He pulled out his phone. "I set my alarm so we'd be here when the sky was at its best."

He settled me near the water then moved out far enough to take the pictures. He asked me about my family, my friends, and finally, the question I should have been expecting but had actually forgotten about—my fiancé.

"Adam?" I smoothed my hands over my dress, wishing I hadn't left my clothes and purse back at his studio. It wasn't like I could run away. "I'm sure he's fine."

"Are you excited to marry the love of your life?"

He probably asked this question of every bride, but he seemed annoyed with it as he asked me. I thought about the question and answered honestly. "Yes. I am excited to marry the love of my life . . . someday."

"What? You don't have the big day set and circled in hearts on your calendar?"

And there it was. He finally asked a question that couldn't be answered without a direct lie. The photo shoot would be expensive, but it would have a much greater cost if I didn't confess my lie. I'd have to tell the truth, put the day on my credit card, and pay for it until I was in a retirement home.

"Actually . . . there is no date."

Jack made a *psh* noise. "Figures."

I frowned. "What figures?"

"Nothing, sorry. Forget I said anything."

"No. Tell me why you said that."

"It's just—" Jack pulled the camera away long enough to roll his eyes and scrub his fingers through his hair. He immediately put it up again as if hiding behind it. "Adam doesn't ever really follow through on things. He's not the kind of guy who comes to mind when I think of *commitment.* It's not surprising he hasn't pinned down a date yet. Look, I'm sorry. I know it's rude to say anything like this to *you* of all people, because, obviously, he's finally got some sense, or he wouldn't have been able to catch a girl like you."

Sucker punch.

Adam *didn't* have a girl like me. He had someone else.

I bit my lip, trying to keep it from trembling. Tears stung hot in my eyes. I looked away, trying to keep Jack from seeing them before they fell. The sky had gone brilliant with color. The clouds reflected a melting kind of sherbet into the water of the turtle pond.

I suddenly felt cold and wrapped the green scarf tighter around my shoulders.

Deep breath.

Time to tell the truth, without letting Jack jump to his own conclusions again.

Who knew the truth could be so hard?

Four

*J*ack's eyebrows were knitted together as he slowly lowered his camera. "I'm really sorry, Juliet. I didn't mean to make you cry. Please. I'm so sorry."

I turned and shook my head. "You don't have anything to be sorry for. I should be the one apologizing. The truth is, there is no wedding date, because there is no wedding."

"I . . . wait a minute. What?"

I blew out a long breath and focused on the water, not wanting to see Jack's face when I explained the horrific lie. "Adam called off the wedding last week. He decided he liked the girlfriend he was seeing behind my back better than he liked me."

Silence came from behind me, which felt worse than anything. How did I come to this? I wasn't a bad person. I was the kind of person who picked up litter on the streets and in the subways. I tossed quarters to street performers and never complained about my next door neighbor, the little old lady who played her television at volumes that suggested she wanted to share her viewing experience with the people in New Jersey.

Finally Jack said, "I don't get it. Why are you here? Why are we doing this?"

So I confessed it all—the fact that I was stuck paying for all those deposits, that Adam had no consequences for his actions at all . . . except this one. The fact that the dress showed up right after he broke off the engagement. The fact that the dress was beautiful, and I felt like such a nothing after Adam left that I needed something to make me feel *valuable* again.

I even admitted to desperately wanting revenge.

I don't know what I expected to happen.

But I didn't expect for Jack to start laughing.

"Really?" I was mad now. "I just poured my heart to you, told you my darkest secret and my greatest shame, and you think it's funny?"

He laughed harder.

Which really ticked me off.

I narrowed my eyes, tightened my grip on my scarf, and stomped away. I'd get a cab to his studio, get my stuff, leave him my credit card number, and move to a mud hut in Africa.

He grabbed my arm and spun me back toward him, into his arms which he wrapped around me.

I tried to struggle out of his grasp, but he held me tight. "What are you doing? Let me go!"

"I'm giving you a hug. You need one whether you want it or not. Now stop acting like I'm mugging you, or someone will call the cops, and your ex will be paying for bail as well as pictures."

I pulled away enough to look him in the face. "You can't charge him for the pictures."

"Sure I can. He signed the contract."

"He's a family friend. That won't go over very well."

Jack pulled me back into the hug, but kept talking. "Don't worry about that. Adam won't want to admit to his parents or my parents that he was a creep about this. He likes them to think he's a nice boy—even though everyone knows better."

I kept up the tension, trying to pull out of his arms while arguing the point. "Okay, fine. But I've had a change of heart. I really can't go through with this. Anger getting the better of me isn't who I am. I'll pay for your time . . . and the hot dogs."

"Juliet?"

"What?"

"Stop talking. You're ruining my hug."

"Oh." My face warmed again, which was okay because there were no mirrors here. Jack would never know about this particular blush.

He stayed there with his arms wrapped around me for a long time, long enough for me to give in and relax against him. It was nice being held by him. Nice in all kinds of ways that didn't make sense. I was just out of a relationship. How could my emotions move on so quickly?

The answer was the obvious one—the one Alison had been repeating over and over again. Adam had been wrong from the beginning, and deep down, I knew that. Jack's embrace was long enough, it should have been awkward and uncomfortable. Instead, the seconds pulling through minutes during the simple act of being held by another human who cared gave me something I hadn't had on my own. Through this embrace, this strange exchange of energy, Jack had loaned me his strength.

He pulled away so he could see my face. "You absolutely do not need a dress or a few pictures to prove you're valuable. I've just spent one of the nicest days I've ever had in my life, with a woman who is smart, funny, capable, and very beautiful."

I took a sharp breath when he let his finger softly drift over my bottom lip and then stepped away from the circle of us that he'd created. He took my hand.

Wow.

I wanted to say something, to thank him for literally holding me together, but no words came.

"I've made a decision," he said, tugging me down the path. "I'm not going to charge Adam for the pictures—even though he's a jerk and deserves it, and I'd love to finally have something to hold over him for all the misery he's caused in my personal life over the years, but I'm only *not* charging him because I don't want you to be uncomfortable. You give me the go ahead, and I'm totally billing the guy. But I'm not taking your money either."

He squeezed my hand, stopping me before I could fully get my mouth open to protest. "Uh-uh!" he said. "No arguing with me. We're going to do a trade instead. I have a gallery showing coming up in the next couple of weeks—one that requires my images to be unique, yet realistic views of our fair city. You've got a great dress. The green shawl adds a nice visual touch, and now that I know you're not really engaged, it makes sense as to why you wanted a splash of color."

I tried to interrupt again, but he went on over the top of my questions. "You are now my model. I get to use the images I create with your pretty face in my show and in any advertising I want. If I sell your image to a stock photo company, and your picture ends up being used in a magazine ad for lipstick, you can't sue me for compensation or get mad, because it isn't my fault you've got great lips."

He stopped walking to turn and look at me. I rolled my eyes at him, took my hand back so I could cross my arms over my chest, and said, "Este Lauder is not going to buy a picture of me for a lipstick ad."

"Why not?" he asked.

I rolled my eyes a second time in response, but he leaned in to whisper in my ear. "You really do have great lips, which is why I'm not apologizing for being glad you aren't engaged, and I'm not apologizing for the fact that I've been thinking about those lips since the first time you smiled at me." He moved away again, almost before I could register how he'd made my legs feel much less steady than they'd been before.

He was flirting with me.

And I didn't mind. At. All.

"You don't have to worry about anything. You'll get copies of all the pictures. We'll even do a big blow up of whichever one is your favorite. So . . ."

He gave me a smile wider than any of the others and took my hand again. "Let's get you dinner, on me this time, since you didn't actually get lunch. And put that pretty face and pretty dress to work."

I barely knew the guy, and he had me feeling better about myself than I'd felt in, well . . . ever. How had he done that to me? I tried to give him one last out. "Jack, really, I can't let you do this. I can pay for your time. You don't need to make me a charity case."

But he waved me off like I hadn't said anything. He led me around the great lawn and the obelisk.

We ended up at the Metropolitan Museum.

"I'm a little overdressed for the café," I said, thinking maybe he'd change his mind and let me put the whole day of shame on my credit card.

"We aren't going to the café." We headed to the fourth floor with Jack stopping every few minutes to arrange me in various locations throughout the museum so he could get a photo. I laughed, shook my head, but complied. There were worse things than being a model for Jack Montague.

Things like still being engaged to Adam.

Things like the day with Jack coming to an end.

I didn't want this to come to an end.

Jack was recognized upon entering the restaurant. Not only recognized, but treated as an honored guest. I shot him a look that showed I was impressed, but he gave me a one shouldered-shrug and placed his hand at the small of my back to guide me to our table.

After we'd been seated by the windows overlooking the park, Jack said, "I would have booked the chef's table if I'd known we'd be doing this tonight. But there wasn't enough time to get that kind of reservation. Next time, though."

Next time. He'd said there would be a next time!

Not wanting my excitement to be embarrassingly obvious, I turned to gaze out toward the park which was still highlighted by the sun's afterglow.

I heard the click. Jack was taking more pictures. I laughed. "Do you ever put that thing down?"

"I put it down when life ceases to be interesting. Or sometimes, I put it down when I want to participate in life, rather than watch." He set the camera down. "Like right now, I'd love to know what you're thinking."

I took a sip from my glass before answering. "I'm thinking that today was a nice surprise. I haven't had a nice surprise in a long time. Thank you."

"Sounds like you were due for a nice surprise. I'm sorry about Adam."

I looked down at my place setting and fiddled with the napkin on my lap. "You mentioned he caused you misery before in your personal life. What did he do to you?"

Jack furrowed his brow. It was the first time his response hadn't been one of amusement and smiles. "You don't want to know about all that."

"Are you kidding? You've heard all about my issues. It could be cathartic, like an Adam's Anonymous group rehab."

Jack leaned back in his chair with a great exhalation of breath. "He's not a great person. Which is baffling. How did this not-great-person end up with you?"

It was my turn to squirm, though I recognized he'd shifted the conversation back to me rather than giving any information about his dealings with my ex. I answered anyway. "His dad's company was involved in a small lawsuit regarding intellectual property. My law firm handled the cleanup. He was charismatic and . . . pushy, now that I think about it. I was caught up in the relationship before I even knew what was happening." I frowned into my wine glass a moment. "You know, his parents never even knew about the suit because Adam worked hard to settle it all rather quietly. They didn't even know their company was in trouble."

"Sounds like Adam. Get in trouble, and buy your way out."

I leaned back in my chair, mimicking the brooding kind of posture Jack had taken. "Which brings us back to you. What did Adam do to you?"

"Do I get another subject change?" he asked.

"Nope. You've used them up."

He opened his mouth to tell me, but the waiter showed up at that moment to take our orders. Jack hurried to pick up his menu and studied it like he was trying to pass the Bar exam.

So, Jack got another subject change option after all, but that didn't mean he was off the hook.

The waiter took our orders and finally went away.

"I didn't forget," I said.

"That's too bad because I kind of hoped you had. Fine. Adam and I are actually second cousins, so more family than simple family friends. Our moms were close friends as well as cousins, and that meant Adam and I spent a lot of time together as kids. His mom and dad were a lot like my mine. Both sets of parents wanted us to graduate from Harvard in business and then come home to run the mini empires our fathers had been running for their fathers."

The waiter returned with a basket of warm rolls. Jack waited until he'd stepped away from the table to continue. "So anyway, while in our first year of school, Adam told me how much he didn't want to be his dad's minion and that he wanted to do something else with his life. I thought we were being sincere with each other and so told him I'd already lined up a studio opportunity and had no plans to return to school the following year because I'd decided to be a professional photographer."

Jack fell silent a moment and looked pretty ticked off.

"And?" I prompted when it seemed he might not continue.

"And he told my parents. They were furious, they managed to shut down my deal for the studio rental, and insisted I go back to school like a good son."

I straightened, horrified. "Are you kidding? Your parents cancelled your rental contract?"

He nodded. "To be fair, they thought they were doing the right thing for me. They just didn't get it. It's kind of water under a burned bridge now. I *didn't* go back to school—no matter how much they shouted—and found another place for my studio. It actually worked out for the best, because the new studio came with the garden. I've had some great images come out of that garden."

"How are you with your parents now?" I asked.

"Strained, but it's getting better. The fact that my personal business has been successful enough to merit nice media attention has allowed them to overlook the fact that I went against the family. But it was ugly there for a while. I have Adam to thank for that."

"I'm sorry," I said, feeling somehow connected to the crime due to association with Adam.

"Not your fault. Anyway, it's water—"

"Under a burned bridge," I finished for him. "Something we have in common."

We fell into contemplative silence for a few moments. When Jack started talking again, it was to change the subject. I let him have his subject change.

The rest of the conversation stayed focused on our careers—why we liked what we did, annoyances with the day-to-day details of our jobs, which for him was bossy mothers of the bride and for me was unscrupulous corporations. He made fun of me for being a young lawyer, so I explained how I graduated from high school with two years of college credit already earned.

The chef visited our table and joked around with Jack giving the impression that they were friends and that Jack ate at this restaurant often.

It fascinated me to watch him interacting with someone else, to see his easy way of making others comfortable, of turning conversations so they were about the other person and not him. It wasn't just me he changed subjects on, but everyone. Putting other people first in a conversation seemed to be a talent.

When dinner was through, Jack kept his word about making me his model. We hit the streets running. He found a Harley motorcycle on the street and asked the owner if we could use it as a photo prop. The owner agreed. Soon I was leaning over the handlebars while he clicked away.

On the subway, he had me leaning against the poles, putting my feet up across the aisles to the seats on the side, and staring out the graffiti covered windows. He had me leaning over the old man he'd seated me next to and reading from the guy's newspaper, which had made the old man laugh.

In Times Square, he had me looking bored while sitting on the stairs at TKTS, pretending to buy dinner at a falafel vender, wearing a policeman's hat and kissing the cheek of the officer we'd borrowed the hat from while the policeman looked stoic. He had me stand over vent shafts with their steam rising up out of the street, in front of construction barricade signs, and in front of boards littered with advertisements and playbills.

JULIE WRIGHT

"My feet hurt," I admitted as we took a cab to Grand Central Terminal so I didn't have to take the dress back down through the subway. That had been a little scary when the dress was so brilliantly white, and the subway was so . . . not. The dress had a couple of war marks that I hoped would come out.

"This will be our last stop." He checked his phone for the time. "It's late enough now, that crowds should be pretty thin. We'll get a few more shots, and I'll let you go home. You've been a great sport today. Thanks. Not many girls would be willing to take that dress into Times Square."

"Or the subway." I reminded him.

He laughed. "Definitely not the subway. Or eat hot dogs. Or climb trees. Really, you're kind of the perfect model—still young enough to be adventurous."

"It's nice to know that even though I turn twenty-five next Saturday, I can still claim to be young and adventurous. If anyone argues it with me, I'll have them call you."

"Ah, a birthday coming up. Any great plans?"

I blinked at him. There *had* been great plans. Adam was supposed to take me to Niagara Falls for a weekend road trip. Now I had no plans. I gave a smile that likely looked as uncertain as I felt and turned my attention to the taxi window instead of answering.

Thankfully, he didn't press the issue.

We arrived at the Grand Central Terminal where Jack led me inside. I smiled at all the people filtering through the terminal. Though it was later, and there were fewer people than there might have been during the commute, it was still plenty busy.

I didn't question Jack on his choice, though. This was his job.

At least, I didn't question him until he lay on the terminal floor. "What are you doing? You're going to get trampled!"

108

"Stand over my legs. It'll keep people from walking on me."

I grunted and blew out a long breath. We would end up spending the night in the hospital with this kind of antic. But I stood over him, placing my feet on either side of his hips, which meant he was nearly entirely covered by the skirt of my dress—everything but his arms and head.

And his camera.

He was immediately taking pictures again, giving me directions for tilting my head, different facial expressions he wanted, how to lean my body so he'd get the right angle— with me in the foreground and the constellation ceiling in the background.

I couldn't see how a shot of this sort would actually look decent but complied with his every instruction.

"Got it. We can go home, now." He started to squiggle out from under my dress, which had to look pretty shifty to anyone else looking on, but who cared? The chances of me seeing anyone I knew here were pretty slim.

Then the small world we lived in shrank considerably.

"Juliet? Juliet, what are you doing?"

Adam's parents stood across from me, staring bug-eyed as I stood in the dress their son was supposed to have married me in.

I think I stopped breathing.

Five

"Mrs. Verona. Mr. Verona . . ." I stammered as Jack removed himself from my skirts, stood, dusted himself off and smiled at my ex-future-in-laws. "Hello. How are you?"

If heat was any indicator, I had to be as red as a fresh lava flow.

"We're fine," Mrs. Verona said slowly. Her eyes sketched over to Jack, then back to me. Mr. Verona had looked at us but then looked away as if we weren't worth his notice. "We're just dropping off a friend here at the station. We met them in town for dinner and a show."

They probably had a cab waiting outside. The Verona family didn't do public transportation.

Her gaze trailed down my dress. "You look . . ."

I don't know what she planned on saying. Was it a compliment? An insult? But instead of finishing her thought, she smiled and shook her head as if the devil himself couldn't drag the next word from her lips. She turned instead to Jack.

"And just what are you doing here?"

"Taking pictures." Jack held up his camera as if Mrs. Verona required evidence.

"Are you prepared for the art show?" she said. "After all the work I went through to set things up, I'd hate it if you weren't ready."

"I'm ready." He assured her. "Just getting a few last minute additions. Juliet here was kind enough to be my model."

She forced herself to turn to me again. "Is that why you're wearing your wedding dress? I did wonder . . . it seemed strange that you'd have it on after breaking off the engagement with Adam."

I fell back a step as if she'd given a slight shove. "Wait. What? He told you *I* broke up with *him*?"

"He did say that—"

Jack placed a hand at the small of my back to try to offer me comfort, or maybe to keep me from flying off the handle. I wasn't certain. He couldn't have known that this woman brought out the worst in me.

Her eyes narrowed as they drank in the scene with Jack and me being at the terminal together. "Well . . . He said you had a wandering eye . . . I see that's true. How very pedestrian of you to go after the photographer we set up for you."

If Jack hadn't known that Mrs. Verona brought out my worst, he should have suspected it with that statement. My heart rate jacked to a point that my chest hurt. For several stupid moments, all I could do was stare at her.

"And I'll be talking to your mother about this, Jack," she said.

Really? She really just threatened to tattle on him? After insulting me?

I moved to step closer to her, feeling anger surge through my veins when Jack pressed my arm to steer me away from them, maybe worried I'd take a swing if left to my own devices.

"For your information," I said, jumping in before Jack could move me too far. "Your pathetic excuse of a cheating, lying son broke up with *me* because the girl he was seeing behind my back didn't like that he was getting married. You should be proud. He's just like his father."

The couple's eyes widened, but I plowed ahead. "But I'm not *really* worried about it, because happily, he's not my problem anymore. I'll be sure to send him a thank-you note, unless that's too pedestrian for your son."

Jack continued to push me toward the exit. He turned back to Mrs. Verona for a brief moment with a shrug while calling out that he'd tell his mother she said hello.

He hailed a cab while I fumed and contemplated going back inside to yell some more. I had barely ever spoken above a whisper to Mrs. Verona before. It felt good to allow myself to be angry.

"Well, that was unexpected," Jack said once he'd hailed us a cab and safely ushered me inside.

I crossed my arms over my chest and closed my eyes. "He told her I'd been the one to cheat! How could he say that about me, especially when it wasn't me at all? That . . . *snake!*"

I felt Jack's eyes on me as he said, "The Veronas are a proud family. They believe whatever they have to in order to continue feeling superior. Don't let it bother you."

My eyes flew open. "Oh no. What about you? They're friends with your parents. You're *related!* She said she was going to talk to your mom. Please forgive me for causing a scene. I can't believe I yelled at her. I didn't even yell at Adam when he'd called off the wedding. Why did I lose control like that now?"

"I'd guess it's because you've had time to think about it, and probably because he lied to his parents by making you the bad guy. That's enough to make anyone angry. It didn't bother me. We're good."

But were we good?

"You don't believe Adam's mom, do you?" I asked. "What she said about me?"

He looked startled by the question, and then he laughed. "I've known Adam my whole life. Trust me. I don't believe anything his mom says about him."

He acted fine, like he didn't really care that I'd called out Adam for being a cheater like his dad. *Did I actually say that out loud?* I was such an idiot!

Mrs. Verona said she'd talk to Jack's mom. Was he worried about that? Had I ruined something for him with my temper flare? I kept thinking of ways to apologize, but couldn't say anything more than I had without sounding desperate.

"Wait here," Jack told the cab driver as he handed him enough to cover our tab as well as my ride back home, still leaving a sizeable amount left over for a tip.

"I can pay for my own cab fare," I said once we were out of the cab. "And I'd really like to cover the cost of the pictures. I want to do the right thing."

He ignored me as he unlocked the studio door and let me in.

"Really. I can pay for myself."

"We've already had this conversation," he said.

And we had. But that was before Adam's parents. Before I'd embarrassed myself by behaving badly in public.

"Did I . . . make things bad for you?" I asked.

"How could you have done that?"

"She said she was going to tell your mom."

"I'm an adult. I don't live in my mom's basement." He said it like he was joking, but after spending a day with him teasing and joking, I knew the signs. He wasn't joking. So I might have ruined things for him, and he wasn't planning on telling me either way.

"Fair enough," I said, feeling like life wasn't fair at all. It had only been a day. How did someone really know how they felt about a person after only one day?

But in that one day, I'd shared more conversations with Jack than I had in all the months of dating Adam. And somehow I knew that if I had a chance to have more than one day, I'd want another. And another.

Jack was the kind of guy I didn't want to say goodbye to. Yet here we were, at the end of our one day, doing exactly that.

We'd made it to the dressing room where my clothes lay folded up on the chair. I tossed an uncomfortable smile before closing the dressing room door so I could change clothes again. Time for Cinderella to get back to reality.

When I realized Cinderella had no way out of her gown. "Jack?" I called out, hoping he still stood by the door. When he answered, I admitted, "I need help getting out of the dress."

I opened the door, feeling stupid.

He twirled his finger to let me know he needed me to turn around. I did, closing my eyes as his fingers worked the buttons down my back. He moved slower than he had this morning, more uncertain. There was fire in the places where his fingertips connected with my skin.

He undid all the buttons, so I wouldn't have to get acrobatic to change, and then he hovered a moment, the energy between us almost searing before he stepped away, cleared his throat, and raked his fingers through his hair.

"Thank you," I said, horrified by the heat in my whisper. *Get a grip, Juliet.*

I changed clothes quickly, zipped the dress up into the bag it was likely never to resurface from again in my life, and moved out to the studio to say goodbye. I gave Jack a hug and thanked him again, wondering if he would bring up the idea of spending time with me later.

He didn't.

He merely accepted the hug and the gratitude with a nonchalant nod and smile.

This was definitely goodbye.

I accepted it and left without making it any more awkward than it was.

And went home feeling a million times worse than I had when Adam told me there would be no wedding.

Six

"So," Alison said, looking at me with her pity face again. "You met the guy of your dreams, who happens to be related to the biggest loser on the planet, and had a run in with the loser's parents. Sounds like quite the adventure."

It had been nearly four days since I'd met Jack. Alison had been out of town that entire time which meant I'd had to marinate in my own misgivings with no one to vent to until she returned. In the meantime, I'd stalked Jack mercilessly online, scrolling through the photo gallery he kept on his personal website so many times, I felt like the people in the pictures were family.

Again, people who say things always look better in the light of a new day are horrific liars. Things looked hopelessly worse. I missed him.

How could I miss someone I'd known for only one day?

"An adventure," I echoed, not knowing how to deal with all the weird feelings. "What should I do?"

She scooted herself onto the kitchen counter and kicked off her heels. "You said he has an art show tonight?"

I nodded.

She took a sip of her raspberry tea. Her pause before responding comforted me. It meant she was considering every possible outcome of my half concocted plan. Finally she nodded along with me. "I think you should go. You need to see him again so you can figure out what it is you're feeling. More importantly, he needs to see you. I'll go with you."

That was that.

We spent the rest of the day unpacking her from her trip, cleaning the apartment in case Jack decided to drop by in the near future, and getting ready for the evening event.

By the time Alison hailed a taxi, and it had deposited us in front of the gallery, I reconsidered the plan. "Doesn't this seem sort of brazen to show up here where all of his friends will be present?"

"You're such a lawyer. Did you just use the word brazen? In a real sentence?" Alison opened the door and waited for me to enter the gallery.

I whispered as I led the way inside. "Would you prefer cheeky, shameless, assuming, *obvious*? How about ballsy? Does that one work better for you?" I stopped almost instantly.

Alison started to grumble at being forced to run into me when she gasped with a quiet, "Oh."

We were face to face with a life-sized framed picture of *me*. It was the one in front of the turtle pond by Belvedere Castle. The sky, and the pond's reflection of that sky, looked like it had painted by an artist. I had the green shawl wrapped tight around my shoulders as if warding off an unseen cold. My eyes were downcast. A single, full tear trailed down my cheek.

So much was said in that single photo. It spoke of loss, regret, shame, all the while the sky blazed with hope and promise. The castle added a romantic sort of backdrop.

The gold plate under it read "Juliet's Reflection."

It felt like my soul had been flayed open to the world in one simple portrait.

I cast a quick glance around. Did anyone recognize me as the girl stretched out on canvas? No one appeared to be looking askance at me, well . . . no one but Alison.

"You look amazing. I'm so glad I talked you into going to that photo shoot," she said. She then pointed. "Hey! There's more of you!"

I slapped her hand down and hissed a "Shh!" at her.

But she was right. There was more of me. Not a lot when compared with how many pictures Jack had taken that day, but enough to make me blush. And they were all equal to the first. They breathed emotion and captured the heartbeat of the city in a way that left me humbled to have been part of it. There were lots of other pictures too, animals, insects, flowers, scenery, city skyline. As I neared the end of the displayed works, the one word that kept coming back to me was *honest*. Jack spoke honesty through his camera.

Alison went ahead of me as I moved slower with each picture. And then a voice came from behind me, but not the one I'd been hoping to hear.

"Fascinating, isn't it?"

I turned slowly. "Adam." I glanced around to try to find Alison, hoping she'd rescue me. She was too far away to call over without drawing the attention of the entire room. "Fascinating?" I said, realizing no rescue would be possible.

"Yes. Fascinating that you're in so many of these little pictures. And now you're here tonight. What happened? Got a little rebound crush going on?"

I narrowed my eyes. "I'm pretty sure a person has to be heartbroken to end up on a rebound. Since I'm grateful to be out of our relationship, I think any feelings I'd develop for anyone else would be genuine. I'm not remotely heartbroken."

He blinked, shocked to find I had any nerve left in me. It made sense for him to be surprised. He'd never seen anything remotely resembling a backbone in me before. But everything I'd said was true. I *was* grateful to be out of that toxic relationship.

"So you seriously do have feelings for him?" His voice was flat, angry.

I didn't deny it. There were definite feelings for me to explore. I only hoped that they weren't one-sided. I took a cleansing breath and smiled, shouldering past Adam to continue through the gallery.

But Adam caught my arm in a grip too hard to be friendly. "Really? Genuine huh? You got a thing for a guy you called too expensive? For a guy you only met because I set up the appointment? For a guy you met while wearing a dress you bought for me? Tacky, Juliet. Really tacky."

"Drinking much?" I said. "Does your mom know you're blowing your rehab treatment?" I tried to yank my arm from his grasp, but he held on tighter.

"My mom told me all about your little fling in Grand Central Station. She said she felt an enormous amount of embarrassment for you."

I finally pulled my arm free, though it hurt to do so. What was Adam doing? He dumped me weeks ago and now had the nerve to act like an enraged, jealous boyfriend?

And then it hit me. "She dumped you. The girl you left me for dumped you, and now you're ticked because I'm not around to be your fall back girl? That's pathetic, Adam."

I moved away, back toward the door where Alison had ended up. Adam followed me. "If you really do have feelings, then you ought to consider that my mom is one of Jack's biggest patrons. She set up this little show. She made his career happen. And if I tell her that Jack is consorting with the wrong kind of girl, she'll pull the plug and drain his career dry."

There was an evil sort of triumph in his words, a hate I'd never heard in his voice before. Yet I knew he spoke the truth. Mrs. Verona had mentioned it when we'd run into each other.

Adam didn't follow me further, but I felt his eyes on my back as I wound through the patrons to where Alison stared at another picture. "This Jack guy totally has you figured out," she said when she saw me. I glanced at the picture she had been surveying. And stopped short. It was me giving the hot dog to the homeless man, his hand wrapped around mine, our eyes bound in a moment of something real, something pure.

I hadn't known Jack had seen, let alone captured that moment.

The gold-plated caption called it, "The Patron Saint of the People."

"Juliet!" Jack had seen me at last and wove his way to me. "Juliet! What a fabulous surprise! What do you think? Do you like it?" He looked genuinely happy to see me, happy to have me seeing him.

His arms opened wide, and I stepped into them without thinking, closing my eyes, feeling a belonging I hadn't ever felt anywhere else. When my eyes opened, I saw Adam, standing behind Jack and making sure I knew he was there. He shook his head in warning.

I tried, and failed, to smile and act upbeat. "Everything looks great! You're really talented, Jack. I'm glad to have seen it all, but I really have to go, sorry I can't stay longer. I'll see you around, maybe."

I turned my back on his confusion, grabbed Alison's hand and forced my way through the doors of the gallery. I looked back only once and saw Jack frowning, and Adam nodding his approval.

Seven

 ou're seriously listening to the serpent tongue of Adam Verona?" Alison had been rolling her eyes and lecturing at me ever since we got home.

"I don't want to mess up anything for Jack. He's a good guy."

"Exactly. He's a good guy. Good guys like good girls. You're a good girl. Good guys like making good choices. You're a good choice."

I hugged the pillow and tucked my legs underneath me, listening to the lectures that had only just begun.

I fell asleep on the couch, certain Alison had kept going long after I'd closed my eyes on her.

The next morning, I opened my eyes to face my birthday. Twenty-five years old. And feeling wretched about it.

Alison hummed from the direction of the kitchen. It smelled like she'd made me a cake. She was sweet that way.

A knock came at the door.

"Go get it!" Alison yelled, likely her way of making me

get off the couch for the day instead of wallowing.

On the porch was a vase with multicolored roses. A lot of roses. I glanced around, saw no one, and picked them up. I pulled the card from the holder and started reading when Alison came into the living room and saw the bouquet.

"Your mom sent you flowers for your birthday?"

My eyes and heart rate shot up at the same time after reading the name at the bottom of the card. "It's from Jack!"

She vaulted the couch to squeeze in next to me so she could read over my shoulder.

Dear Juliet,
Happy Birthday.
Twenty-five years.
Twenty-five roses
Twenty-five colors
To represent the
Twenty-five ways you made me smile on our one day together.
~Jack

"Oh, now that's cute!" Alison squealed.

The bell rang again. Alison shoved me toward it. "Forget the ex, Juliet. Take a chance on something meaningful for a change!" She then disappeared back to her room to give me privacy.

I put down the flowers and opened the door to reveal Jack standing there with a bouquet of photos—each one taped to a decorative stick poking out of a vase. The pictures were all of me. I didn't have to count them to know there were twenty-five.

I had to bite my lip to keep it from quivering. "You remembered my birthday."

"Of course I did. You have plans today."

"Plans? I don't—"

"With me. You have great plans with me. And before

you can argue," he said over my protest. "I know what Adam said to you. And he's wrong. His mom helped me set that one show up, but she didn't do it for me. She did it because she needed to do something to make it look like she'd helped the arts community. It was for her. So stop worrying, and let's go out and have a great day, okay?"

"Why?" I asked.

"Why what?"

"Why me?"

His face softened as he touched my shoulder. "I knew I liked you more than was appropriate for me to like a girl coming in for her bridal sitting when you showed up in flannel. Then you asked me to keep the books in the trees. I liked you even more when you had the courage to ask for help with your dress right from the start rather than making me wait a half hour while you tried to figure it out on your own like other girls always do. You knew when you needed help and felt no shame in asking for it. But the clincher was when you willingly gave a hot dog to a hungry, homeless man. I knew then I'd go crazy if I couldn't get to know you better."

He put down the vase of pictures. "So how about it? Want to spend another day with me?" He stood close enough for me to feel the warmth of his breath, close enough for me to know he preferred wintergreen. "And truthfully, I really have been thinking about those lips since the first time you smiled at me."

He closed the distance between us, his feathery light kiss deepening as I responded to the warmth of him.

Wow.

I broke away and started laughing, loving that he stood on the same doorstep where a UPS man had stood several weeks before.

"What's so funny?" he asked, confused.

"It's the light of a new day, and suddenly . . . *everything* looks better."

ABOUT JULIE WRIGHT

Julie Wright started her first book when she was fifteen. She's written over a dozen books since then, is a Whitney Awards winner, and feels she's finally getting the hang of this writing gig. She enjoys speaking to writing groups, youth groups, and schools. She loves reading, eating, writing, hiking, playing on the beach with her kids, and snuggling with her husband to watch movies. Julie's favorite thing to do is watch her husband make dinner. She hates mayonnaise, but has a healthy respect for ice cream. Visit her at her website: www.juliewright.com

The Meltdown Match

Rachael Anderson

*For my beautiful, talented,
and only slightly superstitious niece, Courtney.
I love you, girl.*

Other Works by Rachael Anderson

Prejudice Meets Pride

The Reluctant Bachelorette

Working It Out

Righting a Wrong

Minor Adjustments

Divinely Designed

Luck of the Draw

All I Want

One

The air smelled woodsy and fresh, exactly how Courtney remembered. A light breeze grazed her face as she walked, and she smiled. This was exactly why she loved coming home—to smell this smell and feel the wild, untamed feeling that made Heimel, Alaska, the perfect place to return home to.

At least for a little while.

An uncomfortable pit settled in Courtney's stomach, the same way it did every time she thought of leaving again in a few months. Would she ever be able to stay for good?

Hannah's arm nudged hers as they headed down Main Street, sipping strawberry smoothies. "Glad to have you back, sis, even if it's only for the summer." She sucked the last of her smoothie with a slurp. "Where next? Oregon? South Dakota? What about Canada? You haven't been out of the country yet."

"Who knows?" Courtney shrugged. "It all depends on where my next book will be set. Which is why I'm here—to get inspired. And to catch up with my favorite sister, of course."

"How nice to be an afterthought," Hannah said dryly.

Courtney laughed. "I didn't mean it like that."

"Yeah, yeah." Hannah swished her long, ebony hair behind her shoulder and lifted her face to the sun. "If you feel so inspired here, why not move back for good?"

It was a question she'd asked herself many times, but as much as she'd love to move back, she couldn't. It would ruin everything. Courtney sipped the last of her smoothie then tossed the empty cup in a nearby trashcan.

Hannah would laugh and call her superstitious, but each of Courtney's four published, and two soon-to-be published books were born in Heimel—*after* she'd left.

The feeling of coming home was like magic, permeating her soul and leaving her rejuvenated. In only a matter of months, she could outline a story and pound out a rough draft. It was like gliding through the skies and seeing everything stretch beneath her in one big beautiful, interconnecting pattern. But eventually, she always found herself back on the ground where, like the effects of a drug, the feeling diminished.

So she'd developed a foolproof system to keep her writing going strong: Return to Heimel, outline and write a rough draft, and move to the place where the book was set for research and revisions. Several months later, after she'd handed over the completed manuscript to her agent, she'd return to Heimel and start the process all over again.

Although moving around was exhausting, Courtney had lived in New York, Virginia, Texas, Colorado, Maine, and, most recently, California. She'd met different people, experienced new cultures, and had become a better writer. But every time she came home, Courtney couldn't help but look around with a feeling of longing, wishing things could be different and she could finally stay put. What she'd once considered an adventurous life was getting old.

With a sigh, Courtney pulled a leaf off a nearby bush and ran her fingers across the smooth, silky surface. "Maybe someday I'll move back for good. Just not yet."

"I'll believe it when I see it." Hannah stopped to look at a banner that spanned the road in front of them and pointed. "Hey, you're going to be here for the Solstice Days this year."

"So?"

She turned to Courtney, and a slow, almost devious, smile spread across her face. "So . . . that means we can both enter The Meltdown Match."

Courtney shook her head. "No way. That contest screams desperation, and I'm not desperate. Neither are you. Don't you already have a date lined up for Friday?"

"And Saturday." Hannah grinned. "But who cares? This isn't about looking desperate. It's about doing something spontaneous and having fun." She grabbed Courtney's arm, tugging her along, and Courtney's gaze dropped from the banner to the empty field across the street, where a moose stood grazing—the first moose she'd seen since her return.

Courtney smiled. Truth be known, she'd always thought of The Meltdown Match as a romantic, even magical, tradition. The so-called legend stated that on the day when the sun shined the longest, two unsuspecting hearts would be brought together in a union created by the universe. Furthermore, if they married under the sun of the summer solstice, they were promised a lifetime of happiness.

Or something like that.

Every year during Heimel's Solstice Days, on the morning of June 21, the first official day of summer and longest day of the year, hundreds of vases made of ice, each holding a stick with the name of a man or woman between the ages of twenty-on and twenty-nine, were left to melt in the warm summer sun. The first male and female sticks to fall were matched.

For Courtney, writer of romances with a magical twist,

it sounded like a novel-worthy beginning to a wonderful love story. Who wouldn't want to say they were matched by the greatest source of light? She'd always wanted to enter the contest and win, but one thing had always held her back. What if her vase didn't melt first? What became of all the names the sun didn't recognize as worthy of true love? She didn't really want to find out.

Granted, only a handful of the matches had ever ended in a lasting union, but a part of her couldn't help believe that the sun didn't make mistakes—only people did.

Lost in her thoughts, Courtney didn't realize where they were headed until Hannah pulled her inside the musty-smelling city office building. She planted her feet and tried to pull her hand free. "Are you deaf? I told you, I'm not entering the contest."

"Are too," Hannah countered.

"Are not."

"Too."

"Not."

"Well if it isn't Salt and Pepper arguing in public," said a deep voice behind Courtney. "Some things never change."

Courtney grinned as she turned around to meet Mitch Winter's teasing eyes. Only a few years older and a good friend, he'd made a habit of giving Courtney a hard time over the years. "We hardly ever argue, especially in public. You just have bad timing."

Mitch chuckled as he pulled her into one of his signature hugs, making Courtney feel warm, cozy, and more than content to stay there forever. Yet another reason she liked leaving and coming home. Only Mitch hugged her like this when she came back.

"Welcome home," he said.

Courtney breathed in the clean, outdoorsy scent that always seemed to surround him. Not for the first time, she found herself wishing she were Mitch's type—willowy, classy, and a brunette—not average and blonde, something he loved to point out with the annoying nickname he'd given her of "Salt."

She reluctantly pulled free and studied his handsome, mischievous face. Green eyes. Dark, curly hair that hung just over his ears. A teasing smile that often taunted her. She slugged him lightly on his arm. "When are you going to grow up? Do we seriously have to dye our hair to get you to stop using those awful nicknames?"

"Speak for yourself," Hannah said. "My hair rocks, and I like being called Pepper."

Mitch tugged on a lock of Courtney's straight, blonde hair. "Dye it red, and I'd just start calling you cinnamon instead. But I like Salt better, so I hope you'll leave it alone."

"Someday I'm going to think of an equally lousy nickname for you, and you're going to rue the day you ever started calling me Salt."

"I look forward to it." Mitch grinned and glanced at Hannah. "You home for the summer too?"

Hannah rolled her eyes. "Awesome. I'm the afterthought again. And yes, I am home for the summer, maybe even for good. I did just graduate, you know."

"From college?" Mitch shook his head. "No way you're old enough for that."

"You're just bugged because it makes you feel ancient. What are you now, thirty?"

"Twenty-nine," Mitch returned.

A large smile spread across Hannah's face as she shot her sister a meaningful glance. "Hear that, Court? Looks like Mitch can enter The Meltdown Match too."

He leaned against the wall and folded his arms. "No, I can't, and neither can you, if that's what you're here to do. Deadline was yesterday."

Hannah cocked her head again and gave him a sultry

smile as she moved closer and adjusted the collar of his navy and grey plaid shirt. "Oh, but I'm sure big-wig Mr. City Engineer can find a way to sneak our names in."

"Leave me out of this," Courtney said. "I don't want my name anywhere near those ice vases."

"She's lying," Hannah said. "Ignore her."

"And if I could get you in?" Mitch said. "What do I get in return?"

"A plate of my mother's to-die-for-cinnamon rolls," Hannah said. "Straight from the oven."

Mitch nodded as if mulling over the offer. "Consider it done." He pushed away from the wall and pointed a finger at Hannah. "But those rolls better be hot."

"They will be."

He moved to walk away, but Courtney stopped him with a hand on his arm. "If my name ends up on one of those sticks, there's going to be a lot more than just cinnamon in those rolls."

"Like what?"

"Like, I don't know, salt maybe? You do like it better than cinnamon, right?"

Mitch leaned close, giving her one of his mischievous smiles laced with hidden meaning. "Actually, I like Salt better than a lot of things." With a wink, he was gone, striding away and leaving Courtney's stomach flip-flopping like crazy.

⁂

Mitch jogged up the stairs, feeling like his day, and possibly summer, had just gotten a lot brighter. Courtney was back in town and had basically handed him a golden opportunity.

He rounded the corner, stepped into a small cubicle, and planted his hands on Alyssa's desk. As the administrative secretary, she had the unlucky responsibility of being in charge of The Meltdown Match. "Hey, Lys, I have a few more names to add to the contest."

She continued her typing without a glance at him. "Sorry. Deadline's passed. They'll have to wait until next year."

"But I'll be thirty then."

Her chubby fingers stopped typing, like Mitch knew they would. She looked up and studied him through thick, black-framed glasses. "I'm sorry, did you just say you *want* to enter?"

"Sure, why not?"

"Because last week you called The Meltdown Match an embarrassment to Heimel."

Mitch shrugged. "I've had a change of heart."

Alyssa pursed her lips as she continued to watch him. Although she only had about five years on him, the way she peered at him made him feel like he was back in elementary school, in trouble with his teacher. "You said a few names. Who else?"

"Courtney and Hannah Spaulding. I ran into them downstairs."

The wariness in her eyes disappeared, replaced by a slight, knowing smile. "Ah. Everything just got a lot clearer. You do know we have over one hundred entries, right? Your chances of getting matched with Courtney aren't that great."

Mitch pushed off the desk and stood. "Yeah, well, I was thinking we could increase my odds."

"And how are we going to do that?"

"With salt, obviously."

She blinked. "To you, maybe."

Mitch smiled, more than a little satisfied with himself. What better way to score a date with Salt than with salt? It was perfect. A slam dunk. "Did you know that nifty little substance lowers the freezing point of water?"

Realization dawned in Alyssa's slightly magnified eyes. "Well, aren't you regular genius." Her expression turned calculating, making Mitch suddenly wary.

"It's going to cost me, isn't it?" he said.

She nodded. "I need someone to take the burger-flipping shift from eleven to two tomorrow, and you're just the man to do it."

Mitch paused. Why was he willing to jump through so many hoops for a date with Courtney? It would be much less complicated to pick up a phone, ask her out, and avoid the hassle of burger duty and frozen salt water. But there was a reason he'd always kept things at the teasing, just friends status. Something about her intimidated the heck out of him, and he'd never been able to bring himself to say, "Hey, I like you. Want to go out sometime?"

He'd much rather let the sun take the risk, and if flipping burgers for three hours is what it took to make that happen, so be it.

"Count me in," he said.

Two

The clock on Courtney's nightstand registered 4:20 AM. She blinked sleepy eyes at it as sunlight filtered its way around the outer corners of her blackout blinds, daring her to go back to sleep and miss the dawning of a wonderful, unique day. Today, the sun would shine down from its highest annual altitude, creating the longest day of the year. For those in Heimel, sunset wouldn't come until close to midnight.

Courtney's arms stretched over her head as a small smile touched her lips. She rolled out of bed and opened her blinds, allowing the sun to wash over her face for a few moments. Then she reached for her netbook and plopped down on her bed, tucking a few pillows behind her back. The air felt charged with creativity, as if inspiration waited for the perfect moment to strike.

She stared at the blank computer screen, her mind whirring with possibilities for a new story. What about something set at a dilapidated castle surrounded by enchanted woods? Ireland, maybe? Hannah always suggested she try something international.

135

Then again, that sounded too much like a fairytale. What about a story involving The Great Wall of China, or those mystical-looking islands off the coast of Vietnam?

Courtney's fingers fluttered against the keys, not hard enough to make letters appear on the screen. Her expression brightened. What about New Zealand? She could write about a filmmaker who goes there to shoot a documentary about snow skiing then meets a mysterious woman who can control the weather.

She bit her lower lip. That could work—cool setting, lots of potential for intrigue and romance. Yes, that could definitely work.

For the next three hours, Courtney thought, typed, deleted, typed some more, and deleted some more. Something was wrong. Off. The story refused to come together the way her stories usually did. Was it the setting? The plot? The characters? All of the above?

Ugh. She pushed the netbook aside and frowned at the sun outside. So much for inspiration striking.

When the smell of bacon wafted into her room, she highlighted the remaining text, clicked delete, shoved her feet into her slippers, and headed downstairs with an attitude much less optimistic than it had been a few hours earlier.

"Hey, Mom, something smells good."

Dressed in a rose-colored floral apron, with matching curlers in her hair, her mother poured pancake batter onto a skillet. "You're up early. I figured you'd sleep in today and I'd have to keep your breakfast warm."

Courtney move to the stove and stirred the homemade syrup that simmered there. "I think it's going to take a few days for my body and mind to acclimate to the early sunrise. I've been up since 4:30."

"Good grief, what have you been doing?"

"Writing," Courtney said. "At least trying to. I woke up feeling inspired, only to come up with a whole lot of nothing."

"Sorry to hear it." Her mother flipped over a pancake. "Maybe getting out will help. You and Hannah are going to the June Solstice Days aren't you? That might trigger something."

Courtney turned off the stove and moved the pan to the counter. She dipped her pinky in the syrup and licked the sweet liquid from her finger. "Let's hope so. I promised my agent I'd have a rough draft ready by the end of the summer."

Her mother smiled and patted her cheek. "And you will; I'm sure of it."

Courtney returned the smile, feeling slightly encouraged. Her mother was right. She was in Heimel, after all, and sooner or later, something solid would come to her. It always did. She just hoped it would happen sooner than later.

❧

Courtney eyed the cylindrical ice vases that covered the tops of several tables—probably about two hundred in all, and not much to look at shape-wise. But the way the light sparkled off the glossy surfaces made for an impressive sight. Located in a central, roped-off section of the fairgrounds, throngs of people milled about, watching and waiting, as if staring at the vases would somehow make them melt faster. Courtney, on the other hand, knew the vases still had hours to go and cared more about whether or not her name appeared on one of the many sticks resting in the vases.

She sighed, knowing Mitch had probably made sure her name was there, intermixed with all the others. Or worse, maybe he'd used "Salt Spaulding," which was something he'd be likely to do, since he liked to annoy her. Regardless, if The Meltdown Match came to an end and her name wasn't announced, she wouldn't look at the remaining sticks. She preferred to believe that if hers didn't fall first, it didn't exist.

"Look!" A little girl beamed as she pointed. "That vase is almost melted!"

Courtney took a few steps to the side and looked where the little girl pointed. Sure enough, in the men's section, a vase definitely looked smaller than those surrounding it.

"Hey, that one seems to be melting faster, too," a woman said, pointing to another vase, this time in the women's section.

Courtney's heartbeat quickened when she saw the stick in the second vase already leaning precariously to the side, waiting for a few more inches of the ice to liquefy. Unable to pry her eyes away, Courtney stood there in awe, feeling like a miracle was happening right before her eyes. Was it coincidence, or was the sun really working its magic, bringing two unsuspecting hearts together? Whose names were on those sticks? She didn't dare hope one was hers.

Before she caved to the temptation to duck under the ropes and be disappointed, she turned and weaved her way through the throng, in search of Hannah. Her eyes scanned the crowed until they settled on a tall, curly haired guy flipping burgers. Without meaning to, she started forward, forgetting all about the taco salad she and Hannah had agreed on later for lunch. A greasy hamburger suddenly sounded much better.

Courtney paid a few dollars for a plate with chips, potato salad, and a hamburger bun, then made her way to Mitch.

"Hey, aren't you the city engineer?" she teased.

He looked up and grinned. "You obviously have me confused with someone else. In case you couldn't tell, I'm a master chef with mad hamburger-flipping skills. Check this out." He scooped up a patty, tossed it in the air, watched as it flipped a couple of times, and caught it with his spatula. His grin widened. "See? No mere city engineer could do that."

138

Courtney laughed. "You're right. You couldn't be the same person. No one in their right mind would ever let *him* near a grill." She leaned closer and lowered her voice. "Back in high school, someone made the mistake of putting him in charge of the hamburgers at a summer party, and he—well, let's just say that he gave 'well done' a whole new meaning." Courtney stood on tiptoe and leaned forward to see over the top of the grill. "Those aren't burnt, are they?"

"Very funny." Mitch lowered the lid to block her view and raised an eyebrow in challenge. "Has anyone ever told you that your hair is the color of salt?"

Courtney barely refrained from rolling her eyes. "It's blonde, not white. And no, not many people get that mixed up. Only you and that other guy who burns things."

"Maybe I should leave your burger on a little longer. You know, for old time's sake."

"And maybe I should enter your name in the karaoke contest—you know, for old time's sake," Courtney said, reminding him of the time she'd done exactly that.

Mitch laughed. "Only if you're planning to pass out ear plugs."

"Oh, you weren't that bad." Courtney smiled and held up her plate. "One hamburger, please. I need to hurry and eat this before Hannah yells at me for having lunch without her."

He nodded toward the table next to him. "Take a seat. It'll be ready in a sec."

Courtney walked around the grill and sat on the table, letting her legs swing beneath her as she admired how good Mitch looked in jeans and a snug-fitting T-shirt. When he glanced to the side and caught her staring, she cleared her throat and averted her gaze.

"How did you get roped into doing this, anyway?" she said.

"Haven't you heard? I'm a saint."

Courtney opened her bag of chips and pulled one out, then held the bag out to Mitch. "Alyssa put you up to it, didn't she?"

"Maybe." Mitch grinned as he stole a chip. "But I agreed to it, so that has to count for something."

Courtney laughed, something she did often around Mitch. Moments later, he slipped an unburned patty on her bun with an exaggerated flourish, and she laughed again. Instead of taking her plate to the designated eating area, she stayed put, preferring to eat her lunch next to Mitch.

While he cooked and slapped burgers on peoples' plates, he entertained her with story after story of humorous things that had happened around town during her absence. She listened, loving the sound of his voice and the way he could make any situation comical.

Something about him had always drawn her in. His good looks, definitely, but Courtney had dated plenty of handsome guys. It was more than that. The way he teased her. The way he looked at her and smiled just that way—as if he'd reserved it for her alone. His natural vibrancy and charm always made it difficult for Courtney not to do something stupid like fall for him. But Mitch could have his pick of anyone, and although he made jokes about salt being his favorite, his actions proved that his tastes always ran more toward cinnamon and pepper.

Besides that, come the end of the summer, Courtney would be leaving again—which was exactly what she should do right now. Get away before she let herself fall under his spell even more.

She brushed crumbs off her fingers and hopped off the table, but as she opened her mouth to say she'd see him later, a voice crackled over the loudspeaker.

"The Meltdown Match has officially ended. If you would please make your way to the middle of the fairgrounds, the winners will be announced."

Three

Suddenly feeling conspicuous, Mitch avoided Courtney's gaze. The results of The Meltdown were usually announced later in the day, typically around four or five. Not—he glanced at his watch—at one. He'd told Alyssa not to add so much salt, but would she listen to him? No. And now, not only did two vases melt way faster than the rest, but the city engineer so happened to be one of the winners.

That didn't look suspect at all.

"That was fast," Courtney murmured.

Mitch sneaked a glance and found her staring toward the middle of town with a faraway look in her eyes, probably wondering who'd manipulated the contest. He ducked his head and concentrated on flipping a burger that didn't need to be flipped.

"You did listen to me, right?" she finally said. "You left my name out of it?"

"Yeah. Of course."

"Good." Her voice sounded hesitant, as if she didn't believe him. Which she shouldn't. "So . . . you coming?"

He shook his head, grateful for an excuse to stay. "Can't. My shift doesn't end for another hour."

"Oh." She threw her plate into a nearby trashcan. "Well, thanks again for the burger and company. It was . . . really good."

Was she talking about the burger or his company?

Mitch bit his lip as he watched her go, wondering what she'd think when she saw how fast their vases had melted compared to the others. Would she be happy? Disappointed? Would she suspect him? With a roll of his eyes, Mitch returned his attention to the grill. He should have stayed out of it, just put their names in and let the sun decide their fates. Or better yet, he should have manned up, left both of their names out, and just asked her out.

⊚≫⊙

Courtney lay on her bed, staring dreamily at her bedroom ceiling. She'd won. She'd actually won the contest. And not only that, but Mitch—the man she'd been half in love with for as long as she could remember—had been chosen as her match. Her heart beat wildly at the thought, just had it had all afternoon, ever since the results had been announced. She'd tried to talk her heart down, but it was no use. No matter how many times she told herself it was only a coincidence, that the sun really didn't moonlight as a matchmaker, her heart wouldn't listen. It didn't want to listen. It wanted to believe in magic.

If she and Mitch were meant to be, then it would follow that she could finally stay put in Heimel, and her writing wouldn't suffer as a result. The universe had promised a lifetime of happiness, right?

An almost giddy sensation started in her stomach and spread throughout her body. She couldn't help but feel like she'd been granted her most-desired wish. On the nightstand, her cell chimed with a text. She picked it up and smiled when Mitch's name appeared.

Looks like were MFEO. Maybe that's why I like salt so much.

Courtney's smile widened, for once not bugged by the nickname. *You lied,* she wrote back.

His response came moments later. *I wanted those cinnamon rolls. So . . . pick you up at four? Too early?*

Too late, more like. But he probably had to work. Courtney would take what she could get. At least he hadn't said six or seven.

Four it is.

Four

Courtney drifted to sleep, dreaming of a beautiful, outdoor solstice wedding, in full view of the big, bright, blessed sun. Wildflower garlands lined the aisle, and Mitch had never looked so handsome, standing beside her in a black tux. When they were pronounced man and wife, he took her in his arms and lowered his mouth to hers. The long-awaited moment was finally happening.

But his lips had barely brushed against hers when a drummer in the band started banging on his drums, ruining the moment. Courtney drew back and frowned. Why would someone do that during the middle of her wedding?

The banging came again, this time louder.

Her eyes blinked open slowly, and the beautiful scene vanished, along with her smile. The banging continued, only it wasn't the drums, it was something else. A knocking—on her window?

Groggily, she rolled from bed and stumbled forward then pulled her heavy curtains aside. Someone stood out there, directly in front of her. She gasped and jumped, letting the curtain fall back. What was Mitch doing here? Heart pounding, she moved the curtain aside again, throwing it over her shoulder so she could open the window. Chilly, early morning air blew in as she stared at him in confusion.

"What are you doing?"

He wore an orange hoodie and a lopsided smile. "Picking you up for our date."

"But you said four."

"Right." Mitch pointed over her shoulder at the clock on her nightstand. The digital numbers glowed 4:05.

She spun back toward him. "You meant in the *morning*?" Who plans a date for four in the morning?

He shrugged, looking sheepish. "Sorry, I guess I should've clarified. I thought you'd understand, since this is a solstice date, and the sun rises a little after four."

Courtney blinked through the dim early morning light, her thoughts frantic. Watching the sun rise with Mitch sounded perfectly romantic, but . . . her hand flew to her hair at the same time she looked down, taking in her oversized T-shirt and flannel pajama bottoms.

When her eyes met Mitch's again, his lopsided smile returned. "You look cute," he said. "Just put on some shoes, grab a jacket, and meet me outside. You can come back later to change. Hurry, though, or we'll miss it."

Courtney let the curtain fall and raced to her bathroom where she ran a brush through her hair at the same time she brushed her teeth. She tugged on socks, shoved her feet into sneakers, grabbed a jacket, and ran outside, where she found Mitch on her front porch, leaning against a post, looking handsome and put-together in the early morning light. She suddenly wished she'd taken another minute or two to throw on some jeans.

"About time." He reached for her hand and tugged her toward his dusty blue Jeep. "I'm blaming you if we miss it."

"Two letters, Mitch. Two. A—M. Seriously, how hard

would have that been to add those to your text?"

Mitch chuckled. "Give me some credit, Salt. Why would I wait until the afternoon when I could pick you up in the morning?"

She let the nickname slide. "Because that's when normal people start their dates?"

Mitch opened her door and paused, looking into her eyes. "I think right now is better." The way he said it, without a hint of sarcasm, made Courtney feel like he meant it. Warmth spread through her body, forcing away the chill. She almost forgot to breathe as she climbed into his Jeep.

Mitch drove toward the other end of town and down a winding road toward the lake before pulling to a stop in front of a beautiful rambler that looked more like a ski chalet than a cabin. Not too small and not too big, the combined stone and wood architecture made a picturesque sight nestled between pines and aspens.

"Where are we?" Courtney asked as he led her up the steps and along the wrap-around porch.

"My house."

She stumbled, tightening her hold on his hand to keep from falling. Did he just say this was his house? "But I've never even seen this place."

"It didn't exist until I built it." Mitch stopped by a wooden table on the back patio and gestured for her to sit down. "I moved in a few weeks ago."

"You built this?" Courtney walked toward the window and peered through it. Thanks to a light on inside, she could make out knotty wood cabinets, granite counters, and a massive stone fireplace. For a second, she caught a glimpse of herself curled up on the leather sofa with her netbook. Slowly, she turned around to face the lake, trees, and mountains in the distance.

"Wow. It's uh . . ." How could she possibly describe the awe she felt? There were no words for it. "You really built this?"

Mitch sat down and pulled out the chair next to him, gesturing again for her to sit down. "Most of it. It took a few years, but my dad and brothers helped a ton, so I've got some major sweat equity to repay. I've always loved this property."

Courtney somehow found her way into the seat. "I . . . had no idea. It's amazing. You're amazing. I don't know what else to say. I'm in awe."

"Glad you like it."

"Like it? I love it." She peeked over her shoulder and pointed. "I'm so going to borrow that sofa when I start working on my next book. The view is incredible."

"You're welcome to it whenever you want." He reached across the table for a carton of juice and filled two plastic cups then pulled a package of doughnuts from a bag. "Orange, pineapple, and strawberry juice and old-fashioned doughnuts—your favorites, right?"

Courtney's breath caught in her throat as she stared at the table, feeling like she'd been dropped into an alternate reality. An amazing alternate reality. "How did you know?"

"You always brought them to snack on during our group hikes way back when. It was kind of hard to miss."

Old-fashioned doughnuts were her guilty pleasure—something she'd always brought along to help combat the jealousy from watching him hold another girl's hand or put his arm around another girl's shoulder. Mitch never failed to invite his girlfriends along on their group outings.

But now, here she was, on her own date with Mitch Winters.

"Look, here it comes." Mitch pointed at the horizon. "Try telling me that isn't a view worth waking up for."

The sun emerged over the horizon, casting a shimmering glow over everything it touched. As Courtney watched, something awakened inside her, breathing new life into her soul and making her feel a connection with everything around her. She felt so peaceful, so full of an indescribable feeling that made her want to stay right here, with Mitch, forever. The sun was working its magic.

"It's beautiful," she murmured. Could Mitch feel it too? She sneaked a glance at him then immediately wished she hadn't. He looked happy and content, but that was about it. Her heart deflated.

She squinted at the sun, willing the wonderful feeling back. "Do you still hunt?"

"Every now and then, but I'm more into fishing these days. A couple of times a year, I head down to Kenai for a week, charter a boat, and stock up. I've become pretty good friends with the guy who owns the boat, so he always takes me to the best places."

"That's great."

"Just wait until tonight. I have some salmon marinating in the fridge for dinner. I know how much you like salmon." He seemed to know a lot of things.

"I do, although it's been a while since I've had it. You'd think, living near the coast in California, I would have eaten more seafood, but it doesn't taste as good as it does here."

Mitch polished off the last of his doughnut and brushed the crumbs from his hands. "Are you planning to head back at the end of the summer?" He said it casually, as if he didn't care either way. It shouldn't have, but it stung.

"No, I'll try somewhere new. I haven't figured out where yet."

"What do you mean?"

Courtney attempted to smile, but it probably looked as fake as it felt. "It's sort of my thing. I start working on a story in Heimel then move to wherever I decide to set the book. I get to know the area, typically get a job, meet people, and work on my manuscript. When I finally submit the book, I come back home to start the process all over again. It sounds kind of crazy, but it's—"

"Exhausting?"

"I was going to say an adventure."

Mitch leaned back in his chair and tossed his plastic cup in a garbage can. "So basically, you're a commitment-phobic drifter."

"I'm also really superstitious," Courtney added.

A smile sprang to his lips, and a teasing glint appeared in his eyes. "Does that mean you really think there's something to this Meltdown Match thing?"

Courtney's face flushed. "I'm not *that* superstitious," she said quickly, although the words sounded like a lie to her.

Mitch leaned closer, resting his elbow on the table. "You're either superstitious or you're not. Take your pick."

Courtney forced herself to look him straight in the eye. "Not."

He laughed—a deep, almost melodic sound that seemed to echo off the lake and surrounding mountains. She loved hearing him laugh, even if it was at her expense.

She pushed the bag of doughnuts away and changed the subject. "Now that you've gotten me up at an obscene hour, what's on the schedule for the rest of the day? Hopefully a nap?"

Mitch shook his head. "And waste precious hours of the day? I don't think so. First I'm going to take you home to change, and–" He leaned over and sniffed the air around her. "—shower."

"Not funny." She slugged his arm, making him grin.

"Then it's a day jam-packed full of stuff to remind you why Alaska is the best place on earth to live."

"I already know that."

His eyebrow rose. "All evidence to the contrary, Miss Commitment-Phobic Drifter who's planning to move away by the end of the summer."

"Maybe I'll surprise everyone and decide to stay this time." Thanks to the sun, maybe she really would.

"That's my goal."

Courtney shot him a look, trying to gauge his motivations. Was this just fun banter to him, or something more? She couldn't tell. "So in only one day, you think you can convince me to stay in Alaska for good?"

He shrugged. "I'll start today, and we'll see how long it takes."

"What if it takes all summer?"

"Then it takes all summer." Mitch leaned back in his chair and gestured toward the sun, grinning. "According to that large round ball of fire, we're meant to be together. How's that going to work if you up and leave?"

Yet another comment Courtney had no idea how to take. Was he joking like he usually did, or did he, like her, want to believe there were some elements of truth in what he said? While part of her hoped that he did, another part—the doubting part—couldn't help but worry that by agreeing to this date, she'd set herself up for a whole lot of heartache.

If only she could read him better.

Five

itch bit back a smile at Courtney's look of concentration as they floated in his small fishing boat in the middle of the lake. Fishing was supposed to be relaxing, but she appeared rigid and tense, as though everything hinged on whether she could get a fish to take the bait.

"This isn't a competition," Mitch reminded her.

Courtney offered a fake smile and went right back to furrowing her brows as she slowly reeled in her line. "Sorry, this just brings back memories of fishing with my dad. He used to get so frustrated with me because I was always tangling the line or catching the hook on something. It made me never want to—"

She gasped and lurched forward, nearly toppling out of the boat. If Mitch hadn't been quick to grab her arm and pull her back, she probably would have.

"I caught one!" She turned the reel quicker, almost frantic. "I can't believe I actually caught one! This has never happened to me before." Her lips widened into a huge smile.

"I totally get it now—why you like this. It's actually fun when you catch something."

Mitch couldn't help his answering smile. If anything could be counted on in life, it was that Courtney would do or say something to surprise him. She was the most unpredictable person he'd ever met, which was probably what made her such a great writer.

When the fish finally broke the surface—a big, ugly catfish—Courtney dropped her fishing pole in the boat and moved away from it as though it had bitten her. Mitch couldn't hold back his laughter as the reel spun like crazy while the fish tried to make its getaway. He grabbed the pole and started bringing the fish back in.

"What was that thing?" Courtney said.

Mitch laughed again. "Congratulations, you just caught one of the vermin of this lake. That was a catfish."

"It had whiskers."

"That's probably why they call it a catfish."

Courtney shot him a glare before shifting positions. She eyed the line with a nervous expression, squirming a little when the fish resurfaced. "What are you going to do with it?"

"I thought we'd fry it up for dinner instead of the salmon."

"Very funny."

He worked to loosen the hook then tossed the slimy, wriggling fish back in the water before holding out the fishing pole for Courtney to take. She shook her head, refusing to accept it.

"I don't understand what you see in this sport. You could spend all day here and not catch anything—or worse, catch something like that."

"What happened to the talk about it being fun?"

"Call it temporary insanity."

Mitch laughed again, something he didn't usually do while fishing. Typically, this was his time to get away from life, to think and let nature rejuvenate him. But being here with Courtney, listening to her, and watching her crazy antics, made him feel lighter and happier than he'd felt in a long time. He liked having her along.

With a thunk, he set her pole on the floor of the boat and rested his elbows on his knees. "Okay, so I obviously didn't sell you on fishing, but don't give up on it just yet. Maybe you could even think of today as fodder for your next book and write a story about a fisherman who talks to fish or something."

Courtney drew her lower lip into her mouth, as if seriously considering his suggestion. "A fisherman with a sixth sense who knows right where to fish every time. That's actually not a bad idea."

Mitch raised an eyebrow. "Really? A guy who can talk to fish?" It sounded pretty lame to him.

"Not talk," Courtney said. "More like feel."

He shrugged, still not seeing it. "Let me guess, he'll fall in love with a mermaid."

Courtney shook her head. "I write magical realism, not fantasy. So no. She'll be a journalist or a photographer—someone who's heard stories about a guy that has never had a bad day of fishing. She'll want to investigate."

Mitch still wasn't sure about the idea. "Just promise me you'll throw in some pirates or something."

Her lips twitched. "I don't think so."

"What about a shark attack?" Mitch said. "Or maybe the guy could get swallowed by a whale and have to talk his way out of it. That would be cool."

Courtney laughed. "Remind me to never come to you for plot ideas. They're terrible."

"Hey, who suggested the fisherman idea?"

"As a *joke*." She smiled then leaned over the edge of the boat and ran her fingers through the water, probably working through plot ideas. Mitch took the opportunity to watch her, admiring her profile and the way the breeze whipped her hair behind her, like one of those magazine covers. Only with Courtney, she didn't need fans or heavy makeup. She was one hundred-percent real, and he couldn't pry his eyes away.

Mitch wanted to see that smile every day, to make her laugh, and to listen to whatever it was she had to say. He wanted to run his fingers through her silky hair, hold her close, and taste her lips. He wanted her in his life for longer than a few months out of the year.

But ever since high school, her MO had always been come and go, come and go—something that had a bipolar effect on him. Whenever she showed up, Heimel became vibrant and exciting, like three-dimensional renderings of a construction design. When she left, it all flattened back to a dull, lifeless two-dimensional line drawing.

If only he could convince her to stay for good.

Courtney looked his way and caught him staring. Mitch quickly averted his eyes, moving to secure the hooks on both fishing poles. Then he started the small engine and steered the boat toward the small dock. It was time to move on to something else—something he knew she'd like.

*C*ourtney accepted the helmet with a grin and put it on. She climbed on the back of the 4-wheeler, scooted close to Mitch, and wrapped her arms around his muscular waist, resisting the impulse to bury her face in his back and breath in the intoxicating scent that was all him. Hopefully this would be a long ride.

"You good?" Mitch called as he started the engine.

"Perfect." She held on a little tighter just because she could.

They spent the next several hours climbing trails, racing through meadows and pointing out moose, elk, eagles, and even a bear. Courtney hadn't felt this content in a long time.

When Mitch drove them to a peak that overlooked Heimel and killed the engine, Courtney reluctantly let go of her hold on him and climbed off to admire the spectacular view. The valley stretched out below them in a lush blanket of greens and browns. Birds chirped, and that raw, earthy scent she loved filled her senses.

"Coming?" Mitch said.

Courtney turned around to find him sitting on a blanket, patting the ground next to him. She smiled and sank down beside him, wishing she could snuggle up and rest her head against his shoulder. Instead, she accepted the sandwich he held out.

"Thank you," she said, peering out over the valley again. "This place really is beautiful."

"You're only now noticing that?"

She smiled. "No, I've always noticed. But there's something different about leaving and coming home. I'm always in awe of how it feels, like a dormant part of me suddenly comes alive. I love that feeling."

He shifted positions to look at her. "I don't get it. If you love it so much here, why not move back for good? You can write anywhere."

Courtney took a small bite of her sandwich and munched it slowly. "I like seeing new places."

When she said nothing more, he shook his head. "Sorry, not buying it. You can always put down roots and still travel to your heart's content. Why do you feel the need to keep moving away?"

She let out a breath and bit her lip. Did she dare tell him the real reason? Would he laugh? Find new material to tease her about? Probably. Still, for whatever reason, she wanted him to know, to understand. "Remember how I told you I'm superstitious?"

"Yeah."

"I wasn't joking." She paused, plucking the leaves off a nearby bush. "From the time I was little, I've always known I wanted to be a writer. In high school, I started submitting my work to agents, but they all shot me down. So I stayed here and went to college for a year in Anchorage, took every creative writing class I could, and went to every writing conference anyone offered. Then I applied what I learned and wrote my first magical realism novel. I thought it was great, but still, no bites. Out of desperation, I took the plunge and transferred to NYU the following year, where I wrote another novel, again with no luck.

"But then something amazing happened. I came back here for the summer and felt that feeling I just told you about. I had never felt so inspired. I wrote a rough draft quicker than I'd ever written one. But by the end of summer, the feeling had faded. So I had my records transferred to Texas—the place where the book was set—and went to school while I finished my revisions. Then I sent it out and about died when ten agents requested it—five of whom offered to represent me. Two months later, I signed my first publishing contract."

Courtney paused, wondering what was going through Mitch's mind. Did he think she was crazy, or did he understand?

He picked up a rock and chucked it over the ledge the way you'd throw a rock to skip it across a lake. "Let me get this straight," he said. "When summer ends, your inspiration runs dry and you have to move away to be re-inspired the next time you come back." Surprisingly enough, his words didn't sound mocking.

She nodded. "I know it sounds crazy, but writing is my career, and I can't afford for Heimel not to stop inspiring me."

Mitch shifted positions, turning around so he could face her head on. He raised his knee and rested one elbow on it as he studied her. "Have you ever considered that maybe your earlier books weren't accepted because you weren't ready? That it wasn't the right story, or you didn't have enough experience yet?"

"Of course," Courtney said. "And I know that has a lot to do with it. But it still doesn't change the fact that I really do feel inspired when I come home—and it's a feeling that doesn't last. Sometimes I feel like I'm cursed."

Mitch scooted closer and tentatively picked up her hand, running his fingers over hers and tracing them. Tingles ran up her arm, making Courtney feel like she'd be catapulted back to her beautiful dream from that morning. She clamped her mouth shut and held still, too afraid that if she moved or said the wrong thing, he'd stop.

Mitch's fingers finally closed around her hand as his gaze met hers. "You could always try to stay this time, just to see. You never know, maybe the change of seasons would give you the same renewed feeling." His eyes took on an uncharacteristic vulnerability, as if he really did want her to stay, that part of his happiness might even depend on it.

Her heart beat faster as she stared back, not wanting to break the connection. Little did he know how much Courtney wanted him to be right. How much she wanted The Meltdown Match to be a sign that she could finally stay—with him.

Ever so slowly, Mitch leaned closer. His hand moved from her fingers to her face, tucking a stray lock of hair behind her hair and sending wonderful chills down her spine. Courtney's heart pounded. She willed him to lean closer still, to brush his lips against hers. Her eyes drifted shut, and she felt herself tilting forward.

Please kiss me.

His hand moved to the back of her neck, but his warm lips didn't cover hers. Instead, they landed on her forehead, giving her a lingering kiss before drawing away. Cool air rushed between them, reminding her of that morning, when her wonderful dream had been rudely interrupted.

Courtney's eyes flickered open to see uncertainty in his expression, possibly even regret. Her face flushed as heavy disappointment settled in her stomach. A forehead kiss was something you'd give a sister, a child in need of comfort, or the girl who'd never be more than a friend.

She knew all about forehead kisses—she'd written plenty of them into her books.

Seven

$\mathcal{S}$ almon juices sizzled on the grill as Mitch watched Courtney from the corner of his eye. Ever since he'd sort of kissed her, things had been beyond awkward between them. He didn't like it. Why hadn't he just given her a real kiss instead of chickening out? At least then he would have known from her response whether she'd wanted it or not. Now he was stuck wondering if she'd been disappointed or grateful.

He'd tried to dispel the awkwardness by taking her to the fairgrounds for some flea market browsing, but it only made things worse. As the couple who'd won The Meltdown Match, they saw people sending one too many knowing smiles their way, so he'd finally brought her back to his place for dinner. Now she sat on the railing surrounding his back patio, dangling her feet while taking in the views, saying nothing.

Mitch bit his lip, mentally kicking himself yet again for being such a wuss.

Courtney twisted around, swung her legs up and over the railing, and hopped down from her perch. She approached him with slow, hesitant steps, her hands shoved inside the pockets of her skinny jeans. "Are you sure you don't need any help?" She leaned her shoulder against a support post, looking beautiful in that casual way she had. "I feel lame sitting here while you do all the work."

His arms itched to pull her to him and kiss her long and hard. Maybe then this nervous tension would go away and leave them alone. Maybe then he'd know if she was as crazy about him as he was about her.

Frowning, Mitch scooped the salmon from the grill, turned the heat off, and lifted the plate. "Everything's ready," he said, setting the plate on the table. He went inside and retrieved a salad from the fridge and twice-baked potatoes from the oven.

When he emerged from the house, Courtney eyed the table. "Wow, this looks amazing. When did you learn to cook so well?"

"You haven't tasted it yet."

"If it tastes as good as it smells, it's got to be fantastic."

Mitch pulled out a chair for her and sat down, racking his mind for something to say— preferably something funny that would make her laugh. When he came up empty, he focused on his food and rebuked himself yet again for botching things so badly earlier. Of all the dates to go wrong, this was the worst. It was too important—*she* was too important.

After some painful small talk to get them through dinner, Courtney insisted on doing the dishes. "It's the least I can do after all you've done today," she said, picking up his plate. "Besides, I've wanted to take a peek inside ever since you brought me here, and this is my chance."

Mitch followed with the glasses. "I'll give you a tour if you want."

"Okay."

Together, they made quick work of cleaning up, and once the last dish had been loaded, Mitch held out his hand. "Ready for the tour?"

She hesitated a second, then placed her hand in his. It felt soft and small and perfect, especially when her fingers tightened around his as she returned the pressure of his grip. Mitch let out a breath of relief, feeling like she'd given him a second chance.

He gave her hand a tug and led her down the hall. "The house has four bedrooms, two and a half baths, a den, vaulted ceilings, and a lot of stone and wood. With so many cabins around, I wanted it to have more of a chalet feel."

Courtney peeked inside each bedroom as they passed. Although they were pretty much empty, with little to no furniture, she seemed to like what she saw. In the master bedroom, she relinquished his hand and took her time looking around. Mitch shuffled his feet as he waited, wondering what she thought. With only a bed and nightstand, there wasn't much to see, but the stone fireplace was cool, along with the wooden beams on the vaulted ceiling.

Courtney finally faced him and cocked her head. "This room is beautiful, but it feels sort of empty. Take that fireplace, for example. It's gorgeous, but where's the loveseat to curl up on? And these hardwood floors—" Her foot tapped the boards. "Spectacular. But it could really use a rug to cozy it up. And those windows." She gestured toward the floor-to-ceiling windows that spanned the far end of the room. "Talk about an amazing view. You need a comfy recliner right there."

A teasing glint appeared in her eyes as she approached him, resting both hands on his chest and shaking her head in mock disappointment. "I have to say, I'm feeling a little let down. After seeing the outside, I expected more. You could really use a woman's touch in here."

With her standing this close, touching him and smelling faintly of citrus, he had to disagree. His room had never felt less empty. "Are you volunteering?" he said.

"Give me some time and a decent budget, and you'll wonder how you ever called this place home before."

Mitch covered her hands with his and peered into her beautiful green, almost blue eyes. "It's feeling pretty homey right now."

A moment passed when they booth stood there, saying nothing. Mitch's heart sped up to the point where Courtney could probably feel it pounding beneath her fingers. Now was his chance to do what he should have done before, to pull her to him and find out if her heart was racing as wildly as his.

Right as he was about to lower his head, confusion appeared in her eyes, and her hands pulled free from his, dropping back to her side. "You said there was a den?" Her voice sounded a little shaky.

Mitch resisted the impulse to curse and nodded toward the doors. "Yeah, that way." Without taking her hand this time, he led her back down the hall and to the right, toward a small alcove outside a set of dark, wooden doors. He paused with his hands on the handles, hoping against hope that she'd like what was on the other side. Then he drew in a breath and swung them wide, stepping aside.

Courtney's eyes widened as she walked into the room and turned a slow circle around, taking in everything. Mahogany bookcases spanned one wall, floor-to-ceiling windows spanned another, a chair sat adjacent to a small fireplace opposite the windows, and a beefy desk stood off-center, angled toward the windows.

Mitch had taken his time with this room.

"Okay, I was so wrong," Courtney breathed. "You don't need a woman's touch, not if you could come up with something like this." She walked to the bookcase and ran her fingers along the spines of several of the books. "This is seriously the most beautiful room I've ever seen."

Her fingers stilled over the spine of a few of the books, and pulled one out. She turned to face him, a look of surprise on her face. "You have my books."

Mitch pushed away from the desk and moved toward her, taking the book from her hands. "I like them all, but this is my favorite."

Her eyes snapped to his. "You've read them?"

"Every last word. You're an amazing writer."

Courtney sucked in a quick breath and looked quickly at her feet, but not before Mitch caught a glimpse of moisture pooling in her eyes. She half laughed, half snorted. "I can't believe I'm crying." She shook her head. "It's just . . . Well, the fact that you've read them all means . . . a lot to me."

Mitch replaced the book on the shelf before taking her hands in his, drawing her close. "Want to know why I finished this room first?"

She nodded, her eyes searching his.

A pit of nervous anxiety settled in Mitch's stomach. "Because of you."

Silence. Only the widening of her eyes indicated that she'd heard him.

Mitch felt as though he'd just gotten off the ski lift at the top of a steep mountain with nowhere to go but down a steep run. He drew in a deep breath and pushed off. "Courtney, I've always been crazy about you. But when you come back to town, you're never here long, and you're always so busy writing that I don't get to spend much time with you. When I designed this room, I sort of did it around you. I made it the type of room I hoped you'd like." He paused, his fingers trembling in hers. "Now, every time I'm in here, it reminds me of you, and makes me feel like you're not so far away and out of reach."

"Really?" More tears glistened in Courtney's eyes, but this time she didn't blink them away. One slipped out and trailed down her cheek, followed by another.

Mitch's thumb moved to her cheek, wiping the tear away. "Really."

She sniffed and blinked away the tears. "Then why did you kiss me on the forehead earlier? I wanted it to be a real kiss, you know? And when you didn't—I thought it meant that you didn't care. At least not as much as I did."

Her words worked their way into Mitch's heart, filling and expanding it. Not wanting to waste another second or let this moment pass, he dipped his head and covered her lips with his, showing her just how much he did care. Her arms wound around his back and her fingers clung to his shirt as she responded in a way Mitch could have never imagined possible.

Her lips moved against his with increased pressure, searching, seeking, and tasting. A feeling of exhilaration flowed through Mitch's body, filling him with an amazing energy. It was a kiss unlike any he'd ever known. Nothing had ever felt so good, so right. Courtney belonged here, in his arms—not in New York or California or anywhere else, but here, with him.

She couldn't leave again. She couldn't.

Courtney finally drew back, looking up at him with an expression filled with warmth and joy. Mitch smiled as his fingers traced along her jaw line. "If you only knew how long I've wanted to do that."

"If you only knew how long I've wanted you to do that."

He chuckled and leaned in for one more kiss, more lightly this time, then led her out of the den and to the great room, where he closed the blinds, dimmed the lights, and started a fire in the fireplace. They spent the rest of the evening snuggling, talking, and kissing.

When the sun finally approached the horizon close to midnight, Mitch took Courtney outside to the front porch. He stood behind her and wrapped his arms around her shoulders, pulling her close as the sun slowly disappeared behind the mountains, marking an end to one of the longest, and now best, days of the year.

Courtney relaxed against him and rested her hand on his arms. "This is the most perfect ending to any day I've ever had."

Mitch couldn't agree more.

Eight

Mouth-watering smells of homemade cinnamon rolls filled Courtney's senses as her eyes blinked open. She stretched her arms over her head and smiled at her bedroom ceiling. With dreams of Mitch and a new plot for a book fresh in her mind, it was easy to leave her bed behind and make her way to the kitchen, where her parents and Hannah were eating breakfast.

Her father eyed her from over the top of his paper. "What time did you get in last night?"

"Around one."

Hannah wiggled her eyebrows. "Was Mitch trying to make a new Guinness world record or something, because that had to be the longest June solstice date ever."

Courtney only smiled. She dropped a huge cinnamon roll on her plate and slid her chair in next to her mother's. "Thanks for breakfast, Mom."

"You sure look happy this morning," her mother commented.

A giddy feeling zipped through Courtney's body as she pulled apart the roll and popped a piece into her mouth. Morning had never been so cheery and bright, and cinnamon rolls had never tasted so good. "Probably because I'm happy," she mumbled between bites.

Hannah and her mother gave each other knowing smiles, and Hannah started chanting, "Courtney and Mitch, sitting in a tree, K-I-S-S-I-N-G—"

"We were in his house, not a tree," Courtney corrected.

Hannah burst out laughing while her father lowered his paper once more, giving Courtney a you've-got-some-explaining-to-do look. "You went out with Mitch Winters?" A man of few words, he'd always been a little behind when it came to keeping up with his daughters' social agendas.

"We won The Meltdown Match."

Her father harrumphed as her mother asked, "So . . . you and Mitch . . ."

"Will be spending a lot more time together," Courtney finished. "In fact, I'm heading to his house this morning to get some writing done. Since he's got to work, it will be quiet there, and wow, you should see his new place. It's gorgeous!"

Her mother nodded, lips twitching. "I take it you've settled on a plot for your next story, then?"

"I won't know for sure until I get it down on paper, but yeah, I think so."

"Let me guess," Hannah said dryly. "Mitch gave you the idea."

Courtney couldn't help the grin that sprang to her face as she nodded. She felt like a silly, twitterpated teenager who couldn't control her emotions. "Let's just say he's definitely inspiring."

Hannah and her mother exchanged another look, making Hannah giggle. "Somebody's in love," she said in a singsong voice, swirling her juice.

Although Courtney rolled her eyes, a warm feeling spread through her chest, making her wonder if her sister was right. What she felt for Mitch was definitely stronger than anything she'd ever felt before, but was it the always and forever kind of love? The kind she'd written and dreamed about?

It sure felt like it.

An hour later, Courtney knocked on Mitch's front door. When no one answered, she pulled out the spare key he'd given her from her pocket and let herself inside. Her footsteps echoed off the hardwood floor as she made her way to the kitchen, where she put a bag of groceries in the fridge and set a plate of her mom's cinnamon rolls on the counter. Adjusting the strap of her bag with her netbook on her shoulder, she walked to the den. The double doors were already open, the blinds raised, and the chair beckoning. Courtney inhaled the smell of paper and ink, mixed with a hint of Mitch, and smiled. Then she sat down and got to work.

The story came together like no other story had before. Scene after scene played out in her mind, and characters became fully formed as her fingers flew over the keys, failing to keep up with her thoughts. Although she'd always been told to write what she knew, Alaska had never seemed that exciting of a place to set a book before. But now, it was perfect.

As the hours passed, her stomach started rumbling. Courtney leaned back in her chair and stretched her arms over her head in satisfaction. Then she rose and went to the kitchen, where she pulled out the bag of groceries and chopped vegetables for gourmet hoagie sandwiches. Mitch had mentioned that he sometimes came home for lunch, and she wanted to have something ready for him, just in case.

Soon the rumblings of the garage door sounded, followed by Mitch walking in the door. He tossed his keys on the counter and headed straight to her, taking her in his arms and kissing her soundly enough to make her toes curl. How many times had she dreamed of this happening? Mitch holding her, kissing her, wanting to be with her.

Too many times to count.

Excited flutters ran through her stomach as she smiled against his lips. "I could really get used to this," she murmured.

"Me too." He drew back and ran his fingers up and down her arms. "Get much done on your story?"

She nodded. "I practically have the whole thing outlined, and I owe it all to you. Not only did you inspire me with the idea, but you gave me the most wonderful place to write it."

"Yeah, well, don't think it doesn't come with strings attached." Mitch said, pulling her close.

"What kind of strings?" She nodded her head toward the counter. "Because I brought you some of my mom's cinnamon rolls *and* made you the best sandwich you will ever taste in your life."

His gaze flicked toward the table and back to her. "That should cover about half."

"Only half? Well, that won't work." Her fingers traveled from his waist to his chest to the back of his neck, where they interlocked. She backed him against the counter and pulled his mouth to hers in a kiss that hopefully made up for the other half. When she finally pulled back, she felt weak and had to tuck her head against his chest as she struggled to catch her breath.

His arms tightened around her back, and he rested his chin against the top of her head. "Wow, Salt, that was really . . . wow," he said. "I'll take one of those anytime."

She poked him in the ribs. "Not if you keep calling me that."

He chuckled. "But it fits so well. I mean, think about it. Salt makes almost everything taste better, the same way you make my life better."

Courtney muffled her laughter in the fabric of his shirt before peeking up at him and shaking her head. "Nice try, but my name is Courtney. Say it with me now. Court—ney."

"But it doesn't have the same ring to it," he joked, dipping his head to try and kiss her again.

"I don't think so." She broke free and took a few steps back, pointing her finger at him. "Just wait until I come up with an equally fitting nickname for you. You're going to be sorry you ever called me Salt."

He pulled out a barstool, sat down, and reached for one of the hoagies. "I'm quivering with fear."

Nine

ourtney entered the city offices and took the stairs two at a time. Only thirty minutes earlier, she'd officially finished her rough draft, and it was time to celebrate by taking Mitch out for lunch. The book was coming together quicker than any of her others, and although she still had mountains of revision ahead of her, she'd reached a huge milestone and couldn't wait to tell Mitch the news.

Ever since The Meltdown Match, her scattered life and question mark of a future had become a little less scattered and a little more certain. For the first time since she'd left for college, she wasn't afraid to stay in Heimel permanently. In fact, she wanted nothing more than to sink her roots more deeply into the place she'd never really pulled them from and continue to live the life Mitch had shown her during the past couple of months.

Every day had been as close to perfection as she could have hoped. Filled to the bursting point with inspiration, she'd spent her days writing, and the evenings hanging out with Mitch. They did everything together. Fishing, 4-wheeling, biking, hiking, shopping, rappelling, swimming—even hunting, although Courtney wouldn't let him actually shoot anything, so it was more like animal watching. They played games, cooked dinner, hung out with both of their families, and read books together. The added romance had catapulted a good friendship into something truly amazing, and Courtney had never felt more connected to anyone. Which was exactly why she couldn't wait to see him now.

She rounded a corner and smiled when she spied Mitch's secretary. "Hey, Alyssa, how are you?"

Alyssa twirled a pen between her fingers as she returned the smile. "Better and better, thanks to you."

"Me?" Courtney asked, unsure as to why she'd been given credit for Alyssa's good day.

"Thanks to you, I now have the happiest, most pleasant boss in the world." Her eyes narrowed as she peered at Courtney through her glasses. "Don't you ever dump him, or I might kill you."

Courtney laughed. Only yesterday, Hannah had pretty much told Mitch the same thing. "Why would I dump him? According to the sun, he's my perfect match."

"The sun and a whole lot of salt," Alyssa said dryly, returning her attention to the paperwork on her desk.

Courtney's smile faltered as she tried to make sense of Alyssa's words. Did she mean Salt, as in her, or the stuff people dumped on French fries? Either way, it didn't make sense. "What does salt have to do with anything?"

Alyssa glanced up. "Didn't Mitch tell you? We added salt to the water to make your vases melt faster."

"Oh." Courtney strained to keep a semblance of a smile on her face while Alyssa continued talking, saying words like *romantic* and *sweet*. Courtney's head felt foggy all of a sudden, as though she'd taken too much cold medicine. She couldn't think clearly.

It suddenly felt as though she were eight years old on Christmas Eve, when Courtney finally got to stay up and see Santa Claus instead of having to go to bed. She'd looked forward to the moment for years, envisioning how magical and life-changing it be. Would Santa bring some of his elves? Would she get to see Rudolf and his glowing nose? Would he give her a hug, set her favorite toy under the tree, and tell her she'd been a really good girl?

Turned out it was none of the above, because Santa wasn't real. Just like The Meltdown Match.

Her heart felt as though it had been poked with a pin, and now it slowly deflated, wrinkling like a balloon.

"Courtney, are you okay?" Alyssa's voice sounded through the fog.

Voices approached from somewhere down the hall, and two men appeared—Mitch and someone else.

"Hey, beautiful, what are you doing here?" Mitch put an arm around her and kissed her cheek before making introductions. Courtney was vaguely aware of trying to smile and shake the man's hand before he left, his footsteps sounding loud on the hard, marble stairs.

Courtney turned to Mitch, trying to talk herself out of her emotions. The Meltdown Match was just a silly contest. It didn't mean anything. She and Mitch were meant to be together because they were meant to be together, not because some huge ball of fire decreed it so. No one in their right mind would place any stock in it at all.

No one except someone stupidly romantic and superstitious, like her.

Mitch rubbed his hand up and down her arm. "Hey, what's wrong?"

Courtney shook her head slowly, trying to clear it.

"I, uh, need to go make some copies." Alyssa was out of her seat and down the hall in seconds.

Unable to put a stop to her overreaction, Courtney blinked at Mitch, needing to say something. "The Meltdown Match . . . you added salt . . . to the water?"

His face took on a sheepish expression as he nodded. "I guess I needed a reason to finally have the courage to ask you out. You're not mad, are you?"

"No." What she felt didn't resemble anger, more like a keen disappointment that she didn't quite understand. She wasn't eight anymore. She was twenty-seven and should know better than to believe in something like The Meltdown Match.

Why, then, did she suddenly find herself questioning everything? Was her relationship with Mitch even real? Had she conjured up intense feelings because she thought the universe had said she should feel this way? And what about Heimel and her well of inspiration? Would that run dry yet again? She'd been so confident about everything only moments before, but now, not so much.

More than ever, she hated the nickname of "Salt."

Courtney drew in a deep breath and took a step back. She needed to get away from Mitch, away from everyone. She needed fresh air to breathe and time to figure out what in the heck had just happened. "I'm sorry, but I've got to go. I just remembered I have to do something."

Mitch moved toward her, but then he stopped. His expression reflected confusion and concern, but he didn't try to stop her from leaving. "I'll call you when I get off work."

Courtney nodded then turned and made her exit as quickly as she'd come. Only this time, instead of her spirits rising with each excited leap up, they plummeted with each step down.

Ten

hen Mitch called after work, Courtney didn't answer. When he called again ten minutes later, she rolled to her side and curled into a ball, hugging her pillow as she gripped her phone, still unsure of what to say. Her cell buzzed with a new text.

I'm coming over.

Her fingers reacted quickly. *Now's not a good time.*

A few minutes passed before the phone buzzed again. *We need to talk.*

She stared at the words. Mitch deserved an explanation—he did—but what could she say? Her feelings still felt so jumbled and cloudy. *We do, and we will. Later. I just need some time.*

This is killing me.

Sorry. It was all she could write. And she was. Very sorry. But even after spending all afternoon trying to talk herself out of feeling this way, she couldn't keep the doubting questions or worries at bay. There were no threatening tears, no emotional outbursts. She simply felt empty inside, as though part of her soul had up and left.

A knock sounded at her door before it opened, and Hannah's voice echoed through the quiet room. "Hey, you sick or something? You've been in here for hours."

Courtney said nothing, just gripped her pillow and clutched her phone as if it were her last link to sanity. Her bed moved as Hannah sat down. "What's wrong with you?"

"I'm a mess," Courtney mumbled into her pillow.

A pause. "Wanna talk about it?"

"No."

"Fine, I'll go get Mom. No wait—make that Dad."

Courtney twisted around and glared at her sister. "Don't you dare."

"Me or him—take your pick." Hannah shifted, making herself comfortable. "But since I already know you're messed up, I'm probably the lesser of the two evils, so I'd choose me if I were you."

Courtney sighed and pulled herself up, hugging her knees to her chest. Maybe talking it through with someone would help, and Hannah was the preferred choice. "I just found out that Mitch made our vases out of salt water so they'd melt faster."

Hannah's eyes widened at the same time her smile did. "Are you serious? That's awesome!"

"No," Courtney said. "Not awesome. All this time I've been thinking that we were, you know . . . destined to be together or whatever, and now it turns out we're like every other couple out there who met randomly and happened to make a connection."

The smile faded from Hannah's face, replaced with a look of disbelief. "You can't be serious. Court—hello! You make love sound like an everyday occurrence, when you, of all people, should know better. You've dated and walked away from a lot of guys in the past, but now you're finally with Mitch—a guy you've always liked—and you've never been happier. Don't you dare walk away from him just because you weren't really matched up by the sun." She threw up her hands. "I can't believe I had to say that. Now you're making *me* sound crazy."

Courtney sighed. "Believe it or not, I know all that—I do. I just can't make my illogical feelings see logic, if that makes sense. It's like with my writing and Heimel. I could never stay here permanently, because then this would become the place I live, not the place that inspires me. Then The Meltdown Match and Mitch happened, and I finally thought that everything had changed. But now I don't know anything anymore."

Hannah's mouth parted as she stood there, blinking at her sister. "Oh my heck. You're like one of those athletes who won't cut their hair or wash their socks the entire season because they think it will jinx them."

Courtney brought her knees to her chest and frowned out the window. "Told you I was a mess."

"I'll say." Hannah shook her head in disbelief. "Know what? I think this is one of those times when your over-active imagination is getting the best of you. You live in the real world. You know that, right? A world where apple trees don't grow fruit during the winter, the wind doesn't have healing properties, and the sun's definitely *not* a matchmaker."

Courtney frowned. She'd always liked to believe that her books had the power to inspire, but maybe they didn't. Maybe they only created daydreamers with unrealistic expectations. Like her.

So much for thinking this talk would help. It had only made things worse. "I know," she finally muttered.

"Do you? Really? Because I'm not so sure." Hannah rose to her feet and walked toward a small bookcase where she pulled out the copies of each of Courtney's four published books. She held one up. "Remember what inspired this one? You came home for the summer, and Mitch organized a camping trip. It was windy, and I sprained my ankle, but no one had an ace bandage in their first aid kit, so Mitch made a joke about how if wind could heal, it would be better in no time. The next day, you started writing this book."

She tossed it on the bed and held up another. "Remember when you took a semester off and came home in the dead of winter? It was below freezing outside, and to help pass the time, Mitch invited everyone over to his house for games. You said you were craving an apple, and Mitch said not to worry. He had a tree out back that grew apples all year long. Then he disappeared and came back with an apple."

Another book landed by the first before Hannah held up the next. "And this one, about a small town that produces amazing artists? That story came about after Mitch made us all go to see Lilly's painting at that gallery in Anchorage. While we were there, he said that Heimel must have something special in the water, because not only did Lilly's painting make it in a gallery, but you'd just published your first book."

The book landed on top of the others as Hannah held up the last one. "What about the time we went spelunking? Don't you remember?"

Hannah's voice seemed to fade into the background as Courtney's gaze dropped to her hands. She did remember now. Everything. The apple. The healing wind. The magical town. The cave of truth, where no one could lie.

All this time, she'd been giving Heimel credit for her inspiration when it had really been Mitch—the same person who'd inspired her with her latest idea. How had she been so blind? So stupid? So wrong?

Tears sprang to her eyes at the same time Hannah's hand came to rest on her knee, bringing Courtney back to the present. "Don't you see? What you have with Mitch is way more miraculous than winning some stupid ice-melt contest. What you have with him is something some people look for their entire lives and never find."

It was true. Even with tears marring her vision, Courtney could see more clearly now than ever before. A warm feeling spread through her body, taking away the heaviness and weaving in peace and joy—the kind of joy that trumped everything else. Her sister was right. What she and Mitch had went way beyond superstitions and magic and fantasy.

What she and Mitch had was real.

Her arms went around her sister as she simultaneously laughed and cried. "Thank you so much for pointing out how stupid I am." She sniffed and wiped at her eyes. "You really are the best."

"Duh."

Eleven

itch sat in his boat in the middle of the lake and flung his fishing pole forward, casting his line as far as he could. Then he reeled it in, too fast to actually catch anything. Not that he wanted to. What he wanted was for the unsettled feeling in his gut to go away and for the image of Courtney backing away from him to leave his mind.

Normally after a bad day, fishing had a calming effect on him, but today was different. Today he'd lived with the worry that Courtney could walk out of his life yet again. That she'd show up at any moment with the news that it was time for her to move on.

His stomach in knots, Mitch cast the line again before turning the reel as fast as he could, as if retrieving the hook would somehow bring Courtney back. But when the hook resurfaced empty, all it did was serve as a reminder of how he felt. Empty.

Over and over, he cast and reeled, cast and reeled, looking for a solace he couldn't find. She needed some time. She needed space. She needed distance.

From him.

The sick feeling returned with a vengeance, and Mitch threw his fishing pole to the bottom of the boat. It was no use. The only thing that would help would be for Courtney to tell him she wasn't going anywhere.

"Mitch!" The faraway voice seemed to echo off the lake and surrounding trees.

He looked around, finally spotting long, blonde hair blowing in the breeze and two arms waving at him. Courtney was here. Ready to talk. About what? Queasiness filled his stomach as he started the engine and headed for the dock. He pulled up moments later, avoiding her gaze, too afraid of what he'd see.

"Hey," she said, sounding happy and light.

Mitch glanced up, caught her smile, and felt more confused than ever. He tied up his boat slowly before stepping onto the dock and eyeing her warily.

She started to move toward him, but stopped and clasped her fingers together, looking suddenly nervous. "I guess you probably want an explanation."

"That all depends on what your explanation is," Mitch said, shoving his hands into the pockets of his khaki shorts.

Courtney took a tentative step toward him and drew in a deep breath. "Okay, so here goes. When I found out that you were behind the contest, I sort of freaked out about, well, everything. I wanted to believe the contest was real, that we really were destined to be together, and then I found out it wasn't. It threw me a little."

Mitch wanted to stop her, to pull her to him, give her a good shake and tell her that they *were* destined to be together. It was something he'd known for years. But his hands remained at his side and his mouth shut.

"But then Hannah bluntly pointed out that I've been wrong about everything. Especially you."

Him? She'd been wrong about him? What was that supposed to mean? That she wanted to be with him, or that she didn't? The way she looked at him gave him hope, but her words didn't match. "I don't understand," Mitch finally said.

Her head cocked to the side as she approached him and took his hands in hers. "You're my inspiration. Not Heimel. Not coming home. You."

For the first time since Courtney had walked out on him earlier, Mitch felt his chest lighten. He had no idea how she'd come to that conclusion, but if it meant she wasn't going anywhere, he'd take it. Or did she mean that?

"Wait, so where does that leave me, exactly?" Mitch said. "Do you still feel the need to move away? And if so, then what? Come back to me instead of Heimel? Like I'm some . . . I really don't know what to compare it to. All I know is that I wouldn't be okay with it."

Her lips drew into a smile. "What I'm saying is that I'm here to stay. For good."

"But what about the whole needing to be re-inspired thing?" Mitch wasn't quite ready to believe her.

Courtney intertwined her fingers with his and peered up at him. "Look, I don't know what the future holds for me, for us, or for my writing. But what I do know is that from here on out, I'm choosing to believe in us rather than some silly superstitions. I'm in love with you, Mitchell Winters, and I want to stay here with you. For always and no matter what."

A light breeze blew past, making Mitch wonder if the wind really did have restorative properties. As it came and went, all of the heaviness and worry and heartache seemed to leave with it, making him feel better than ever. He lifted Courtney's hands, bringing her closer. "You'll really be happy living here with me forever?"

"And ever," she said without hesitation. "Although I do still want to travel and research places for my books. I'm just hoping you'll come with me."

The corners of Mitch's mouth tugged up into a smile. "So long as you don't mind checking out the engineering side of things while we're there."

"Of course not." A teasing glint appeared in her eyes. "In fact, maybe my next book will be about an engineer."

"Yeah?"

"Yeah."

"Will his name be Mitch?"

"Definitely."

"Will he have x-ray vision and be able to see through roads so people know exactly where to dig?"

Courtney's lips twitched as she shook her head. "No."

"Will he be a brilliant mathematician who never has to use a calculator?"

"No."

"Oh." Mitch shrugged, out of ideas. "Then I guess he'll have to be the guy who can sense when two people are supposed to be together and manipulates the situation so they are." He grinned as he tugged on a lock of her hair. "Like with salt."

Her forehead creased in thought, and she drew her lower lip into her mouth for a moment before letting it out. "You mean like Cupid?"

Mitch frowned, picturing a naked cherub with a pink bow and tiny white wings. "No, not like Cupid. That was just a joke—a bad one."

"Well, I like it. And considering how all of my ideas have been inspired by one of your bad jokes, it definitely has merit."

If that was the case, Mitch really needed to stop joking, especially when it came to characters named Mitch. "What about Hercules instead? He's pretty cool."

"No, I like Cupid."

"Zeus? Poseidon? I'd even take Hades."

Her fingers threaded through the hair at the nape of his

neck. "I think I've finally found your nickname—one that will be as fitting and endearing to you as Salt is to me." She grinned. "Cupid. It's perfect."

This conversation was getting out of control. "No, it's not perfect."

"It totally is. I can't believe I didn't think of it before." Her fingers pressed on the back of his neck, trying to pull his head toward hers, but Mitch resisted.

"Oh, c'mon, Cupid," she said with a slight pout on her lips. "Don't you want to kiss me?"

Mitch grasped for something—anything—to make the nickname go away. "Okay, fine, you win. I promise to stop calling you Salt if you never say that word again."

"Cupid, Cupid, Cupid, Cupid, Cupid, Cupid—"

Mitch's mouth covered hers with a kiss meant to erase all thoughts about engineers and books and Cupid. However, as her lips moved across his and her fingers worked their way through his hair, Mitch was the one who forgot about everything but her.

Epilogue

The day of June Solstice dawned overcast and rainy. Through her window, Courtney frowned at the skies as she smoothed her fingers against the soft satin of her wedding gown. This was all wrong. According to the weather report, the skies were supposed to be clear, the day sunny. A perfect day for an outdoor wedding.

Her mother kept promising that it would clear up, that Courtney needed to finish getting ready, but the clouds didn't break, and the rain continued to splatter lightly against her window.

Not good.

Courtney's stomach twisted into knots at the implication. She forced herself to take a deep, calming breath. This was not the universe telling her that she shouldn't marry Mitch or to pick another wedding day. It was just an unlucky coincidence. That's all.

Horribly unlucky.

Her phone rang with Mitch's ringtone, and Courtney quickly brought it to her ear. More than ever, she needed to hear his voice.

"No, this is not a bad omen, and yes we're still supposed to get married today," Mitch said without preamble. "In fact, this is actually a good sign. It means our married life together will be full of surprises and never dull."

Courtney couldn't help her answering smile. She loved that he knew where her crazy thoughts were headed—and that he still wanted to marry her. More than that, he knew exactly what to say to erase the worried lines from her forehead.

"I was just thinking the exact same thing," she said.

"Liar."

Her smile widened. "Okay, Mr. Know-it-all, so where are we going to have the wedding now?"

"Outside, near the lake, as planned. It's already set up, and the food is under that gazebo thing you rented, so we're good."

"So long as the food stays dry," she said.

"Exactly."

Courtney rolled her eyes and looked down, picturing rain splattering all over her dress while her short train skidded across the muddy ground. What would her hair look like after a few minutes in this weather? Not like it did now, that was for sure. "But what about my dress?"

"I don't see a problem. It's not like you're planning to wear it again, are you?"

"Well no, but—" It was beautiful and white, and she didn't want it to get muddy. She wanted it to look clean and perfect for the day her future daughter tried it on. Did she really have to explain that?

"But what?"

Courtney sighed. "My hair will go limp, and the pictures will look awful."

"Oh please. You couldn't look awful if you tried, and the pictures will give us a great story to tell our kids one day."

An almost hysterical laugh escaped Courtney's mouth, mostly because she actually found herself considering his suggestion. She threw up her free hand and plopped down on her bed. "Okay fine, Mr. Cupid Man, let's get married in the rain."

"That's my girl. See you in an hour." At least he'd let the Cupid comment slide.

The phone went dead before Courtney could tell him she was only half serious. She frowned out the window once more before turning toward Hannah and her mother. "Looks like the outdoor wedding is still on."

"Sweet!" Hannah said at the same time her mother excused herself to make a few phone calls and track down some umbrellas.

An hour later, Courtney found herself sitting in her dad's car as he pulled into the muddy mess of the designated parking area. She'd exchanged her satin heels for tennis shoes and stepped into the squishy mud, holding her dress high while her mother positioned a large, multi-colored beach umbrella over their heads.

They squished their way to a large tent, where Courtney made her final preparations. Her mother cleaned off her shoes with wet wipes while Hannah fiddled with her hair. Thankfully, someone had brought a clear, plastic umbrella for Courtney's father to carry down the aisle so they could dispense with the brightly colored one.

In no time at all, her mother disappeared, the music started, and Hannah left the tent, carrying a bouquet of fresh wildflowers.

Courtney's dad held out his arm for his daughter. "Ready to go, sweet pea?"

"As ready as I'll ever be." Her feet landed once more in the mud, and Courtney tried not to cringe as they made their way to the back of the crowd, where a live band huddled under a canopy and guests waited with various colored umbrellas. At least the wildflower garland looked lovely.

Through the drizzle and beneath her veil, Courtney's eyes met Mitch's. He stood at the front, looking beyond handsome wearing a black tux and holding a matching clear plastic umbrella. Her breath caught in her throat as all thoughts of rain and mud and limp hair faded. In a matter of minutes, she would be his, and he, hers. They would leave this scene as man and wife and spend the rest of their lives together.

It really did feel like a miracle.

Her father led her to Mitch's side, where she relinquished her father's arm and kissed his cheek. Then she placed her fingers on Mitch's warm palm and smiled when he held out his umbrella so she wouldn't get wet.

"You look beautiful," Mitch said, drawing her close. "Are you ready for this?"

"More than ready."

"Me, too." He tucked her arm in his and turned to face the pastor. In what seemed like minutes, they were pronounced man and wife beneath a dense canopy of clouds. Although the sun remained hidden, the warmth that spread through Courtney's body made it feel as though it shone down on her with the promise of happiness.

Mitch handed the umbrella to the pastor, and raindrops dotted Courtney's face and arms. But it didn't matter, not when his hands framed her face and he looked at her in just that way, as if she were his everything. Courtney raised her mouth to his, smiling when his lips moved gently over hers in a kiss that would be forever engrained in her memory. He kissed her as though she were fragile and precious—something to treasure. Her heart swelled with the kind of love she'd only ever imagined in her mind and written in her books.

In that moment, Courtney's world seemed to align, as if she'd finally been able to bridge the gap between fiction and real life. She'd always been a wisher, a hoper, a believer in something greater than the ordinary, but today it was no longer wishful thinking. It was reality. Her very own real life fairytale come true.

She couldn't wait to live it all out.

ABOUT RACHAEL ANDERSON

Rachael Anderson is a *USA Today* bestselling author. She's the author of four novels and two novellas. She's the mother of four and is pretty good at breaking up fights, or at least sending guilty parties to their rooms. She can't sing, doesn't dance, and despises tragedies, but she recently figured out how yeast works and can now make homemade bread, which she is really good at eating.

You can read more about her and her books online at RachaelReneeAnderson.com.

Golden Sunrise

Annette Lyon

Other Works by Annette Lyon

Band of Sisters

Coming Home

A Portrait for Toni

At the Water's Edge

Chocolate Never Faileth

The Golden Cup of Kardak

The Newport Ladies Book Club Series

There, Their, They're:
A No-Tears Grammar Guide from the Word Nerd

One

The cab stopped at yet another red light in the snarled Las Vegas traffic. Natalie checked the time on her cell phone for at least the hundredth time since she'd boarded the plane at LaGuardia. Assuming Sierra was keeping to the schedule—and she always did—the wedding rehearsal started five minutes ago.

Without me. Natalie was the maid of honor. She crossed her ankles, hating that in the blistering Nevada heat, her legs were sticking together. The air conditioning in the cab apparently didn't reach past the driver. He looked perfectly comfortable, while Natalie dripped with sweat and stressed out over missing her best friend's rehearsal.

She loved Sierra, but really, what had she been thinking planning a wedding in Vegas—at the hottest time of the year? Vegas was out of the way for everyone attending the wedding, and most would be traveling significant distances. No way would Natalie have ever made such a trip for anyone but her best friend. She and Sierra had been tight since junior high, and during high school, they'd dated a pair of best friends. The four of them—the Quartet, as they called themselves, had been nearly inseparable.

Nearly, but not quite. Sierra and Jason were about to marry all these years later, while Natalie was very much single; she and Adam had parted ways after graduation. Natalie had asked Sierra whether Adam would be at the wedding. It would make sense, but she had no idea whether the male half of the Quartet was still close.

What if she did see Adam again? His crooked smile, the way he laughed with his head thrown back, the warmth and safety she felt in his arms, the silly quirk of one eyebrow whenever he was surprised or amused.

Natalie shifted in her seat. It was time to think of something—someone—else. Except that her foot had kicked some trash on the floor of the cab, including pieces of stale popcorn. The sight triggered a memory about the night the Quartet had hung out at Sierra's house, watching an old movie Adam was assigned to write a paper on. The film was boring beyond belief. They'd watched it in silence for a good half hour, and then out of the blue, Natalie found herself being pelted with pieces of popcorn by Adam, who sat beside her on the floor.

Three pieces hit her straight in the face, one after the other. She laughed and brushed off her shirt then jabbed Adam in the ribs with her elbow. "You *eat* popcorn," she told him, grabbing some from the bowl he held in his lap then lobbing the pieces at his face one at a time. Her aim wasn't as good as his, and the pieces stuck in his hair instead. She covered her mouth and stifled a laugh.

Adam brushed his hair out with his fingers. "This is *cold* popcorn. It's basically salty Styrofoam. The only thing it's good for is ammunition."

"Oh, really?" Natalie said with a challenging tone and a grin. She snatched the bowl and ran off with it. She and Sierra hid behind the couch, throwing popcorn missiles over the couch then dodging popcorn coming from the boys, who were using the other bowl of popcorn, which Sierra and Jason had been eating from. Fortunately, Sierra and Jason had eaten most of their popcorn, so the boys ran out of ammo much earlier than the girls did, and started throwing whole kernels until their bowl was completely empty.

The end result was a total mess. Natalie still had no idea what movie they'd been watching, except that it was black and white. To this day, she had a hard time eating cold popcorn. Not because it tasted bad, but because it brought back many memories she'd rather keep buried.

She sighed. Why was she thinking about all of that now? It was ancient history. Besides, Adam was almost certainly *not* going to the wedding. For years, Sierra did the duty of a best friend, going out of her way to avoid talking about Adam to Natalie, and it had worked, except for the pictures of the three of them from their five-year class reunion, with Natalie noticeably absent. She hadn't gone because the symphony was getting ready for a tour. Not that she'd needed much of an excuse to avoid the reunion. And she'd appreciated Sierra keeping any mention of Adam out of their relationship, it had meant that Natalie hadn't known until recently whether Jason and Adam had stayed in touch. But when Natalie agreed to be maid of honor, she had to ask the big question for the sake of preparing for anything awkward: would Adam be best man?

Turned out that while he and Jason were still tight, six months ago, Adam had committed to fly out that same weekend to Brussels to meet with a software company for a potential merger. If he could get out of the trip, he'd come to the wedding, but last Sierra heard, the chances of that were slim to none.

Which was just as well. Seeing Adam again would have been uncomfortable. Not that she couldn't handle it. What was done was done—long ago.

Adam was surely married and off doing his technology stuff. He'd gone to Cal Tech to study computer science, and she had no idea where he'd settled after that. All she knew was that a few months before high-school graduation, she'd been accepted to Juilliard, and he'd been accepted to Cal Tech. They went off to study on opposite sides of the continent.

After the graduation ceremony, the Quartet spent the night playing goofy games, eating pizza, and laughing themselves silly. They stayed up all night to watch the sun rise on their new lives. The four of them walked from Jason's house to a nearby hill. They climbed up a steep road to a park at the base of the foothills, and stood there looking east at the Rocky Mountains of their hometown. Jason had his arm around Sierra's shoulders. Natalie stood in front of Adam and leaned back against his chest as he wrapped his arms around her waist.

The sun never really came up that morning. Night ended, and the day lightened. But the sky was overcast, so they never saw the sun peer over the mountain peak.

"Well, now, that's ominous," Jason said as a joke. Only Sierra laughed. Natalie smiled wanly, trying to appreciate the humor, but a seed of dread had settled into her middle, and she didn't know why. Sierra kissed Jason, took his hand, and together the two of them headed down the hill.

Natalie and Adam stayed at the top, unmoving. She hardly dared breathe. Jason's comment about a bad omen continued to ring in her ears. What *did* the future hold for her? For them? If only they could stand right there on that grassy hill, forever, and not worry about heading to opposite coasts for the next four years, but instead, jump over those years and land in the future, still together.

She'd be leaving in a couple of days for an early summer program. He wouldn't go to Cal Tech until later, but the next day, his family was headed out for a final trip before he went off to college. This was their last day together.

Adam sighed and whispered, "I'll miss you."

"I'll miss you too." Natalie swallowed and soldiered up, broaching the subject they'd both been avoiding. "But we can stay in touch with email and texts, and we can Skype . . ." Her voice trailed off, expecting Adam to chime in with agreement, adding more things they'd use to stay close across the miles. Maybe a phone call every night. But he stayed eerily silent. With her back against him, she leaned to the side and looked up at his face. His jaw had tightened, and sadness seemed to circle his eyes. She wanted to ask what was wrong, but the words caught in her throat. She turned back to the mountain range with its gloomy gray clouds and again wished for the moment to hang on a bit longer. Forever would be just fine.

Eventually, Adam spoke. "Nat . . . I don't think this will work."

There it was. She held her breath until she had to swallow, and then she took in a gulp of air and held it, waiting for the shoe to drop. She couldn't—wouldn't—ask what he meant. Even though she knew.

"We both have a lot of intense schoolwork ahead of us, and we'll be *three* time zones apart." He said it as if they would be in different solar systems. She closed her eyes and braced herself as he went on. "How often will we get to actually see each other? Once a year? Twice? Even with texting and all that, it isn't enough to maintain a relationship. We'll probably meet other people and change, and . . ."

She didn't want to meet someone else. They could make it work.

Unless *he* wanted his freedom to date whomever he wanted to in California. Who was she to stop him? They were only eighteen, and while she loved him with all her heart, a part of her knew that they were still young. She probably didn't know what love was, although she couldn't fathom that it could mean something deeper than what she felt for Adam—what she was sure he felt for her, too.

But maybe in a year or two, all of that *would* change. She couldn't imagine ever loving someone like she loved Adam.

"We don't have a chance of making it. We're too young." He swallowed hard. "You'll meet some guy out there, you know," he said. "Probably several."

She turned around, shaking her head. "No, I won't. I—"

"You can't know that," Adam insisted.

"And do you have a crystal ball that says you'll meet some other girl?"

He closed his eyes and breathed out, not saying anything for a while. What did that mean? If he didn't *want* to break up with her, maybe she could convince him not to do it. But before she could be sure of anything, he went on.

"I can't do this." His eyebrows drew together, and his brown eyes looked glassy, like maple syrup. Oh, how she loved those eyes. "It's over, Nat. It's been great, but it's over."

Before she could protest, he pulled her close into a long, tight embrace. Then he pulled back, lifted her chin, and kissed her. It was much briefer than many of their kisses, barely more than a peck. If he hadn't kept it brief, she would have used it to try to change his mind. But then he'd pulled back, leaving her lips tingling and her heart racing—with love, anxiety, and fear all jumbled up inside her.

He squeezed her hands, released them, and walked away. Natalie wanted to call out, to make him come back, but the pit in her chest told her that he was serious, and that it was over between them. With her chest feeling hollow, she waited for him to turn around, to come back. But at the bottom of the road, she saw his car pull out of Jason's street and drive away.

He'd really broken up with her.

All of these years later, Natalie couldn't hate him for it. They were really young. It was probably the right thing for him to do. If he didn't want a long-distance relationship, it wouldn't have lasted.

That morning, after he'd left her on the hill, she'd sat on the dewy grass, intensely aware of being alone, something she wasn't used to after spending most of her free time with Adam for the better part of the last two years. They'd practically grown into adults together. She stared at the mountains, where a beautiful pink and orange dawn should have broken over them, and she cried hot tears. Jason was right; the overcast morning *had* been a bad omen.

The cab pulled up to the hotel and stopped with a jerk, pulling Natalie out of her memories. "Here we are. Let me get your bags."

"Thanks," she said as she got out. She waited by the trunk for the driver to get her suitcase and carry-on. She checked her watch again. She was already fifteen minutes late for the wedding rehearsal. When she'd booked her flight, she thought she'd timed everything perfectly. She'd bring her luggage to symphony practice, which would end in time to catch a cab to the airport. Barring traffic, she'd get there with enough time to get through security and catch her flight, which would then land in Vegas with thirty minutes to spare. She was supposed to use that extra half hour to check in at the hotel and freshen up. But then the plane was delayed by an hour, and to top it off, the Vegas traffic was a beast. Instead of showing up fresh and relaxed, she was late, travel worn, and looked entirely wilted.

"Here you go, miss." The driver handed over her bags and closed the trunk as Natalie handed over enough bills to cover her tab and a tip.

With a quick thanks, she was off racing into the hotel, her carry-on slung over one shoulder as she ran, rolling her suitcase behind her. No time to get her room key now; she had to head straight to the wedding salon for the rehearsal. With luck, she hadn't missed much—or maybe Sierra had waited for her, so Natalie wouldn't miss any of the rehearsal after all.

No big deal. I can freshen up before dinner.

She raced down the hall, which was lined with crown molding, lush carpets, expensive furniture, and sparkling chandeliers. To the right was one of many wedding salons in the Wynn. She stopped short at the door, hearing sounds of an organ and people talking. They'd started. Of course they had, but that didn't keep her from feeling disappointed. She peered in so she wouldn't interrupt. Jason stood in position at the end of the aisle, looking much as he had in high school, only his hair was lighter, and his face was tan.

Beside him stood the best man—taller than the groom, with broader shoulders. He noticed her peeking in the door, and his eyebrow quirked when he looked up at the door. Natalie's heart stopped cold; her jaw went slack.

Adam. He wasn't supposed to be here.

He looked different. Better, even, with cut cheekbones and jaw; she hadn't realized that his teenage face had a boyish softness to it until she saw the grown man at the end of the room. Her insides buzzed, and her stomach flipped over itself.

Why, oh why, hadn't Sierra told her that Adam was coming after all? She swallowed against a parched throat.

Adam nodded toward the back of the room and smiled broadly. "Guys, she's here." He turned to the bride, who wore a short black dress and pearls. "Hey, Sierra, want me to walk down the aisle again, this time with your maid of honor?"

Wait, what? Natalie had thought she'd be walking down the aisle alone, with the best man—who was supposed to be Jason's little brother—already standing beside the groom.

She'd seen weddings done this way, but it wasn't what she was used to.

And it was *Adam* she'd be walking down the aisle with.

Her carry-on slipped from her shoulder, and she put it on the floor inside the door as Adam walked toward her. As he approached, she could tell that he'd left any shred of boyhood behind him. He was all man now—and so much better looking than she remembered. She had to force herself not to stare.

He was just an old friend, and this was nothing more than a friendly reunion.

Adam took the handle of her suitcase and rolled it to the side beside her carry-on then took his place at the head of the aisle and put out his arm expectantly, his eyebrow quirked again, this time in expectation. Oh, that eyebrow. The last time he'd stood like that—arm out, waiting for her—had been right before the promenade on their senior prom.

"Ready?" He looked over, still smiling casually, as if there hadn't been seven years of silence. Seven years since he'd broken her heart on the top of the hill.

Natalie shook away the thoughts and mustered a smile. "Ready. Sorry I'm late." She stepped forward and slipped her arm through his, terrified that he'd feel her trembling.

The music began, and they walked down the aisle. Everyone around them was dressed well—not in wedding finery, but in dresses and slacks, while she wore capris, sandals, and a sweaty fitted tee—comfortable flying attire—with a ponytail that drooped and probably had wisps of hair flying around it.

She kept a fake smile plastered to her face, wishing she could hide under a rock from the gazes of all of these people. She prayed that she was, at the very least, hiding her real emotions.

No way could she let anyone know that right then, she

felt as if she was the same vulnerable eighteen-year-old she'd been so long ago.

Two

Judging by the look on Natalie's face—jaw slack, eye wide—she was shocked at seeing Adam. He just couldn't decide if it was *good* shocked or *bad* shocked as he stood at the top of the aisle with her. He hadn't known until yesterday that he'd be here—after walking out on his job at Web Works in Seattle, where he'd been a senior software architect. He was lucky he found a seat on a flight at all.

He'd been building up his freelance and consulting work over the last few years, but never had the means to make the leap to go solo. Then yesterday, Storm, a company based close to his old home town in the Rockies, had offered ongoing freelance work and plenty of money to go with it, and that was all Adam needed. He'd add to his client portfolio, but in the meantime—tada!—he'd made it to his best friend's wedding after all. Jason's little brother Brett hadn't wanted to be the best man, and he freely gave up the job.

Someone started the music again. As he wrapped Natalie's arm through his and walked between the rows of seats, he tried to keep his eyes forward, but he couldn't help taking a peek at her. She looked travel worn and a bit flushed, but she was still the same beautiful woman he'd loved and sent away, only more mature. Maybe more elegant, too. Over the years, he'd periodically clicked over to her Facebook to see what she was up to, but he'd never dared friend her. He waited for her to click the friend button, if and when she decided to.

He checked her page with increasing frequency of late. She didn't have a relationship status listed, or pictures of anyone who might be a boyfriend, only fellow symphony members. That might not mean anything, though; she'd always been the private type. Maybe she simply didn't post personal stuff.

A few months ago when Sierra and Jason had come to visit, they'd walked in on him checking her page. Jason proceeded to razz Adam about it, but after dinner, Sierra found him alone in the kitchen and dropped a little fact Adam hadn't considered.

"She'll never friend you, you know," Sierra had whispered, glancing over her shoulder as if Jason might hear. She dropped an ice-cream bar wrapper into the garbage.

Startled, Adam looked up from the sink, where he'd taken a break in loading the dishwasher to check Nat's page on his phone. He clicked it off and shoved it into his pocket. "Why not?"

"Because *you* broke up with *her*, genius." She threw a significant look at him and walked out.

Now, as he and Natalie reached the end of the aisle, Adam squeezed her hand and released her to go to her spot. He took his place by the groom.

I did the breaking up. He was hardly able to keep his eyes off Natalie, although she seemed pretty adept at avoiding eye contact with him. *Worst mistake of my life.* Even though he'd done it to be selfless, to let her be free to have a life in New York. To be *fair* to her.

Sierra got a chair for Natalie, who sat on it and seemed to be keeping an almost unnatural focus on the rehearsal—on Sierra and Jason in particular. Not the best man. Adam kept trying to catch her eye, but it never worked.

She probably hates me. Seeing her again—touching her hand even for that brief walk—had brought back a shower of memories and feelings. He'd wanted to hold her close, smell her perfume. Somehow reverse time so they were at senior prom again, swaying to the music, before he'd been stupid enough to cut her from his life.

It wouldn't have lasted, and you know it.

Yet again, he reminded himself of the reasons he'd broken up with her: high-school romances almost never made it. He couldn't ask Natalie to put herself in cold storage for four years on the off chance she'd still want him in four years.

And even if she did, then what? What about her career? She'd be playing with some world-famous symphony and traveling the world, while he'd be programming somewhere on the west coast for a big technology company.

Natalie had always wanted to be a professional flutist. Had he asked her to give it up to marry him and settle down in suburbia with a picket fence and 2.5 kids, she probably would have.

But he'd never have forgiven himself for it.

That didn't mean he hadn't wished for that very thing every day since walking away from his soul mate.

Today, for the first time in years, he let the past wash over him. Adam remembered the time she'd taught him to crochet so he could help make hair clips for a charity project at school. At the time, he'd worried about losing his man card, but Natalie had said there was something incredibly hot about a guy willing to wield a crochet hook.

Or the time they got lost in a Halloween corn maze and used the unexpected privacy of a dead end for an impromptu make out.

The notes he'd push through the vents in her locker—silly stuff, sometimes nothing more than a smiley face or a couple of words. She'd done the same for him. He still had every single note.

Sierra's mother clapped her hands to get everyone's attention. She wore a purple blazer with a matching skirt, which contrasted with her obviously dyed red hair. "Thank you all," she said, clasping her hands at her chest and smiling across the room. "The wedding will be marvelous; I just know it." She checked her watch. "We have about forty-five minutes until the rehearsal dinner, so you're free to do whatever you need to—check in to your rooms, whatever."

She glanced at Natalie with the last part. Adam detected a hint of another blush creeping up her cheeks. She'd never liked sticking out, or having a room's attention just on her.

Back in high school, he'd suggested she try out for the school musical. "I love theater," she'd told him. "But I'd much rather be in the orchestra pit than on stage." Apparently she still didn't like being the center of attention.

"Dinner will be in the other wing of the hotel in the SW Steak House restaurant. We have an entire section reserved. Bring your appetites!"

Everyone started gathering their things, mulling around and heading for the door. Adam wanted to be sure to talk to Natalie before she could escape; she looked ready to bolt for the door. But first she approached Sierra. Of course.

Natalie waited a minute as Sierra finished talking to her aunt then held out her arms to Sierra. "I need a decent hello from my bestie."

"Oh, it's *so* good to see you!" Sierra said as they hugged.

When Natalie pulled back, she said, "I am so sorry I'm late. You were right; I should have taken the earlier flight."

Sierra waved the worry away. "Don't sweat it. The rehearsal went fine, and tomorrow will be great. I'm just glad you could make it."

"Anything for you."

"Let me help you with your stuff," Sierra said, turning to head back up the aisle.

No way. If they left the room, Adam would miss his chance for his own "decent hello." He stepped forward, ready to block their way.

"I can get my things just fine," Natalie said, waving away Sierra's help. "I'm sure Jason wants a little time with you. Besides, I need to freshen up before dinner."

Jason laughed. He walked over and put an arm around his bride-to-be, effectively cutting off Adam by forming a semicircle. "Can't deny I'll take any second I can with her, but I also know the importance of girl time."

Natalie stepped forward and gave Jason a hug and a peck on the cheek. "As long as I get her sometimes for girl talk, I'll be happy. That, and as long as you're always good to her." She poked a finger into his shoulder in a mock threat.

"Yes, ma'am," Jason said with a nod and kissed Sierra.

The room was nearly empty, and Adam still hadn't really spoken to Natalie. Standing behind Jason, he got desperate. He cleared his throat, hoping to enter the circle.

Jason and Sierra stepped to the side, providing a space. "Hey, sorry, dude."

Adam smiled and held out his arm like Sierra had. "Do I get a proper hello too?"

Natalie seemed to hesitate for a fraction of a second before putting on a smile. "Of course." Her voice sounded unnaturally high. He met her halfway and held her longer than he meant to. There was the scent of her perfume—

feminine but not too floral or sweet. Perfectly Natalie. He breathed it in, hoping he wasn't being too obvious. When she pulled back, she didn't give him a peck like she had Jason—clearly intentional.

Message received: She sees me as a platonic buddy. After all these years, what did I expect?

"It's really good to see you, Nat," he said, holding her hand for a second and hoping she could sense his sincerity and wishing she could sense his regret.

She cleared her throat and reclaimed her hand, awkwardly tucking a stray piece of hair behind her ear.

Adam looked around the small circle of the original Quartet as silence descended over them. Sierra and Jason were perfectly comfortable—and nuzzling each other—but Natalie looked uneasy. Adam broke the silence for her sake. "I'm looking forward to dinner. I'm so hungry, I could eat cold popcorn."

Wrapping her arms around Jason, Sierra laughed. "I can't believe you still remember that."

Natalie's eyes had widened, and her head tilted, as if she, too, was surprised he'd remembered. Of course he did. He was willing to bet he remembered more about their relationship than she did; he'd replayed it in his head more times than he could count.

How much did she still care—if at all? Judging by the hug and no peck on the check, he was clearly in the friend zone. She didn't wear a ring—he'd noticed that right away as he took her suitcase. But that didn't mean she was available. She could easily have a boyfriend. Social media was too much like the stage instead of the orchestra pit.

He'd never dared ask Sierra about Natalie's life, not even after she'd dropped that vague comment in his kitchen. But maybe he could change that. Find Sierra alone, even briefly, and ask if Natalie was available. The next twenty-four hours could be his only chance to win her back.

So what if she has a boyfriend in New York? We belong together.

Three

Natalie somehow made her excuses, got her key, and found her room. Inside, she threw the suitcase onto the bed and rummaged through it for the dress she'd planned to wear to the rehearsal—a sassy chiffon, navy-blue number that didn't wrinkle. She hung it in the closet then pulled out her makeup bag and flat iron. She couldn't change her first impression on the wedding party, but she'd look fantastic for the rehearsal dinner if it killed her.

She set an alarm on her phone so she'd know when dinner was five minutes away—just enough time to blot lipstick, spritz perfume, and put on earrings before heading downstairs. As the flat iron heated up, she worked on her makeup: lots of concealer under her eyes, foundation, eye shadow—the works. She pulled out a brand new tube of mascara. But no matter how carefully she tried to apply it, she got smudges around her eyes. Stupid to try a new brand on a trip like this. The wand was so thick it felt like applying mascara with a hairbrush. She would *not* go down to dinner with Adam looking like she had two black eyes. With her makeup finally done, she spent twenty minutes wrestling with her hair, because her usual trick for making soft curls with the flat iron wasn't working. It was probably the dry air; she was used to some humidity.

Her phone beeped, startling her. She narrowly missed burning herself. She put down the flat iron, turned off the timer, and studied herself. Her makeup was passable, but her hair was only half curled—with dinner in five minutes. In a panic, she swooped it up, twisted it, and lucked out with a nice French roll on her first try. She jabbed several bobby pins in, covered it all with a cloud of hair spray, stood back, and nodded. Much better. She tugged out a bit of hair in front of each ear and curled it. Even better.

She quickly put on her perfume and jewelry then shoved her feet into a killer pair of red heels she'd bought last week. At the last second, she remembered her phone and key card. Flustered but ready, she headed out the door, pausing before she went out to take a cleansing breath.

Tonight will be fun. A chance to catch up with old friends and bask in her best friend's happiness.

On the elevator ride down, Natalie couldn't help but vacillate between two emotions. On the one hand, ever since she'd laid eyes on Adam in the rehearsal hall, the same hope she'd felt as a young woman kept bobbing to the surface— that she and Adam could have a glorious future, something romantic, passionate, and straight out of a movie. But the grown woman she was now countered that with the reality that Adam hadn't tried to cross the divide since breaking up with her. He hadn't had the decency to even friend her on Facebook.

First the breakup. Then years of silence. In spite of his charm and good looks—possibly even more *because* of those things—she needed to keep her inner teenager on a leash until she arrived safely back home in New York.

Natalie found her table in the steakhouse. She and Adam sat across from each other at the same table as the bride and groom. The room's square tables were draped with white linens and had elegant, gray-backed chairs. Above each table hung a gold light fixture.

The bride and groom arrived at the same time Adam did, thankfully, so Natalie didn't have to be alone with him.

Jason stood by their table and looked at the light fixture. "Looks like one of those collars dogs wear after surgery."

Sierra batted his arm and laughed.

During the first part of dinner, Natalie managed to keep her emotions level and her gaze away from Adam. She prided herself on chatting with Sierra and Jason, as well as getting up to introduce herself to guests she didn't know. When she returned to her seat, she managed to make small talk with Adam, all while remaining totally unflustered. The French roll made her feel classy and confident. She worked the feelings for all they were worth.

During a lull in conversation, Adam stood, lifted his fluted glass of white wine, and tapped it with his spoon. "A toast," he said, and conversation gradually subsided, with everyone's attention on him. Adam looked at the happy couple. Jason had his arm around Sierra, and their heads were nearly touching. "When we were pimply sophomores, Jason told me that Sierra was the girl for him. They were *fifteen*. I thought he wanted to *date* her. I didn't realize at first that even back then, he meant he planned to *marry* her. When I did clue in, I laughed. Didn't I?" He looked at Jason, who chuckled at the memory.

"You totally laughed at me." Jason held Sierra close and kissed her cheek. As he did, she closed her eyes blissfully and smiled.

"And who could blame me?" Adam said. "We were young, with hormones and acne but no common sense. The chance of high-school sweethearts making it was almost zero."

He'd said almost the exact thing the morning he broke up with her. Natalie's throat was suddenly dry. She reached for her glass and sipped some champagne. The glass rattled against the edge of the china; her hands were shaking.

The chance of them making it *hadn't* been zero. Jason and Sierra were proof of that. Except that the two of them had attended the same state university. They hadn't faced a long-distance relationship. Natalie couldn't stand to look at Adam right now—she couldn't bear to see the smile she remembered all too well, couldn't bear thinking of what might have been. What if she'd gone to the USC Thornton music program? What if Adam had attended MIT instead of Cal Tech?

His voice broke through her emotions, almost echoing her thoughts. "But *almost* no chance isn't zero. These two right here beat the odds."

You didn't even let us try.

"Here they are at twenty-five instead of fifteen, about to marry, and, I believe, become the stuff of fairy tales. May we all be so lucky. A toast to Jason and Sierra." He nodded at first the groom and then the bride and lifted his glass.

The other members of the wedding party did the same, with the chorus of, "Hear, hear!"

Natalie lifted her glass along with everyone else, and she supposed she cheered along, but she couldn't be sure; her movements seemed mechanical, and her eyes burned. Seeing Adam again had sent her world spinning off its axis, leaving her with questions and feelings she didn't know what to do with.

Maybe I should change my flight to an earlier one. Leave right after the wedding.

Adam sat down, shooting Natalie a smile—not the one he'd given the rest of the party, but the one that was the real

213

him, the one only close friends saw. She hadn't seen it in ages, but now as it flashed across the table, it made her feel like she'd stepped into a time machine. As if she and Adam were still going together, as if they'd barely ordered their caps and gowns.

We're just friends, she told herself.

She smiled back and took a sip of water. The years that had turned his faced from boy to man hadn't changed that smile. It used to make her knees weak. With the way her was mind spinning, it was a good thing she was sitting.

Remember, he probably has a girlfriend back in— wherever he lives. Natalie returned to her salad, stabbing it with her fork. She hated his girlfriend, whoever she was. Yet feeling that way made no sense; it's not as if she had a claim on Adam. And of course he'd moved on. So had she.

Yes, I have. I have. But it's crazy how seeing him again brings back old thoughts and feelings. I'll be fine after this is over.

As soon as the wedding was over, she'd pack up and fly home. She'd return to her life as a professional musician, and this surreal fantasy world of feeling like she was back in high school would be over. Adam and his smile would go on the shelf once and for all.

A few tables over, Lindsey, one of Sierra's college roommates, got up from her seat, apparently finished with her salad. She'd been hired as the official wedding photographer, and she began snapping pictures of the guests. She shot all the guests, plus the food and centerpieces, then gestured toward one of the ivory-colored draped columns in the room. "Hey, let's get one over there of the couple with the maid of honor and best man. The four of you stand over there and scoot together."

Natalie walked to the column and put her arm around Sierra at the same moment Adam put his arm around Jason.

GOLDEN SUNRISE

Their hands touched, which shouldn't have meant a thing, but she still caught her breath.

Stop it. She smiled broadly as Lindsey snapped at least half a dozen pictures. She took a few of just the bride and groom. "Oh, these look great," she said, scrolling through the images on the camera screen. "Okay, let me take some of the maid of honor and best man. Weren't you guys an item in high school?"

"Sure were," Adam said as Natalie's stomach twisted and her face turned warm. Her cheeks would be bright red for this picture.

"We definitely need a shot of the two of you, for old time's sake."

Adam's right eyebrow went up in its quirk, which made Natalie's stomach twist deliciously. "Absolutely." His voice seemed eager, and his eyes actually twinkled.

Natalie's stomach continued to turn and twist in spite of herself. She stepped beside Adam, who was already waiting by the ivory column. He put his arm around her waist, and for a moment, Natalie felt like they were at a school dance getting their picture taken. Only then did she remember that she'd worn her hair in a French twist for senior prom, complete with a ringlet on each side. This whole thing was too much like reliving the past.

"I know!" Sierra said suddenly. "Pretend it's senior prom again. Remember your picture? Stand like that."

Natalie gave her best friend a flat look. Of course she remembered. "Here? Now?"

Adam chuckled. "Anything for the bride." He turned to Natalie. "For old time's sake?" He wrapped his arms around her waist and turned his cheek to her, waiting for her to kiss it as she had in their prom picture. The feel of his hands around her waist, the smell of his cologne this close, were all too much.

Sierra is so going to pay for this.

215

Everyone was waiting, so Natalie laughed awkwardly and went onto her toes. Even though she wore four-inch heels, Adam was significantly taller than she was. He pulled her close with one arm and leaned in to help her reach his cheek. She had to balance herself with a hand on his shoulder, which was firm and muscular under her hand. She meant to give him a quick peck and call it good, but Lindsey had other ideas.

"Hold it right there. I need to change the F-stop. Okay, ready."

Natalie ended up on her toes, lips against Adam's cheek, for a good thirty seconds. She couldn't help but breathe in his cologne. *Man, he smells good.* At the feel of his skin on her lips, with the slightest hint of evening stubble, a shiver tickled her spine.

It's just memories triggering all of this, she reminded herself. *You're dealing with ghosts. None of these feelings are real.*

"Got it." Lindsey again scrolled through the pictures, nodding, and the room erupted in applause.

"Thanks for humoring me, guys," Sierra said with a grin.

"No problem," Adam said.

Was it Natalie's imagination, or had his voice been emphatic on that point? Before she sat down, Adam squeezed her hand and gazed at her, their eyes holding for a moment. Her insides lit up like Times Square on New Year's Eve.

The servers brought in the main course, and conversation around the room picked up. Natalie ate her steak—medium rare, just how she liked it—in silence. She didn't dare look up for fear of catching Adam's eye again and having him see her still blushing over reenacting their prom picture. He'd pity her for hanging on to a crush for so long when a normal person would have moved on. *He* had surely moved on. As Natalie had. Her cheeks were betraying her.

And yet. Would indulging in her teenage fantasy for a day or two be such a horrible thing? She could flirt with Adam, have a little fun, and leave it all behind. She debated the issue as she ate. For a moment she found herself regretting—regretting!—moving so far away, even if getting into Juilliard had been a dream come true. But what would kissing Adam be like now that they were both grown? Not a peck on his cheek for the camera, but a solid, strong, *long* kiss on his lips. Like that would be happening.

At least she could let herself flirt until the wedding. Then it was back to reality.

Or maybe thinking about Adam at all was a mistake. She'd do better to curl up in her hotel room and watch a bunch of movies. That was safe. But instead of feeling excitement over the prospect of flirting with Adam, she felt dread. She grabbed her steak knife and cut the rest of the meat with far more force than necessary; she had to work off her nerves somehow.

Stupid wedding in stupid Vegas in the stupid summer. It was hot enough to fry your eyeballs just walking outside. Who got married in Vegas anyway, unless it was to elope at some drive-thru Elvis chapel? Too bad she hadn't brought her flute so she could take out her frustrations on it. Forty-eight hours from now, she'd have her flute. Plus several big mugs of Mexican hot chocolate. The combination might do the trick.

Four

After dinner, Natalie excused herself—and handily avoided Adam, as she was in no condition to be flirting. She should have drunk more of the champagne. Maybe then she'd have loosened up. And not cared. But she didn't like losing control like that, so she rarely drank much of any alcohol.

She headed up to her hotel room, only to discover that the chatter in her head was even louder when she was alone. She tried to watch TV, read a book, listen to music on her phone. None of it worked. She turned off the TV and headed to the tub for a bath. She got the water nice and hot, dumped in one of the mini bottles of shampoo, and let bubbles form. She sank into the water and forced all thoughts of prom and cold popcorn and the sunrise that wasn't out of her mind. Soon she breathed nice and slow and could feel knots of stress unwinding in her upper back and neck. She stretched luxuriously then reached for her toiletry bag on the bathroom floor and pulled out her razor. Whenever she indulged in a bath, she shaved her legs. Drying off with silky smooth skin added the cherry on top for feeling that she'd pampered herself.

She smoothed some of the bubbles along her left leg and began the long, easy strokes with the razor. Four strokes in, her eyes landed on an old scar below her knee, and her hand stopped. The scar had become another part of her body, something she gave no thought to. But with Adam and her high-school years on her mind, the history of the scar came roaring back.

It was her junior year. She was driving home after a band concert—a great night, with a complicated flute solo that she got to perform. Half a mile from home, she'd rounded a dark bend. Her next memory was of waking up with EMTs working on her. She had no memory of the accident, which was caused by a drunk driver. As she sat in the bathtub, images from that time flashed through her mind. Needing surgery on her left leg and knee. The pain, the worry. The relief when her bumps and bruises healed and she knew for sure that her arms and hands were fine, that she hadn't lost the ability to play the flute.

Adam had stayed at her side in the hospital every chance he got. He made jokes about how her black eye made her look tough. When she was released, he pushed her around school in a wheelchair. For her first week, before she had the strength to maneuver the wheelchair, he even got a hall pass allowing him to leave his classes early so he could help her to hers. Over spring break, when her family went to Disneyland, Adam asked to come along. He stayed in a hotel room with her little brother, next to the one Natalie, her sister, and her parents stayed in. He pushed her chair from ride to ride for three days to make sure she wouldn't miss out on a thing. She'd teased him that the only reason he did it was to get on the rides faster through the wheelchair entrances, but she knew that wasn't true.

Drawing a finger along the scar, Natalie swallowed

against a knot of emotion in her throat. Adam had been kind and caring and selfless. He'd gotten her through a really rough time. It was during that trip when she'd first thought that Adam might be the one. They were inseparable from that point until graduation.

She shook her head and tossed the razor into her toiletry bag then quickly rinsed off her leg. So much for distracting herself with a bath. She drained the tub and dried off, trying to decide what to do now. She needed a distraction. She had no flute. Maybe she could find hot chocolate at one of the hotel restaurants. She was suddenly glad she hadn't gotten her hair wet; it was still up in the twist from earlier.

After getting redressed, she touched up her makeup and hair then flipped through the guest book to decide on where to go. She decided to go to the hotel bar she'd passed on her way in. She needed a place with a crowd, where she could be an anonymous face and the noise would drown out her thoughts and she'd be less likely to bump into other members of the wedding party. That bar would do. Some of the other bars in the hotel wouldn't—they had couches and cushioned chairs, which encouraged groups to gather and chat. The bar she'd passed had tables and chairs too, but it also had a nice long counter she could sit at, so she could blend in unnoticed.

She hoped it would be nice and crowded, and that the noise would be a nice surrogate for the buzz and hum of the city, which always helped distract her. Maybe some guy would flirt with her and buy her a drink. The thought lifted her spirits a tad, although as she stepped out of the elevator and clutched her purse, she realized what she'd been thinking and scowled. Was she so shallow as to let a total stranger make her day, with or without a free drink? What would she really do if a guy ordered her a beer, when she couldn't stand the taste of the stuff?

Soon she found herself slipping onto one of the dark brown stools. Each had a bright red seat, matching the red and purple decorations, which complemented the gold accents and dark wood, as well as the winding staircase along one wall. The room was blessedly crowded and noisy. She found a stool on the far side of the bar, away from the staircase, and hoped to not only blend in with the crowd but to shake the thoughts she'd been having ever since seeing Adam in the wedding salon. Touching his arm. Smelling his skin. Kissing his cheek.

Stop it! She closed her eyes sharply and shook her head, ordering herself to knock it off. If hanging out in the bar didn't work soon, maybe she could go see a movie, or at least rent one in her room and order room service, including that big mug of hot chocolate. The bartender came over to ask for her order. Natalie opened her mouth to answer, but words fled her. She almost found herself ordering a virgin pina colada, as if she were a designated driver or something. But she wouldn't be driving any time soon.

When she hesitated, the bartender raised his eyebrows, waiting for her answer. "Just holler when you've decided," he said, and took a step away.

"She'll take a Shirley Temple, and I'll have a beer," a voice said behind her. Adam. "And a large fry. Oh, and could you melt some cheese on it?"

So much for escape. But she couldn't decide whether the jolt in her chest was annoyance or the electricity of attraction.

Five

dam slid onto the stool next to Natalie's. She seemed to brace herself before putting on a smile and turning to face him. "I didn't expect to see you here."

"I could say the same about you," he said grabbing a few peanuts from the bowl on the counter. "You never did like alcohol back in the day."

"Back in the day, I wasn't legal." She followed his lead, reaching for the bowl and picking out a couple of pretzels. She turned her back to him and looked at a mounted television, which broadcast a baseball game. Unless she'd changed drastically over the last seven years, she was faking her interest; she'd never liked baseball. In high school she'd come to cheer him on during his games, but that was the end of her interest in the sport.

"Which team are you rooting for?" Adam asked, nodding toward the TV. He'd call her out on her bluff. He could tell she was trying to avoid him, and he wanted to know why. Nerves? Anger? Did she despise the very thought of him?

Natalie's mouth moved for a couple of seconds as if searching for the right thing to say. She faced the counter again and picked apart a pretzel. "Okay, fine. Neither. I came down here for a break."

He could tell it was the truth. The question hung in the air, though: What did she want a break *from*?

"I needed a break too," Adam said. The bartender delivered their drinks. Adam thanked him then scooted the Shirley Temple in front of Natalie. "Here. I can get you a beer if you want it, but I remember how much you couldn't stand it that one time we tried some at Jeff's party. If I remember right, you wanted to puke after one swallow." As he took a swig from his beer bottle, he noted the slightest hint of a blush on Natalie's cheeks. He had an unruly urge to kiss them.

"In my defense, it tasted gross. And after drinking a whole can, Sierra said it made her brain feel fuzzy."

Typical Nat—always the perfectionist, never wanting to be out of control. She used to plan out every day, and didn't like spontaneous anything. Which was why for her sake, he probably should have discussed their post-graduation relationship over several days. Except that if he'd done that, he wouldn't have had the guts to make it stick. Taking her off guard was the only way to protect her future happiness.

At least, that's what he'd thought at the time. He'd been miserable away from her during college. Maybe he'd been wrong for both of their sakes.

He remembered how, after that one night of experimentation when they were sixteen, Nat had left alcohol alone for the rest of high school. Adam was willing to bet she hadn't changed much even after turning twenty-one. At the rehearsal dinner, he'd paid attention to how she'd only sipped at her champagne, and mostly after toasts. Which made it all the more odd that she'd purposely seek out a bar for a distraction.

They sat in silence for a bit, each drinking here and there, and watching the game. He finally broke the silence after the bartender slid the plate the cheese fries onto the counter. He scooted the basket between them so Natalie could reach what used to be one of her favorite treats.

"Kind of wild to have the four of us all together again, huh?" He took a fry off the top, let the cheese stretch and break, then bit the end.

"Just like old times." Natalie pulled a cheese-covered fry off the pile and put it into her mouth.

"But it's not *really* like old times, is it? We've all grown up and changed."

"True," she said, and ate her fry.

Adam eyed her, wondering just how much she'd changed. They'd both matured, grown up. But were they, at the core, the same people they used to be? He wanted to believe they were. The Shirley Temple and cheese fries had been a guess on his part, and the fact that she seemed to still like both gave him hope—perhaps a silly one—that other things were still the same too.

Like maybe she still had feelings for him. *I'd better act fast, though; we don't have much time together.* He wiped his fingers on a napkin and tried to sound casual. "It's even weirder to be at Jason and Sierra's wedding in the middle of nowhere."

At that, Natalie turned from the TV to face him. "I know! Why Vegas in the dead of summer?"

"Jason says it's a special place to them. They met here or something, didn't they? I don't get it, but I'm here to support them."

"That's why I'm here too." Natalie stirred her drink with the thin red straw then tried to pierce the cherry at the bottom, but it spun away. "It's good to see you guys again. It's been a long time. I keep in touch with Sierra, of course, but you and Jason not so much."

Actually, me not at all.

"It's been *way* too long," Adam said, hoping she'd sense his eagerness to reconnect. But Sierra's comment rang in his ears; their lack of communication was *his* fault. Nat wouldn't friend him on Facebook or contact him because *he* broke up with *her.*

He cleared his throat and tugged the fry basket toward him and then pushed it away, as if that would get rid of the nervous energy building inside him. Nat glanced over, eyebrows together, as if she was surprised he looked nervous. Yet he was so nervous, he felt as if he stood on the edge of cliff. And he was about to jump off it. Tonight was his only shot at getting her back. *Here goes nothing.*

"Do you remember the night we won the state basketball championship?"

Natalie smiled in spite of herself. "Of course."

It was early March of their senior year, one year after her accident. Graduation already loomed in their future. They'd already gotten their acceptances to Juilliard and Cal Tech. That night, after watching their team take the state title, she and Adam had celebrated with takeout from their favorite hamburger joint. Adam had brought along a blanket, and they ate their very late dinner under the stars at a park.

Nat lay beside him on the blanket. They both stared up at the bright pinpricks of light. He had no idea what she'd been thinking about, but already he dreaded June, when they'd be heading off for different universities, thousands of miles apart.

"Just think," she'd said. "This fall, when we're apart, we'll be able to look up at the same sky." The thought seemed to give comfort at the time, but Adam couldn't answer her. She'd go to Julliard and be wooed by some cellist. And that would be that.

Natalie laughed. "I also remember getting kicked out by the cops because the park had an eleven o'clock curfew, and it was nearly midnight." She shook her head. "My parents still don't know about that."

But that wasn't the part of the evening Adam was focused on. He swallowed back his nerves and touched her arm. She looked at his hand, then lifted her eyes to his questioningly. She didn't pull away. A good sign, he hoped.

"Do you remember our promise?" With his other hand, held up a French fry to remind her.

She blinked a few times and nodded without words. Her eyes looked watery. What did that mean? Was the memory a happy one, or sad one?

Finally, she spoke softly. "Of course I do."

Emotion filled her voice. He would have given anything to know *which* emotion.

They were both twenty-five now. He'd been an idiot, hoping she'd forgive him enough to contact him first. He was done with waiting. He had to act. Grab the brass ring if he possibly could. He tried to appeal to the eighteen-year-old who'd gazed at the stars with him that night—the one who took seriously deals made by teenagers under a romantic moon.

Adam selected a particularly long fry from the basket and held it between them, just as he had that night so long ago. After a pause of hesitation, Nat smiled and took the other end. Adam started breathing again, only then realizing he'd been holding his breath.

That night on the blanket, he'd broached the idea that they might not make it. In the back of his mind, he'd already decided to set her free, but just in case, he proposed a deal: When they turned twenty-five, if neither was married, they'd get hitched.

It had seemed ridiculous at the time even to him. Of course they'd be married. Or Nat would be. No way would someone so amazing and talented and beautiful not be taken by then. It was silly, and he knew it at the time, but making the deal gave him the guts to break up with her when June came.

As they had seven years ago, they both pulled on the fry, like a wishbone from a turkey. It broke almost exactly in half. Their eyes met. After a beat, Adam looked down at the broken fry. "So what does that mean?"

"It means we were young and silly, but we had *great* taste in fries." Natalie dipped hers into the little plastic cup of dipping sauce and popped it into her mouth.

Adam's heart deflated a bit. He tried to come up with another way to broach the subject, but failed before Natalie went on. "So . . . are *you* still single?"

Now his heart rate picked up as a tiny beam of hope shot through him. He cleared his throat. "Sure am." Praying she wouldn't pull away, Adam reached for her left hand, which was resting on the bar, and stroked her bare ring finger. "You?"

She looked at their hands and turned hers to hold his. "As single as they come." She smiled wanly. "Except that Sierra says I'm married to my flute." Her cheeks were flushed bright red now. Adam was dying to know what she was feeling. She hadn't pulled away, which was a very good sign. But maybe she held his hand simply as a friendly gesture.

Adam's mind whirled. How to move from here? They were both single. And he was no longer tied to Seattle. As long as he had an internet connection, he could handle his freelance clients from anywhere. But he couldn't just jump into all of that randomly, throwing himself into her life. Maybe she didn't want marriage anymore. She'd made a great life for herself in New York, a life he had no part of.

The silence between them stretched on, but it wasn't uncomfortable; he stroked the back of her hand. It felt familiar and warm. Natalie breathed out, relaxing around Adam for the first time since her arrival.

As she reached for her drink Adam knew he had to blurt out what he wanted to say or regret never saying it. "We could do it, you know. Here. Tonight."

She sputtered on her drink and coughed as she set the glass down. "You aren't serious," she said, pulling her hand back so she could grab a napkin and cough into it.

But he was serious. He had no way of answering her question without looking like a fool.

She lowered the napkin. "You *aren't* serious, are you?"

He lifted one shoulder in what he hoped was a casual a shrug. "We're in Vegas. Why not?" *Stupid, stupid. You're sounding like marriage is nothing but a tourist activity.*

"Because we're adults," Nat said. "With lives and responsibilities. Because that would be *insane*." She picked up the napkin and began worrying it into shreds. Why was she suddenly nervous again? "What would we do? Get married, say good-bye, and go home?"

Adam couldn't answer; it did sound stupid. But marrying her tonight would give him a chance to fully woo her later. He could reignite the old spark. If her pink cheeks were any indication, she still cared. At least a little.

"We both have lives to go back to, right?" she said under her breath.

He leaned in and put his arm around her waist, gently pulling her near. She didn't resist. "Would it be so awful?" he whispered into her ear.

He stayed there, smelling her hair and wanting to move just enough to kiss her. She closed her eyes. What was she thinking? Feeling? Was it her flute holding her back?

The thing is portable! He wanted to shout it, but he knew it wasn't just her flute. It was her life with the symphony.

Her eyes sketched over to his beer glass—he was on his third refill—as if wondering whether his words were ones of a drunk man.

When she said nothing, he pressed his lips to her jawbone, just under her ear, something that used to, in her words, make her "toes curl."

"What do you say?" he whispered.

"We hardly know each other anymore." Natalie argued, but her voice was breathless.

He stroked her hair and pulled away a few inches. "You don't seem to have changed that much, and neither have I." When Nat began fiddling with the napkin again, he released her. "We've both grown up, but at the core, you're still the old Nat, and I'm the same old Adam." He licked his lips with disappointment and took a pull on his beer. "But I suppose it would be a crazy, stupid thing to do." With his thumb, he wiped some condensation from his mug.

He couldn't help but look over and gaze into her eyes with all the hopes and fears and love he still felt—and hoped she sensed it and felt the same love in return. "It could be crazy. But it could also be pretty great." She chewed her bottom lip as if she was seriously considering his idea. He took both of her hands in his and gave her one last thing to calm her worries. "We wouldn't have to tell anyone if you wanted to give it a trial run."

Natalie looked at their clasped hands then stared back into his eyes as if warring emotions clashed in her chest. Did she feel the same old emotions he did? She leaned closer, her gaze dropping to his lips. His heart hiccupped in its rhythm. Was she about to kiss him? When she didn't pull back, he drew nearer, until their lips almost touched. He hesitated, wanting to be sure she wanted this. Nat closed the distance, pressing her lips hard against his. He cupped her head in his hands and poured seven years of longing into his kiss. As it intensified, his hands slipped around her waist, and hers wrapped around his neck as her mouth sought his with an emotion he hadn't dared to hope he sensed in her.

The noise and buzz in the bar faded into the background as fireworks erupted in his veins. Kissing Nat was familiar, yet strange—and better than his fantasies. She pulled back before he was ready to end it.

Her eyes shot over to his mug and back again. Yes, he'd drunk almost three beers. He wanted to say that no, he wasn't drunk, that he'd wanted this for years. Her hand came to her lips as if the kiss still burned there. Then, suddenly, as if her mind was made up, Nat took the straw out of her glass, downed the rest of her drink, and popped the cherry into her mouth. She pulled out the stem, tossed it onto the counter and said, "Let's do it."

ith the ghost of Adam's kiss lingering on Natalie's lips, she took his hand and pulled him toward the exit before she could change her mind. Or come to her senses. Or both. Because she did care. Always had. From the moment she first saw Adam today, she'd known the truth. The kiss, which had left her feeling heady, had only cemented that knowledge

"You're serious," Adam said with a surprised laugh as he tossed several bills onto the counter to cover their tab.

"It was your idea." In the lobby, Natalie stopped and looked up at him. "Unless, you know, you were kidding." She tried to keep her voice light, but her eyes pricked with the thought. *I'm probably going to be Mrs. Adam Bradford in a few minutes.* It might not last, but somehow, she couldn't shake the idea that this would be worth the momentary insanity of marrying in Vegas on a whim. Even if she was the only one who really cared. Adam obviously felt something; she doubted he would have looked at her and touched her the way he had if he didn't find her at least passably attractive. But she'd been the one to initiate the kiss . . .

Adam squeezed her hand, shaking his head as he laughed. "Maybe you have changed. The old Nat hated spontaneous stuff." He tugged her hand and led the way outside. "Come on. Let's get a marriage license."

Marriage license. Marriage. Natalie's insides felt like she was headed down a giant hill on a roller coaster. She clung to Adam's hand to steady herself. He must have interpreted the action as happiness or something, because he squeezed back and grinned.

The sun was setting, but the bright signs the strip and downtown Vegas were lit up. Even with the fading sun, the air was hot and dry; Natalie felt like she was walking—nearly running, now—through a wall of heat. Adam moved left and right between pedestrians, pulling her behind him, like they were moving along a slalom course or a racetrack. Then he stopped, and she nearly ran into him. She managed to climb into the cab Adam had just hailed.

"We need a marriage license," Adam told the driver. "And then a ride to the nearest wedding chapel that isn't cheesy."

"No Elvis?"

"No Elvis," Adam repeated.

"You got it," the driver said with a nod.

Natalie had no idea if you could get a wedding license at a wedding chapel or what getting one involved, but clearly, they weren't the first couple to make a similar request. She almost added that the chapel couldn't be drive thru either, but bit the words back and leaned against the upholstery of the cab. What did it matter where this crazy thing happened at this point?

The cabbie pulled into a parking stall and gave directions to the correct office in the red building. In a bit of a haze, Natalie followed along through the halls, produced her ID when needed, and returned to the cab, which took off through the city streets again. Her mind kept trying to argue that this was foolish, that she'd regret it, and that of course this wouldn't work out. Why was Adam so insistent on marrying her now anyway? Was he hoping for a wild wedding night before filing for an annulment? Her eyes burned with tears from a million emotions.

The cab ride was both the shortest and longest of Natalie's life. Before she knew it, Adam was leading her into a miniature white chapel. Natalie eyed the banner over the receptionist's desk: "Chapel O Love." A step up from Elvis, she supposed. And not a drive-thru.

In no time, they filled out the paperwork, selected a wedding package, and the minister, wearing a clip-on tie and sneakers—and his wife, the receptionist-turned-organist waited in the chapel proper.

Natalie stood at the head of the aisle, just like she had earlier today—yet everything was different. She held a bouquet of fake flowers. How many other last-minute brides had held the same bouquet? She looked across the small room, which was flanked by three rows of pews, all empty. With relish, the minister's wife began the bridal march on the old organ.

At the first note, Adam looked over from his spot at the end of the aisle and grinned. Natalie felt as if her heart had been jump-started by the organ. She forced herself to take a step forward, and then another, but each was harder than the last. Did that smile of Adam's mean this really was a big joke? Some blast from the past, wild thing to do for old time's sake?

Halfway down the aisle, she was painfully aware of the empty white pews. Her parents and siblings should be here to see her married. And Sierra. But the bitter feeling growing inside her was more than that.

Does Adam really love me?

And two steps, and she stopped at the minister. She

looked up at Adam and searched his face, but didn't know what she read there. She still cared for him as much as ever, but if he really loved her back, why hadn't he ever contacted her? Why had he broken up to begin with?

None of this is real. And it's not worth it.

The minister held a Bible open with what looked like a cheat sheet for his script resting on top. "Dearly beloved, we are gathered here today to witness the joining of . . ." He had to consult the paper to get their names right.

Pastor Jones from home should be performing the ceremony. He'd known her since she wore pigtails.

The minister's voice droned on, but Natalie's brain seemed to be yelling at her. *What do you think you're doing?!*

She'd felt drawn to Adam all day, finally admitted that she'd never gotten over him. She still loved him. And yes, she wanted to be with him. But *not* because of a silly promise they'd made on a spring night more than seven years ago. Not as a joke. Not temporarily.

And most importantly, not if Adam didn't love her the same way.

His three beers came back to her mind. Adam had to be drunk—tipsy, at least. He'd surely lost his inhibitions. That was what had landed them here. That, and one amazing, intoxicating kiss.

The minister paused and looked at her, and Natalie realized that it was probably her cue.

She shook her head and pushed the bouquet toward the minister. It hit the top of the Bible and fell to the ground. "I'm sorry. I'm really, really sorry, but I can't do this."

Natalie raced out of the wedding chapel. She hailed the first cab she saw and climbed in, giving the driver instructions to just drive, but fast. She locked the door, and the cab raced away.

She covered her face with her hands. *What an idiot I've been.*

Seven

"Where to now?" The cabbie looked at her through the rearview mirror. "Driving for a long time ain't cheap."

"I just need a minute."

"Alright," he said, pressing the gas pedal when the light turned green. "It's your money."

Natalie leaned to the side and rested her forehead against the cool glass of the window separating her from the desert heat. She didn't care what this ride cost. She couldn't return to the hotel yet; the chances of running into Adam were too great. He might even be waiting for her in the lobby. She couldn't face him right now. Not when he'd made a joke out of marrying her.

Or maybe he'd figured out that she still had feelings for him. She could *not* abide his pity.

The cab stopped at another red light. "You sure you want me to keep going?" the driver asked. He nodded toward the ticking fare.

The total had crept up awfully fast. Natalie choked. She checked her watch. It had been over half an hour. Surely Adam had gone back to the hotel by now. He could be in one of the restaurants, but it was probably safe to slip through the lobby and get to her room without seeing him. "How close is the Wynn?"

"Just a couple of blocks. Should I drop you off there?"

"Yes, thank you."

After paying a tab close to the cost of her flight, she went into the hotel senses on high alert. She hurried along the elegant hallway to the elevators and successfully made it inside. When the shiny doors slid shut and the elevator began moving, she leaned against the back and let out a huge breath. No more facing Adam. Ever.

Except that in a few hours, she'd not only have to face him, but she'd have to walk down the aisle with him as Sierra's bridesmaid. She hadn't thought that anything in the world short of death could keep her from her best friend's wedding, but jilting Adam at the altar might be enough.

No. I have to be there for Sierra.

Just like Adam had been there for her after the accident. *Not Adam again.* In frustration, she hit the elevator wall with her fist. She had to stop thinking about him and everything about him she'd fallen in love with. Tomorrow at the wedding, she'd ignore him and pray to whatever powers that be to not blush. Then she'd escape after the ceremony.

Maybe Adam will ditch the wedding. That was a vain thought. Adam wouldn't miss Jason's wedding any more than Natalie would miss Sierra's.

The doors opened to her floor, and Natalie stepped out of the elevator, only to freeze at the sight of a dark-haired man. He had Adam's build, but on closer inspection, she relaxed; he wasn't Adam. She headed down the hall to her room with shaky legs, fishing through her purse for her key card and wishing she knew which floor he was staying on.

When she was safely inside, she kicked off her shoes and undid the twist in her hair. She sat on the bed and massaged her aching scalp as she took in the gorgeous view of the city from the window.

The next several hours were painful. First Natalie lay on her pillow, still in her dress, and stared at the ceiling. The luxury of the Wynn was entirely lost on her. She didn't care about the slippers laid out by the bed or the other amenities. She wanted to hide. Too bad she couldn't tell Scotty to beam her to Manhattan and be done with it.

She'd be miserable even at her apartment, though; she knew that as well as she knew anything—like the fact that she still loved Adam Bradford.

Refusing to cry, she sat up and massaged her feet, realizing that after the day she'd had, they were beyond sore. With her knee up, her hem slid down her thigh, revealing the old scar. A flood of emotions crashed through her again. Her index finger carefully traced the pale pink line.

I kissed him today. The thought brought a twinge of joy along with pain. She could hold on to that brief moment, relive it over and over in her tiny apartment. Alone. The old hole in her heart felt bigger than ever, gaping. With a fierce shake of her head, she lowered her knee and pulled down her hem. No more thinking about Adam and what might have been. Of what she'd thrown away. Yes, she loved Adam and always would. Might as well accept the truth that this was no teenage crush.

If he'd ever felt the same, he wouldn't have broken her heart on that hill. He wouldn't have been silent. In spite of the hurt from the past, she thought of the chance she'd almost taken—the chance to *marry* Adam.

"What did I throw away?" It came out as a whimpered plea, and the answer hit her with a thud. She'd thrown away nothing. Not really, because the marriage wouldn't have meant anything to him. But oh, how she would have given anything—even her flute, which cost more than many cars—for Adam to love her back.

The thought was sobering. She'd given her *life* to her instrument.

She stood and paced. This whole thing was making her nuts. What she needed was someone to talk to. A good chat with her best friend would clear her mind and make everything better. Natalie grabbed her phone from the mattress but hesitated. She couldn't call Sierra now, wake her up and cry on her shoulder hours before her wedding.

She sat on the bed and lay back again staring at the ceiling and wishing away the ache in her chest. At some point she must have fallen asleep, because she opened her eyes groggily and checked the clock. It was after five. Her body was sore from being in an awkward position for too long.

As she tried to orient herself, the kiss, the marriage license, the chapel—all of it rushed back. She closed her eyes to block it out, to fall back asleep, but her mind spun, not letting her rest any longer. She needed something peaceful and calm to distract her. Maybe looking at the slow, winding lines of traffic and glowing lights below would do the trick.

She got up, deciding to check out the observation atrium she'd noticed on one end of the floor, a glassed-in area where you could look eastward over the city. She grabbed her phone and key card but left her shoes by the bed.

When she reached the atrium, she was in luck—it was empty. But then, only crazy people would be city gazing at nearly six in the morning. She stepped inside, right to the edge of the glass. The view was breathtaking, but it wasn't what she'd expected—a black sky and bright lights from the Strip. Instead, night was gradually yielding to morning, and the sun was making its appearance, peeking above the mountains. The gold, almost orange, glow seemed to be pure light and took Natalie's breath away. She'd always thought Manhattan sunrises were gorgeous, with shades of pink and purple. They looked like Debussy's "Claire de Lune" moving across the sky as an Impressionist painting.

This sunrise held none of the mystique, but all of the wonder. It looked more like Grieg's "Morning Mood," a favorite because it not only brought the power of morning claiming victory over night, but it also had a strong flute part. The light quickly took over the darkness, just like in *Peer Gynt*, dissipating the night like a hand gently drawing a blanket of light over the valley.

A creak sounded behind her—the glass door. So she *wasn't* the only crazy person wanting to use the atrium this early. She coughed to clear her throat and turned to excuse herself, only to stop short.

Adam stood there, his tie untied, and the top two buttons of his dress shirt undone. The shirt hung rumpled. His eyes were rimmed with red; he looked at tired as she felt.

"Sorry," she said. "I won't be in your way." She took a step toward the door, but instead of moving aside, Adam reached for her arm. His touched seemed to burn her skin.

"Nat."

She closed her eyes and willed herself not to cry. "I'm sorry I ran out. I should have stopped everything before it got that far. I'll pay you back. I couldn't . . ." Another word, and she'd burst into tears.

He didn't let go. "No," he said. "*I'm* sorry. I shouldn't have assumed . . . I mean . . ." He sighed and tried again. "I've never been good at being serious, at showing my feelings."

Her gaze snapped up, and her eyebrow arched. "You did quite well expressing your feelings the morning after graduation." Anger replaced sadness. She ripped her arm away and tried to push past him.

"Nat, let me explain. Please."

Emotions battled inside her. Half of her wanted to stay to hear every word. The other half wanted to slap him and run away. She took a step back and folded her arms tightly—the only way she could feel protected—and waited.

"You scared me when you ran out and I couldn't find you. I worried all night that something had happened to you. Without your cell number, I couldn't call you. Jason and Sierra wouldn't answer their phones . . ."

She looked over, surprised, and noticed that his hair was mussed up, as if he'd run his fingers through it several times. A shadow of stubble outlined his jaw. The combination made him more attractive than ever. She forced herself to look away. Why had he looked for her? To be sure she was safe on the streets of Vegas, like a decent human being would do. Nothing more.

Adam ran his fingers through his hair again. "I walked all over the Strip, through a bunch of casinos. Through all the restaurants and bars in the Wynn, asking if people had seen you. I even went to the registration desk, but of course, they wouldn't give me your room number, and it was so late that they wouldn't put me through, either. I called and texted both Jason and Sierra probably a dozen times . . ." His voice trailed off.

"If you're feeling guilty and pity, you don't need to. I'm sure you're sober now, and you can see that you dodged a bullet last night." Natalie was tired and just wanted to leave.

"I wasn't drunk." He stepped further into the atrium and let the door close behind him. He took her hands in his. "I should have told you this a long time ago. Listen now. The morning after graduation, I honestly thought I was setting you free. Figured it was selfish to ask you to put yourself in cold storage for four years on the off chance we'd make it until we both graduated. And then what about our careers? I knew you'd be playing with some world-famous symphony, traveling the world, while I'd be programming in California

240

or Washington or somewhere at the big technology companies. It was the hardest thing I'd ever done, but I was sure that within a few weeks—months at most—a musician or actor or dancer in the big city would sweep you off your feet, and you'd feel obligated to the techie nerd from high school. I didn't want to hold you back."

She shook her head, brow furrowed, studying his face, trying to unravel his words. "You didn't *want* to break up?"

"No. I *loved* you," he said. "I couldn't bear the thought of being dead weight in the life you had ahead of you. But a few months passed, and I loved you as much as ever. I knew I'd never, ever get over you. And then yesterday, there you were, walking into my life again."

The memory of Adam in the wedding salon flashed through her mind, including the quirk of his eyebrow when he first saw her. He stepped even closer. The scent of his cologne muddied Natalie's senses. He slid his hands up her arms and rested them on her shoulders, making her heart thump like an entire percussion section.

"Last night in the bar, I knew *exactly* what I was doing when I asked you to marry me. I figured I'd better win you back fast, when the universe had brought you back to me, or I'd lose you forever." He shook his head. "I guess it was dumb to think that maybe, after making the biggest mistake of my life, I'd be lucky enough for you to forgive me, and that you still cared." He dropped his hands and stepped back; she wanted to reach out and pull him close again. "Nat, I'm sorry. It was dumb to think that after so long, you could still love me that way . . ." His voice hitched. "The way I *still* love you."

The way he . . . She didn't dare believe she'd heard right. "What?" Her pulse throbbed in her ears.

He gazed into her eyes, and for a moment, she could do nothing but gaze back. "I love you. I always have. Always will."

Say it, she commanded herself. *Or you'll lose* him *forever.*

"I've always loved you too. Always have, always will. I'll swear it over a fry if you want me to."

His voice lowered. "Really?" When she nodded, joy coursing through her veins, his face relaxed from the tense worry it had held a moment before, and a smile—oh, that smile—spread across his face. "Then basically, we've been fools for seven years?"

She nodded mutely. Maybe she needed those years to chase her dream, to tour and hear the applause and feel the pulse of the city. But she was done being alone, using the chaos of the city to drown out her thoughts and true feelings. She'd go anywhere to be with Adam now.

A shiver went up her spine as he closed the gap between them and put his arms around her and gently pulled her closer. She raised her lips to meet his, threading her fingers through his deliciously disheveled hair. The fire of their last kiss was nothing compared to the pyrotechnics going through her body now.

She finally pulled back, because part of her couldn't quite believe she'd heard right. Her eyes teared up, and a drop fell down one cheek. "So last night wasn't out of pity? It wasn't a joke?"

He shook his head and wiped her tear away with one thumb. "It was because I love you. I just couldn't say it before."

He nodded at the window, where the sun had risen with its brilliant golds and oranges. "Maybe we can start over. I think that's a good omen for what comes next." He put his arm around her shoulders, and she leaned in, resting her head on his chest.

But the practical side of Natalie cut through the bliss of the moment. "What about our careers?" She'd go anywhere for Adam, but she didn't necessarily have to leave the symphony.

He leaned down and kissed her quickly, stopping her protestations. She smiled as she looked into his eyes, amazed at how quickly their old closeness had returned, at how natural all of this felt.

"I quit my job," Adam said. "That's how I was able to come to the wedding."

"You quit—"

"I do enough freelance work to live on now," Adam hurried to clarify. "So I'm not tied down to a location. And I'm not *about* to lose you again." He pressed a kiss to her temple then released her to reach into his suit coat pocket.

He pulled out a plastic container that was clearly from one of those machines kids gets toys from for a couple of quarters. Inside was a cheap plastic ring. "Found this last night when I was looking for you. We'll have to replace it with something much, much nicer as soon as we can."

Natalie laughed at the toy ring—pink with an adjustable band made of some easily bent metal. "Wear this, and I won't need a French-fry oath." She held out her left hand, but he shook his head. "You deserve to have this done the right way." He got down on one knee and presented the ring. "Natalie Conner, will you marry me?"

She threw her arms around him and held him tight. "Yes, yes, of course."

They kissed soundly, and then he stood to put the ring on her finger. It fit perfectly. She straightened her arm to look at the toy ring. "Should we tell Jason and Sierra?"

"Let's let them have their day. I have a feeling they won't have eyes for anything but each other anyway."

"I know the feeling." Natalie rested her head against his chest and breathed in the scent of Adam. "Maybe we can make them travel all the way to Manhattan for our wedding."

"Turnabout's fair play."

Natalie never wanted to leave his embrace. "Somehow I think a wedding in the Big Apple is kinder than one in the middle of a desert," she said. "Even if Vegas does have fantastic sunrises."

ABOUT ANNETTE LYON

Annette Lyon is a Whitney Award winner, a two-time recipient of Utah's Best in State medal for fiction, plus the author of ten novels, a cookbook, and a grammar guide as well as over a hundred magazine articles. She's a senior editor at Precision Editing Group and a cum laude graduate from BYU with a degree in English. When she's not writing, editing, knitting, or eating chocolate, she can be found mothering and avoiding the spots on the kitchen floor. Find her online:

Website: http://annettelyon.com

Blog: http://blog.annettelyon.com

Twitter: @AnnetteLyon

Tide Pools

Heather B. Moore

Other Works by Heather B. Moore

The Aliso Creek Novella Series

The Newport Ladies Book Club Series

Heart of the Ocean

The Fortune Café

Published under H.B. Moore

Esther the Queen

Finding Sheba

Beneath

Daughters of Jared

One

$\mathcal{L}$ exi held the phone away from her ear as her best friend, Sydney, screamed into it.

"You're coming?" Sydney's voice was higher pitched than a scavenging seagull.

"Yes," Lexi said, laughing.

Sydney had always been way over the top—probably why they got along so well. Lexi rarely found anything in life that could pull her away from studying. Only the ocean could—but even that was homework; Lexi's major was environmental science.

Currently, Lexi's best friend and roommate was in Hawaii with her fiancée, Apelu, meeting his family for the first time. And apparently the introductions had gone so well that Sydney and Apelu had decided to get married on the spot. Well, in three days.

This was on the spot for Lexi, who did nothing without careful planning. Spring term just ended, and she'd intended on moving in with her mom to save money and so she wouldn't have to work during a full load of classes summer term. She could graduate from San Diego State in December if she loaded up on credits for the next six months.

Summer term didn't start for a week, so in theory, Lexi didn't have anything stopping her from going to Hawaii and being maid of honor. She'd have to leave her job at the marina early, though she'd already given her two weeks' notice. There was the matter of money, but Sydney said she could use her Skymiles.

When Lexi hung up, after another round of squeals and gushing details she would never remember, Lexi looked around their apartment. Lexi loved the quiet, but she had to admit that the last week without Sydney had been *too* quiet. She didn't even mind Apelu hanging around—a force on the San Diego State football team, yet quiet and well-mannered without the uniform. He was perfect for Sydney—he kept her down to earth, not floating a couple of feet above as usual.

Since Sydney wouldn't be coming back before the end of the month—and she'd be *married*—Lexi would have to move out Sydney's stuff too, get the deposit back, and turn in their keys. She'd have to store Sydney's stuff at her mom's house until they returned and found an apartment. Moving a wedding up three months complicated matters.

Lexi glanced at her laptop and stack of science books, where she'd been researching for one of her classes, before Sydney had interrupted with her call. Plans had changed drastically, and Lexi wouldn't be getting the head start she'd planned on. Hopefully the week in Hawaii wouldn't set her back too much.

Maybe she could bring one or two textbooks and catch up on reading. Or she could spring for the extra fees to download them. But Lexi preferred paper to the computer screen; it was easier to flip pages to compare ideas and definitions.

However she decided to get ahead, Lexi promised herself that she'd be there for Sydney, even if it meant doing all of those "fun" things she'd always managed to avoid.

Two

*L*exi straightened in her seat and looked out the window as the plane descended toward Honolulu. Beaches stretched in every direction, bordered with hotels and other large buildings. The last couple of days had been chaotic clearing out the apartment and getting ready for the trip. Sydney had said to bring a swimsuit. Any normal college girl would have grabbed hers from the dresser.

But Lexi hadn't worn a swimsuit in years, maybe since high school. She couldn't stomach the thought of trying one on. She'd bought three swimsuits in three sizes, left the tags on, and decided she'd figure it out in Hawaii. It wasn't that Lexi had poor body image. If anything, she was skinnier than most, which didn't help in the breast department, but it wasn't like she was trying to impress anyone. She just didn't have time to play at the beach. When she went to the ocean, she collected samples from tide pools and recorded data.

After leaving the plane and entering the terminal, the first thing Lexi noticed was the moist air. San Diego had some mild humidity, but Honolulu was vastly different. It was warm, so moist she could almost touch it. She redid her eternal pony tail, which kept her long, brown hair out of her face. She never bothered with styling it, just kept it straight and all one length so it needed no upkeep. She knew the humidity was about to wreak havoc on her normally smooth pony tail. She had a bit of natural curl that came out on the most humid days in San Diego, and she'd probably need to wear an iron-clad bun here. Lexi had walked about fifty feet, dodging people greeting each other, when she heard Sydney's unmistakable voice.

"Lexi! Over here!"

Sydney dashed toward Lexi and scooped her friend into a bone-crushing hug. Apelu was a bit more calm in his greeting, kissing Lexi on both cheeks Samoan style. Seeing the two together was always a bit of a contrast. Apelu towered over Sydney's curvy, petite figure, and her coloring was the exact opposite of Apelu's. Where Sydney was platinum blonde, Apelu was dark. But they were both stunning in their own ways, and together, they made an attractive couple.

"Welcome to Oahu," Apelu said with a grin then placed a gorgeous white-flowered lei about her neck.

The smell was heavenly. "Wow," Lexi said. "What kind of flowers are these?"

"Plumeria, my fav," Sydney answered, linking her arm through Lexi's. "Apelu will get your suitcase, and then you *have* to see his parents' house. It's right. On. The. Beach! Did I tell you that?"

"Quite a few times," Lexi said with a laugh. It was good to be with Sydney. She was like a hyper kid sometimes, but Lexi had missed her.

As they walked to baggage claim, Sydney continued to chatter about the advantages of having a house on the beach, along with disadvantages like cockroaches. The idea of pests didn't bother Lexi much, and she looked forward to exploring the shoreline . . . maybe even collect data that would be useful for her upcoming marine biology class.

She tuned back in to the conversation as they climbed into an old Ford truck.

"You have to meet him," Sydney was saying. "I already told him all about you."

"Who?"

Apelu chuckled, and Lexi threw him a glance.

"Tell her about David," Sydney said to Apelu.

"He was my best bro growing up," Apelu said, starting the truck's engine. "But he's got a crazy girlfriend right now. She's no good for him." He pulled out into traffic.

"What does that have to do with me?" Lexi asked.

Sydney turned to face her. "Because you're perfect for David. He needs someone smart and mellow—if you knew Angel, you'd want to rescue David."

Lexi was used to her best friend's antics, but this was way past the norm. "Sounds ridiculous."

"Angel *is* ridiculous," Sydney said.

"No, it's ridiculous that I show up in Hawaii for my best friend's wedding, and she's lining me up to rescue her husband-to-be's childhood friend from a crazy woman?" Her chest tightened at the surprise on Sydney's face. Lexi had probably been a little too honest.

"When you put it that way, I guess it does sound pretty stupid," Sydney said, her voice subdued for once. She turned around and faced the front windshield.

"Lexi's right. We should probably drop it," Apelu said.

Sydney sighed. "I guess so."

Dear, dear Apelu, Lexi thought. *I'm so glad you're marrying Sydney.* When Sydney went into pout mode things always turned gloomy. It wouldn't last long, although Lexi hoped it wouldn't be due to a revival of Sydney's insistence of Lexi somehow wresting the unknown David from a mysterious loony girlfriend.

Still, she wanted to dispel the sting of her rejection. "Is David Samoan?" She didn't know what was offensive to ask, but Apelu hadn't ever been the easy-to-offend type.

"He's Haole, even though he thinks he's Samoan." Apelu laughed. "He claims he's got Maori in him, but I've seen no proof."

Sydney turned to look at Lexi again, her eyes bright and mischievous. "His eyes are the darkest brown I've ever seen—not as gorgeous as Apelu's, of course." She took her fiancé's hand. "I totally believe he's part Maori. You'll have to see for yourself. No pressure. Promise."

"I'm not going on a date." Lexi wasn't anti-dating. Well, maybe she was. The few she'd had in high school and college had amounted to awkward good-byes, especially when the guys expected a make-out session after they'd paid for her meal.

"No date," Sydney rushed to say. "He'll be hanging around, and you'll meet him naturally." She grinned.

Lexi smiled back, but inside, her stomach was in knots. For once, she wished she had a boyfriend or some other excuse. How hard would it be to convince Sydney that she'd met and fallen in love with someone back home in less than a week? Her mind scanned through the guys in their apartment complex, someone convincing. No one came to mind that Lexi hadn't outwardly voiced her strong opinion about—using descriptive words like *jerk* or *idiot*.

Sydney wouldn't buy it.

Apelu turned onto a highway, and the scenery changed from businesses and hotels to masses of trees and flowers. Simply put, it was gorgeous.

"Are those hibiscus?" Lexi asked of the giant red flowers edging the sides of the road.

"Yeah. Aren't they amazing?" Sydney said. "They grow wild here."

Lexi was glued to the window and barely followed the conversation up front—about the wedding cake Apelu's auntie was going to make. Maybe Lexi should have been a better maid of honor by contributing to the conversation, but the hibiscus made her think about a past ecology class, and plants in their native habitats versus growing in controlled conditions. She wanted to come back to check out the terrain. "What's the name of this road?"

"Kamehameha Highway," Apelu said.

"Isn't it a great name?" Sydney said. "I love saying it. *Kamehameha, Kamehameha*. Like a tongue twister. It's named after a Hawaiian king."

Lexi nodded, committing the name to memory so she could come back when she had a break. "The plant life is incredible."

"The whole island is like this. We'll take you on a hike to some waterfalls. You'll fall in love," Sydney said. "In fact, we've decided to move back here after Apelu graduates next year if he doesn't get drafted to the NFL."

"Really?" Lexi said. Hawaii seemed too remote, too small for Sydney's huge personality. Since high school, Sydney had always talked about moving to New York and working for some big fashion designer. Lexi guessed that's what relationships and marriage did to a person. Their goals changed.

Sydney smiled back at her. "Really. I can't wait."

Lexi believed it. If *radiant* should ever be used, it described Sydney now. She was definitely in love, happy, and seemed to have everything she wanted. For a second, Lexi felt envious then reminded herself that she had everything she wanted in a full-ride scholarship to a great university with a prestigious biology program. She'd been thinking lately of getting a graduate degree.

Apelu pulled off the highway, and they drove through a copse of trees. Moments later, the road opened onto a row of houses. Behind them, the ocean stretched as far as she could see.

"Wow," Lexi said. There was really nothing else *to* say. Blue water glittered in the late afternoon, moving back and forth against pristine sand.

"Isn't it fabulous?" Sydney practically bounced in her seat. They climbed out of the truck, Apelu grabbed Lexi's suitcase, and they followed him into the house.

Stepping inside, Lexi entered into a whirlwind of introductions, kisses and hugs. She met Apelu's parents, a couple of aunties, an uncle, and a horde of cousins, ranging from little kids to a guy about her age—maybe another cousin. She couldn't remember his name apart from the others'. Was this David?

Sydney hugged everyone as if she hadn't been gone only a short time. Lexi could see the connection between Sydney and her new in-laws immediately. No wonder she wanted to move here. Sydney's home life was sparse—her parents had divorced, and a sister several years older lived on the east coast.

After the greetings, Sydney led Lexi to the back door, where they literally stepped out onto the sand.

"What do you think?" Sydney asked.

Lexi was speechless at first. The Pacific expanded before them, moving gently in colors of blue and gold as the sun began to set. Palm trees collected at the left and on the right, and the beach extended as far as she could see on both sides—pure white sand, immaculate. It looked like a postcard.

"Not all beaches are created equal, huh?" Sydney said.

"Beautiful." Lexi lifted her cell phone and snapped a picture then saved it as the wallpaper on her phone. "I need to get my notebook."

"Oh, no you don't," Sydney said. "You're here for *me*. For my wedding *and* to have fun."

"But the light's perfect." Lexi snapped another picture. "And the tide is going out."

Sydney heaved a big sigh. "Okay, you have *one* hour. The barbeque will start then, and I expect to parade you around Apelu's family as my maid of honor."

"Didn't I just meet them?"

"Ha. You've met only a fraction of them. Just wait." She laughed. "David will be here too, probably with Angel." She rolled her eyes.

"I thought he was in the house. Who was that guy I met?"

"One of Apelu's cousins. You will *know* when you meet David." Sydney lowered her voice. "If I weren't engaged already . . ."

Lexi stared at her. "Apelu is perfect for you."

"I'm just saying, you will have no doubt when you meet David."

"You know what happens when you set someone's expectations too high?" Lexi said. "They're sure to be disappointed."

"You'll just have to trust me, then," Sydney said.

"Does David know about your plan to break up him and his girlfriend?"

"Apelu bugs him about it all the time. David just laughs about it. He doesn't think Apelu's serious."

Lexi shrugged. "I said I'd meet him. But you know my record with guys."

"You think they're all jerks."

"Except for Apelu, of course," Lexi said.

Sydney laughed. "Of course."

Three

exi heard Sydney call her name, but she wasn't
finished inspecting the tide pool. She had her
phone trained on the small pool of water,
recording two tiny crabs fighting over a mussel shell.
Sydney's voice floated over the wind again, which had picked
up in the past few minutes, tugging Lexi's pony tail free. But
Lexi held her phone steady and didn't bother to fix her hair.

She only need a few more minutes. Lexi sensed
someone—likely Sydney—walking on the reef toward her,
but she continued to focus on the crabs as the person walked
up and crouched next to her.

A quick glance brought Lexi up short. Unless Sydney
had muscled calves and dark leg hair, a man was beside Lexi.
Keeping her phone trained on the battle below, she slowly
lifted her eyes. Definitely not Sydney.

He had the darkest brown eyes she'd ever seen. They
reminded her of tide pools on her midnight explorations in
San Diego. The man looked more tanned than Polynesian,

and his hair was lighter than Apelu's, touched by the sun, so golden highlights were woven in with the dark brown.

"Hi," he said. "I was told to confiscate your notebook and escort you to the barbeque." His deep voice had a bit of a lilt—the way Apelu's family spoke too.

Lexi must have been staring at him open-mouthed, because he smiled, and said, "Sorry to startle you. I'm David, by the way."

Of course.

He held out a hand, and she maneuvered the phone to her left so she could shake his with her right.

"You're Lexi, I assume?" he said.

It was a question, but she couldn't speak for a second.

What's wrong with me?

"Uh, yes, Alexis, actually. But everyone calls me Lexi."

Why did I just say that?

Here she was spouting useless trivia to someone she'd just met, a man her best friend wanted to set her up with, even though he had a girlfriend. What did he know about her?

David nodded and looked back at the tide pool, giving Lexi a view of his profile. His dark eyebrows pulled together as he watched the crabs. "Feisty little guys, aren't they? Maybe we should drop another mussel in so there's enough for two."

"No!" Lexi said, a bit too strongly.

David looked up, surprise on his face.

"I mean, I'm observing their natural reactions. To disturb their habitat would make it unnatural."

The sides of his mouth tugged up, as if trying not to laugh at her. She felt like an idiot. For the second time. She had turned on full scientific-geek mode. The heat of mortification flashed through her.

Lexi paused the video recording. She was done with this tide pool now.

"Don't you want to see who wins?" David asked with a mocking tone.

At least she could tell Sydney that while David was attractive, they had nothing in common. A single date was sure to end in disaster.

"I'd better get back," Lexi said. "Sydney wanted me to meet Apelu's family, and you . . . but since I already met you, I guess I'd better go." She turned and picked her way across the reef.

"Hey, check this out," he called after her. "The mussel opened."

Lexi froze, wanting to see it. David sounded sincere this time, but what was he really thinking? And why did she care? She turned and hurried back to the tide pool, tee-ing up her phone to record. She crouched by David and aimed her phone at the scene.

The crabs were practically climbing on top of each other to reach their feast. Lexi watched, fascinated by the desperation and brutality. David sat quietly next to her, and she was grateful he didn't feel the need to make some sarcastic comment.

Several minutes passed, and the recording stopped, running out of memory. Lexi would have to download the video to her laptop before recording anything else. She rose. "I think I got everything."

David stood too, and Lexi was struck with how tall he was, even taller than Apelu. But he was leaner, where Apelu was stocky but well built.

"That was pretty crazy," David said.

Lexi nodded. Did he mean crazy-dumb, or crazy-cool, or something else?

"Apelu told me you were a science nut," David said.

Lexi swallowed. "I guess you could say that," she said, keeping her tone even. She turned and started walking toward the beach.

David kept pace with her. "I think he meant it in a nice way. I mean, he grew up here, so I guess he's not all that fascinated. I grew up here, too, and it's just kind of normal for me."

They came into view of Apelu's side yard, which was adorned with tables, chairs, and platters of food arranged on a long table.

"I grew up next to the ocean, and I *am* fascinated," Lexi retorted then immediately regretted her sharp tone, but she was seriously getting annoyed.

"Wait, I didn't mean—" David was cut off by Sydney walking toward them.

"There you are. Didn't you hear me calling you?" She didn't look put out. In fact, she grinned, looking from Lexi to David.

Lexi wanted to tell Sydney to save her eager speculating, but couldn't right in front of him. They were interrupted by a gorgeous, honey-skinned woman practically sashaying over to them.

"That's Angel," Sydney said, her smile about as fake as Lexi had ever seen.

The crazy girlfriend. But she didn't look crazy. She looked like she did regular photo shoots on Waikiki beach. She was tall and curvy in all the right places, and her dark eyes were framed by incredibly long lashes. Angel's black hair tumbled over her shoulders in soft waves. Her name fit her appearance.

"Hey, baby," she said to David in a sultry voice. "Where did you go?"

One side of his mouth lifted. Any man would smile if he had a woman like Angel attached to him.

"I had to do an errand for Sydney and fetch the errant Miss Alexis," he said.

Lexi had to restrain herself from groaning. Why had she told him her full name?

"Oh, I've heard all about you," Angel purred. She snaked her arms around his waist, and his arm settled easily about her shoulders. Angel gave Lexi a satisfied smirk. Why shouldn't she be affectionate with her boyfriend? Still, Lexi's stomach rolled. Either she was disgusted or hungry.

She glanced at David; he didn't seem fazed by his girlfriend's adoration.

"Come on, baby," Angel said. "I want some of that teriyaki chicken you made." She looked at Lexi. "Nice to meet you, hon."

Lexi could have sworn Angel's eyes narrowed for a moment, but then widened again in sweetness.

As the couple walked over to the food table, Lexi didn't realize she was staring after them until Sydney nudged her.

"What did I tell you?" she whispered. "Was I right?"

"About David being good-looking?" Lexi said. "Yeah, but he's taken. And he pretty much made fun of me."

"How?" Sydney asked as Apelu crossed to them.

"I'll tell you later," Lexi said. What she'd tell Sydney was to give up hope of intervening between Angel and David.

Lexi didn't want anything to do with either of them.

Four

"$\mathcal{I}$t's beautiful," Lexi said, watching Sydney spin in her wedding dress. It wasn't what Lexi had envisioned for her friend, but the white muumuu with tiny pearls and lace couldn't have been more perfect.

"Apelu's mom wore it when she got married," Sydney said. "It's a little big, but Apelu's mom is a fantastic seamstress, and she'll take it in a little. She's also making me a haku to wear on my head."

"You'll be gorgeous," Lexi said.

Sydney squealed and hugged her, then left the room to go change.

Wow. This is really happening. My best friend is getting married. A stab of loneliness shot through Lexi. She'd always been fine not having a bunch of friends or a major social life, but Sydney made up for all of that. Now . . . things would be a lot different. At least they'd still have the rest of the year together at SDU, although not as roommates.

"We're leaving in twenty minutes for the hike to Maunawili Falls," Sydney called from the other room. "David's picking us up."

Lexi drew in a breath. She'd thought the hike was going to be the three of them—Apelu, Sydney, and her. "What about Angel?"

"We didn't invite her," Sydney said, coming back in wearing shorts and a tank top.

"You guys are really pushing it by not inviting her. What will she think if she finds out that I came along?" Lexi pictured the dark-eyed woman. "I don't want to make her mad."

"Why would it?" Sydney said, lifting an eyebrow. "You said there was nothing between you. So nothing for her to be jealous about, right?"

Lexi opened her mouth then shut it. There *was* nothing between them. But she'd seen how Angel acted around David . . . Lexi wouldn't be surprised if the woman had real claws. "Right."

"We'll have fun, then. Don't forget your notebook," Sydney said. "You should wear one of my tank tops. You'll sweat like mad on the hike."

A horn blared from somewhere outside.

"David's early," Sydney said. "I'll meet you out front."

Lexi turned to the mirror on top of the dresser. Her t-shirt was already damp with sweat from her sojourn to the tide pools that morning. She quickly changed into one of Sydney's tank tops, not caring for the way it clung to her small curves. One more way she was nothing like Sydney—or Angel. Lexi pulled on the only pair of shorts she'd brought, ones with a floral print—who knew where she got them? Her capris were still wet from the morning's excursion to the ocean, so the ugly shorts were her only real option.

Again, why did she care? She wasn't here to impress.

She grabbed her phone and notebook, wishing she would have brought two notebooks; she'd already filled a good portion of this one. But she couldn't lug her laptop around a mountainside.

When she walked into the front yard, the others sat in a battered yellow jeep. Its body rested at least a foot above the massive tires. What was this, monster trucks? David sat in the driver's seat, and Apelu and Sydney cuddled together in the back.

Apparently Lexi would be sitting up front. David grinned as she climbed up and into the jeep. "Look at you," he said. "Dressing like an islander already."

Apelu laughed from the back seat. "She just needs a flower in her hair."

David jumped to the ground and picked a hibiscus bloom from one of the many flowering bushes. He climbed back in then leaned toward Lexi and tucked it behind her right ear.

Lexi tried not to flinch when his warm hand touched her.

"You wear it on the right side if you're single," he said. "And on the left side if you're married."

"Uh, thanks," Lexi said, feeling every part of her body heat at all the attention. *Just relax,* she told herself. *This is what they call having fun.* She smiled, and he winked.

Wow. She was so not going to read anything into that. But David seemed to have forgotten her anyway as he pulled onto the highway. He and Apelu called back and forth to each other, debating the stats of some rugby players they were friends with.

Lexi refused to look back at Sydney to see if her friend had noticed the wink. She let her gaze slide ever so slightly over to David. Without fully looking at him, she could see his right hand and arm as he shifted gears, gaining speed. His arms were tanned and muscled, as was the one leg in her view.

She looked away, focusing on the right side of the jeep. *The humidity must be getting to me.* She gazed on the gorgeous scenery speeding by as the wind rushed through her hair. Lexi tried to concentrate on the types of plant life she could make out.

When David pulled off the road, he reached over and touched her arm. "Hold on, it's going to get really bumpy."

Soon they were on a dirt road that looked pretty smooth, but a moment later, David took a detour that looked like it went straight up the mountain. Sydney had the advantage of clinging to Apelu in the back, but Lexi could only grip the dashboard.

The jeep careened on only two wheels, tipping on toward the left, then slammed back down, maneuvering over deep ruts. Apelu let out a whoop; Lexi gritted her teeth.

David glanced over. "Don't worry. I've done this a hundred times."

The knowledge didn't lessen the tightness in her stomach.

His hand grasped hers, and Lexi found herself gripping back. Somehow, he continued to climb the jeep up the ridge using only his left hand to steer. Then he turned sharp right onto a flat spot and braked.

"We're here," he said, grinning at her.

Lexi realized he was still holding her hand. They both looked down. She pulled hers away. "That was . . . I don't even know what to say. I'm dizzy."

David laughed. "I'll help you out." And he did. While Apelu and Sydney apparently felt the need to kiss for a few moments—maybe they were grateful to be alive—David helped Lexi climb down.

"You all right?" he asked, his dark eyes holding hers.

Lexi was breathless, even though all she'd done was sit in a bumpy jeep. "Yeah, I'm good." She had a few aches now that she thought about it, but she wasn't about to mention them.

By the time Apelu and Sydney joined them, David had loaded up a backpack with water bottles.

"I can carry some," Lexi offered.

"Oh, let him," Apelu said. "He needs something to do after wimping out on playing college football."

"Whatever, man." David shoved Apelu's arm, but he was smiling. "Some of us have a life, you know."

"You used to play football?" Lexi asked.

David glanced at her, his smile dropping.

"Three years as starting quarterback in high school," Apelu filled in. "Then he decided to leave his bro hanging while he stayed on the island to cook."

"Look who's leaving who hanging now?" David fired back, his tone teasing. "I'm not the one getting married in two days."

Apelu grinned and drew Sydney against his side. "Yep. Payback."

Sydney laughed. "Knock it off, you two, or Lexi will want to go back to the beach."

"I'm fine." Lexi didn't want to be in the middle of anything. Based on their surroundings, she'd be completely happy if she could wander along this ridge for hours.

Apelu grabbed Sydney's hand, and they set off, hiking down the other side of the ridge from where the jeep was parked.

David slid on the backpack and looked at Lexi. "Ready?"

Five

exi followed David along a barely perceptible trail that wove through thick undergrowth. "You played football with Apelu?"

"Yeah," David said.

He didn't seem want to talk about it. Lexi was fine with that. There was plenty to distract her—flowers, plants, and the sounds of birds.

They walked for several moments, Apelu and Sydney getting farther and farther ahead, when David said, "I got a scholarship to San Diego State, same time as Apelu. There was no doubt in his mind that I'd take it."

"You turned it down?"

"Being a quarterback might seem cool when you're in high school, but in college, you redshirt the first year, and you're lucky to get in a few plays for the next two. If there isn't some other hotshot recruited after you, you might play first string your senior year."

"I can see how that would be a deterrent," Lexi said.

David stopped and turned to face her. "Really?"

Her pulse quickened for some reason. He seemed to want to know her thoughts, needed someone to understand him.

"Sure. It's a big risk," she said. "And if it doesn't work out, then you get pounded on in practice for nothing."

David exhaled. "Exactly. Maybe I wasn't as big of a meathead as everyone thought."

"So what did you do?" Lexi asked. "Apelu said something about cooking."

"Yeah," David said, starting to hike again. The terrain became steeper, and they had to move single file. "I walked onto the team at the University of Hawaii, mostly sat on the bench for two years, and then quit to get serious about school. Plus, my dad was sick, and I had to help my mom run the restaurant."

This was not the David she thought she'd met yesterday, who she'd been annoyed with. "I didn't know your family has a restaurant."

"My dad started it, and I grew up working in it. My mom taught me to cook, and I guess it was in my blood. I majored in business management, intending to take over someday. That day came a lot faster than I expected."

Lexi was quiet for a moment. "Your dad?"

"He died last year, a couple of months after I graduated." David paused. "I was glad I quit football—I wouldn't have been anywhere close to graduation with all of the traveling and interruptions with school."

They'd reached an overlook. "Sorry about your dad," Lexi said quietly.

David nodded, and they walked for a few more minutes in silence. Then he stopped, and Lexi took a couple of steps to the edge of the ridge. Below, vines and trees seemed to tumble for hundreds of yards until they met the coast. The sight was breathtaking.

She snapped a few pictures with her cell phone.

"I'll take one of you," David said.

Lexi handed him the phone, and she smiled for the shot.

"Beautiful," David said.

Lexi scrunched up her nose. "If you're referring to the scenery, then I agree."

David arched a brow. "Don't like compliments?"

She lifted a shoulder in a shrug. "I'm a science major, remember? I deal with facts."

David studied her for a moment, making Lexi feel self-conscious, so she turned away and gazed over the valley. "How much farther to the waterfalls?"

He came to stand by her. "Another twenty minutes. Apelu and Sydney are probably already there."

Strangely, Lexi was hyper-aware of how close David stood. Not that he was all that close, but maybe she was paying more attention because of the personal stories he'd shared.

"Do you hike here often?" she asked.

"I usually come here on my days off. Or I surf the North Shore."

Lexi looked over and found his brown eyes on her, looking thoughtful. "You traded a football for a surfboard?"

"Like Apelu said, I have to do *something*."

Lexi smiled. Being around him today had made her do that a lot for some reason. He handed her a water bottle, and she took a long drink. "I guess you get used to the humidity," she said.

"I don't know anything else," David said. "Come on, let's catch up, or they'll come looking for us."

They set out again, and Lexi found herself becoming more and more curious about David. "Have you been off the island?"

"Only for recruiting trips," David said with a shrug. "The restaurant business is too busy for extended vacations."

"How many recruiting trips did you go on?"

"Three."

It was Lexi's turn to arch a brow. "I can see why Apelu gives you a hard time."

David nodded. "Yeah, but I think staying close to home was the better choice." He looked over. "What about you? Did you always want to be a scientist?"

"After a failed stint at ballet, it seemed the better option."

"Do you still dance?" David asked.

Lexi sighed. It had been a long time since she'd even thought about her past dancing craze. "Not since high school."

"You're just naturally skinny?"

Lexi shot him a look, but noticed him smiling.

"I'm not that skinny," she said. "Just around here, it seems."

David nodded. "Come to my restaurant. I'll fatten you up in no time."

Lexi laughed. "You only have three days."

"Sounds like a challenge," he said, grinning. His cell rang, and he fished it out of his pocket.

Lexi was surprised that cell service worked way out here. From the tinny sound coming through the phone, she guessed the person on the other end wasn't happy. Maybe it was his mother, and David's day off was about to be cut short.

His answers were short, then he hung up.

"Do you have to get back to work?"

"No . . . it was Angel."

They lapsed into silence for a few moments. Lexi could hear the sound of water—they must be getting close to the falls. Pretty soon they'd be with the others, and she wouldn't be able to ask David much more of anything. "How long have you guys been dating?"

"Off and on for about a year." He let out a sigh. "It's complicated."

Lexi stayed quiet. She couldn't believe she'd asked him in the first place.

"She's an . . . interesting person," he said.

"*Interesting*?" Lexi caught David's gaze. "I'm not sure that's how I'd describe her."

He smiled at her.

"Come on, you guys!" Sydney's voice cut through the humid air.

Lexi looked up as Sydney came into view. She wore a bikini top and shorts and was soaking wet. Lexi didn't know she was supposed to wear a swimsuit.

"The water's perfect!"

She heard a shout from Apelu, followed by a huge splashing sound.

They rounded the corner and came into view of a massive waterfall tumbling into a deep blue pool of water. The noise of the powerful water seemed to vibrate through Lexi. It was spectacular.

David slipped off his backpack and pulled off his shirt. Before Lexi knew it, he was running toward the edge of the pool, then jumping and diving into the water below.

"You are totally checking him out," Sydney said.

Lexi blinked, clearing the image of David's muscled back as he'd run and dove into the pool.

"Don't worry, if I weren't engaged, I would be too."

Lexi elbowed Sydney and changed the subject. "This place is incredible. No wonder he comes here a lot."

"He does? How do you know?" Sydney asked, following Lexi as she walked to the edge of the cliff.

It was at least twenty feet down to the water. Apelu was swimming, while David had just climbed out. He shook his hair and looked up at them. Lexi was definitely staring now.

"Come on! It's perfect!" he called up to them.

Lexi swallowed nervously, not just at the image of David's torso gleaming with water, but because she'd never jumped off anything. Not even the high dive at the public pool. She enjoyed having her feet on the ground. Which might explain why she didn't go beyond high-school ballet— all that leaping into the air with a partner. Not to mention her stomach was still in knots from four-wheeling up the mountain.

"Come on, Lex," Sydney said, tugging her arm.

And then it dawned on her. If she got wet then . . . Well, she was wearing a white tank and a white bra. Not good.

"I really don't want to get wet."

"You don't have to jump. Just swim," Sydney said. "The water is amazing."

"I don't think—"

"Hey," David said, interrupting. "Do you need help?" He'd climbed up the bank and stood there, dripping, a few yards away.

"See ya, guys," Sydney said and jumped off the cliff with a scream. Apelu laughed below then paddled over to her where she'd landed in the water.

Lexi crossed her arms. "I'm not a big swimmer." Which was true. That wasn't the reason she didn't want to get wet. But the water did look great.

"I can hold your hand, and we can jump together," David said. "I won't let go."

She shook her head. "It's not that . . . I'm not really dressed to get wet."

David's eyes moved down, then quickly back up. His face reddened. "Do you want to wear my shirt after?"

Because he was blushing, now she was too.

This is not happening.

"M-maybe if we come back another day, I'll be better prepared," she stammered. "I'll just check things out while

273

you guys swim."

David's cheeks were still red, and he nodded. He turned and did another dive off the edge. Lexi paused to admire his form, and well, his arms . . .

"Come on, Lexi! Jump!" Sydney called from below.

"I'm going to look around for a bit," Lexi called, waving at her.

Before Sydney could respond, Apelu dunked her. There was a sputter, and she came up with a scream. Sydney appeared sufficiently distracted, so Lexi busied herself scanning the flora. The scent of the greenery and flowers was heady. Paradise. If Sydney could stop squealing and splashing, Lexi could envision taking a nap here.

She took another swallow of her water bottle then got out her notebook. A group of jasmine shrubs grew nearby, and she crouched to examine the waxy green leaves. She didn't know a lot about jasmine, but she wrote down a description of it and the surrounding plants blended it with.

"What are you writing?" said a voice behind her.

Lexi turned to see David. He was dripping wet from his second foray into the water.

"Just writing notes about jasmine." She straightened as he walked toward her.

"For a class or something?"

"Not specifically, but I'm sure it will be useful at some point."

"We use jasmine flowers to make leis," he said, picking a few blossoms. "It's my mom's favorite."

Lexi moved over slightly to the side. David was quite close to her, and with his bare torso and wet body . . . She didn't want to be caught blushing again. "When I arrived at the airport, Apelu gave me one made of plumeria. The smell is addictive. It's still in my room."

"Ah. That's my favorite scent," he said with a smile.

Her eyes met his, and it seemed to take forever to pull

hers away.

David held out the handful of blossoms, and Lexi bent over to smell them. "Mmm. Nice," she said. The scent was heavenly, but she decided she favored plumerias.

She drew away, and David tossed the blooms into the bush.

"If you change your mind, I left my shirt on the rock right next to the water."

Lexi met his gaze. His expression was amused and sweet at the same time. She could hear Sydney and Apelu having fun in the water, while she was burying her nose in her notebook. Not that she didn't enjoy it . . .

"Okay," she said, surprising herself.

David's brow rose. "Okay?" He grinned and held out his hand. "Let's go."

Before Lexi could think twice about what she'd agreed to, she was sailing over the edge, hand in hand with David as they plunged toward the water.

Six

$\mathcal{L}$ exi couldn't remember ever laughing so much in her life. They were driving to David's restaurant, where he said he'd feed them his specialty—some sort of teriyaki chicken—and Apelu and David wouldn't leave each other alone.

First they'd ribbed each other about stunts played in high school, and then Apelu made fun of David for choosing an apron over football pads, and David gave Apelu a hard time for becoming Haole-ized on the "mainland."

"You don't even eat island food over there, bro," David said. "No wonder it took you two years to make starting linebacker."

"Little good did your cooking do for you," Apelu shot back with a laugh. "Your arms are skinnier than Lexi's."

"Hey," Lexi said, and everyone laughed. David's arms were far from skinny. She knew, because she'd been all too aware of them, especially since putting on his shirt. Her shirt was probably dry by now, but it was hard to tell with the humidity. Besides, she was quite cozy in David's shirt as the wind pushed all around them.

Lexi was ravenous by the time he pulled off the road into a shopping complex.

"Uh oh," Sydney said as David turned into a parking spot in front of The Grille.

Angel stood in front of the restaurant, arms folded over a fitted hot-pink shirt, her lipsticked mouth drawn into a pouty circle.

Lexi felt about an inch tall. She'd been laughing and smiling with David, not to mention she was wearing his shirt.

Everyone went dead quiet as David turned off the engine and climbed out of the jeep. Lexi wanted to disappear. She couldn't watch David greet Angel. She heard his greeting, and her clipped response of, "I need to talk to you."

They disappeared inside, and Lexi let out the breath she'd been holding.

"That's one mad woman," Apelu said.

"Do we need to call 911?" Sydney said, in a half-joking, half-serious tone.

"Nah," Apelu said. "My bro can handle himself. But I'm not waiting for food. Let's go inside and order."

Lexi followed the two into the restaurant, her stomach knotted with both hunger and worry about what might be happening between David and Angel—and if she was part of it. She hoped not. They were nowhere in sight, so they must be out back.

A woman came from around the counter, all smiles. She was tall, thin, and looked like David. She greeted Apelu and Sydney with kisses then turned to Lexi, clasping her hand.

"Welcome. You must be Lexi," she said. "David told me you were coming. I'm his mom, Frankie."

David told his mom about me?

"It's nice to meet you," Lexi said. Frankie seemed warm and open, like most of the islanders Lexi had met.

"David will be out in a minute," his mom said, her brow creasing for a fraction of a second. Then she smiled again. "He wants you to try the chicken."

I know, she thought. *He hasn't shut up about it.* "Sounds great."

"Sit, sit," Frankie said. "I'll bring you your plates."

Moments later, they were seated at a well-scrubbed, dark wood table. It was about 3:00 in the afternoon, and the lunch rush seemed to be over. There were only a few others at tables at the restaurant. While they waited, Lexi glanced around, impressed with the neatness of the place.

She saw a restroom sign and excused herself. In the ladies' room, she could hear a man and woman arguing. She glanced up—a small window above the sinks must have connected to the outside. She froze when she recognized Angel's voice. Lexi couldn't quite make out the words, but the woman sounded livid.

Lexi hurried, then left as soon as she could. When she returned to their table in the restaurant, Frankie had brought out the food, and Apelu and Sydney had already begun eating.

Lexi's stomach clenched as she thought about what was happening between David and Angel. Her heart went out to him, but she could see Angel's point of view; she didn't look happy about being left out of the excursion. Maybe she didn't recognize David's shirt on Lexi—she could hope.

Even though Lexi figured her appetite was completely gone, one bite of the teriyaki chicken, and she was hooked. "Wow," she said around a mouthful. "I could eat this every day."

Apelu laughed, scooping a large helping of steaming sticky rice onto his plate. "This is the best of the best."

Lexi took another bite then ventured to taste the other dishes on the table. One was battered chicken with a delicious tangy sauce, and the other looked like short ribs. But she kept coming back to the teriyaki chicken.

When she knew she was full, but still eating, she wondered how long David and Angel would be gone. "Is David coming back, do you think?" Lexi asked.

Sydney looked up from her plate then over at Apelu.

"Don't know," he said. "Looks like she's got her claws into him good this time."

"Apelu." Sydney said, her voice sharp.

But it was plain that Sydney agreed. Her expression was the most serious Lexi had seen it since she'd gotten engaged. Everyone at the table was quiet.

After a few minutes, Frankie came over to them, her face pulled into a frown. "David said he'll be awhile and for you to take his jeep back to your place. He'll catch up with you later."

Apelu stood. "What's going on? Is he all right?"

Frankie lifted her shoulders then sighed. "He's a man now; he has to figure it out."

"We can walk home," Apelu said.

"No, take the jeep. You guys had a long day."

Lexi was grateful for the offer. She hadn't realized how tired she was—and sore—until they sat down to eat.

Frankie cleared some of the plates then walked away, mumbling something about "that woman."

For a wild instant, Lexi wondered if she should go and talk to David. But Angel was probably there, still yelling at him.

Besides, what could Lexi possibly say?

꙳

Back at Apelu's house, Lexi sat down with Sydney and a myriad of Apelu's female relatives and helped string leis.

Apparently every invited guest would get a lei at the wedding. From the looks of the piles of flowers, there would be a couple of hundred people there.

Even though the chatter was lively, Lexi felt gloomy. Her mind was still on David, on the fun they'd had, and then what he'd come home to. What was he was doing right then—cooking? Still arguing with Angel?

She'd changed out of his shirt and had it folded up on her bed. She hadn't planned on doing laundry on such a short trip. A small smile played on her lips as she thought about the subtle way David had talked her into swimming. But still her heart was heavy—odd that something with David would affect her so much. Why was she thinking about him anyway? She barely knew him, and his life and relationship with his girlfriend were none of her business.

The evening passed in a flurry of stringing flowers and baking sponge cakes. The Grille was catering the main dishes, but Apelu's mom insisted on doing the desserts herself. Pretty much everything Lexi had eaten on the island was delicious. No wonder most of the woman were larger than Lexi's size six. A few months here, and she would be in the market for new clothes.

By the time everything quieted down for the night, Lexi was exhausted from being around so much commotion, but she was too keyed up to sleep. It was close to 10:00 when she slipped out the back door and walked barefoot toward the water. It was too dark to see anything in the tide pools, so she walked along the beach, watching the moon move slowly across the sky. The salty air was still warm, and the breeze was almost nonexistent.

In two days, her best friend would be married, and Lexi would return home alone . . . Her life would be very different. She wouldn't see David again either. She hoped he'd be okay, and that Angel would be nicer to him.

Letting out a sigh, Lexi again wondered why she cared so much.

After turning back, she wandered through the side yard. In the moonlight, she saw someone walking along the lane leading to the front yard. Lexi stopped, recognizing David. What was he doing here, and so late? He was probably coming to get his jeep.

She hesitated. Should she slip around back and pretend she hadn't seen him? Or should she say something?

Is Angel done yelling at you? Do you want your shirt back?

Lexi took a step forward. Maybe if she talked to him, she wouldn't have to worry about him anymore, and she'd be able to sleep.

David walked slowly, hands in his pockets, head down. He looked up as Lexi approached.

"Lexi," he said.

The way he said her name washed over her with warmth. How did he do that?

"How are you?"

"Better." David stood there, not making any move to hurry past her. Maybe he did want to talk.

"The teriyaki chicken was amazing," Lexi said.

David smiled, and Lexi's heart pinged. The sight was like smelling the sweetest flower.

"I think I'm still full from eating so much, but the weird thing is that I'm craving it too," Lexi said.

He chuckled, and relief coursed through Lexi. Maybe she'd overheard the worst of it between him and Angel, and everything was okay now.

"I told you it was the best."

"You were right," Lexi said. "You may want to patent that recipe."

He smiled but remained silent, his eyes taking on a thoughtful expression as he looked at her. Lexi felt her face and neck grow warm. Thankfully, it was dark, so there was no way David could know what his gaze was doing to her.

Finally he said, "So what are you doing out here?"

"I, uh, went for a walk." She motioned toward the house. "It's been crazy inside tonight."

"I can imagine." David looked over at the house for a second. "Tomorrow I'll start the chicken."

"Not much of a relaxing day for the best man, huh?"

"No," David said.

"I can help," Lexi offered then realized that Sydney likely had a full day of preparations planned for Lexi to help with, not to mention the little fact of David's irate girlfriend.

But he was shaking his head. "I've got some teenagers coming in to help. They need the money. Besides, aren't you the maid of honor?"

"Yeah," Lexi said. "Who knows what Sydney has planned for me?"

David nodded, watching her closely again. "I broke up with Angel."

Lexi didn't know what to say. "Oh," she managed. Her mind caught up with her senses. "I'm sorry."

He lifted a shoulder, not like an I-don't-care gesture, but in defeat. "Apelu is wiser than I gave him credit for."

Lexi wasn't sure how to answer.

"Don't tell him that," David said, one side of his mouth lifting.

"I won't." Lexi had a thousand questions but didn't think it was her place to ask any of them.

"I had a great time today . . . I'm glad you decided to swim." His gaze seemed to soak her in.

"Me, too," Lexi said, her voice sounding small. Her mind kept chanting: *He broke up with her. He broke up with her.*

"Well, I'd better get the jeep out of here."

Lexi nodded numbly.

He stepped past her, and his hand briefly touched her arm. "Thanks, Lexi."

For what?

"See you tomorrow," he continued then dropped his hand.

"Okay." She watched him walk toward the jeep. He climbed into it with one swift movement, and the engine roared to life. She took a few steps back, getting out of the way. As he drove past, he lifted his hand in good-bye, and she lifted hers.

When the jeep turned out of sight, she realized that the thundering in her ears hadn't been the engine, but her heart.

Seven

ut Lexi didn't see David the next day. She assumed he was busy with cooking, and Lexi was plenty busy with Sydney, decorating the yard. Apelu recruited a bunch of kids in the neighborhood to rake and mow the lawn then set up chairs and tables.

Lexi watched Sydney and Apelu together with a bit of a pang in her heart. Even when something went wrong, they laughed together. Lexi didn't say anything about the visit with David last night, or about how he'd broken up with Angel. There wasn't a good time to mention it.

A whole day passing without seeing David felt strange, which was strange in itself. So when she woke up Sunday morning, knowing she'd see David for sure that day, she felt breathless.

What's wrong with me?

The solution for intruding thoughts about a guy she wouldn't see after the wedding was to stay busy. Lexi climbed out of bed and headed for the beach, even though it was still early, wanting to explore the tide pools before the day got underway. The wedding was at 5:00, followed by the reception, but there was plenty to do before then.

She spent about an hour at the tide pools—not recording, just observing and thinking about when she'd met David here. The beach was not taking her mind off of him, so she returned to the house to help.

If she was honest, she was happy that David had broken up with Angel. Not because she enjoyed hanging out with him, but if Apelu was his best friend, and *he* thought the relationship wasn't good, David would be better off without Angel.

Lexi remembered how David had said it was on-again and off-again; maybe they'd been through breakups before. Maybe this was their cycle, and Lexi should stop analyzing it.

The rest of the day passed in a flurry, topped off with the arrival of Sydney's family. The only time Lexi caught her breath was when she helped Sydney with her hair. Her long hair was piled on top of her head, with plenty of curls, which Lexi pinned in place.

The final touch was the haku, a halo of tightly woven flowers. It completed the ensemble with the white muumuu dress, making Sydney look like a Hawaiian princess.

"What do you think?" Lexi said, turning Sydney around to look in the mirror.

Sydney grinned. "I love it." She hugged Lexi. "I'm so glad you came. It means everything to me."

Lexi squeezed her back. "I've loved it here." Which was true, in more ways than Sydney knew.

Music started up outside. "Sounds like they're ready for you," Lexi said. "Are you ready?"

"Yes," Sydney said, her eyes looking a bit moist. She gripped Lexi's hand.

"Let's go." Lexi led Sydney down the hall. Her dad was waiting at the door to escort Sydney down the aisle. For a second, Lexi thought about her dad and wondered if he'd come to her wedding if she got married. He'd taken off when she was about six; the only communication since had been a few birthday cards.

They stepped outside and walked to the side yard, where the ceremony would be. Two flower girls, Apelu's little cousins, were waiting. They looked adorable dressed up.

Everything was beautiful and exactly like a tropical paradise. The sun was starting to set, casting golden light on the assembled guests. Lexi waited for the flower girls to start down the aisle first. Then she followed, aware of everyone's eyes on her. She looked straight ahead, where Apelu waited, looking handsome. Lexi's heart pinged at the happy look on his face. She knew he'd take good care of her best friend. Then Lexi's gaze moved to David, who stood next to the groom.

Their gazes met, and David smiled. Lexi's heart was definitely melting now. He looked amazing, and she was suddenly extremely glad he was now single. Not that it would affect her in any way, but he was better off without Angel, so she'd be happy for him.

Lexi took her place at the front, across from Apelu and David, and then it was Sydney's turn. Everyone turned to watch the bride walking down the aisle with a huge smile on her face, arm in arm with her dad.

The ceremony was beautiful and touching, and there were congratulations all around. Lexi didn't have a chance to say anything to David because of the crowds. The music struck up again as the chairs were moved to the side.

Sydney and Apelu led out on the first dance, and then others joined in. Lexi watched with a smile on her face then realized she was looking for David. Her face flushed at the thought. She was leaving in two days . . . Still she looked through the crowd, and found him.

He was behind one of the serving tables, arranging fruit on a platter. Of course he was on work duty, his restaurant did the catering. Someone moved in front of Lexi, blocking her view of David.

She found a chair to sit on, but that didn't last long. One of Apelu's cousins/uncles/friends asked her to dance, and from that point, she danced most of the time. During a break, she went through the food line and piled up a plate with teriyaki chicken, rice, and fruit. David was no longer serving, so Lexi glanced around, thinking he might be dancing.

He was nowhere to be seen. Was he in the kitchen? Had Angel called? Maybe they'd get back together. Lexi was distracted by whistling, and she turned to see Sydney dancing solo, Apelu sitting in a chair, watching. Guests tucked dollar bills into her dress wherever they could make them stay.

Lexi found a table. She sat and ate at while watching the dancing. She wished she'd had some cash with her so she could participate. When the song ended, everyone clapped and cheered. By the time Lexi finished eating, Sydney and Apelu were about to cut the cake.

All of the remaining guests gathered around to watch. The couple made good work of smashing cake into each other's faces amid laughter. All too soon, Sydney and Apelu said good-bye to everyone. They were taking a late flight to Maui.

When Sydney hugged Lexi, she said, "You've been the best friend I could ever have."

Lexi squeezed back, swallowing sudden tears. "You, too. Have a blast, and I'll see you back home."

After Sydney and Apelu took off for the airport, most of the guests left. A few hung around to clean up, but it didn't take too long, because Apelu's mom said they needed to wait until morning to do the tables and chairs. Lexi talked to Sydney's parents for a few moments before they left for their hotel. Then she was left alone to wander the beach. Even though it was dark, the bright moon provided plenty of light on the sand.

She hadn't even reached the sand when she heard someone call out her name. *David.* She turned to see him walking toward her. He'd changed into shorts and a button-down shirt. Her heart skipped a beat as she waited for him to catch up.

"I was hoping to catch you," David said, stopping in front of her.

He smelled like he'd just showered; not that Lexi was noticing. At least he wasn't with Angel, but where had he been?

"What happened?" Lexi asked. "You missed a bunch of stuff."

"Yeah, there was a bit of an accident in the kitchen," David said.

"Are you okay?"

"Nothing that can't be fixed in the laundry. One of my employees dropped a platter of chicken, and I thought I could catch it in time . . ." He shrugged. "I guess my football skills are rusty. Ended up with sauce and chicken all over myself."

Lexi smiled. "I'm sorry."

"I'm surprised you missed it," he said.

"I am too."

He laughed. "I'm sure you are." He looked toward the yard. "How did it all go? The cake, the dancing, throwing the bouquet?"

"The cake was delicious, once we had a chance to taste it after Sydney and Apelu decided to stop smashing it into each other's faces," Lexi said. "Sydney's mom caught the bouquet, and the dancing was okay."

"Just *okay*?" David said, an eyebrow rising. "What's dancing like back in San Diego?"

"I wouldn't know. I'm not much of a dancing-party-girl." Lexi glanced away, feeling her face heat up. "Although the dance Sydney did for money was pretty cool."

"That always gets the crowd worked up," David said.

It had been really sweet, actually, now that Lexi thought about it.

"Want to dance?" he asked.

She snapped her head up to look at him. "What?"

"You know, dance. With me." David moved closer, his eyes on her. "Since I missed everything."

"Dance . . . now?" Was he serious? And if so, why did he want to dance? "The musicians already packed up. Everyone's gone."

David didn't seem pay attention to her protests. He pulled an iPod out of his pocket and scrolled through some songs. Finding what he wanted, he pressed play. The sound was surprisingly loud—easy enough to hear without speakers. He slipped it back into his pocket. David held out his hand. "What do you say?"

He was serious.

Lexi looked past him into the yard, feeling self-conscious. But no one was outside. Lights spilled from the house, plus the occasional burst of laughter. Lexi took a deep breath and put her hand in his. David slipped one hand around her waist, and with his other hand holding hers, drew it against his chest.

They swayed to the music coming from his pocket, which made Lexi want to laugh. She could have never created this scenario in her mind, ever—dancing to an iPod at the edge of the beach with a guy she'd just met.

"What's so funny?" David asked.

Did I laugh out loud? "I just . . . I've never danced like this before."

"Hmmm," he said quietly. "What do you think about it?"

"It's okay," Lexi said, matching the quietness of his voice. In truth, her heart was about to pound out of her chest. Being this close to David, dancing with him, added a new dimension to her pulse. She probably shouldn't let this go on much longer. It was far safer to go into the house, where there were a lot of people and tons of distractions.

He drew back, his gaze capturing hers. His mouth quirked into a smile. "Only *okay*? You're hard to please."

Lexi shook her head. "Not really." Truth was, she felt out of breath, and being in David's arms made her think crazy thoughts. About kissing . . . He was still watching her.

"Maybe I'm just nervous." What was she saying? She hadn't meant to get personal.

David didn't answer. He released her hand and slipped it around her waist with the other, which meant the only place to put her other hand was on his shoulder. Lexi closed her eyes as they kept dancing and let herself relax in his arms. The music, the tropical scents, David . . . it was like a dream. One she wanted to last a little longer. She slid her hands higher, behind his neck.

His arms tightened around her, and his dancing slowed.

Wow. Lexi's heart beat faster than it had even when she used to dance ballet three hours a night. She wasn't sure where her body ended and his started.

"I'm pretty nervous too," David said.

His words did nothing to slow her heart rate. "You don't seem like a nervous person."

"I'm usually not." David drew away, his hands still at her waist as his gaze met hers.

"What are you nervous about?" Lexi asked, even though the look in his eyes pretty much told her.

"You . . ." He touched her cheek, and his thumb moved slowly along her jaw line.

Lexi couldn't move. His touch seemed to burn through her, but at the same time, goose bumps rose on her arms.

Was he going to kiss her? The thought sent her pulse racing again. She couldn't remember the last time she'd been kissed; it had been that unremarkable. Somehow she sensed a kiss with David would be different.

"I think I have some explaining to do," he said, dropping his hand and releasing her.

Lexi could breathe again, but her heart was in a sorry state. She thought he was going to kiss her.

"Do you want to go for a walk?" he asked, extending his hand.

Lexi looked down at it, and before she could second-guess herself, she slipped hers in his. They walked toward the pulsing surf, where the moonlight made the water gleam silver.

David stopped a few yards from the shore line, then turned to face her. He let go of her hand and shoved his hands in his pockets. If the iPod was still playing, she couldn't hear it above the waves. "I know tomorrow is your last day, but getting to know you has been . . . unexpected."

Lexi agreed, but where was David going with this?

He looked toward the ocean, rubbing the back of his neck. "This is going to sound crazy, but I think you are why I broke up with Angel."

Lexi stared at his profile. "But we just met."

"Yeah," he said, looking over at her. A fire in his eyes made Lexi catch her breath. "We hardly know each other, but I already know you're a hundred times the person Angel is. It's like a light switched on in my head, and I saw what was missing in my relationship with her."

How is that possible? Lexi was flattered if he admired her qualities, but surely it couldn't be deeper than that. "Maybe it's just a coincidence that I'm here when it happened," Lexi said, although it sounded lame even to her as she spoke.

"Maybe," he said, "But I think it's mostly you."

Lexi's heart pinged. "That does sound crazy."

"Not so crazy." His voice was quiet, thoughtful. "I didn't realize I could be so relaxed around a woman and just be myself. With Angel it's always . . ." He shook his head like he was trying to clear away some memory. "In the end, I realized that if I was thinking about kissing you, I should probably break up with Angel."

"You were—" Lexi cut off before she completely embarrassed herself. He'd been thinking about kissing her? And he'd broken up with Angel because of it?

He looked at the ocean again. "But I didn't want to act on anything, because you're leaving, and it wouldn't be fair to you . . . or to me. I mean, we'll probably never see each other again, right?"

She'd had the same thoughts as well, but coming from him, it all sounded pretty gloomy. But she couldn't forget that he wanted to kiss her. What would one kiss hurt? He was single; she was single. She was definitely curious, and maybe smitten, too. And she didn't expect anything—one kiss wouldn't break her heart. Right?

She stepped toward him and touched his arm. He turned, and she placed her hands on his chest. She didn't have time to comprehend that his heart was beating as fast as hers before she rose and pressed her mouth against his.

For a second, he didn't move and at first Lexi thought she might have made a mistake. Maybe he really had determined not to kiss her. That he'd be the honorable gentleman and shake her hand good-bye.

That thought was quickly dispelled when his lips responded, taking control. Lexi had read a couple of romance novels in her lifetime but hadn't seen much point in them—men weren't really *that* considerate, totally hot, *and* great in bed, all wrapped up into one fabulous hero. But kissing David contradicted all of the pessimism she'd ever conjured.

His hands cradled her face, then moved behind her neck as his kiss deepened. If dancing with him had heightened her senses, kissing him made her feel like she'd discovered another sphere on earth. It was definitely not what Lexi had expected. While she hoped being kissed by David would be great, she wasn't expecting a floating-above-the-earth sensation.

Lexi found herself clinging to his shirt and foregoing essential breathing in favor of not breaking off. David's hands moved down her back, stopping at her waist, and he pulled her closer.

She let her body fit with his. Lexi had no idea it could be like . . . this. When she was absolutely forced to breathe, she drew away. David's hold relaxed, but he didn't release her.

"It's okay to kiss me if you want to," she whispered.

"Good," he whispered. Then he brushed her neck with light kisses that made her shiver. "But it's definitely your fault."

"What's my fault?" she asked.

His raised his head, looking at her. "That I broke up with my girlfriend, and that I'm here kissing you now."

"Oh." Warmth traveled through her at his words. "Is that okay with you?"

He smiled. "It's more than okay." He leaned his forehead against hers. "Can I kiss you again?"

"Yes."

Eight

hen Lexi awoke, the sun was well on its way to the middle of the sky, and Apelu's house was absolutely silent. Lexi tugged her pillow to her chest. She hadn't fallen asleep until almost dawn. She'd stayed out with David far too late, and when she crept back into the house, it was after 2:00 a.m. But even though she was exhausted, her mind wouldn't shut off from the exhilaration of being with David. She'd never experienced anything like it.

Suddenly, cheesy phrases like *stars in her eyes* or *head over heels* made some sense. She wasn't the same Lexi that walked off the plane at the Honolulu airport. All because of David.

She bolted upright. David was coming over. He wanted to take her kayaking on her last day in Hawaii. She glanced at the clock on the dresser; she had about twenty minutes before he'd get here. She hurried to get ready, and as she let hot water run over her in the shower, she questioned her sanity.

Maybe last night had been a dream—not that she'd been asleep—but did it all happen as she believed it had? Did David really break up with his girlfriend because of her? As the warm water soaked her body, the memories from last night grew hazier. It all seemed a bit unreal. But the kissing had definitely been real . . . at least for Lexi. How did David feel about it? He probably had no problem getting dates or keeping girlfriends. Sydney had been right—a girl *knew* when she'd met David.

Lexi was ready to go, but David hadn't arrived. He was only about five minutes late, but the thought of him changing his mind, and not showing up, sent her heart into overdrive. She'd almost convinced herself that last night hadn't happened how she remembered it. But now, she wanted to believe it had.

She wandered through the kitchen and picked up a banana then found a note on the refrigerator addressed to her. Apelu's mom had left it, telling her to help herself and that everyone would be at work or school until that afternoon. Apelu's mom would take Lexi to the airport tomorrow morning.

Lexi wrote a note back, leaving her cell number and saying she'd be out with David most of the day.

At least she hoped she would.

As she tacked the note up, she heard a vehicle arriving. She peered out the window, and there was David's jeep. He'd come.

Lexi smiled. It had been real. Last night. All of it.

She opened the front door as he climbed from the jeep. When he saw her, he smiled, and Lexi thought she might melt on the spot. He wore a tank that showed off his arms and Hawaiian-print board shorts.

He came around the jeep as she crossed the yard, and for a second, she didn't know how to greet him. A hug? A kiss? Just climb in the passenger seat? She didn't have to wonder long, because David scooped her up in a hug, lifting her off the ground.

She laughed and wrapped her arms around his neck if only to hang on.

"Glad you were waiting for me," David said, his breath tickling the side of her face.

"What else would I be doing?" Lexi asked as he set her down.

He didn't release her, just gazed at her. "Absolutely nothing else."

She felt the intensity of his brown eyes all the way to her stomach. "I'm glad you came."

"Did you doubt I would?" David asked.

She hesitated.

"Lexi?" he said in a soft voice, touching her chin so their eyes met.

"This is all really new . . ." Her heart thundered at his touch as memories of kissing flooded back.

One side of his mouth lifted. "It is. But I wasn't about to ditch you, okay?"

"Okay," Lexi said.

"Come on," David said, grasping her hand and leading her to the jeep. "The kayaks are waiting."

Lexi climbed in and settled against the warm, cracked leather. What would Sydney think if she could see Lexi with David now?

I told you so . . . Or something similar.

David drove out of the yard. They pulled onto the highway and headed in the opposite direction from the day they'd gone to the waterfalls. Lexi's stomach was in knots, both at being alone with David and from knowing that she was leaving tomorrow.

When David slipped his hand into hers, she wished, not for the first time, that she didn't have to leave so soon. But there was no point going there. Last night, when she'd kissed him first, she'd known that whatever was between them had an expiration date. Not that they couldn't email or text, but as Lexi looked at their intertwined hands, she knew nothing could ever make up for being with David in person.

By the time he pulled off to a beach, Lexi realized she already felt comfortable with him. The thought of saying goodbye tonight made her miss him already.

"This is it," David said, releasing her hand then hopping out of the jeep. They'd stopped by a row of sheds between the road and the beach. "We'll grab a couple of water bottles, and then we'll be set. Did you bring sunscreen?"

"I'm wearing some," Lexi said.

"That should be okay until we get back," he said, turning the combination lock on one of the shed doors. When the lock opened, he tugged the door open. He pulled two kayaks from the shed, laying them side by side.

"Let's find you a life jacket," David said.

Lexi walked over to the shed and tried one on.

David watched her zip it up. "You don't want it too loose."

"It's fine," she said.

"Only wear what you want to get wet."

Lexi had a swimsuit on under her clothes. "Okay, I'll take some stuff off." She walked over to the jeep and unzipped the life jacket. She peeled off her t-shirt and shorts. She'd elected to go with the red- and white-polka dotted suit. She hadn't had a chance to get Sydney's opinion on the ones she'd brought, so Lexi chose the one that fit best.

When David came out of the shed, she was zipping up the life jacket again. "You've probably never seen such a pasty white woman before."

David laughed. "Well, maybe you should stick around a little longer and get some more sun."

Lexi's stomach flipped at the comment. He was walking toward her, and her stomach flipped again. When he stopped in front of her, he said, "Everything fit okay?"

She was sure she'd start blushing within seconds if he didn't stop gazing at her. "Um, yeah."

"Let's get going then." He turned and picked up one of the kayaks, lifting it to his shoulder. "I'll be back for the other one."

He walked toward the surf and set the kayak at the water's edge. Before he could turn around, she moved toward the jeep and folded her clothes on the front seat, to avoid being caught staring at David. It was probably a good thing she was leaving. She could imagine a hundred different ways she might make a fool out of herself today, and one was constantly staring at him.

"Got the water?" David's voice broke through her thoughts.

She must have been daydreaming. "Yeah." She grabbed the bottles where she'd set them on the runner of the jeep.

David had hoisted the second kayak onto his shoulder and waited for her. They walked to the ocean together. "We'll head straight out. The cross current doesn't start for about a hundred yards."

"How do we stay together? With a rope or something?"

"No," he said, amusement in his eyes. "Don't worry; I won't let you stray too far from me."

His words warmed her through, and as she walked into the water, dragging her kayak, she didn't even feel the cold. When they reached about waist-deep water, David helped her into her kayak.

"Just do what I do," he said, climbing into his own kayak.

Lexi paddled out with him, copying his movements. The quiet of the ocean was amazing. The farther they paddled from shore, the more it felt like they were in their own world.

After about fifteen minutes of paddling, David pulled over next to her. "How are you doing?"

She was out of breath but enjoying the exercise. "I wish I had a waterproof camera."

"Do you want to go snorkeling?"

"Can we fit that all into one day?" Lexi asked.

David grasped the side of her kayak and pulled it next to his so they were side by side. "Who says we have to do it all in one day?"

Even though they were both in their kayaks, they were close enough to touch. "I *am* leaving tomorrow," Lexi said. "So it would have to be today."

David leaned closer. "Not if you changed your flight."

She was about to protest when he kissed her. His hand tugged at her life jacket, pulling her toward him, and she kissed him back, the kayaks knocking against each other in the water.

"David," she said between kisses. "You're going to tip me over."

He chuckled but didn't release her. His mouth moved slowly against hers, and she closed her eyes. It was like a dream . . . completely unreal. Floating in the water, kissing this man. San Diego, college, and even Sydney and Apelu seemed far, far away.

After spending the next couple of hours in the kayaks, David declared that he was starving. As they started paddling back to shore, Lexi asked, "Are we going to your restaurant again?"

"No," David said, looking over at her. "I'm too selfish for that."

"What are you talking about?" Lexi asked.

"I brought some food. That way, I get you all to myself."

Lexi tried not to blush, but it was hopeless, especially since David was still watching her.

"Are you okay with that?" he asked.

"Did you bring any chicken?"

"Of course."

"Then I'm okay with it." Lexi met his gaze, and something passed between them—a connection she'd never felt before, like something tugged her toward him, although she couldn't define it.

This can't be happening. I can't be so attached to him.

When they were nearly to shore, David climbed out of his kayak then helped Lexi out of hers. When they got the kayaks safely beached, David took off his life jacket, and Lexi did the same.

David tossed both jackets onto the beach then grabbed her hand. Before she knew it, she was in his arms, and kissing him. The breeze from the ocean flowed around them, but Lexi was plenty warm with her body against David's.

He broke off the kiss first. "Stay," he whispered, gazing at her, his hands cradling her face. "Stay here with me."

She stared into his brown eyes. She didn't want to move, didn't want David to release her, and didn't want to say no. But what other choice did she have? "I can't stay. Classes start in two days."

His hands moved behind her neck, his touch soft. "You can transfer to U of H. Or even BYU-Hawaii. Or take courses online."

Lexi shook her head. "I have a scholarship, and I'm set to graduate in December. I can't cut all that out of my life. My credits probably wouldn't transfer fully anyway."

David lowered his forehead to hers. "You're worrying too much." He brushed his mouth against hers.

Lexi closed her eyes, melting against him and kissing him. Being in David's arms was such an incredible feeling—nothing compared to it. But she knew she had to say good-bye. This wasn't real life. Being with David and living in Hawaii weren't part of the goals she'd set for herself. All things David belonged to this crazy Hawaii trip, and she'd be returning to her real world in the morning.

A rush of waves soaked their feet and ankles, and David

tightened his hold, still kissing her. After he pulled back he said, "Give me one more day. If class doesn't start for two days, you can have one more day here. I'll take you to the U of H, and you can talk to a counselor. Just to see what your options are."

She gazed at him, her heart pounding. Saying good-bye would be painful. And what if her credits *did* transfer? Surely U of H had a good biology program; they were surrounded by some of the greatest plant and ocean life in the world.

She'd check out her options—that was all. Not that she'd be changing her mind.

"Okay," she said, hardly believing herself even as she spoke. "I'll stay one more day."

David threw his head back and whooped then he scooped her up and spun her around.

"Put me down!" Lexi squealed, but David ignored her until she was laughing.

*L*exi clenched her hands in her lap as Mrs. Faga typed furiously on her keyboard. The college admissions counselor had already downloaded Lexi's transcripts and seemed pleased with what she'd seen so far. The question was, which classes would transfer?

Mrs. Faga paused then looked up, adjusting her purple-framed glasses. "Almost everything will transfer. We do have two classes here that can be part of your major that aren't offered at San Diego. Only one is required, and the other is an elective."

Lexi nodded. This was good news, right? But there was the matter of the scholarship . . . She couldn't dismiss the fact that she was a nonresident who'd have to pay a higher tuition.

"And," Mrs. Faga said, peering back at the computer screen. "Your grades are good enough that you can apply for an academic scholarship." Her eyes were back on Lexi. "Although you wouldn't be able to apply until after you transferred and paid summer tuition."

Lexi exhaled. "What do you think my chances would be of getting a scholarship?"

"Very good, but I can't guarantee anything," Mrs. Faga said. "So it will be a bit of a setback if the scholarship isn't granted. But we do offer financial aid, of course."

Lexi moved her hands to her knees and leaned forward. "Do you think I'll fit into the program? This would be a big change for me. Out of all the students you see, what is your personal opinion about my case?"

Mrs. Faga raised a high-arched brow. "You'll do very well here. We have excellent professors and a top-of-the-line research facility, but it's your decision."

"Thanks," Lexi said. "I appreciate all of the information."

Mrs. Faga slid over a piece of paper. "This would be what your schedule would look like if you transfer and want to graduate in December. Summer semester starts Thursday."

The schedule on the printout looked neat and organized in black and white.

"Another thing that might help you decide," Mrs. Faga added, "is that if you apply for our graduate program, you won't have to worry about nonresident tuition."

"Oh," Lexi said, not expecting that kind of news. "That's great." It was wonderful, really. She knew she'd have to go into some debt for college but wanted to keep it to a minimum.

Mrs. Faga handed over another paper. "This is information about student housing. Summer apartments always have openings, and that will give you time to find something for fall."

Another complication to consider. She'd have to find a job to pay rent. Was she really seriously considering this? Changing everything? Just to be close to David? He was waiting outside for her, said he didn't want to influence her decision. Grinning when he said that.

"Well, thanks for all of this," Lexi said. "I'll be back in your office soon if I decide to transfer."

Mrs. Faga smiled and stood. "I can help you with whatever you need."

Lexi rose and shook the woman's hand then gathered the paperwork and slipped it into the U of H folder Mrs. Faga had given her.

Lexi walked out of the building and toward the parking lot, her heart rate speeding up. Her credits would transfer. She had a chance to finish out the year on scholarship. Sure, there were other things to consider, but staying wasn't impossible. In fact . . .

She looked up as she stepped off the curb; David leaned against his jeep, arms folded, waiting.

Their eyes met, and Lexi literally felt hope and expectation coming from David. She realized it was her same hope. Even with all of the adjustments she'd have to make, she *wanted* to make them. She wanted to give David a chance . . . give *them* a chance.

Lexi couldn't help but smile as she crossed the parking lot. She wanted to run but forced herself to walk, even though her heart ran full speed. He straightened as she grew closer, his gaze curious.

She stopped a couple of feet away, unsure how to start.

"What did the counselor say?" David said, watching her closely.

"My credits will transfer, but I lose my scholarship."

His brows pulled together. "No tuition break?"

She shook her head. "Not at first. I can apply for a scholarship after I transfer and could possibly get one for fall."

One side of his mouth rose. "That's good, right?"

Lexi lifted a shoulder. "If I get it."

"And if you don't?"

She took a step closer and slipped her hand in his. "Then it might still be okay."

David's fingers threaded through hers. "Really?"

She nodded, gazing at him.

His eyes searched hers. "You're still considering a transfer even without the scholarship?"

"I'd need a job," she said.

"I'll hire you," he said with a smile.

Lexi laughed. "You'll teach me how to make your famous chicken?"

David slipped a hand around her waist, drawing her close. "Of course."

"And I need a place to live," she said, moving her hands to his shoulders.

His smile broadened, and he looped both of his hands around her waist. "You can stay with me."

"Oh really?" Lexi asked with a smirk. "What would your mother say?"

"Then maybe you can stay at Apelu's parents," David said, leaning down and speaking into her ear. "Or another place *very* close by." Goose bumps broke out on her skin as David's breath tickled her neck and ear.

"How would I get to campus?"

"I'll drive you," he said in a low voice.

Lexi drew back, studying him. "Every day? Don't you think that will get old?"

"Never." David tugged her against him, his mouth finding hers.

Lexi's heart hammered as he kissed her. Was she really staying in Hawaii—changing her life? It was a risk, and it was for a man, but it felt right. In David's arms, the complications didn't seem so complicated. Something told her that things would work out.

David pulled back. "You can take the jeep." His gaze held hers. "It's yours. Everything I have is yours, Lexi. Even my heart."

"Good," Lexi whispered. "Because your heart is all I need."

ABOUT HEATHER B. MOORE

Heather B. Moore is a *USA Today* bestselling author. She has ten historical thrillers written under the pen name H.B. Moore. Her latest is *Finding Sheba*. Under Heather B. Moore she writes romance and women's fiction. She's the co-author of The Newport Ladies Book Club series. Other women's novels include *Heart of the Ocean, The Fortune Café*, the Aliso Creek Series and A Timeless Romance Anthology Series.

Author website: www.hbmoore.com
Blog: http://mywriterslair.blogspot.com
Twitter: @HeatherBMoore
Facebook: *Fans of H.B. Moore* or *Heather Brown Moore*

A Regular Bloke

from Stanmore

Sarah M. Eden

Other Works by Sarah M. Eden

Seeking Persephone

Courting Miss Lancaster

The Kiss of a Stranger

Friends and Foes

An Unlikely Match

Drops of Gold

Glimmer of Hope

As You Are

Longing For Home

Hope Springs

One

There was nothing quite as dangerous as a Brit-obsessed romantic planning a dream wedding. For weeks, Abby Grover had followed her sister, the bride-to-be, from one possible venue to the next.

"It's not *English* enough," Caroline had declared of a ritzy hotel.

"A *British* lake would have different trees," she'd said of an upscale country club.

The day they visited a historic-church-turned-reception-hall, Abby thought they'd found the perfect place. It was old and elegant and antique-y. Caroline had seemed almost convinced. She even spoke at length with the event planner. But on the drive home, she deliberately crossed the reception hall off her list.

"No one there has an English accent," Caroline explained quite firmly.

"This is Oregon."

Unfortunately, logic cannot compete with Anglo-mania. "There *will* be accents at my wedding. I must have accents."

My sister is insane. Completely insane.

And so, for the fifth Saturday in a row, Abby and her sister drove to yet another location too swanky for ordinary people. Caroline, however, was aiming far beyond ordinary.

"Sainsbury House was built in 1880," Caroline told her, scanning the venue's website on her phone. "It has gardens. I need gardens."

Abby could appreciate the need for a garden. She loved plants. *Loved* them. She drove down a narrow lane.

Caroline's voice jumped an octave. "And there's a conservatory."

Apparently conservatories were reason for excitement. Caroline sounded ready to jump out of the car and run the rest of the way.

"You realize," Abby warned her. "No one there will have a British accent."

"This will be perfect. I can feel it."

They pulled into the parking lot. Abby had developed a keen eye for venues. *Plenty of parking. Easy to find.* These were points in Sainsbury House's favor. Or would have been if Abby were the one choosing. Of course, there was absolutely no chance of Abby choosing a wedding venue. She hadn't been in a relationship in a year, and the guy she'd been with then had proven to be such a complete jerk that she had no plans of ever dating anyone again. No, the realm of wedding plans was exclusively Caroline's.

She looked at her sister, wondering what she thought of her first glimpse of the Sainsbury House grounds. Everything would probably depend on how historic and English and fancy the house itself looked, and on how well the staff could pretend to be British.

Abby got out of the car and stepped onto the cobblestone walkway. The sooner they had their tour and Caroline ran down her list of requirements with the event coordinator, the sooner they could be on their way again.

"Five acres of land." Caroline was still inhaling every piece of information she could find online. "Five acres."

"Remind me again why you need five acres for a small, family wedding."

"Because."

"That isn't actually a reason."

Caroline shook her head, sighing dramatically. In her "I'm quoting something very English" voice, she said, "Why must every day involve a fight with an American?"

"*You* are an American."

Caroline waved that off. "It's a thing people say."

Abby eyed her sister more closely. "And these people who say this, they don't happen to be British people in period dramas on public television, do they?"

Caroline looked the tiniest bit guilty.

Abby had to smile. "I don't know how Gregory puts up with you."

Caroline's entire face lit up at the mention of her fiancé. "He loves me."

"Of course he does." For all of Caroline's flittiness and fantasies, she was quite possibly the most lovable person Abby had ever known. It was little wonder their great aunt had named Caroline her only heir. Great Aunt Gertrude hadn't been a millionaire by any means, but Caroline's inheritance was paying for her dream wedding.

"Oh, Abby! Look. It's perfect."

They'd only just emerged from the thick canopy of trees to a rather amazing view of the house. *Historic. Fancy.* Two out of three so far. Abby didn't know what qualified a place as "looking English." She didn't see a Union Jack flying out front or Audrey Hepburn selling flowers or anything. Still, if Caroline thought the place looked perfect, Abby wasn't about to argue.

"Fantastic," Abby said. "Let's go inside."

They stepped inside the open front doors and walked,

slowly, eying their surroundings, to the front of the entry hall. Polished tables flanked the room, with fresh-cut flowers in porcelain vases. Old-style paintings hung in gilded frames. A turning staircase with an intricately carved banister led up and past a wide row of tall windows. Even the ceiling was fancy.

She'd been in upscale places like this. Her last boyfriend was rich, with high-class friends and connections. He felt most comfortable in places where Abby felt too poor to even breathe the air.

"Welcome to Sainsbury House," a man's voice said from just behind them—a man with an English accent.

Caroline squealed. Abby did her best not to roll her eyes and looked back. Mr. English Accent was young—she'd guess not yet thirty, and handsome—the man had green eyes, for heaven's sake, and a ridiculously amazing smile; his teeth stood as a one-mouth testament against the widely-held belief in universal English dental issues.

"Have you come for a tour, or do you have an appointment?" he asked.

"Both." Caroline even bounced a bit as she answered.

They'd found a place that was old and elegant and where at least one person spoke with a British accent. Abby couldn't be entirely certain Caroline wasn't about to explode with excitement. Or faint—she'd been doing the whole *back of the hand pressed daintily to the forehead* thing a lot lately.

"You must be Caroline and Abby Grover."

Abby leaned closer to her sister and spoke under her breath. "You gave them my name? This is your tour."

"Don't you love the way he said 'Caroline'?" her sister whispered back. "So elegant."

The Englishman watched them with admirable patience.

"We are the Grover sisters," Abby told him. "That sounds like a lame band, doesn't it?"

"The name is lovely, I assure you."

"I assure you?" Who talks like that?

He looked between them. "Which of you is Caroline, the bride to be?"

Abby didn't wait a single instant. She pointed across herself at her sister. Mr. Elegant's green eyes lingered on Abby. He smiled the tiniest bit, before his gaze moved to Caroline.

"Congratulations, Ms. Grover," he said. "If you will follow me this way, we shall take a moment in my office to discuss your needs and wishes for your wedding before going about the estate to see if Sainsbury House can meet those needs."

Smooth, Brit Boy. Smooth.

Caroline followed almost glassy-eyed. If only the guy realized he'd likely sold her on the location simply by opening his mouth. Caroline would have her English-accented wedding, and Mr. Green-Eyed-Hunk-of-Britishness would get whatever commission came with booking the event.

"My name is Matthew Carlton, by the way," he said to Caroline.

"Matthew?" She sounded ridiculously happy about that. Apparently Matthew was a good name for her fantasy wedding.

Matthew wasn't the least bit weirded out by that. He just nodded and held open a door. Abby stepped through behind Caroline. The office wasn't huge, but it wasn't tiny, either. It was almost as nauseatingly elegant as the entry. They sat in two leather armchairs facing the desk, where Matthew sat.

"Tell me, Ms. Grover, what would make your wedding day perfect?" The man was feeding an addiction.

Abby watched as he nodded in agreement with Caroline's crazy ideas. He didn't even seem surprised when she mentioned the hope of convincing Grandma Grover to wear a bustle. When Caroline spoke of polished silverware, spotless crystal, starched white aprons on appropriately silent maids, Matthew simply said, "Of course."

Of course? No one Abby had ever known would think these kinds of demands were normal or expected or *not insane.*

Matthew took notes, listening closely and asking questions. He was handsome, too good looking, actually, for Abby to stop herself from looking at him again and again. He seemed nice enough, in a snobby sort of way.

For Caroline's sake, and the sake of Abby's future weekends, she sincerely hoped Sainsbury House worked out for the wedding. But for her part, Abby definitely had enough of all the haughtiness and fake fanciness.

The Grovers weren't that kind of people. They were simple, down-to-earth, hovering somewhere near the bottom end of the middle of the middle class. People like Matthew Carlton would never understand that.

Two

att grabbed a cold bottle of beer from the fridge before stepping through the glass doors onto the balcony of his flat. His neighbor was out, watering the impressive herb garden he'd cultivated on his own balcony. Barney had a green thumb, a talent he'd carefully cultivated over his seventy-some-odd years of life.

"Good evening, Barney," he said as he sat in his Adirondack chair. "Your garden is coming along nicely."

Barney's wrinkles clearly showed he'd spent his life happy. "You always speak so proper. Makes me feel like I should be bowing or something."

"You forget, I'm an American citizen now." He raised his bottle as if making a toast. "No more bowing for this bloke."

"Americans don't say 'bloke,'" Barney warned him.

Matt leaned back, settling in for a relaxing evening in the cool summer air. "I thought American citizens had the right to say anything they wanted—that bit was on the test, you know."

Barney pointed at him with his gardening clippers. "You can say anything at all, but you might get beat up for it."

Matt nodded. "We do that in England, as well."

He enjoyed their chats. Barney had been the one to start them not long after Matt moved in. They spent quite a few evenings each week talking across the small space that separated their balconies. He was grateful for the friendship.

"How was your day?" Barney asked, snipping expertly at one of his plants.

"Not bad at all. I booked a wedding for late June."

Barney nodded slowly, his eyes not straying from his task. "A June wedding."

"I know it's very cliché, but I have my suspicions that this particular bride is very . . . particular."

Matt had learned a thing or two about dealing with dreamers and bridezillas and the occasional lunatic. He was certain Caroline Grover fell in the dreamer category. She knew exactly what she wanted on her wedding day, and she was nearly panicked at the thought that something might go wrong or deviate from her imaginings. He'd worked with that before.

"She had a sister, though, who was . . ." He couldn't quite put a word to Abby Grover. She'd clearly been annoyed. She'd also sent her sister more than a few looks of exasperated affection. Abby had managed to toss more than a few zingers during their interview and subsequent tour. "She was *intriguing.*"

"Was she?" Barney was either laughing at him or . . . No. He was definitely laughing.

Matt grinned back. "Not that anything will come of it. She made her dislike of me very clear. I don't know what, exactly, I did to put her off me so immediately."

"Were you wearing that monkey suit of yours?"

Matt chuckled. He knew exactly what Barney was

316

getting at. "I have to wear a suit and tie to work—it's my uniform. Besides, I don't think I look so terrible in a suit."

Barney snipped a rosemary plant. "Not terrible, but it does make you look like a yuppie."

"A yuppie? Is that an American thing?"

"It means square. You look square."

"Square?" Matt hadn't heard of that one, either.

"Stuffy," Barney tried again.

"Ah." That was a word he understood. "People will think I'm trying to be posh."

Barney took a long drink of water from the bottle he always kept nearby while he gardened, all the while giving him a look of confusion.

"When I came to the States, I didn't expect a language barrier." Adjusting to the odd quirks of the American culture had been harder than he'd expected. Still, he wouldn't want it any other way. One of things he liked most about living in America was how diverse the place was, how different people could be one to the next.

"Tell me more about this intriguing woman," Barney said. He turned a bit toward Matt, shifting around on the short stool he always sat on while tending his plants.

It was nice of the old man to humor him, but Matt had no intention of boring him to death. "You don't really want to hear about some random person I met."

Barney let his gloved hands rest against his legs. His expression turned thoughtful. "My wife was . . . *intriguing.*" His smile softened and spread. "Always kept me wondering. I loved that about her." Barney looked across at Matt. "So, yes, I want to hear about this random, *intriguing* woman you met."

Matt often got the impression that Barney was lonely. He could indulge him in this. "Her name is Abby. She's pretty, but not in a movie-star or super-model way."

"A natural beauty," Barney suggested.

"Exactly." He'd especially liked the hint of freckles across her nose. "And I could tell she was annoyed by the entire wedding planning thing, but she put up with it, not poking fun at her sister for her ridiculous demands."

Barney raised a bushy white eyebrow. "More ridiculous than some of the demands you've told me about?"

There had been some crazy brides and mothers- and fathers-of-the-bride over the five years Matt had worked at Sainsbury House. It was always a juggling act to keep them happy while trying to reacquaint them with reality.

"This bride wants a historic British wedding fresh out of a television drama." She hadn't said as much outright, but Matt had quickly gotten the gist.

"I bet she just ate you up then." Barney chuckled deep in his chest.

Matt grinned. He'd seen her glee when she realized she'd found someone in Oregon with an English accent. Caroline Grover had thrown in more cliché British words and phrases than Matt had heard on his last trip back to London.

"Abby was patient with her sister, which was admirable. But she made some of the funniest comments under her breath."

"So she has a sense of humor." Barney nodded his approval.

"And she asked all of the questions her sister should have been asking but was too high in the clouds to think of."

"So she's smart on top of it all." Barney gave him a wizened look. "This one *is* intriguing."

"I confess, I'm hoping she handles more of the arrangements than her sister does."

Barney set his gardening sheers aside and leaned his arms along the balcony railing, facing Matt. "You plan to see her again?"

"If she comes by."

Barney was obviously unimpressed. "When a woman like that walks into your life, Matt, you don't casually let her walk back out."

"I don't have her contact information."

Barney wasn't discouraged by that at all. "You have the sister's information."

"It doesn't work that way. I don't call up clients to ask out their family members."

"Bah." Barney stood up from his stool, waving off Matt's words like a pesky fly. "Youth is wasted on the young."

"Have a nice night, Barney," Matt said as the old man tottered back toward his glass door.

"Call the woman," Barney shot back before disappearing inside.

Matt thought about that as he sat watching the sunset color the sky. Abby Grover wouldn't entirely leave his thoughts. He wanted to see her again, if nothing else to discover if she hated him as much as she'd seemed to. And why. And whether he could do anything to change that.

Intriguing didn't even begin to describe her.

Three

"*I* don't understand why *I* have to do this." Abby held her phone to her ear with one hand and tried to flip through Caroline's three pages of instructions with the other. She'd made the drive out to Sainsbury House with a very detailed list of assignments. Within a few seconds of arriving, Caroline had called to add a couple of things.

"Because I have a fitting today!" Caroline's frantic tone was clear even with the noise of the city echoing through the phone.

Abby could think of a hundred things she'd rather be doing than spending another Saturday at Sainsbury House. "Why not Mom?"

"She's coming to the fitting with me. Come on, Abby. You're maid of honor—you're supposed to help with this stuff."

There should be a law against sisters being maids of honor.

"You're right." What else could she say? "I'll let you know how it goes."

"Thanks. You're the best."

"Yes, I am." She hit the end button and tucked her phone in her pocket. "Yes, I am."

She stopped at the bottom of the stairs leading up to Sainsbury House's wraparound porch. Wedding planning, especially in a place as high-and-mighty as Sainsbury House, wasn't her kind of thing. She'd dragged herself away from her garden that morning to run this errand. She probably still had dirt under her fingernails.

Dirty fingernails and fancy houses don't go together. She knew that well. Dirk the Jerk—her family had given him that name even before Abby realized the kind of guy he was—had lectured her on that so many times.

"At least pretend like you belong here." That had been one of his favorite lines.

Abby stepped inside the entryway. The place was as overwhelmingly fancy as it had been a week earlier. It made a person feel judged, like the paintings and crown molding and polished tables were there solely to remind her that she fit better in a tiny apartment in a solidly middle-class neighborhood than in a mansion.

"May I help you?" A woman Abby thought she'd seen in passing the last Saturday greeted her near the winding staircase. As near as she'd been able to discover, Matthew was the only person at Sainsbury House who spoke with an accent.

"I am looking for Matthew Carlton." She was proud of herself for not calling him Brit Boy or Mr. Elegant or any of the other names she'd been using in her mind the past week.

"He is through here in his office." The woman motioned toward the same room they'd been shown to before.

"If I'm interrupting, I can wait." She wanted to wait. For

reasons she refused to think about, she was nervous. Matthew Carlton had shown up a few too many times in her wandering thoughts recently.

The woman peeked past the office door then looked back at Abby. "No one is in the office but Matthew. You are quite welcome to go on inside."

Perfect. She threw back her shoulders. No snooty Englishman was going to intimidate her. She might not fit in with her worn-out jeans and casual top. The dirt under her fingernails and her complete lack of jewelry probably pegged her as someone not cut out to be a client at Sainsbury House. But she didn't care. Not at all.

Abby stepped into the office. Matthew looked up from his laptop.

He smiled at her. That smile was part of the reason he'd shown up in her thoughts so often. She couldn't be blamed for thinking about it, or for her heart fluttering around at seeing it again.

"Ms. Grover." He stood and came around his desk, indicating the leather armchair nearest his desk. Once she sat, he moved back to the chair he'd occupied before. "What brings you to Sainsbury House?"

"My sister." *Might as well get right to the point.*

His mouth pulled in a thought-filled line. "She did not mention that you would be stopping in."

"Has Caroline been in touch with you?"

That smile returned again. "She emailed me six times yesterday."

"That's Caroline."

"She seems very . . . particular." His green eyes sparkled with amusement.

Abby did her fair share of laughing at her sister, but she didn't like anyone else to. "It's her wedding day," Abby said in Caroline's defense. "She's entitled to be picky about a few things."

"Of course." He gave a short nod. He threaded his fingers through one another. "What may I do for you?"

"What may I do for you?" No one talks like that. If he kept it up, she wouldn't be able to understand him at all. Sainsbury House, apparently, was the place to go if a person wanted to feel poor *and* stupid.

"Caroline sent me to ask about a few things."

"I do not have any appointments for a couple of hours, so we can certainly address those items now." Matthew Carlton could probably sell the stripes off a skunk with those soft eyes and that heart-melting smile. "What is first on your list?"

Yes. Stick to business. Abby laid her papers on the edge of the desk, smoothing them out. "She wants to know if the fountain in the formal garden will be running the day of her wedding."

Matthew nodded. "It is only ever turned off in the winter."

Abby snagged a pen from the pencil cup on his desk and wrote "yes" next to the first item. "Does the conservatory have a sign that says 'Conservatory?'"

"Do you mean like a placard?" The question clearly confused him. She could appreciate that—it was a strange question.

"I think so. She probably wants to make sure the guests know that there is a conservatory at her wedding. She likes the word."

Matthew leaned back in his chair, brows drawn. "I honestly cannot remember whether there is a sign or not. Are there any other details we need to go look at? We can check for the placard while walking around the house and grounds."

Abby scanned her list. "I'm supposed to find out which flowers grow closest to where she'll be standing for the ceremony. Also, which side of the guest chairs will be in the most shade. And she wants to know if the floor in the ballroom is cherry, oak, or pine."

"It is oak but stained cherry."

Abby wrote that down, impressed despite herself that he knew the answer off the top of his head.

She read Caroline's next question word for word. "'Are the walls in the ballroom aqua or moss?'"

"I honestly have not the slightest idea."

Abby put a star by that, as she had next to the conservatory, flower, and shade questions. "Does your in-house caterer make tarts?"

"Tell her the catering options are all on our website. Special requests go through the head of catering, but there is a request form on—"

"The website," Abby finished for him. "That's not very antique-y of you. Shouldn't you be giving that information by telegram or something?"

His smile spread to a grin. A smile like that was a dangerous thing. "We *do* cater to those looking for a traditional event."

"If by *traditional* you mean *old and fancy,* I agree."

His expression clearly showed he thought she was offering a compliment. If she'd said *snotty* instead of *fancy* like she'd meant to at first, he probably wouldn't have been as happy about it.

They went through a few more questions. After fifteen minutes, everything left on the list required a walk around the house and grounds. Matthew took a long coat from the coat rack inside the door of his office, along with an old-fashioned umbrella with a cane-style handle. That brought Abby's eyes to the windows. While they were talking, a steady drizzle had begun.

He held his office door open for her. Dirk had done that when they were out in public. At first she'd liked it, until it became clear he only held the door because not doing it would look uncivilized. She stepped into the entryway, zipping up her jacket as they walked toward the doors. She tugged the drawstrings on her hood so it pulled tight around her head.

One step short of being beyond the roof of the porch, Matthew popped open the umbrella and held it over both of their heads. He seemed to be making sure it covered her, even if it meant getting a bit wet himself.

It wasn't even a hard rain, just enough to be annoying. She didn't know how to respond to a guy opening doors, or pulling out her chair, or holding an umbrella for her. "You don't have to do that."

"Actually, I do. It is in the employee handbook."

She looked up at him. "Seriously?"

He nodded, completely sincere. "I know you think your sister is very particular about things, but I promise you, she has nothing on the owners of this place."

Matthew suddenly seemed relatable, almost like a normal person. Abby couldn't quite put her finger on what had changed, but something definitely had. "What other rules do you have to follow?"

He looked over his shoulder back toward the house before resuming their walk, leaning in enough to talk to her under the umbrella. "We are supposed to avoid contractions whenever possible."

"Like *won't* and *didn't* and that kind of thing?"

"Exactly. Using the full two words is supposed to sound more sophisticated, though I fully intend to contract words as soon as we are out of earshot of the house."

"You aren't afraid you'll get into trouble?" Abby asked.

He gave her a winning smile. "I think you can be trusted to keep my secret."

He led her around a puddle with the slightest pressure of his hand on her back. Another gentlemanly gesture she thought only existed in movies.

"What other requirements do your bosses have for you?"

"I am to, and I quote, 'milk my accent for all it's worth.'" He shot her a look of amusement that brought a smile to her face. "If I ever lost my accent, I'd probably lose this job."

"Are you in danger of losing your accent?" It seemed pretty firmly in place.

"Last time I visited London, my family all told me I sounded like an American."

She actually laughed at that. "They don't talk with many Americans, do they?"

"Clearly not."

They turned up the cobblestone path that led to the spot where outdoor ceremonies were held. Matthew had told her and Caroline about the elegant canopy they set up when the weather was questionable. It wasn't set up today.

"So your sister is very much a fan of traditional, old-fashioned things," Matthew said. "That description doesn't seem to fit you. What would you choose if this were your event?"

"Are you trying to convince me to buy a wedding package? That'll be a tough sell; I don't even have a boyfriend."

"Really?"

She swore he actually took note of that. Was he flirting with her? If so, he wasn't doing a very good job of it. Maybe Brits were terrible flirters.

"No sales pitch, I promise." He tucked the hand not holding the umbrella into his coat pocket. "I'm just curious to know if my hunch is correct."

"What hunch?"

"Sainsbury House is a good fit for your sister, but I have a feeling it would be torture for you."

She felt her defenses going up. He really didn't think she belonged in an upscale place.

"And what *would* be a good fit for me?" She could hear that her tone had turned cold but couldn't help it.

He wasn't fazed at all. "If you were the one planning a wedding, I'd guess you would choose something smaller and simpler—a beach or a garden. And there'd only be a few people, those you care about most, not every person you've ever met."

She had to admit, *silently*, that he was right about that. He was so right that she didn't know if his insightfulness was impressive or a little spooky.

"Okay, Nostradamus, what would my wedding colors be?"

He eyed her closely. His gaze narrowed. She almost laughed at the comical "thinking" face he made. *Almost.* "You wouldn't have colors. You'd tell your bridesmaids to wear whatever they wanted. And you wouldn't wear a traditional wedding dress, just whatever you felt like."

She let her surprise show. "That's creepy."

He flashed her a flawless smile. "I came pretty close, then?"

They'd reached the spot where the bride and groom and minister would stand during a wedding. Abby eyed the trellis and nearby bushes. Did Caroline expect her to list every flower nearby, or only the closest ones?

"Daffodils," Matthew said. "Tiger lily. And, I believe those are Dolly Madison lilies."

Once again she was staring at him. "You know the names of these flowers?" He'd gotten every single one correct so far.

He shrugged a little. "My mum has an extensive flower garden. I probably know more about flowers than almost any person in Oregon."

Probably not more than I do. She wrote down the flowers he'd mentioned. "Do you think I can get away with just saying 'roses' for the rest?"

"I wouldn't bet on it. Your sister is very detail-oriented."

"Tell me about it." She bent over the darkest red roses growing there, taking a deep breath. The amazing scent answered her question. "These are probably Mr. Lincoln roses."

"They are. You know a few things about flowers, yourself."

She took another deep breath of the rose's perfume. *Beautiful.*

Between them, they managed to identify nearly every variety of rose growing around the ceremony area. They likely didn't need to be that extensive, but Abby was enjoying it. Her family's eyes always glazed over when she talked about gardening and flowers. Dirk had told her a few times to "shut up about the plants." While she could tell flowers wouldn't have been Matthew's first choice of topics, he was knowledgeable and didn't seem to mind. It was a nice change.

They timed the walk from the parking lot to the front porch, just as Caroline had requested. They decided that the ballroom walls were closer to aqua than moss, though Abby thought there was at least a little mint in them. The conservatory, they discovered, *did* have a placard.

The longer Abby was with him, the more Abby liked Matthew. He had a dry sense of humor and wasn't nearly as stuffy as she'd thought at first. She wasn't ready to start throwing herself at him or anything like that. But she liked him.

She liked him quite a lot, actually.

Four

"She can identify roses just by scent, Mum." Matt pulled his jacket on while talking on the phone. After a long morning of making arrangements, calming frantic brides, and telling himself the summer rush would be over in only a few more months, he was almost desperate to get away from his desk, if only for the length of a lunch break.

"I very much doubt she only used the scent, Matt. She likely looked at petal patterns and stem anatomy and any number of other things." Mum knew her flowers; no one would argue that. "But the fact that she could identify them at all is impressive. I like this one."

"Because she knows roses?"

Mum laughed. "No. Because you've mentioned her three times in this one call. If she's interesting enough to grab your attention, I will happily cheer her on."

He stepped onto the front porch, grateful for the breeze and fresh air. His office could feel claustrophobic sometimes. "I hate to tell you this, but she doesn't care for me much. Her obvious dislike didn't improve much beyond begrudging tolerance when I last saw her."

"How could she not like you?" Mum always was rather blinded by her loyalty. She never believed anyone could possibly feel anything other than adoration for her children.

"Barney says she probably thinks I'm too posh." He followed the path leading away from the house. He enjoyed taking a slow stroll around the grounds during the day.

"*Posh?* Where does she think you come from, Chelsea?"

His family couldn't afford to *look* at the houses in Chelsea, let alone live there.

"You just tell her you're a regular bloke from Stanmore," Mum instructed.

"I could tell her that exactly, but it wouldn't mean anything to her. She doesn't know anything about London."

"Then you'll have to show her."

He pushed out a breath. "I tried when she was here last, but I could tell I wasn't making a very good impression."

The scent of pine hung on the cool breeze. Matt could feel some of his stress slipping away. There was nothing like fresh air and the outdoors to clear his mind.

"Have you called her?" Mum asked. "Maybe if you took her out for coffee or something, she might get to see the real you. Somewhere away from work."

"I don't have her number."

"So call the sister, the one getting married."

Mum and Barney were both crazy. "I can't call a client asking for personal information about her family members."

"Why on earth not?"

"For one thing, it's unprofessional."

"Then I'll have to start wishing on my star again."

He stopped in his tracks. "Don't do that, Mum."

She had a metal star hanging in her kitchen that, ever since he was a child, she'd made wishes on any time her kids needs to be guilted into doing something.

"Star on my Wall—" Her typical beginning to any wish. "—find Matt a way to talk to this girl who knows a lot about roses but who thinks he's posh. Matt needs a second chance."

"Mum."

"Star on my Wall, convince Matt that he can call this girl and still be a stuffy professional like he thinks he needs to be."

He held back a laugh. "Are you done?"

"For now."

His mother had always been enjoyably nutty. "I miss you, Mum."

"I'd tell you to move back home, then, but since you've gone and made yourself an official American, I don't suppose that's going to happen."

"You should move here." He knew what her answer would be; they'd had this conversation before.

"Maybe if you don't get your act together and find yourself a nice girl, I'll do that and find one for you myself."

That was a threat if he'd ever heard one. "No need. I'm certain I'll—"

The words died. His feet froze. Larry, the Sainsbury House gardener, was talking to someone by the rose garden. It was a young woman in a ratty pair of jeans, and a button-down flannel work shirt, with hair a familiar shade of light brown.

"Matt?" Mum's voice hardly registered.

He was certain that Abby was talking to Larry. But why was she there?

"Matt?" Mum asked again.

"I . . . uh, I gotta go."

"Is everything all right?"

He began walking toward the roses. He lowered his voice. "She's here."

"Abby. The girl I've been telling you about. She's here at my work."

"The star does it again! Go talk to her, dear. Quickly. But call me tomorrow and tell me all about it."

"Sure. Bye, Mum."

He walked toward Abby and Larry with no idea what he meant to say. Larry spotted him before he had time to figure it out.

"Hey, Matt." Larry was the only person at Sainsbury House who didn't call him Matthew.

He nodded a greeting, but turned almost immediately to Abby. "Hi. What brings you around?"

She blushed a little. Was she embarrassed or happy to see him? He hoped happy. He really hoped. "I've come to save your roses."

"Save the roses?"

Larry nodded. "She noticed when she was here that we have black rot in a few of the bushes. She brought a special formula to treat it."

Her cheeks were still red, and she didn't quite meet Matt's eyes. What did that mean? A good sign? Bad?

"Abby works at the Northwinds Nursery," Larry added.

That explained a few things. He was surprised she'd made the drive out just to tend a few rose bushes. Sainsbury House wasn't really near *anything*. "You cannot stand to see an innocent plant suffer, is that it?"

Her blush deepened, but her shoulders straightened. "I only thought your gardener would appreciate knowing what we did to save our bushes from this awhile back. Black rot can be stubborn."

Though he couldn't be entirely sure, Matt suspected he'd offended her somehow. Maybe this was simply more of her assumption that he was arrogant.

Let her see for herself. Mum's advice echoed in his mind. He could do that.

"What's the formula?" he asked.

Larry explained it, but in terms Matt wasn't entirely familiar with. He tried to follow but didn't do a very good job. When the chemicals and explanations wrapped up, he simply threw out an, "Ah," and left it at that. "Does it work?"

"Of course it does," Abby insisted. "I wouldn't have driven all this way for something that wouldn't help."

He'd rubbed her wrong again. It was Sainsbury House that did it. He had to act . . . well, for lack of a better word, *posh* while he was there. Even when he tried to be himself, he couldn't do it entirely.

"I was about to go get some lunch." *Invite her to go.* His stomach twisted a little with nervousness. "Would you like to join me?"

She was clearly surprised.

Say yes. Say yes.

"We're going to look at a few more plants," she said after a moment's pause. "So I'm going to be kind of busy."

"Sure." He tried to shrug it off, but the rejection stung. He couldn't remember the last time he'd really wanted to impress a girl. He had no idea how Abby Grover had reached that point so quickly, and after talking to her only twice. But she had. And he was blowing it. "If you two are going to be working through lunch, maybe I could pick you up something and bring it back."

Larry took him up on it right away. "Are you going by the sandwich place on third?"

"Sure."

"I'll take a club with everything and a Coke."

Matt looked to Abby, hoping she would take him up on the offer. He could convince himself she had reasons to decline his offer—it was too inconvenient or something—but to not even let him bring her back lunch was harder to explain away. Maybe he would have to admit to himself she wasn't interested.

"BLT, no mayo," Abby said.

So she hadn't brushed him off. For a minute, he was too

surprised to even say anything. He pulled himself together. "Anything to drink?"

"No. I brought some water with me."

With an eagerness he couldn't entirely explain, Matt made for his car. He repeated the order in his mind again and again, not wanting to get it wrong. When he got back, he meant to sit by the two of them while they did their gardening, even if nothing they said made any sense. He wanted to be there by her, to try to figure out if she disliked him as much as he was afraid she did.

"You're completely lost on her," he muttered as he pulled out onto the small road leading away from Sainsbury House. He felt like a fool. He hardly knew Abby Grover, and he was already making a fool of himself over her.

Fool or not, he was back in record time with three sandwiches and a Coke. Larry and Abby were still at the roses, but kneeling by the bushes, pruning.

"Ready for a break?" he asked, holding up the bag.

They both agreed, slipping off to a nearby spigot to wash their hands. Matt sat on a bench. Would Abby sit by him or take her sandwich somewhere else and avoid him entirely? Maybe he should try telling her he was just "a regular bloke from Stanmore." It couldn't hurt, right?

He gave Larry his club sandwich. Larry handed him some money.

"Yours wasn't this much." Matt started to give some of it back, but Larry shook his head.

"That's for mine and Abby's. I talked her into letting me pay for her lunch, since she won't let me pay her for the work she's doing."

If Larry hadn't been old enough to be Abby's father, Matt might have been jealous.

She came over. He held out her BLT, fully expecting her to take it and walk away. She sat on the bench beside him. That was promising.

He tried to act casual, eating his sandwich like he couldn't care less that the woman he'd been thinking about almost constantly for a week and a half was willingly sitting next to him. If she knew, she'd think he was a complete idiot.

Abby and Larry talked about plant fungi and insect treatments. Matt listened but had nothing to add. He'd reached the end of his lunch break but hadn't said more than a few words to Abby. He was supposed to call Mum and tell her how things went. "I watched her eat a sandwich, and I looked stupid while she talked about flowers."

Mum is going to laugh at me.

And she did. A lot.

For his part, Matt didn't think it was very funny.

Five

"Matthew asked about you."

Abby examined the apples laid out at the produce stand, pretending her sister's comment hadn't made her breath catch. "Matthew Carlton?" she asked as though it didn't matter.

"Of course. Who else?"

"I do know more than one person named Matthew." Actually, she wasn't sure she did. "What did he have to say?"

"Only that you helped with a fungus or something in the roses and that he thought it was nice of you."

She felt a stab of disappointment. He hadn't really asked about her, then. He'd simply mentioned her.

Abby and Caroline moved to the next booth at the farmer's market.

"The bushes had a little black rot," Abby explained. She bought a small bushel of blackberries from the farmer running the booth.

"Black rot?" Caroline sounded absolutely horrified. "That will be gone before the wedding, won't it?"

"The roses will be gorgeous. I promise."

They walked along. Abby usually enjoyed the Sunday farmers' markets, but Caroline was killing the joy.

"And the flowers for the bouquets—"

Abby jumped in before Caroline could ask the question she'd posed a thousand times in the months since Gregory proposed. "Emily is reliable and talented. You saw her work. I promise you, the bouquets will be amazing."

"How was your last fitting?" Caroline asked.

Abby moaned. "The dress fits fine; it just looks ridiculous."

"It's a perfect reproduction of World War I-era dress. It's perfect."

Perfect was not the word Abby would have used. She would much rather spend her days dressed like she was then, in a comfy t-shirt and running shorts, wearing her worn-out running shoes. "That dress makes me look like a history nerd getting ready for Halloween."

Caroline threaded her arm through Abby's. "It'll be beautiful."

Abby shook her head at her sister's romanticism. "Gregory must *really* like you."

Caroline's eyes turned dreamy. "He does."

"Speaking of which." Abby motioned ahead with her chin. "There he is. It must be noon."

"Isn't he the cutest?" Caroline squealed a little.

"Go ahead. I'm going to walk around the market for a while."

Caroline didn't need more encouragement; she was off like a bolt of lightning. Abby watched her go with every bit as much amusement as envy. Though she'd never been the hopeless romantic her sister was, she did sometimes catch herself daydreaming about finding someone she could be that perfect with and for.

Those daydreams eventually came to an abrupt end.

Dirk the Jerk saw to that. He'd appeared in her life like a hero in a cliché romance novel. He was the wealthy, suave, dreamy hero who somehow decided to be interested in the plain, poor, awkward heroine. Except he turned out to be a complete jerk. She'd been blind about it for a while, but she'd finally realized how he saw her, never quite good enough.

That was a year ago. Quit thinking about it.

She sat on a bench overlooking the sprawling green fields of the park where the farmer's market was held. The blackberries she'd bought worked well as comfort food. By the time she'd finished off half of the little basket of berries, Dirk the Jerk had almost completely left her thoughts. The park was peaceful, one of the things she liked most about coming to the markets. Children played on a nearby playground. People jogged the running paths. A disorganized soccer match covered a field to the left. To the right, people tossed balls back and forth.

It was the greenery, though, that kept her attention. She loved plants. Loved them. The city had done a good job keeping things trimmed back and healthy at the park, but it could do with a few more flowering shrubs.

"Heads up!"

Abby processed the shouted warning just in time to duck out of the way of a flying soccer ball.

One of the soccer guys came hustling over. "Sorry 'bout that."

She shrugged. "No problem." She popped another blackberry in her mouth.

"Abby Grover?" a second male voice asked.

She froze, the berry half-chewed in her mouth. She only knew one person with an English accent. Sure enough, Matthew Carlton was coming in her direction.

Abby swallowed a little too fast and choked a second on the berry. A quick swig from her water bottle had her almost composed by the time he reached the bench.

"Playing a little soccer?" she managed to ask.

He gave her a half smile. "I am playing *football*. The rest of these clowns are playing soccer."

His friend, who had retrieved the ball, laughed and slapped him on the shoulder as he passed. "Whatever you call it, we're still wiping the grass with you."

Matthew stayed by the bench even after his friend rejoined the game. "Did you come for the market?"

Abby nodded. "Never miss it. Caroline was with me."

At the look that flitted quickly across his face, she laughed out loud. Apparently Caroline hadn't calmed down about the wedding arrangements over the couple weeks that had passed since selecting Sainsbury House.

"Don't worry," Abby reassured him. "The future Mr. Caroline has taken her to lunch. She won't stress out on you today."

He chuckled. "I wouldn't bet on that. I'll probably have a half-dozen emails from her waiting for me when I get in to work tomorrow."

"It's good of you to put up with her."

He wiped a trickle of sweat from his forehead. "She's actually not that bad compared to some brides I've had to work with."

"Wow. I almost feel bad for you."

Matthew grinned at that. "*Almost?*"

"Hey, Matt!" someone called from the soccer game. "Either quit flirting over there or bring her over here to play."

Matthew looked a little embarrassed. There was something very odd about a sophisticated, high-class, Englishman turning even the tiniest bit red. Dirk was never embarrassed by anything. Angry, sometimes, but not ever embarrassed.

"Do you play football?" Matthew asked.

"Football? No." Abby shook her head. "But I did play *soccer* in high school."

"Really?" Matthew looked impressed. Dirk had been a field-hockey kind of guy. They'd never talked about *her* sports.

"We took state my senior year."

"I don't know what that means," Matt said. "But it sounds impressive."

Abby made her best superior face. "It means we were *good*. And I played in the city league after that. Champions three years running."

He motioned with his head toward the game. "Would you like to come play? Show these chumps how it's done?"

Her first thought was to turn him down. But why should she? She still liked to play. His friends had invited her first. He was being nice—not the arrogant, stuffy guy from Sainsbury House.

"Sure. Why not?"

He walked with her back toward his friends. He walked *with* her. Dirk would have set his own pace and expected her to match it.

"Hey, boys!" Matthew called out. "We've one more."

She was welcomed heartily. Any concerns she might have had about butting in were quickly put to rest. She was immediately part of the game, treated like one of the guys, though they weren't nearly as rough with her as they were with each other. It was great to play again. She'd stopped while Dirk was in her life, and, though she couldn't say why, hadn't taken it back up again.

Matthew, she discovered, could smack talk with the best of them. And he was funny. Hilarious. She'd seen hints of that during their walk around Sainsbury House the day she'd gone there on Caroline's orders. But during their lunch among the roses a few days later, he'd been quiet and distant.

She'd assumed he didn't want to be there, or he wasn't enjoying her company.

The two of them, who had ended up on the same team, both as forward, trounced the other team. The game wasn't anything official, just a bunch of people trying to score against a bunch of other people, with little regard for rules.

The players began trickling off as the afternoon wore on. The game finally broke up, with the others declaring that Matthew had brought in a secret weapon, that he'd been planning to bring her in all along.

Abby couldn't remember the last time she'd grinned so wide.

"We're *good*," Matthew declared, smiling at her.

"*We're*? I didn't think you were allowed to use contractions."

He laughed lightly. "Away from work, I can use them all I want." Matthew dribbled his soccer ball as they walked away from the field. "Speaking of work, thanks again for helping Larry with the roses. He was having trouble clearing up the fungus you two were working on."

She knew how persistent black rot could be. "No problem."

Matthew opened his mouth like he meant to say something, but then stopped.

"What?"

He slowed their pace. "I have a neighbor, an older gentleman, who is an avid gardener. He has an acre's worth of plants on his tiny little balcony."

Abby could easily picture it.

"He has been particularly distraught lately about spots on his tomato plants."

"On the tomatoes or the leaves?"

"I'm not sure." He shrugged. "Do you think . . . would you be willing to take a look? Give him some advice?"

She hadn't expected this. It was almost as if he valued her expertise. She didn't think the lord of the manor usually talked plants with the gardening staff.

"Do you think your neighbor would welcome the advice?"

He nodded without hesitation. "And you'd like Barney. He's fantastic."

She kept her expression serious. "I prefer *un*fantastic people, actually."

Matthew smiled at her. Somehow over the course of their soccer match, she'd forgotten how devastating that smile could be. Her heart pounded a bit before she managed to get it under control again.

"If you have a little time now, I'm just up the road a bit," Matthew said. Again, a hint of uncertainty hung in his tone, like he was afraid he might be wearing out his welcome.

"If Barney doesn't mind a dirty, sweaty gardener, I'm game."

Matthew gave her a grateful look and even thanked her for it.

Which Matthew was the real one? The personable, humble, joking Matthew? Or the stuffy, arrogant one? And why was it that men were so hard to figure out?

Six

$\mathcal{M}$att knocked on Barney's door, trying to convince himself this was actually happening. Abby Grover, who'd blown him off more times than he could count, and who, until that afternoon on the football pitch, had seemed more or less unapproachable, was with him at his apartment building.

And she was smiling. And talking to him.

The door opened. Barney's thick white eyebrows pulled in a look of curiosity.

"This is Abby Grover," Matt said. "She's something of a plant expert, and I told her about your tomatoes."

To his credit, Barney didn't give any indication the two of them had spent a few evenings talking about Abby. "Did you also tell her that the spots weren't my fault?"

Abby spoke before Matt could. "In my experience, tomato spots are seldom the gardener's fault."

"That's the truth." Barney emphasized the declaration with a quick nod of his head. "If you can save these stubborn plants, you'll be an expert in my book."

Abby's smile was sincere—not the fake, patronizing smile too many people gave the elderly. Everything about her felt that way—honest, real.

They passed through Barney's flat, past furniture he'd probably had for as long as Matt and Abby had been alive. Matt had only been inside Barney's place a couple times, but it was always neat and tidy. Barney was that way with his garden as well. The spots on his plants probably bothered him most because it wasn't up to his standards.

"I put the plants over here that have the problem," Barney said as they reached the balcony. "I didn't want them too close to the others, just in case it's insects."

Abby knelt in front of the plants, looking closely at them. "You were smart to move them. I think it is insects." She carefully turned over one of the leaves, eying the underside. She looked up at Barney. "Do you have a sheet of paper and some kind of magnifying lens?"

Barney nodded eagerly. "I have a lens for reading the morning paper."

"Perfect."

He made his way back inside.

Matt sat on the ground next to her. "What do you need the paper for?"

"I'm going to write the bugs a letter, asking them nicely to leave Barney's plants alone."

She spoke so seriously, without even the smallest twitch to her lips. For just a moment Matt didn't realize she was joking. Then her smile spread. She had a great smile.

"That's how professionals deal with insects?" He let his amusement and doubt show.

"Insects are very polite. They wouldn't ever, you know, talk smack at a soccer match or anything like that."

He chuckled. "You had a few choice things to say as well."

Her smile grew to a grin. "Mostly because we were far better than the rest of them."

"We were, weren't we?" He hadn't had that much fun playing football in a very long time. "We play almost every Sunday. You should come."

The smallest show of a blush touched the skin behind her freckles. "Maybe I will."

I hope so.

"And thanks, again, for doing this for Barney. He doesn't get out much anymore, and these plants are his life, just about."

Her gaze went to the sliding door and the living room beyond. "Does he have any family?"

"His wife died a few years ago, and his children all live out of state. He and I sort of adopted each other—I don't have any family here either."

She looked back at him again. "That's really sweet."

He couldn't think of anything to say. The softness in her brown eyes made it impossible to think at all.

Barney rejoined them, handing Abby the paper and magnifying lens. She shook a leaf over the paper then studied the tiny specks that landed on it with the lens. The specks moved.

"Spider mites." She folded the paper over the bugs, pressing it tightly. "Do any of your other plants seem infested?"

She and Barney spent the next half hour meticulously going through his entire balcony garden. Matt didn't know enough to offer any insights, but he thought he did a good job following directions and retrieving the things they asked for.

After checking the last of Barney's plants, Abby broke the bad news. "The mites probably arrived on one of your plants, but there are signs of them on all of them now."

Barney dropped onto his stool, looking frustrated and tired. "Am I going to lose the whole garden?"

Abby immediately and emphatically shook her head. "We got this, Barney. We totally got this."

"You can save the plants?"

"I won't give up on them if you don't," Abby promised.

A look of relief crossed Barney's face. That garden really did mean everything to him. The plants were almost like family. Somehow, after only knowing him for a few moments, Abby had figured that out.

She smiled at the old man. If Matt hadn't been half gone on her already, that single moment would have done it.

"I have something at home that will help a lot with the mites." Abby stood, wiping soil and bits of crumpled leaves from her hands. "Let me run back to my place and shower— I've spent the afternoon showing a bunch of boys how to play soccer—and I'll be back in, say, an hour. Does that work?"

Barney took one of her hands in both of his. "This is very kind of you, Abby."

"I have loved plants since I was six years old," she said. "I would never let a garden as beautiful as this one get eaten by mites. Not ever."

"Will you let me treat you to dinner when you get back? You and Matt both?"

She glanced Matt's direction. He could see the question in her eyes, so he nodded. Turning Barney down would hurt his feelings.

"That is a deal," Abby said.

Matt walked her to the door. "I'll see you in an hour, then, I guess."

She shrugged. "I guess."

He watched her disappear down the corridor. Barney came and stood next to him.

"Did you know that I met my wife at a nursery?" Barney said. "She loved to garden. Loved it. I'd never grown a plant in all my life."

"Then why were you at a nursery?"

"I was buying a potted plant for my mother for Mother's Day." Barney's expression grew wistful. "Francis convinced me to buy a fuchsia instead of an iris. And over the next forty years, she taught me everything she knew about plants."

Matt set a hand on his friend's shoulder. "I wish I could have known your wife. She sounds remarkable."

"She was." Barney looked up at him, an earnestness in his expression. "When a man meets a remarkable woman, he doesn't let her slip away."

Matt knew what Barney was getting at. "Abby's pretty great, isn't she?"

Barney nodded. "Hold on to that one."

"I'll do my best." But would his best be enough?

Seven

Over the next weeks, Abby saw Matt—she discovered he preferred to be called Matt instead of Matthew—more often than she saw her own sister. An evening here or there, plus Saturdays, belonged to wedding preparations, but the rest of her evenings and Sundays were spent with Barney and Matt. She didn't think she was necessarily a lonely person, but having those two to spend her time with filled a hole in her life she hadn't realized was there.

She learned all about Barney's late wife, how they'd met and fallen in love over plants. He taught her a few things about caring for fuchsia, his wife's favorite flower. Fuchsias hung in baskets all along his roofline.

They saved the tomatoes from mites, trimmed back some overgrown rosemary, and, using Abby's own formula rose food, had his Sunflare roses blooming to perfection. And while she enjoyed every minute of that, and came to adore Barney like a wonderful mixture of grandfather and friend, Matt somehow managed to be an even better part of those evenings and Sundays together.

She found out he talked with his mom a couple of times a week, not in a mamma's boy kind of way, but simply because they liked each other and got along. More impressive even than that, he wasn't embarrassed or ashamed of being close to his family. Abby liked that. A lot.

Matt wasn't afraid to get his hands dirty and help with the gardening. Though he didn't have Barney's experience or Abby's expertise, he knew his way around soil and plants and gardening tools, and he was a quick learner. She couldn't remember the last time she'd felt so at home with two people. Even her own family grew quickly tired of her obsession with flora.

For dinner the Sunday night exactly one month since Abby had begun frequenting Matt and Barney's apartment building, she and Matt introduced Barney to Indian food. Much to the dear man's surprise, he liked it. After a leisurely, casual meal, Barney made his way back to his own apartment, tired from a day of gardening.

"I have a feeling he'll be sending me out for coconut korma on a regular basis now." Matt smiled as he dropped to the sofa. "I would, of course, have to reward myself with a little dhansak for my troubles."

"Of course." Abby pulled her feet onto the couch next to her. "And if I was here, what you bring for me?"

He didn't even hesitate. "Channa masala."

Abby was impressed, but not surprised. Matt noticed little things like that. "What if we were having Thai food?"

"Chicken Pad Thai."

Not bad. "What do I like on my hamburgers?" she asked.

He shook his head. "Nice try, Abby, but you don't eat hamburgers. No red meat for you."

349

SARAH M. EDEN

Not bad at all. Her eyes darted to the entry table near the door, where her keys sat by her phone. "What is on my key ring?"

He turned his head toward the door. Abby moved quickly, scooting over so she knelt right next to him and covered his eyes with her hand. "No peeking. We'll see just how observant you really are, Matthew Carlton. What is on my key ring?"

"Your keys."

"Very funny."

He flashed her his brilliant smile. Even with her hand lamely covering his eyes, that smile was dazzling. She thought she'd become immune to it over the past weeks. Apparently not.

Completely unaware of how distracting the lower half of his face really was, Matt answered her trivia question with her hands still covering his eyes. "You have on your key ring a brass-colored bauble in the shape of the state of Oregon."

That was absolutely correct. She dropped her hand away. "How did you know that?"

His deep green eyes met hers. "Why are you always surprised that I notice things about you?"

"Because you notice *everything*." She wasn't creeped out or worried—Matt was a nice guy, a good guy in a way she'd long ago decided didn't exist anymore. "It's like you're . . ."

"Paying attention?" he finished for her. His smile tipped with amusement. "That surprises you?"

When she really thought about it, the attention he paid her *was* surprising. She couldn't remember the last time someone had really noticed her. Dirk had only ever taken note of what she wore or did or said when she fell short of his expectations.

"Most people don't notice the girl with dirt under her nails," she said. "I work an unimportant job at a hole-in-the-wall nursery." She was embarrassing herself, pointing out her

350

shortcomings, and yet could not seem to stop the list from pouring out of her. "Why would anyone pay attention to—"

"Abby." He set a hand gently on the side of her face.

Her heart jumped to her throat, pounding and pulsing. Heat poured into her cheeks. Matt had never touched her like that before. They'd brushed hands or arms a few times while working in Barney's garden. They'd high-fived after scoring a goal during Sunday afternoon soccer matches. But he hadn't ever touched her that way, deliberately and affectionately.

He said her name again, but slower and softer. He cupped her face in his hand, his thumb slowly brushing along her cheek.

Abby tried to hide the way his touch upended her. If he had any idea how quickly and fully she was falling for him, he would have all the ammunition he needed to break her heart. She wasn't ready to feel that kind of vulnerability again.

"If you keep doing that, I'll think you're about to kiss me." She tried to keep her tone light and joking. She could tell she didn't entirely succeed.

"Maybe I *am* about to kiss you."

Her heart flipped over. Every ounce of air slid out of her lungs. She couldn't look away. Matt moved closer. She met him halfway. The space that separated them jumped and crackled with energy. Anticipation tiptoed over Abby's skin.

I don't know if I'm ready for this. Her mind warned her not to get in any deeper, but her heart pounded too loudly. She wanted Matt to kiss her, she'd wanted it for weeks, though she'd never admitted it to herself.

Why wasn't he moving? Was he waiting? Had he changed his mind already? Abby lowered her eyes. If he was about to reject her before they even had anything between them, she didn't want to have to see it on his face.

"I probably should go," she whispered quickly.

351

But he didn't drop his hand from her face. "Please don't."

She met his gaze again. "But you—"

"—promised my dad years ago to never kiss a girl without giving her ample opportunity to tell me to take myself off."

He was waiting for *her*? "I didn't tell you to take off."

His gaze dropped to her lips. "I noticed."

Matt closed the gap, his mouth brushing over hers. Abby set her palms against his chest. All thoughts of past heartache and disappointment and vulnerability fled from her mind. There was nothing in that moment but him and that kiss. Warmth spread through her like a slow-burning fire.

He held her close, earnest but gentle, as he deepened the kiss. Abby simply melted against him. She hadn't expected this to happen. After Dirk, she'd promised herself that it wouldn't ever happen again. But Matt had found his way past the barriers. Being held by him this way, feeling the warmth of him there beside her, Abby realized she was beginning to fall in love with him. More than just beginning to, in fact.

❧

Abby hadn't seen Matt since their kiss in his living room two days earlier. She'd missed him, but she didn't want to seem desperate. When an order came through at the nursery for Sainsbury House, Abby jumped at the opportunity to make the delivery.

She didn't find Larry in the gardener's shed. She decided to slip inside the house and say hi to Matt. Abby was glad she'd worn her favorite pair of work jeans instead of the ratty ones she'd had on the last time she'd come to Sainsbury House. Her blue t-shirt was in decent shape too. She'd spent the day at the counter and not among the plants, so she was still clean. Not a bad day to drop in on the guy who'd somehow managed to lay claim to her heart.

Abby smoothed her hair as she stepped onto the porch and into the entryway. She hadn't been to Matt's office many times, but she remembered exactly where it was. His voice floated out his open office door. That accent had turned her off when she first met him. He'd seemed stuffy and arrogant. Now she loved the sound of it, loved the way her name sounded like poetry when he said it.

"We can, of course, accommodate you in that," he was saying to someone inside. "At Sainsbury House we pride ourselves on making our clients' experiences as close to perfect as we can possibly manage."

Abby leaned against the wall beside the door, listening.

"And you can guarantee the staff will remain out of sight and unobtrusive throughout the night?" Whoever was in there with them seemed adamant on that point. "We don't want the help getting in the way."

The ones doing all the work have to stay out of sight. Some people are so arrogant.

"I will make note of that," Matt answered.

She leaned around the doorframe, not stepping fully into the threshold. Matt sat at his desk, wearing a suit and tie, hair perfect like a model in a magazine. A couple sat across the desk from him—pearls, cufflinks, polished shoes, snotty expressions. Abby knew in a glance that they were exactly the sort of people Dirk had tried to make her fit in with, the ones who always sighed in dismissive annoyance at her appearance and her clumsiness and her plainness.

She must have made some kind of noise. All three people looked toward her. The same familiar discomfort she'd known every minute she'd spent with Dirk in public came rushing back. When it was just the two of them, things were fine. Not great, but fine. But as soon as someone else was around, she wasn't good enough.

Matt was up and out of his chair in an instant, moving to where she stood. "Abby. What you are you doing here?"

He didn't seem at all happy to see her. "Larry ordered some plants and things from the nursery," she said. "I'm delivering them."

Her eyes darted to the couple. They were watching her, their faces pulled in expressions of disapproval.

Matt slipped a hand under her elbow, moving her toward his office door with obvious determination. "Larry is probably in the shed. You should look for him there."

"I was just there," Abby said. "He was gone, so I came to see you."

Matt glanced back at his office before returning his gaze to her. "He may have returned by now."

"Maybe."

Matt was still lightly pushing her back toward the entryway. He didn't want her going in his office? "I'm interrupting, aren't I? I can just wait out here."

He shook his head no.

He doesn't even want me to wait?

He lowered his voice. "This is a very particular client. They can be very picky about things."

"About things or about *people*?" The question slid unbidden from her lips.

"Both," he said. "They have very particular . . . standards."

She didn't like that word choice at all.

"Let me put it this way—they are not the sort of people to know what a gardening shed *is*, let alone go inside one."

There was no mistaking that. She didn't belong here among his important, highbrow clients. She couldn't have been more out of place in her jeans and t-shirt, the smell of potting soil clinging to her the way the aroma of money hung off the couple seated by Matt's desk. He didn't want them to see him with the "garden shed girl."

Dirk's words echoed in her mind, but in Matt's voice: *Everyone has their level.*

Once again, she'd given her heart over to a guy who looked down on her. He was ashamed to be seen with her in front of his snobby clients.

Abby wasn't about to go through that again. If he was embarrassed by her, hiding her away from the fancy, important people in his life, then so be it. But she wouldn't hang around, enduring the humiliation of it all.

She nodded then turned and walked away. If she kept her shoulders and head up, he might not realize her heart was breaking.

bby wasn't answering her phone. She came by to help Barney in his garden, but only when Matt was at work. She didn't come to the market on Sundays or join him and his friends for their weekly football matches. He hadn't seen her or talked to her in two weeks.

What had he done wrong? He'd talked through it with Barney and Mum and even his sisters, but no one had any idea what had happened. Mum finally told him, in a tone that brooked no argument, that if he couldn't ask Abby why she'd suddenly decided to toss him off, he needed to ask Abby's sister.

Caroline and her fiancé were scheduled to meet with him that week to finalize all the wedding details. He intended to get the business part of it all taken care of quickly so he could ask her what he'd done to make her sister run off.

Caroline's intended, Gregory, wasn't at all like Matt had imagined him. Where she was fussy and, honestly, a little high strung, Gregory was laid back. Looking at him, no one would guess he was only a few days from getting married.

They quickly wrapped up the wedding checklist. Matt closed the lid on his laptop and looked at Caroline, hoping she could see the earnest sincerity in his expression. "May I ask a nonbusiness question?"

She and Gregory exchanged quick, knowing glances. "About Abby?" She sounded very sure about the topic.

Matt nodded. "I don't know what I did, but I can tell she's mad at me, or doesn't like me anymore." He had broken the "no contractions" rule three times in one sentence, a clear sign Abby's defection was getting to him. "I can't get her to return my calls. I don't know what happened."

"Oh, I can tell you what happened," Caroline said. "Dirk the Jerk is what happened."

Though she spoke with conviction, the explanation didn't help at all. Matt looked to Gregory, hoping for a guy-friendly translation.

"Up until about a year ago," Gregory said. "Abby was dating this guy named Dirk. He was a total plague."

"Then why was she dating him?" Another question came to mind immediately. "And what does that have to do with me?" He wasn't a jerk, a bully, or a plague. He didn't think so, at least.

"Abby didn't see him the way we all did," Caroline explained. "Not at first, anyway. When it was just the two of them, or around our family, he was okay. He treated her decent. But around *his* friends and family, or the public in general, she was never good enough."

Matt didn't like that sound of that at all.

"Dirk comes from money, if you know what I mean. His family's very connected and rich and fancy." Caroline was growing noticeably angrier as she spoke. "All dressed up like them, Abby looks like a million bucks. Dirk approved of her, kind of, when she was like that, but he looked down on who she really is. She wasn't supposed to tell anyone where she worked or where she grew up. For the most part, she wasn't supposed to talk at all when they were out together, just smile and look pretty."

"I actually heard him tell her to shut up once," Gregory said. "I almost belted the guy."

A simmering anger began in the pit of Matt's stomach. How dare anyone treat Abby that way?

"She finally admitted that Dirk was, in fact, a complete jerk and found the guts to dump him," Caroline said. "But that kind of thing leaves scars. She still wonders if she's good enough, if she's too poor or ordinary or plain."

"How could she even think that?" It didn't make sense at all. "Abby is amazing."

Caroline smiled. "We think so too."

"So why did you toss her out the other day?" Gregory asked.

"I never tossed her out." What was he talking about?

They both looked instantly confused. Obviously Matt was missing something.

"She came by here," Caroline said. "And, apparently, you were pretty insistent she make herself scarce."

"What?" That was ridiculous. He remembered her visit. The Carlisles were there, working out details of some stuffy dinner party they wanted to hold, and he'd been doing his best not to tell them how idiotic they were. The owners of Sainsbury House valued the Carlisles' business and connections and had been quite clear that he was not to do anything to jeopardize that. He'd managed to hold his tongue throughout the meeting, but not without effort.

"She said you kept trying to keep her out of sight of your clients," Gregory added.

"Actually that part's true." He spoke the realization as he had it. "But because of Abby, not because of *them*. The

358

Carlisles are cold and cruel. They have no qualms about insulting or belittling people they think are beneath them. I couldn't guarantee they would be civil to her." He had, in fact, been very much afraid they would be terrible to her. "There was no way on earth I was going to let her be mistreated. The only way to avoid that was to keep her from having to interact with them."

Both Caroline and Gregory looked surprised, and maybe even a little relieved.

"Then it wasn't that you were embarrassed to be seen with her in front of important people?" Caroline asked.

"The Carlisles are *not* important people, At least, not to me. And certainly not as important as Abby."

Caroline leaned a little closer to his desk, lowering her voice. "Does *she* know that?"

Does she? "Considering how quickly she decided I was ashamed of her, I'd guess she doesn't."

"Show her," Caroline added.

Show her. He meant to. He simply had to figure out how.

⚬

Caroline's wedding was everything any hopeless romantic could wish for. The bridesmaids all wore their 1910s-inspired dresses and only complained about them when the bride wasn't nearby. The men looked, to coin Caroline's phrase, "quite dapper" in their fancy suits and slicked-back hair. The venue was perfect. The weather was perfect. Everything was nauseatingly perfect.

Abby was in a bad mood but couldn't seem to shake it. She was happy for her sister; she really was. But watching Matt—she couldn't bring herself to think of him as Matthew, wanting to remember the version of him she liked best— hover on the edges of every moment of that day only drove

359

the knife of disappointment deeper into her heart. She did her best to look the other way when he came in her line of vision. As the event coordinator, he was everywhere. He was also too busy to talk to her. For that, she was grateful.

She sat at the wedding party's table through the unending dinner, pretending to enjoy the food and faking a smile. She didn't hear half of what was said during the toasts. She raised her glass when everyone else did, laughed when the guests laughed. But her heart wasn't in any of it.

You'll kick yourself for this later, wishing you'd pulled yourself together for Caroline's wedding. But all of the well-meaning pep talks in the world didn't seem capable of pulling her out of her funk.

If Matt hadn't seemed so great, so close to exactly what she was looking for in a man, she wouldn't have been so disappointed. He was kind and thoughtful. He got along with his mother, which she thought was a good sign. He wasn't obsessive about plants like she was, but he liked gardening with her and Barney. He didn't blow off her passion for flowers and plants and gardens the way so many people did. He'd seemed so . . . so *right*.

Maybe you're blowing the whole thing out of proportion. Maybe you should have answered when he called.

She clapped mechanically as Caroline and Gregory began their first dance, but her mind was miles away. Matt was likely in the kitchen checking on the staff or outside overseeing the pavilion takedown. What she wouldn't have given to have been on Barney's balcony instead, letting the sweet old man cheer her up once more.

Despite her heavy heart, Abby could almost smile thinking of Barney and his stories. She'd never heard anyone talk with as much love and adoration as he did about his late wife. Maybe that was what had made her idealize Matt so much. She'd started thinking of him as her Barney, a man who loved her, quirks and all.

The dancing became more general. With fewer eyes focused on the front table, Abby finally felt like she could escape for a moment. She skirted around the room, making her way to the open double doors. The entry hall beyond wasn't exactly empty, but it felt far less suffocating. She needed someplace quiet, somewhere she could be alone even if for a moment.

"Abby!"

She spun at the sound of her name spoken in an achingly familiar British accent. "Hey, Matt." Her voice wasn't entirely steady.

He stood outside the closed door of his office, looking earth-shatteringly handsome in a dark suit. She'd tried to avoid noticing that all day. But those green eyes. They got to her every time.

"I thought you would be . . . coordinating . . . something." The pounding of her heart in her throat made words difficult to come by.

"Actually, I've been waiting for you."

He was waiting for her? Why? That didn't make sense, not when he had clients and important things to see to. Hadn't he made her place on his totem pole painfully clear? "I don't understand."

"There hasn't been a chance to talk to you all day, and I didn't want to risk causing a scene during your sister's wedding," he said. "But I can't let the entire night get away without seeing you. So I've been waiting here, hoping you'd step out."

The few guests wandering the entryway gave her and Matt curious glances. Abby could feel her face heat with the attention.

"Can we talk in here?" Matt asked, motioning toward his office. "I'll only take a minute, I promise."

She was halfway to his door before the realization hit her that if she really thought he was a complete jerk, she wouldn't have agreed to talk with him without so much as a hesitation. Besides, he was being her Matt again, not stuffy Matthew. She could at least find out what made the difference, where the change came from.

She stepped inside, pushing from her mind the memory of the snooty couple who'd sat there the last time she'd been at Sainsbury House. Nothing much had changed in his office. Her eyes settled on a potted plant at the corner of Matt's desk. It hadn't been there before. And she knew exactly what variety it was.

"A fuchsia," she said, gently running her fingers along the petals of one flower.

The same plant Barney gave Francis every year for their anniversary, for her birthdays, as an "I love you" and an "I'm sorry" and everything in between.

"It's a Swingtime Fuchsia," Matt said. "The variety you like best."

This was her Matt, remembering every little thing.

"I brought it for you," he said. "Though I haven't figured out how to give it to you yet."

"For me?" She looked up, her heart already beginning to hope. It would shatter if this didn't turn out well. She cautiously asked, "Why?"

She had never in her life seen a man beg, but the look on Matt's face in that moment came very close. "I miss you, Abby. I miss sitting on the balcony with you. I spend all day Sunday at the farmer's market watching for you. Every time my phone rings, I hope it's going to be you calling." He'd moved to her side but didn't touch her. His eyes studied her face, the pleading in them not lessening at all. "I want a chance to try again. A chance to make things right between us."

A bubble of hope began deep inside. Abby tried to push it down, not ready to open herself up to the possibility of being hurt again.

Matt slowly, deliberately took her hand, clearly expecting her to pull away. She didn't. She couldn't. His touch filled an empty part of her. She'd missed him too. She'd needed him nearby.

"I was something of an idiot about things," Matt said, holding her gaze with his. "When you were here before, I wasn't trying to hide you away. I wasn't embarrassed to have you here or ashamed of you. Nothing like that." His words took on an earnest edge she couldn't doubt was sincere. "The people who were here are quite possibly the biggest snobs on the face of the earth. And they are often cruel. I have no choice but to interact with them—it's one of the more unpleasant parts of my job—but I didn't want you to have to. I was afraid they would be unkind. I didn't want you enduring that. And if they'd been cruel to you, I couldn't have held my tongue. I was trying to avoid all that."

"Really?" She wanted to believe him. She wanted to badly.

"Honestly and truly." He took her other hand. "I should have been clearer about that. I should have explained and let you decide what you wanted to do."

"I would have been very out of place with fancy and sophisticated people."

He lightly laughed. "My mum keeps saying I need to tell you that I'm just a regular bloke from Stanmore."

Abby had no idea what that meant, but he said it so earnestly, she knew it was significant.

"I've never been rich and probably never will be. I'm just an average guy who's, honestly, kind of surprised you let me spend as much time with you as you did."

A ridiculously handsome, well-spoken, successful guy surprised that she liked being with him?

"All we ever did was trim plants and play soccer." She could hardly believe he'd cherished those moments.

He shrugged a single shoulder. "I grew up pruning

plants and playing football. I like it. I enjoy it. And I like and enjoy *you*."

That was something Dirk had never once said to her. Not ever. She'd always felt like she had to prove to him that she was worth his time.

"You brought me a fuchsia."

He nodded uncertainly. "I kept thinking of Barney's stories and how Francis would always forgive him if he gave her a fuchsia. I hoped it would work the same magic for me."

"You want to be my Barney, is that it?" She couldn't say exactly why the question thickened her voice with tears. She wasn't generally a crier.

"I want to try," Matt said. "I would very much like to have that chance."

"And I would very much like a Barney of my own." She wanted a Matt of her own. *Her* Matt.

He brushed his thumb along her cheek just as he had that evening in his apartment. She smiled up at him, a smile that for the first time in a long time came straight from her heart.

The strains of distant music could be heard through the closed door. "Dance with me?" she asked.

He didn't hesitate, didn't debate for the length of a single breath. Matt took her hand in his and settled his arm around her waist. He pulled her up and close to him. She could feel the warmth of his breath rustling her hair.

Abby closed her eyes and leaned in to him. Being with Dirk had always meant constant attention to her posture, to her appearance, to how other people might judge her. But that moment, in Matt's arms, she didn't worry about any of those things.

He swayed with her to the music. "Does this mean I get a second chance?"

"Honestly, you never really lost your first chance. I was working on convincing myself to call you."

He pulled back the smallest bit. Abby looked up at him.

"You were going to call me?" he asked, an eager hopefulness in his tone and eyes.

Abby nodded. "I missed you too. I was embarrassed and a little hurt, but I guess I never completely believed you were a jerk."

His grin grew on the instant. "That's not exactly a gushing compliment but, honestly, one of the best I've ever received."

She pulled her hand from his and wrapped her arms around his neck, holding tightly to him. His arms tucked around her as well. He pressed a kiss to her temple then whispered in her ear.

"Can we start again?"

"No." She almost laughed at the look of surprised worry on his face. "I don't want to start over," she quickly explained. "I want to go back to being happy together and figuring each other out. Back to where we were before things fell apart."

He raised an eyebrow. "You realize 'where we were' was making out on my couch."

She felt a blush creeping up her neck. "Would you settle for being my date for the rest of the wedding?"

"For now," he said.

He kissed her forehead, then the tip of her nose. They'd stopped dancing and simply stood in each other's arms. Matt pressed a sweet kiss to her lips. She loved that he was so often tender and gentle, but in that moment, she wanted him to kiss her like he really meant it.

She shifted her hands to the back of his neck and returned his kiss with fervor. Matt didn't need any more encouragement than that. He kissed her deeply and passionately there in his office against a background of wedding music and the now-cherished aroma of fuchsia.

Caroline had been right all along.

In the end, her wedding day turned out absolutely perfect.

ABOUT SARAH M. EDEN

Sarah M. Eden is the author of multiple historical romances, including Whitney Award finalists *Seeking Persephone, Courting Miss Lancaster* and *Longing for Home*. Combining her obsession with history and affinity for tender love stories, Sarah loves crafting witty characters and heartfelt romances. She holds a bachelor's degree in research and happily spends hours perusing the reference shelves of her local library. Sarah has twice served as the Master of Ceremonies for the LDStorymakers Writers Conference, acted as the Writer in Residence at the Northwest Writers Retreat, and is one-third of the team at the AppendixPodcast.com. Sarah is represented by Pam van Hylckama Vlieg at Foreword Literary Agency. Visit her website at www.sarahmeden.com

Twitter: @SarahMEden
Facebook: Sarah M. Eden

MORE TIMELESS ROMANCE ANTHOLOGIES:

Visit Our Blog:
TimelessRomanceAnthologies.blogspot.com

36567521R00212

Made in the USA
Lexington, KY
27 October 2014